EXPLORING THE WRECKAGE

"Not much to see here, I'm afraid," came the voice from the submersible as the ROV threaded its way carefully through the maze of sharp-edged steel. "We're going to steer him toward the stern now, and hope our access isn't blocked."

The ROV passed through two more huge compartments, the damage becoming far less noticeable the farther the craft moved away from the *Regulus*'s forward area. The image became very confused, with strange shapes lying at odd angles.

Williams moved closer to the monitor, and he instantly became aware of what he was looking at. "It's the division's combat equipment," he said. "If you look closely, General, you can make out a Bradley and what looks like the rear end of a Humvee."

The camera moved in for a closer look. It was, in fact, what Williams had guessed. Beyond there were faint shadows of other pieces of equipment, tossed and turned by the violence of the explosion and the sudden onslaught of seawater filling the decks.

The ROV moved gingerly around the Humvee and ascended slowly until its camera lens came even with the vehicle's still intact windshield. This time there was a loud gasp in the room, and almost everyone simultaneously jumped in their seats. There was a human face, a very lifeless human face, staring back at them from the other side of the glass. . . .

KEN CURRIE

CRISIS POINT

LEISURE BOOKS NEW YORK CITY

To Dawn Marie:
If I didn't have you, I would be lost and blind.
You are my muse, my friend, my love.

A LEISURE BOOK®

September 2002

Published by

Dorchester Publishing Co., Inc.
276 Fifth Avenue
New York, NY 10001

ISBN 0-8439-5107-9

The name "Leisure Books" and the stylized "L" with design are trademarks of Dorchester Publishing Co., Inc.

Printed in the United States of America.

Visit us on the web at www.dorchesterpub.com.

ACKNOWLEDGMENTS

The Twain quote in Chapter Eleven is taken from Mark Twain, *A Tramp Abroad*, ed. by Charles Neider (New York: Harper and Row, 1977), pp. 7-8. The Jefferson quotes appearing in Chapter Thirty-seven are from *The Oxford Dictionary of Quotations* (New York: Oxford University Press, 1979), p. 272, and Thomas Jefferson, *Writings* (New York: Library of America, 1984), p. 289.

I wish to thank Col. Steve Emery, United States Air Force Reserve, for his invaluable assistance in providing insight into American fighter tactics and operations. Col. Emery, of course, bears no responsibility for the manner in which I may have put such information to use in this fictional work.

CRISIS POINT

Chapter One

19 August, 1415 hours Local

Tim Padrillo leaned sleepily on the ship's railing watching the waters of the Indian Ocean stream by as the *Regulus* sped toward Saudi Arabia. He held a well-worn photograph of his wife, Caitlin, and, gazing steadily at the passing sea, he absentmindedly ran his index finger back and forth across the tattered image. He closed his eyes and imagined her lying next to him, very much pregnant with what he hoped would be their son. He had hurriedly said goodbye to her just a few weeks before. There had been no time for a proper farewell. The last time he saw her she had been standing in their doorway, wearing a threadbare robe that she stubbornly refused to throw away, sadly waving as he raced away in a shipmate's car. An hour later, Padrillo and the balance of the *Regulus*'s crew were scrambling madly to prepare the ship for her trip to the Middle East.

The afternoon was mercilessly hot, with the breeze generated by the ship's movement providing little relief. Nevertheless, Padrillo had opted to take his break on deck in hopes of escaping the noise and the even more stifling atmosphere belowdecks. The sky was hazy, but not enough to prevent an unrestricted view to the ocean's edge. Trying to take his mind off his involuntary separation from his wife, he distractedly watched the clouds as they scudded across the sky, hurrying into the distance as if to escape the burning afternoon sun. His attention was slowly drawn to a dark spot on the horizon. At first he thought it nothing more than a seabird that had strayed too far from shore, but the spot quickly grew in size, taking on a more discernible and disturbing shape.

The *Regulus* was one of the original fast sealift ships, aging now but still an occasionally important part of the Military Sealift Command's—MSC's—merchant fleet, because she was capable of carrying great loads at high speeds from the many embarkation points to American forces scattered about an unceasingly troubled world. The *Regulus* had served proudly with her sister ships during Desert Shield/Desert Storm, but she now faced mothballing as newer, faster ships handled the country's rapid deployment requirements. But that end was still a year or more away, and now she was needed once again to support yet another military effort. She had departed Charleston, South Carolina, just a few days before, carrying military cargo for American troops embroiled in the latest Middle Eastern crisis: not-so-veiled Iranian threats to blockade the Strait of Hormuz, the gateway to the Persian Gulf.

Dustups between U.S. and Iranian forces had already occurred. The Iranians had fired a Silkworm cruise missile at a feckless Estonian tanker on her way home with a cargo of Kuwaiti crude. The freighter had been badly damaged, with a number of casualties, including her captain, the son of the Estonian prime minister.

The American president, coming to the defense of one of his country's newest NATO allies, quickly ordered cruise missile strikes on Iranian Silkworm and air defense sites. As tensions ratcheted ever upward, Teheran's Islamic regime ordered a general mobilization, doing its best to whip a skeptical and weary populace into anti-Western frenzy with calls for a *jihad*, or holy war, against the Western infidels. Despite the hysteria and the carefully organized throngs of would-be martyrs flooding Iranian cities, the fighting entered an uneasy lull while Teheran pondered its next move. Meanwhile, the president, battling for a second term in a bitter, very personal electoral contest, huddled with his advisers to plot a course of action they passionately hoped would force the Iranians to back off, while bolstering—or at the least not jeopardizing—his reelection chances.

The spot in the sky was clearly coming closer, and Padrillo felt increasingly uneasy. It was now clear the object was a much larger bird than he'd originally thought. He could now make out a helicopter, and it was rapidly closing on the *Regulus. Still*, he thought, *no alarm sounded on the ship, so it must be one of ours.* While he was trying to reassure himself that everything was in order, two additional spots flashed into view immediately behind the unknown aircraft, and he was certain they were helicopters as well. His quiet unease quickly gave way to sharp pains in his stomach as he was seized by the first stages of panic: A flash and smoke had suddenly appeared at the side of the lead helicopter, and the smoke was on an unmistakable course toward the ship.

Finally the ship's alarm sounded, startling Padrillo into glancing toward the ship's bridge. Chaos reigned. The captain was frantically gesturing and mouthing unheard orders. Padrillo felt the ship heave and shudder beneath his feet as the helmsman began a frantic attempt to maneuver out of the way of approaching disaster.

The *Regulus*'s turbines responded quickly to the captain's orders, but she was a big ship, and at thirty knots she could not turn rapidly enough to avoid an inevitable fate. The missile fired by the lead helicopter found its target. It shredded the bridge, the captain, and most of those standing with him. Those who lived through the blast were now consumed with crawling for the hatches in a desperate effort to survive, certain there was nothing they could do to rescue the captain or the ship.

The missile's impact had thrown Padrillo onto his back.

Ken Currie

All he remembered was the roar of the explosion, the sharp pain as he was knocked off his feet, the howling of metal yielding to explosive force, and the moans of the *Regulus* as she began her death dance. The last he remembered before he passed out was a searing white light and a ringing in his head that kept time with the ship's still-wailing Klaxon. His wife's photograph slipped from his fingers. Caught in the blast wave, it flew over the railing and fluttered quickly away, like a sparrow fleeing a bird of prey.

He regained consciousness slowly, and painfully propped himself up on one elbow. He looked toward the bridge. Nothing remained but blackened, twisted metal. Shards of the ship's superstructure were buried in the deck near him; he had barely escaped impalement. A boot also lay close by, with shreds of cloth and flesh protruding from its top. He immediately felt a wave of nausea and turned his gaze toward the back of the ship. He could just make out the silhouette of two helicopters hovering amidships. He watched in bemused fascination as several fatigue-clad figures jumped in what seemed slow motion to the *Regulus*'s deck. He could hear the steady *whump* of the helicopters' rotors, and the indecipherable shouts of the invaders. He was vaguely aware of the staccato pop of gunfire, mixing with the sounds of the helicopters in a strangely hypnotic melody. He sensed other figures moving quickly about on the periphery of his vision, some running, others crawling.

He felt a sudden searing pain in his chest. He could not breathe. He thought of home. Then he understood the source of the burning, and he realized he would not lie with his wife again or ever see his son. A shadow had blocked the sun, and slowly his eyes adjusted so he could see the grinning, charcoal-blackened, distinctly feminine face of one of the camouflaged soldiers. *Son of a bitch*, he thought. The muzzle of the soldier's automatic weapon was pointing at him, smoke drifting from its barrel, reminding Padrillo of the clouds he had been watching. She continued staring at him. He somehow found the energy to smile back. He lifted his hand with the middle finger upraised and slumped dead onto the deck.

19 August, 0520 hours EDT

Back at the MSC Operations Center in Washington, the duty officer noted a garbled fragment of a message coming across the comms circuit reserved for the fast sealift ships. It clearly was from the *Regulus*, but it made zero sense. The lieutenant immediately picked up his secure phone and tried to place a call to the ship; the beeping sound of a busy signal was all he could hear. He tried several more times, with the same result. Finally, he set the message aside and made a short entry in the duty log telling his relief to try to contact the ship after the duty turnover in a couple of hours. "I don't have time for this shit," he thought out loud, and quickly went back to preparing the briefing he had to give in a couple of hours to the MSC commander and the VIPs coming in from one of those "damned House oversight committees."

At the headquarters of the U.S. Transportation Command, Colonel Blair Williams, the senior officer on duty in the Mobility Control Center, was busy preparing for his morning briefing to the deputy commander in chief, the DCINC, when a message was laid in front of him, interrupting his train of thought. He impatiently looked up into the face of Lieutenant Colonel Tom Mulkey, who clearly was agitated over what he'd just placed on Williams's desk.

"Yes, Tom?"

"I know you're busy, Colonel, but you need to see this before the DCINC walks in. It's a message fragment from the *Regulus*. To say it's confusing is an understatement. But it could mean trouble, and I mean very big trouble."

Williams looked down at the message:

```
FROM: T-AKR 292
TO: CINCUSTRANSCOM SCOTT AFB IL
INFO: MSC WASHINGTON DC
```

SUBJECT: INCIDENT REPORT
1. RADAR INDICATES UNIDENTIFIED AIR-
CRAFT IN THE AREA, ON A DIRECT HEADING
TO REGULUS. UNABLE TO CONTACT AIR-
CRAFT. INTENTIONS UNCLEAR. NO OTHER
US SHIPS VICINITY. REQUEST

"This is it?" Williams asked his subordinate with unchar-
acteristic sharpness. He had known Mulkey a long time and
was used to getting all the details from his section chief.
Clearly, he was not going to get the usual data dump, and
he was irritated over the prospect of having to interrupt the
morning routine to straighten out a last-minute glitch.

"Yes, sir," Mulkey replied, quickly reading his boss's body
language and tone. "I understand your frustration. We've
tried calling the MSC duty officer, but the lines are busy.
We've tried contacting them on the other circuits, but no
response yet, and I'm gettin' really pissed. Their damned
status reports were due twenty minutes ago. I don't know
what the hell is going on back there." Then Mulkey added,
only partially joking, "Maybe they're out playing volleyball
or taking a coffee break to watch the ESPN exercise shows.
Who the hell knows? In any event, we've received nothing
else from the *Regulus* here. I'd say there's a little cause for
concern, but apparently all this isn't causing any conster-
nation to our Navy brethren inside the Beltway."

"Okay, Tom," Williams said. "Keep trying to get what
information you can. Keep bugging the hell out of MSC.
Somebody there has to know what's going on." And then
Williams added, with the slightest hint of a sigh of resignation, "It would be nice if just once in a while they'd remember who the hell they work for. In the meantime, I've
got to notify the J3 and the DCINC to tell 'em what we've
got, even though it isn't much. And, Tom, call the J2 and
bring him up to speed on what's going on. Find out what
the intel folks know, if anything, and ask them to get one
of their folks over here, ASAP."

"Roger that, Colonel."

Mulkey had wheeled to walk away, but Williams stopped him with one last question.

"Remind me one more time, so I don't have to go through all these damned slides to find the answer—what was the *Regulus* carrying?"

"Give me twenty seconds, and I'll have an answer for you," Mulkey called over his shoulder as he quickly sat down at his computer terminal, submerging his balding head in the screen's whitish glow, all the more pronounced in the darkened room. The information he wanted popped up on the screen. He stared in disbelief, and entered a new query. The same answer came up. He sucked in his breath, pushed himself away from his desk, and walked back toward his boss.

Williams looked up and knew immediately he wasn't going to like what he was about to hear. "I take it you found the answer?"

"Not the one I expected. She's carrying the bulk of the remainder of the 24th Mech's equipment. No surprise there. But she's also carrying several hundred artillery rounds and two dozen joint air-to-surface standoff missile canisters."

Williams's forehead furrowed as he raised his eyebrows. "JASSMs?" he asked, barely audibly.

"Yes, sir. I can only assume the JASSMs are intended for transloading at Dharan, but I'll have to verify that. Since we've been popping the things off like crazy against the Iranians, these must be intended to replenish the Positive Ally ships. The port congestion at Augusta Bay could also have been a factor."

Williams's eyes narrowed and his ears turned crimson. He was quiet for a moment. "Jesus, Mary, and Joseph." Then he continued, rapidly warming to his subject but still holding his anger in check.

"Could someone please tell me what rocket scientist decided to load ammunition on a ship strictly prohibited from carrying ordnance?" Williams raised his voice so that everyone in the center could hear the next comment. "No one in TRANSCOM decided to put ammunition on a ship with the 24th's equipment, correct? I think our procedures are pretty clear on that point, right? So we can assume the culprit—or should I say idiot?—was someone at MSC or at the port of Charleston?" Williams turned his chair slowly back toward his computer as he continued. "You've just made me very unhappy, Tom. If *Regulus* is in trouble and we can't establish a comms link, everybody from the CINC on down is going to be puffing down our damned necks. And then you can bet I'll have the ass of whoever did this. Get me some answers, and get them damned *fast*."

As Mulkey walked away from his boss, he muttered to himself, "So much for our fantastic positive location and tracking system. I hope to Christ somebody can tell us where on God's blue water she is before General Allen walks in."

Chapter Two

19 August, 0830 EDT

President Noonan's mind drifted elsewhere as he listened to the morning briefing by the team from Langley. Although he was staring at the briefing charts, most of the images went by without registering. He was wondering whether the intelligence community would tell him something he didn't already know or hadn't read about in one of the journals adorning the Oval Office tables. As the briefer droned on, Noonan also pondered the unsettling events of the past few days. He was trying to convince himself he remained in control of events.

Richard Mathias Noonan was an oddity among recent occupants of the White House: an academic. He had never been a lawyer, a "shortcoming" he noted with pride in his speeches bashing the Trial Lawyers Association and the ACLU. His blunt intellectual style and his imposing personal appearance—his tall, muscular build served as a reminder of his less intellectual days as an All-American quarterback at the University of Virginia—had played well with the voters of Virginia, and they had overwhelmingly voted him in as their junior senator before he embarked upon his unlikely but successful bid for the White House. An economy once again in the doldrums and a series of international setbacks for the previous administration had set the stage for what at first had seemed an improbable campaign.

Noonan wore his Ph.D. in history from George Washington University proudly, precisely because it did set him apart from his predecessors. He had spoken at every spring commencement at GW since becoming president four years earlier, the annual return to his alma mater a welcome retreat from the demands of the presidency. And because he was one of them, the university students always welcomed him warmly, even though for many of them he came from the "wrong" party. He thoroughly enjoyed wearing the gown and stole that went with his academic credentials while listening to the strains of "Hail to the Chief," a bit of vanity he would never confess to anyone.

Because he was an academic, Noonan considered himself his own expert on American foreign policy. He had been a key architect of arms control and defense policies during the Bush presidency. His rapid rise to deputy secretary of defense at the age of thirty-two confirmed his self-assessment, while whetting his appetite for still more power. The chance to run for the Senate had simply fallen into his lap. In short, Noonan appeared to be blessed by the gods.

His successes as president only served to sharpen his self-image as the anointed one. The economy had recovered dramatically, for reasons he knew had very little to do with his policies or Congress's actions. The White House may be a "bully pulpit," but it was basically powerless to effect real economic change. The best Noonan could hope for was a public perception that his policies and the inevitable economic rebound were related. Timing is everything, and events had borne out his optimism.

Noonan had received an unexpected bonus in the serious economic problems besetting the European Economic Community and Japan. The dollar's strength had soared. Despite the much-touted interdependence of the world's economies, Europe's and Japan's economic travails had helped fuel America's economic recovery as the United States swept up markets formerly dominated by its economic rivals.

His successes in foreign policy proved equally dramatic. Armed with his overpowering—many would say over-bearing—intellectual prowess, he browbeat his European partners into accepting all of the former Warsaw Pact countries—including Russia—into NATO, while resisting Franco-German attempts to weaken the United States's position within NATO's military and political decision-making organs. He now urged these same partners to accept the new NATO allies fully into the European Economic Community, a step he was convinced would be good for the former states of the Soviet Union as well as for the United States. He judged that the inclusion of Russia and her former imperial possessions into the European Economic Community would diminish the influence of the major European economic powers—and America's principal economic rivals—within the continent's political structure. It was a tricky and perhaps dangerous game, but Noonan had proved himself a most adept player, and—most important from an electoral perspective—the American public loved it. The United States, at last, was acting like the world's only super-power, and the American economy was surging forward.

Noonan overcame Russian opposition to including the former Soviet colonies into NATO by securing Moscow a key decision-making role in NATO. In exchange, Noonan locked in Moscow's cooperation in a global campaign against terrorism, a campaign that rapidly expanded into frequent military strikes on suspected terrorist targets, including several in the Persian Gulf. Noonan convinced his Russian counterpart, President Milyutin, that it was time for Moscow to turn its back on its traditional "friends" in the Middle East. In turn, Milyutin—ignoring protests by his Security Council and the more nationalist forces within the Foreign and Defense Ministries, especially Defense Minister Gromov—vouchsafed his democratic credentials by sacking his

11

foreign minister, a holdover from the old regime and a former KGB operative who had enjoyed a close personal relationship with several of the virulently anti-American leaders in the Middle East.

Milyutin's increasing apprehension about growing Iranian political and economic inroads into Central Asia also played into Noonan's hands. The thought of Russia's southeastern borders beset by fundamentalist Islamist regimes caused no surcease of nightmares for the leaders within the Kremlin.

If pledges of influence within NATO and fears of Persian revanchism weren't enough for the often-divided Russian leadership, Noonan further sweetened his arguments with promises of expanded economic aid and support for several Russian policy initiatives once Moscow had entered the European defense alliance, a fact unknown to the other European leaders. Noonan's behind-the-scenes machinations, their general outlines if not details frequently covered in the press, certainly contributed to the public view of a president possessing unequaled foreign policy acumen. Noonan and his advisers calculated that the promise of resolute joint action against international terrorists would be a boon to his upcoming reelection campaign.

Two suspected terrorist camps inside Iran already had been struck in a joint U.S.-Russian air attack, and additional military operations were in the planning stages. These strikes and the unexpected Iranian reaction—to say nothing of the reaction from America's traditional NATO partners, who decried the "unilateral" action by the United States, ignoring the Russian role in the military actions—had been the genesis for what had now become a full-blown crisis in the Persian Gulf. Noonan reasoned that the Iranians would talk a brave game, perhaps fire a few warning missiles at non-U.S. targets, but would do little else. They no longer had access to advanced weapons now that Russia had joined the Western alliance. Moreover, Noonan had recently dispatched his secretary of state on a mission to Beijing, where she had successfully—and, surprisingly, even to Noonan—convinced the Chinese to stop supplying Teheran with surface-to-surface missiles. Noonan was convinced, with Moscow and Beijing in hand, that he had thoroughly outflanked Teheran.

The Iranian attack on the Estonian oiler had upped the ante, and now the president was deliberating the next steps in the face of Iranian mobilization. His seeming invincibility on foreign policy had not yet cracked, but the armor was beginning to wear a bit thin. The public had loved Noonan's bold talk and diplomatic skills, but now it was faced with the uncomfortably imminent reality of rubber actually hitting the road. Noonan's popularity was eroding—even his party's own polling showed evidence of a decline—and the political opposition was capitalizing on the shift in public attitude. The Senate minority leader was decrying Noonan's "brinkmanship" and urging Congress to look into the administration's "hysterically exaggerated" claims of Iranian involvement in recent terrorist attacks. Catcalls now greeted the president on some of his public outings, even during forays into the party's traditional strongholds. What was worse, Noonan was now beginning to share the public's unease, because events were not proceeding as he had anticipated. However, it still wasn't the time to panic.

The president's daydreaming had not gone unnoticed. The briefer, quickly sensing Noonan's disinterest, hurried through the next several briefing boards, sensing an opportunity to cut short the daily ordeal. As the focus shifted to a projection of Iran's anticipated actions over the course of the next forty-eight hours, however, the knot returned to the briefer's stomach. Noonan was once again fully engaged, sitting ramrod straight in his chair, almost glaring at the briefer, who paused momentarily, cleared his throat, then continued.

"Based on the activity at the Silkworm sites located along the coast near the Strait of Hormuz, we believe additional missile strikes against shipping will occur during the next two days. Our air attacks have so far failed to neutralize all the Silkworm sites. We estimate that sixty percent of the sites remain operational. Iran retains the capability to strike at will against targets in the vicinity of the strait. Given these capabilities, the intelligence community cannot rule out attacks against U.S. and allied naval combatants operating in the area."

The president pressed his fingertips together and leaned forward in his chair. The corners of his mouth curled ever so slightly upward as he started his daily cross-examination, a painful ritual that had assumed legendary proportions within the Washington intelligence community.

"So, Colonel Underwood, if I understand you correctly, you cannot rule out attacks against U.S. military forces? Does that mean your people rule them in? Does the weasel-wording mean our troops will get hit, or not? Weigh your answer very carefully, because decisions of supreme national importance will be made based upon the sound judgments you and your colleagues provide me and my staff."

The corners of the president's lips curled upward even more, but his expression was anything but friendly, and the final sarcasm in his comments did not go unnoticed by anyone in the room, especially Underwood. Underwood shrank back in his chair, sensing he was in the presence of a predator growing weary of playing with his prey.

"Mr. President, we believe the remaining Iranian missile sites are fully operational and ready to launch a strike against targets in the area. We believe they have the will, and probably the intent, to react to our recent air attacks with a strike of their own against friendly targets, including U.S. Navy ships operating in the area."

"Probably the intent? Tell me, if you please, Colonel, just exactly what that means. Are they going to hit us or not?"

"We believe there's a strong likelihood they will. Yes, sir."

The president leaned back in his chair, looked at Underwood intently for a moment, and then shook his head. "Everyone in the community agrees with this assessment?"

"All agencies agreed, Mr. President. The only exception was State. They rate the possibility of attacks against U.S. forces as very low."

The president smiled.

"Well, Colonel Underwood, I'm pleased to see that at least one agency is willing to swim against the tide. I guess this is as good an answer as I'm going to get from you folks today. Personally, I share State's skepticism, and I would hope that some of the other intelligence agencies would do a little more research. I don't think the Iranians will undertake such a course of action, because they are fully aware of the deadly consequences of striking directly at our forces. In fact, I would be very surprised if they launched any more Silkworms against targets in the area, given the scope of our military preparations. Since he didn't join us today, tell the DCI that I hope your analysts can do a little better in the future. I expect more from my intelligence experts, who, I assume, are reading the same information I am. Now, do you have anything else to tell me, something that might be of value during my discussions with the NSC later this morning?"

Underwood shifted uncomfortably in his chair. He was perspiring heavily under his jacket and had the awful feeling his suit pants had become stuck to the leather chair in which he was sitting, making escape from the presidential inquisition an embarrassing, though welcome, prospect.

"Just one additional item of interest, Mr. President. We have a report, wholly unconfirmed, that Iran is planning a major terrorist strike against a prominent target in the United States. No further information on the target or the precise date, although the source indicated it was likely by the end of the month."

"Meaning it could take place within the next three weeks?"

"That would be the timing. If the report is correct, sir." Underwood winced as soon as the words left his mouth. He had unwittingly provided the president an opening. Noonan promptly stepped through.

"And who, or what, is the source, Colonel Underwood?"

Underwood had to force out the words. "It's a report from Uzbeki intelligence, sir."

Noonan had just lifted his coffee cup to his mouth and the spray from his lips covered his desk, barely missing Underwood, who had involuntarily snapped back in his chair.

"Mr. President, I understand your skepticism, but this particular source appears to have some credibility. The Uzbeks have had some axes to grind in the past, given their dislike of the Russians. But their relatively close ties to most of the countries in the region, especially Iran, give them a unique access. Admittedly, there's been a lot of misinformation, or even disinformation, in the material they've provided us in the past. However, given the nature of this particular report, the director personally felt it important to bring it to your attention."

"Noted," Noonan said, as he wiped the coffee from his lips and made a halfhearted effort to clean off the top of his desk. The president's chief of staff had quickly leapt to his feet and started sopping up the presidential mess.

Obsequious little toady, Underwood thought as he watched Jeff Farley blot up the coffee on Noonan's desk. He quickly realized his unspoken judgment had been redundant, but then, he thought, so was Farley.

"Okay, Mike, thanks for the briefing. We'll see you tomorrow. Bring me some good stuff, then, okay?" The president had already stood up and was quickly walking out of the Oval Office as he delivered his parting shot.

Underwood frowned at the president's sudden familiarity but was unable to come up with a more erudite response than "We'll try, Mr. President." He felt like kicking himself. He sounded just like Farley.

As Underwood walked out, he gave a nod to General Phil Hannah, the chairman of the Joint Chiefs of Staff, who had sat quietly through the morning briefing. Hannah proffered a compliment on the briefing, then managed a minor smile and a barely noticeable shrug.

"We'll just have to see who's right, Mike. I know most of the analysts at the Pentagon agree with what you said, but the president makes some pretty persuasive arguments. He always does. From one blue suiter to another, I thought you did a great job this morning, as usual."

Underwood attempted a smile. "Thanks, General Hannah, I do appreciate that."

*   *   *

Underwood felt only marginally better as he and his fellow briefer and subordinate, Joshua Evans, walked out of the office and made their way to the waiting staff car. As they stepped outside the White House, Underwood spat out his summation of what had just transpired.

"Arrogant fucking son of a bitch. I don't need this bullshit, Josh. To think I volunteered for this. I should have stayed at the air staff. The chief of staff was a jerk, but at least he was willing to listen and accept the judgment of his experts. Noonan won't listen to anyone except Noonan. He talks to himself and thinks he's talking to God. Academic, my ass. Hell, the bastard is about as anti-intellectual and intolerant as you can get. The Germans have a way of summing up his character."

Underwood touched his index finger to his thumb in a circle, but the symbolism appeared to elude Evans. He looked quizzically at Underwood.

"Let me put it as delicately as possible. The president is an asshole."

Evans looked quickly around. "Good Lord, Colonel, don't you think you should tone it down a little? I'd think you'd want to be a bit more careful, given the location." Evans motioned with his shoulder toward the executive mansion just a few yards away. "Anyway, I thought you people in uniform couldn't talk about the commander in chief that way. Don't you have rules about such things?"

Evans had only recently joined the presidential briefing staff. Despite his reputation as a skilled political analyst and hard charger, to Underwood he still seemed very much—perhaps too much—in awe of the responsibilities associated with his job and of the president. Underwood attributed Evans's seeming skittishness to never before having been this close to the centers of power. He was afraid, Underwood concluded, that his boss's indiscretions would reflect on him and lead to an early termination of his recently acquired access to the Washington power brokers. And that, Underwood knew, would be the kiss of death for an aspiring member of the Washington elite.

Ken Currie

Underwood looked at Evans for a moment, quietly considering then discarding his subordinate's remarks. "Josh, my young friend, you clearly need to get around Washington a bit more. We'll get you over to the Pentagon one of these days, so you can catch a glimpse of the outer edges of the real world. However, let me put your mind at ease by recanting a bit in my judgment. Noonan's a son of a bitch, but he has a presidential aura. How's that? Does that pass the respectfulness test?"

Evans winced. Underwood continued his tirade.

"One more thing, about Noonan being the commander in chief. I've heard this line ad nauseam from the little weasels on his staff who continually call us up demanding this or that 'on behalf of the president.' From now on, you can take those calls. You can experience their practiced insolence for a while. I'll give the bastards credit for one thing: They've honed their skills in that area to a fine edge. So in one respect, Noonan's staff is simply carrying on a recent tradition of the cluster of young academic dilettantes who descended on this city in the early nineties. Best and brightest, my ass. There's only one kind of cluster they're good at."

Underwood paused to catch his breath and fish a pack of cigarettes out of his suitcoat.

"Foul, stinking habit," he mumbled as he lit up. "Every time I try to quit, I have to come here." He shrugged in the direction of the White House. "Anyway, I'm certain you're too young remember this, but years ago General McCaffrey—"

"The former drug czar?" Evans asked.

"Very good, Josh, now shut the hell up and let me finish. Before he was the drug boss, while he was still wearing the uniform and working at the Pentagon, he was greeted at the White House one morning by a prepubescent staffer who told him 'We don't like your kind.' I'm afraid that whiny-ass attitude is alive and well under Noonan. His staff reeks of it."

At that moment, one of those very same preadolescent staff members walked brusquely between Underwood and Evans, gently bumping against them, totally oblivious to their presence, as if to underscore Underwood's point.

Underwood shook his head and muttered "Excuse you" as he glowered at the young man, who wandered on without a look back.

"Just to set the record straight," Underwood continued heatedly, "nobody needs to remind me Noonan's the boss. But forgive a poor airman's disdain—it's a terrible character flaw, I know—for people who've never served a day in uniform but insist on all the military trappings, and the president's the worst, especially when he climbs aboard his helicopter or *Air Force One*. I wouldn't be a bit surprised to see him try to put general's stars on his academic robes the next time he makes his annual pilgrimage to his alma mater."

Evans's feeble attempt to chastise his boss had clearly struck a nerve. Underwood had never been so worked up, even though it was not the first time the president had nailed him on a briefing point. Evans moved in the direction of their pickup point, but Underwood stood his ground near the entrance to the executive mansion.

"I'll give Noonan the respect he's due by virtue of his office, nothing more," Evans went on. "And in November, I'll hold my nose and vote for the guy from the other party. Just because I can't stomach the thought of America going down the tubes because of Noonan's inability to listen to anyone other than himself. His majesty's supposed omniscience is going to bring us a boatload of trouble, someday, very soon. Bet on it, Josh. And when that happens, it'll be God help—not bless—the United States of America."

Chapter Three

Tom Mulkey shot a glance at his boss, received a nod, and began the briefing: "Good morning, General Allen. Here is the first of our status slides, showing the locations of the fast sealift ships. As you've already been partially briefed, the *Regulus* is unlocated. We were finally able to contact the MSC Ops Center, but they were unable to provide any amplifying information. Both MSC and the Mobility Control Center are trying to establish contact with the *Regulus* using all available means. The Global Transportation Network has received no signals for over six hours from the *Regulus*'s location transponder, and that is cause for concern, since the transponders normally relay position data to GTN every fifteen minutes. Central Command was, of course, alerted to the situation. CENTCOM has dispatched ships and rescue aircraft to the *Regulus*'s last reported position. We have provided a brief update on what we know to the National Military Command Center. We learned a few minutes ago that

20

the NMCC responded a bit zealously to our update and briefed the Deputy SecDef."

General Ray Allen, TRANSCOM's Deputy Commander in Chief, quickly diverted his eyes from the screen. "So the CINC can expect a call from the SecDef's office. Anything else? What about intel?"

Mulkey continued, "Sir, Lieutenant Colonel Waters is here to provide an update. Do you wish to move on to the intelligence portion of the briefing now, or hold off?"

"Let's hear it now. Morning, Bill."

"Good morning, General," Waters said in a grave tone as he stepped to the lectern. "We have some very limited information. We've been in contact with our counterparts at CENTCOM and at the National Military Joint Intelligence Center. They've provided some data, but it's sketchy at best. You've seen the partial message from the *Regulus*. We have some incomplete radar tracking data that may correlate to the aircraft the *Regulus* reported, but we simply don't know the identity of the aircraft at this time, or whether they continued on in the direction of the *Regulus*. We have no way of knowing whether their presence is connected to the loss of communication with the ship. Some of our folks believe that is the case, but there is no confirming evidence at this point. The only thing we can say with some degree of certainty is that the aircraft were slow movers and their point of origin was Yemen."

"And I know you're about to tell me the significance of that fact, correct?" General Allen asked, his tone letting Waters know he understood the significance of what he had just been told.

Waters looked straight into General Allen's eyes. He let out a small cough, and in the stentorian manner that was his trademark when he wanted to emphasize a point, said, "As you were briefed last week, sir, Yemen announced its solidarity with Iran in the current crisis. It has promised to do whatever it can to help its allies in Teheran. The fact that these aircraft originated in Yemen and were tracked heading—at least for a time—in the direction of the *Regulus*

21

suggests that the Yemenis may have decided to act on that threat. If they have, that has profoundly serious implications for the current level of tensions in the Gulf and for the safety of our assets operating in the area."

Allen nodded slowly. He briefly considered chiding Waters for his melodramatics, but decided that in this case the histrionics probably were warranted. Even so, he glanced at Brigadier General MacBride, the director of Intelligence, seated down the conference table, and smiled ever so slightly.

The J2 shifted in his chair, leaned forward, and began, "As Lieutenant Colonel Waters has so effectively pointed out, General Allen, there's a strong circumstantial case that loss of contact with the *Regulus* may be due to a hostile act. Our folks and yours are burning up the comm lines trying to nail this one down. We don't want to raise the alarm prematurely in Washington, of course, but at the same time, we don't want it to be business as usual if our ships are facing an immanent—and imminent—land-based threat from the Yemenis."

"Absolutely, Hank," the general replied. "But tell me, can your staff or the analysts at CENTCOM or in Washington figure out why the Yemenis would go after the *Regulus* rather than some other ship? Assuming it was the Yemenis?"

At this point, Mulkey interjected, "General, perhaps I can answer that. The *Regulus* is slower than most of our other ships, she was unescorted, and her course took her reasonably close to Yemen. There was no thought given to altering her course since, quite frankly, no one took Yemen's threats very seriously."

Allen shot Mulkey a skeptical look. "And now we are?"

Mulkey turned to Waters, looking for help.

"Sir, Yemen's military capabilities are very limited," Waters said. "Even though they have access to the Indian Ocean, their capabilities are roughly the same as those of Afghanistan whose provisional government also announced its support for Iran. For very good reasons, we all judged the threat to be low. That has changed, but we still don't know the precise nature of the threat, because we don't know what types of aircraft these may have been and whether in fact they were Yemeni. And, again, we can't confirm that they had anything to do with the loss of communications with the *Regulus*."

"Okay, okay, gentlemen, no need to be defensive here," Allen said as he raised his palm toward the briefers. "No one's being accused of dropping the ball. Yet. That will come later in Washington when word about this leaks out, and I can guarantee you all that it will. For now, this command will keep the lid on it until we have more facts we can present to the CINC and the NMCC."

General Allen turned to his executive officer. "Paul, since the CINC is traveling, I'll need to make the call to the Pentagon. As soon as we leave here, get me on the line with the SecDef's office. I'll try to impress on him the need to play this one close to the vest until we know exactly what's going on. The situation in the Gulf is bad enough without throwing more fuel on the fire."

Allen then returned his attention to MacBride. "Hank, your people have done a good job, and I know they're working in a virtual information vacuum here. But keep pumping the system and see what you can find out. Let me know anything, and I do mean *anything*, that intelligence can discover."

"Yes, sir."

"Gentlemen," General Allen continued, "let's dispense with the remainder of the briefing. I'll review the rest of the slides in my briefing book later when I have the time. Needless to say, this is issue number one as far as everyone on the TRANSCOM staff is concerned." Allen pushed himself away from the table and quickly stood to depart. He stopped as Colonel Williams raised his index finger. "Yes, Blair?"

"Sir, General Lee asked that I bring this to your attention. The information is in your book, but in case you're delayed in getting a chance to look at it, we wanted you to be aware of some items in the *Regulus*'s cargo. You're aware she was carrying the balance of the 24th's equipment?"

Allen nodded.

"She was also carrying some live ammunition and JASSMs. We're trying to find out how that happened. The problem did not originate here at Scott, we know that for certain, but the decision to mix the cargo—whoever made it—slipped past us."

General Allen raised his eyebrows and sat back down in his chair, gripping the edge of the table. "That's unfortunate. I expect more from all of you. I don't understand how something like that could slip past you. This is a major violation of procedures, and you're telling me no one noticed?"

Williams tried his best not to sound defensive in his answer. "General, we've already started reviewing the database and the logs to find out what happened. A preliminary check indicates the cargo manifest was updated within the past twenty-four hours to reflect the true nature of the *Regulus*'s cargo. We don't know why the discrepancy suddenly appeared, but someone in MTMC or MSC is going to tell us. Very soon."

"I'm only partly reassured, Colonel." Allen looked up at General Lee, who was hovering nearby. "I expect Operations to stay absolutely on top of this one. Let me know the minute you hear anything?"

"Of course," Lee responded.

Allen looked pensive for a moment, then continued. "So if *Regulus* was attacked by these unidentified aircraft, maybe from Yemen, maybe not, then the hazardous cargo may have complicated their chances. A catastrophic event would explain why you haven't been able to contact the ship. How many in the crew?"

"About forty-five, sir," Williams answered.

"All right, I need to know ASAP when you hear anything from CENTCOM regarding search-and-rescue efforts. Don't be shy about prodding them for answers. I'll also want an update as soon as you have one on how you think the snafu in the manifest came about. If I have to get on the horn to the MTMC and MSC commanders, so be it, but I want everything you can find out first."

"Absolutely, General," Williams responded, and wheeled away.

General Allen looked around the room as folks scurried back to their duty locations. This was getting very ugly very fast.

Chapter Four

Underwood continued to be haunted by images, distorted pictures of a past he thought he'd forgotten. The images tugged at the edges of his mind at first, but then they consumed him. It became difficult to focus on his work. What he had loved before now became a painful chore, and the burden was increasingly reflected in his ill humor toward others. His waking moments became reveries about times he remembered as much happier and more ordered. He recalled events as if they were snapshots, or bits of a crazy quilt of memories, and then his mind spun them into the whole cloth of lives he had never experienced but desperately wished he had. He wanted passionately to escape a present that had become unbearable. But how, and where would he hide?

He closed his eyes and dreamed of being in the sun, a warm breeze, and then lips, gently touching his skin. When he opened his eyes nothing had changed, but the imaginary touch of soft lips lingered, and made him even more desperate. He wanted to scream, throw something, hit something. Then he set his thoughts adrift once more, once again seeking solace in the past.

Ken Currie

* * *

Fifteen years ago. He passionately believed he had found what he sought while stationed in Guam. He had volunteered for the two-year tour on the remote island, hoping the distance from his problems would make them vanish while he was gone. When he returned stateside, he fervently hoped, everything would look different, be different. He could start all over. Fresh. No remorse. No looking back. He had been searching only for an escape on Guam. He had expected the isolation and solitude of the island to afford him the respite he craved. He had not expected that it would bring him much more.

He had been at Andersen Air Force Base for a month, concentrating on his new job, learning how to cope with the challenge of dealing with combat aircrews for the first time in his short military career. Despite a boss—a short, irrepressibly jovial lieutenant colonel in charge of the support squadron—who tried repeatedly to shove him out the door, urging him to take a break and enjoy what the island had to offer, he spent long hours in the office. He convinced himself—and finally his boss, though more through stubbornness than reason—that there was too much work to let him get away. And indeed he found, or rather made, the work to fill the time and keep him chained to his desk. The hours passed quickly, and forgetting everything except work became easy.

Seductive as seclusion at work had become, there came a point where not even his obstinacy could hold off his supervisor. Frustrated that his suggestions went unheeded, the squadron commander finally ordered him to take a three-day break away from the office. The commander lectured him, with only partly mock seriousness, that he would be court-martialed if he showed his butt in the office during the next seventy-two hours. He started to protest, but the deepening frown on the lieutenant colonel's face told him discretion was the far more valorous path to take. What the hell, he thought, he'd be back in the office on Monday. It wouldn't kill him to humor the old man for three days.

It would have been easy to transfer his hermitlike existence to his quarters, as he had done every evening since his arrival, and at first he thought of doing just that with his three-day reprieve from the office. But something urged him out the main gate, and he decided to embark upon a brief exploration of his temporary island home, if only to find a book or something to fill his time when he returned to his quarters.

He had driven to Tamuning to see what cities were like on Guam. He ended up walking the streets, peering into store windows, mindlessly examining the local merchandise.

That's when he saw her.

She was leaning on the counter, her body turned slightly toward him, holding a gold necklace in slender fingers. She was wearing Navy whites, and he could make out the lieutenant's epaulets on her shoulders. He noted with pleasure how the semi-opaque white skirt and blouse accentuated her figure. He felt a stirring within, and it propelled him into the store. As he pulled open the door, she glanced up, smiled, and returned to her shopping.

He feigned interest in the store's wares, wandering from display to display, drawing closer in an ever-tightening circle to where she stood, watching her as discreetly as possible. He took in the softness of her auburn hair, the fullness of her curves, and the smoothness of her skin. No wedding band, he quietly noted with pleasure. Finally, as the clerk walked away to locate a box for the item she wanted, he moved next to her. She turned to him as he had hoped, a renewed smile lighting up her face. He couldn't call her beautiful, but he sensed a smoky sensuality that caused a dryness in his mouth, a tightness in his chest, and a growing awareness on his part that he was close to being struck dumb, and quite possibly terminally stupid. He knew he should say something quickly, but discovered he was transfixed by intensely green eyes. *Her eyes are made of jade*, and he almost blurted out the thought as it flashed through his mind. He knew he was staring, but he couldn't stop.

Thankfully, she broke the silence and his growing embarrassment with a voice he judged the perfect match for everything else he had noticed about her. If she was uncomfortable from his stares, she did not show it.

"Hi. Stationed at Agana?" she asked, referring to the naval station southwest of the city.

He guessed he'd been betrayed by his haircut. "No, afraid not," he answered. "Very good guess, however. I'm up at Andersen. Permit me to introduce myself," he said, and he couldn't resist bowing slightly and sweeping his right arm around in front of him in a grandiose display of chivalry. He blushed as soon as he had made the gesture, but recovered from his embarrassment enough to continue the introduction. "I'm Mike Underwood, captain, United States Air Force, and lowly intelligence puke." He extended his hand in eager anticipation of being able to touch her slender fingers.

"Hi again," she responded, taking his hand with a wonderfully firm grip. "I'm Carolyn Younghart, Navy intel weenie." She smiled warmly, and they laughed together, he more than necessary, betraying his nervousness. "Normally, I'm out on the *Theodore Roosevelt*, but the Navy decided to send me out to Agana to help out on a special project. Seems I'm indispensable." She continued smiling.

Only at the last split second did he catch himself before he nodded emphatically.

He was thrilled by his good fortune. Normally, he had great difficulty screwing up enough courage to talk to women, despite his undoubted and well-known attraction to their wonderful diversity. In the past, his reticence had served his desires well; not a few women had been attracted to his seeming shyness. This was decidedly different. He was frankly amazed that his usual shyness had retreated enough to have brought him into the store. For him, it had been a bold step, and the shared background had been fortuitous—it made conversation, usually a horrible chore for him, relatively easy.

His job faded from his thoughts altogether. He was very much aware he was being drawn to her. What's more, he realized as he continued to gaze into her incredible eyes, he wanted her, desperately. Anticipation of wonderful possibilities emboldened him even more.

He invited her to a cup of coffee, once again astonished by his directness. To his delight, she accepted. They searched briefly and found a nearby café. For the next three hours they talked of work, where they came from, and where they hoped their respective jobs would take them. He was certain he found even more in common with her in terms of their aspirations. They both professed a strong desire to keep focused on supporting the "operator," and disdained those who thought only of what was good for their careers. To that end, they fervently voiced the hope of avoiding service in Washington. When the subject of possible assignments to the Pentagon arose, she made a cross with her index fingers, as if to ward off a demon.

"I know I'll probably end up there eventually," she conceded, "but I don't want to become just another mindless participant in the bureaucratic games they seem to love in the Pentagon. Every time I read the *Navy Times*, I have to remind myself that all that garbage isn't the real Navy, although sometimes I wonder whether there is such a thing. For now, military politics are well above my pay grade. Wouldn't it be nice if it could stay that way? Just stay focused on getting the job done? I think I'd quickly go nuts in a job where most of the people, especially the civilians, are clueless about what goes on in the field."

"Well," Underwood said, "if *I* have to leave the operational world for a while, I think I'd like to end up in a job where I can influence intelligence policy, rather than just pushing papers around. You know, make people keep their eyes on what's important. I think I could do that in a policy job. I have a feeling I'd be pretty good at that. But that's probably a bit too much to expect. Maybe somewhere down the line."

For just an instant, a very seductive instant, he thought that perhaps a job in Washington might not be the end of the world he imagined it would be. If he couldn't influence policy, he could bury himself in work and continue his anonymity. He had been told by others some Pentagon jobs offered splendid isolation. One could hide from the outside world forever, it seemed. He wasn't the least bit troubled by the inconsistencies between what he professed and what he desired. Just then he looked into her eyes again, and all thoughts of isolation—and most everything else—slipped far away.

He asked why she had joined the Navy. He confessed, admitting openly that perhaps he was still influenced by old stereotypes, that it was puzzling to him that a woman would want to serve in what was still a male-dominated service, especially aboard ship. He had sensed the pendulum of public sentiment changing direction once again. A consistently conservative Congress had been making abortive attempts for years to make it tougher for women to find their way into combat-related positions. But here, clearly, was someone managing to buck the current trend, at least so far, and it was clear she believed—or at least hoped—it would continue.

"My older brother was in the Navy," she said, and there was a mixture of sadness and pride in her voice. "In fact, he was a fighter pilot. He was killed in the closing days of Southern Watch. Folks started getting a little careless. Less watchful, I suppose. Anyway, he was jumped by a MiG-29. Before he could do anything, the Iraqi pilot had fired a missile. A bunch of guys on the AWACS were hung out to dry. We fired a few missiles at Iraqi SAM sites. I guess someone higher up judged those were fair trades for my brother . . . some poor schmuck sitting in front of a console. I applied to the Academy but was turned down. I ended up at Notre Dame, in ROTC."

Her smile returned as she concluded, "The rest, as they say, is history."

He was impressed. He had applied for the Air Force Academy because he wanted to get the hell out of Nebraska, even though it was only a state away from Colorado. His grades were good, and he had been a creditable football player in high school. The Air Force said yes. Four years of carrying a football. He had also carried a four-point, and that was good enough to get him into graduate school after graduation. But his classmates remembered him as a running back whose blond-headed good looks and athleticism led him to score more than touchdowns—not a scholar. There had been nothing as noble as following in a heroic sibling's footsteps.

"So why aren't you wearing wings? Or did you ever give that a thought?"

"My eyes," she replied. "They aren't good enough."

Again he stifled the urge to say something about her eyes.

"I wear contacts, so at least I can read intelligence reports."

Although she was happy with her assignments thus far, she admitted she still experienced problems being a Navy woman. She was gratified by the emphasis the Navy brass had given to alleviating problems of sexual harassment and discrimination. Despite that progress, she argued, it was still very much a male-dominated world. The old boy network remained a potent force, with emphasis on *boy*. Her eyes caught fire as she described in vivid detail the various people she wanted to murder. There were still those who believed they could make barely veiled suggestions about how she could guarantee herself a more promising future.

"Do you believe it?" she asked. "They still do it. Oh, they're not open about it, mind you, but the implications are clear. And they always make sure no one else is around. What's worse, it's usually the guys with the sterling records, on paper, the fast burners, who are the worst. Maybe they feel that gives them the license, or the cover, to do whatever they want."

She paused and gave him a smile, as if she sensed her bashing of men was going too far. "Don't get me wrong. They're not all knuckle-draggers. I've worked with and for some great male officers. But some of them have evil twins, and I do mean evil. How would these creeps like it if someone grabbed them by the crotch and told them there was a way they could guarantee their next promotion?"

He couldn't resist. "Actually, some of them probably would be thrilled." He instantly regretted the remark.

She grimaced, then forced a smile. "You know what I mean. How about a little turnabout?" Then she added, with a vehemence that startled him, "In any event, I've decided

I'm going to take the Chief of Naval Operations up on his word. I'm going to adhere to my own zero-tolerance approach in dealing with my male counterparts. You heard it here first, Michael Underwood, captain, U.S. Air Force. So if you read about a bitchy Navy lieutenant trying to bring up some randy admiral on charges—"

"It'll be Carolyn Younghart."

"Roger that."

He had frowned briefly during her small diatribe, but not perceptibly. Too many of his male colleagues acted the same way, and he sure as hell wasn't exactly innocent. He told the jokes, made the remarks about the lookers in uniform with great sets of wheels or headlights. He therefore wasn't about to do or say anything about their actions, even when he knew several who had crossed well over the line. He had done nothing, even then. He hadn't really thought much about it, until now. Those feelings, that past inaction, now stood in the way of what he wanted. He suddenly felt a twinge of guilt, because he knew that he explicitly wanted the same thing from her other men had only suggested. But he salved his conscience by telling himself he was seeking no favors and could promise nothing in return. He simply wanted her. Period.

She glanced down at her watch. "Oh, good Lord. I totally lost track of the time, Mike. I've got to get back to the base." She gave him her warmest smile. "It's been absolutely great. You Air Force guys aren't so bad, contrary to Navy pilots' reports."

"Well, I should warn you about the rest of them, I guess."

She declined his offer of a lift back to Agana, but only because she had a rental car.

"You can drive next weekend, Mike, when we go exploring the island. Does that sound like a plan?"

He grinned, most certainly like an idiot, thrilled their first encounter had gone so well that *she* did not hesitate to propose their next meeting.

"A terrific plan, Lieutenant!" He took her proffered hand, holding it longer than he should have. She pulled it away, but very gently and slowly.

He felt wonderfully smug as he drove back to the base with the car top down and the radio going full blast. Images of her whirled through his mind until he came to rest upon one particular vision of his hands exploring the contours of her breasts. He was instantly aroused, and he could think of little else except doing everything he possibly could to make that vision a reality. He'd never be able to concentrate when he got back to work, he mused happily. He was convinced he would be hopelessly distracted by thoughts of the afternoon and expectations of the coming weekend.

But he did work. In fact, he didn't think much about her until Friday afternoon, immersing himself once again in reports, briefings, and debriefings. He swapped stories with a few of the crews, totally forgetting the vow he had made. As quitting time finally rolled around, he stuck his head in the boss's door to wish him a good weekend.

"Same to you, Mike. Enjoy the local scenery. Try to meet someone." Then he added with a smile, "For God's sake, Captain, get a life other than this place, okay?"

"Yes, sir," Mike said, and smiled back. He snapped the squadron commander a sharp salute and headed out the door. *I have met someone*, he thought, and by the time he reached his car, he was thinking of nothing else. Like a mental light switch, he had cut off all thoughts of work. When he reached his quarters, he could no longer control his impatience to see her. He couldn't wait until tomorrow. He called the base operator at Agana in search of her phone number. He happily punched it in, then was bitterly disappointed when there was no answer. He slammed down the phone.

Ridiculous, he told himself, but he unsuccessfully fought jealousy. He absentmindedly flipped through the TV channels and rummaged through some journals, throwing the last one at the TV set in frustration. His mind wandered to less noble thoughts. He imagined she was out with someone else, that the arms he wanted so desperately around him were around another. The thought angered him more than it should have, more than he could explain. They had barely met and had talked only a little while. But he knew he wanted her. He ached for her. In his wanting, she became his and his alone. No one else could have her.

He could bear the tension no longer. He called it quits and went off to bed, where he punched his pillow angrily and rolled under the sheets in a seemingly hopeless battle. Finally, more out of exhaustion than anything else, he fell asleep.

He dreamed of being naked and pursued by a pack of wolves, snarling ferociously and biting at his heels as he ran through unfamiliar city streets. The wolves called to him to stop, and as he turned, they were transformed into men in strange attire. He looked down at himself; he was no longer naked. At first he seemed to be wearing a uniform, but he couldn't recognize it. The uniform turned quickly into a long, white, flowing robe. As he stood before them, examining himself, looking at the robe hanging down from his arms, one of the wolf-men said, "You will become as one of us."

He shook his head vigorously and tried to shout, but he could already feel the changes taking place within his body. Hands reached for him, and cold fingers wrapped themselves about him. He began to scream. He snapped awake and felt the cold, sweat-soaked sheets wrapped tightly around his arms and legs.

She was waiting by the curb as he drove up. Her glowing smile forced him to put the discomfort and suspicions of the night before out of his mind. She was wearing shorts that showed off even more of the wonderful legs he had noticed during their first meeting. The top several buttons of her bright yellow blouse were undone, and he had to force his eyes to look elsewhere. He was disappointed to notice that she was wearing aviator-style sunglasses; he would have to wait until later to see those emerald eyes once again. She held a picnic basket in her hand.

"Hey, you puke," she said as she climbed into the seat beside him, setting the basket on the floor between her legs.

"Hey, yourself, weenie."

She settled back into the seat and propped her arm on top of the door.

"I've really been looking forward to this, Mike. It's been one lousy week. But I'm not going to depress you with the details." Then her voice brightened noticeably, and she almost sang out, "As you can see, I have packed us a feast. And one guess as to who *thou* is."

She opened the top of the basket to reveal some baguettes, two small wheels of cheese, and a bottle of wine. She held up the bottle. "I trust you like Australian wines, *mon Capitain*. This is a Shiraz. One of my all-time favorites."

"Nope, never had it. But I'll trust your professional recommendation. My compliments to the chef, Carolyn. This looks absolutely great."

She tucked the wine back into its pocket, set the basket back on the floor, and reclined comfortably into the passenger seat. "Okay, Underwood, I'm at your mercy. Let's blow this joint!"

"Aye-aye," he said, and chuckled. He stole sidelong glances at her, hungrily taking in a different part of her with each look.

"Watch the road, Mike!" she shouted as he bounced the front wheel against the side of the road. "Where *is* your mind?" She caught him looking sheepishly at her. Her knowing smile revealed a total awareness of where his thoughts had been wandering.

They found a spot overlooking the ocean. There were two other couples, but they were as preoccupied with one another as Mike was with Carolyn. He rummaged around in the car's trunk and found an old blanket, relieved it was clean. He made a grand ceremony of spreading the blanket for her.

They feasted on the wine and cheese and, propped on their sides on the blanket, talked for hours more. He felt giddy, but he was sure it was Carolyn and not the wine producing the feeling. He had talked her into removing her sunglasses, finally having to confess how much he loved her eyes. Then he admitted they were only two of the many things he liked about her, and his eyes involuntarily drifted down to the opening in her blouse. He caught himself and abruptly brought his attention back to her face.

He felt embarrassed, but he also felt aroused. He leaned forward on his elbow and was pleased when she leaned toward him as well. Her lips on his were wonderfully soft. He felt the curve of her breast as she rested against him.

"I think it's time to go," she said. Her voice had dropped an octave. She placed her hand on his inner thigh and gently rubbed his leg.

He quickly packed things away. He struggled to place the car in first gear, then discovered how much better it worked when he pushed on the clutch. He slapped the accelerator, and the car kicked small coral stones into the air as he sped away from the picnic spot.

"Slow down, Mike, there's plenty of time. We have all weekend, and you don't want to kill us before we get back."

He steered the car into a spot in front of her building at Agana. They had stopped talking. He opened the passenger door and followed her quietly to her door. She momentarily lost her composure as she fumbled for the key in her bag. Having found it, she quickly opened the door, reached back without looking, took his hand, and pulled him into the room. She closed the door as he stood dumbly just inside. She turned slowly and smiled, then reached up and pulled him toward her. As their bodies touched, there was no longer any secret about the effect she was having on him. Their lips still locked, she led him to the couch. He had never been very good at getting through this moment, but in this case he had no trouble removing her garments; she provided all the help he required. He quickly disrobed, and even though the apartment was chilly from the air-conditioning, he discovered he was perspiring heavily.

His hands and lips made their way to her breasts, and as he moved between her legs, he wondered what he was doing. Any lingering questions to that effect disappeared, however, as she wrapped her legs around him. He had what he wanted.

He spent the remainder of the weekend in her room, exploring every part of her. He finally, very reluctantly, left her late Sunday night. She told him that as much as she would like to spend the rest of her TDY in bed with him, they both had better get some sleep. He held her body tightly and gave her a goodnight kiss, then leaned down and kissed her breasts one more time.

"You know I don't want to leave," he said. "Next weekend?" He struggled against a momentary fear she would say no.

She smiled. "Of course next weekend. And every weekend after that. Kiss me again, you crazy man. Then get the hell out of here so I can get some sleep."

As he walked toward the car, he looked up into the Pacific sky. There was no moon. He was convinced he could see every star in the universe, and they were all smiling at him. "Thank you," he mouthed. He returned to his quarters and fell exhausted into his bed, still dressed.

He dreamed of the women he had known, asking first one, then another to marry him, unconcerned that each said yes. And then he dreamed he was falling off a cliff, and as he slowly tumbled, he looked down and could see nothing below.

His daydreaming was interrupted by the ringing of his phone. He was only vaguely aware of the voice at the other end.

"Colonel Underwood, you're wanted in the director's office."

He replaced the phone, had one last fleeting thought of Carolyn, and hurried down the hall.

Chapter Five

19 August, 1030 hours EDT

One can get lost in Washington. Nothing seems out of the ordinary. The unusual, the eccentric, the outrageous is the rule. So no one noticed the tanned, muscular young man and his two canine companions on the Ellipse on this very hot, muggy summer's day. He was dressed in cut-off, slightly tattered Levi's, a Grateful Dead T-shirt, and a red bandanna tied about his head. He wore a gold chain with a pendant that vaguely resembled a cross between an ankh and the symbol for the "Artist Formerly Known as Prince." In short, he blended right into the crowd. A somewhat comatose rottweiler lay serenely at his side, its mouth twitching periodically to ward off the occasional fly that tried to land on its nose. The other dog—an aptly named springer spaniel—bounded happily, and idiotically, around the young man, hoping that they would once more play fetch with the bedraggled Frisbee his master had so thoughtfully brought along.

The young man tried in vain to get his overly playful pet

to sit still. He wasn't angry or frustrated with the dog's behavior; in fact, after a few ineffective attempts to get the dog to sit, he turned his gaze back toward the skies along the Potomac, watching attentively as the endless stream of passenger aircraft headed into Reagan National Airport. The spaniel continued to dash madly about, oblivious to the airplanes and the noise, running up to strangers and then dashing away as they tried to pet him.

Reagan National Airport was the bane of all sane airline pilots. The approaches to the airport took aircraft over heavily populated areas, although attempts were made to keep the planes on a clearly delineated path up and down the Potomac. Strong winds would frequently force the planes off the desired course, and they would periodically stray over the high-rise office buildings in Reston, Virginia, or come perilously close to the "restricted" airspace over the Pentagon. The pilots would crab their aircraft in a sometimes perilous attempt to stay in the landing pattern; from the ground one gained the distinct impression that the planes were flying sideways. Takeoffs and landings required great skill—and nerve—especially in bad weather. It was the kind of approach only a carrier pilot could love. And, to the discomfiture of the passengers, there was the occasional airline pilot who thought he *was* bringing it down on a carrier deck.

There had once been strong public sentiment to close the airport, or at least sharply curtail flight activity. But congressional support—the thought of all those VIP parking spots so close to the Capitol was too hard for senators and representatives to resist—kept the airport open. And multimillion-dollar expansion and renovation of the airport had sealed its future once and for all. So the endless flow of passenger traffic along the river continued unabated.

If there was anything remarkable about the young man on the Ellipse, it was the state-of-the-art cellular telephone he pulled out of his well-worn backpack. He spent most of the morning of his stay in front of the White House speaking on the phone, inaudible to all except the party at the other end of the line. Around noon, as the temperature climbed and the humidity became unbearable, he packed up his belongings, awakened the still-snoozing rottweiler, succeeded in getting the springer on its leash, and walked quickly toward the parking space he had successfully procured by arriving before Washington's rush-hour nightmare had begun. He loaded everything, including his animals, into a bright red BMW 750. He eased the car into the noontime traffic and disappeared. No one really noticed.

Chapter Six

Underwood peeked around the corner of the DCI's door, since there was no one in the outer office. The director was huddled with his secretary, the deputy director of Intelligence, the director of Near Eastern and South Asian Analysis, and the chairman of the National Intelligence Council. Off to the side sat an analyst Underwood had seen several times around the headquarters building; he placed the face but couldn't remember the name. *Not important,* he thought, given the rest of the cast gathered in the room. The DCI caught sight of Underwood hovering outside the door and motioned him in.

"Mike, we wanted to get you in here as quickly as possible, because it looks like you'll be heading back down to the White House this afternoon to brief the vice president. President Noonan has departed for his afternoon campaign trip to Philadelphia. He'll be back in town in time for the state dinner tonight, but there won't be an opportunity to get to him on this. You'll have to brief him on this subject tomor-

41

row. I called these folks together so we can provide you an overall picture before you huddle with the analysts to finalize the briefing. The analysts are working on a draft script and graphics right now, but you may have to wing this depending on how much time we have. The vice president is over at the Hill right now, but he's due back at the White House in an hour. You need to be ready by then."

Underwood's quizzical expression turned quickly to concern with the director's announcement of the short-fused nature of this new tasking. He had until tomorrow morning to prepare for Noonan. Briefing the vice president would be a snap, however. Everyone in Washington held Robert Terryfield in universally low esteem. Terryfield's main claim to fame had been a book on the environment that simultaneously warned of the danger of global warming, a coming ice age, and the perils posed to the earth by asteroids and comets. The small, generally indecipherable, and wholly undistinguished volume had won him a place of honor in the pantheon of radical heroes. It had also secured for him the role of favorite target of America's political humorists, a status he already enjoyed because of his notoriously wooden speaking style. Of the many mysteries surrounding how vice presidents were chosen, Terryfield's selection ranked as one of the greatest. If Noonan had sought anonymity in his running mate, he had clearly found it with this political cipher.

The DCI turned to Walter Cummings, the head of Near Eastern and South Asian Analysis. "Walt, why don't you go ahead and tell Mike what NESA knows about the situation. Everybody sit down, since this is likely to take a while." The DCI got up from behind his desk and joined the others in the leather chairs clustered around the centrally located coffee table.

Underwood settled back in the softness of the fine leather, admiring the director's taste in furniture. The office presented a marked contrast to the spartan surroundings of the DCI's predecessor.

Cummings began, "We have a report from a very good and very reliable source—"

"Don't worry, Mike, he's not an Uzbek," the DCI interrupted with a mischievous grin at Underwood. "I'll tell you later, Walt," he said in response to the confused smile on Cummings's face. "Something that happened this morning. Sorry for the interruption. Please, go ahead. I'll be good."

"Sir, it's your nickel, anytime you want," Cummings continued. "As I said, we have a very solid, reliable report. It appears to corroborate the Uzbeki report that was briefed to the president this morning." At this point Cummings cast a cautious glance at the DCI. "According to this particular source, a hitherto unidentified terrorist group, whose name means 'Fist of God,' is planning a major operation within the continental United States. The likely target is a government building, or buildings, in Washington. The entire operation is being funded by Teheran. It is reportedly intended as retribution for our military attacks against Iran."

Underwood shifted in his chair, uncrossing then recrossing his legs. He had heard this story before. Dozens of times. Such reports constantly poured through the door, and since the start of the Gulf crisis, they had turned into a deluge. Although he wasn't a terrorist analyst by training or trade, Underwood's years as a military analyst had drilled into him the importance of being skeptical, even about the most "reliable" sources. He had fought a pitched battle with NESA about the report the president had burned him on that morning, and here was the head of NESA handing him another story.

Underwood raised his hand and looked at the director.

"Yes, Mike."

"Sir, maybe it's time to tell Mr. Cummings about the president's reaction to the briefing this morning?"

The DCI contemplated the proposal for a moment, then nodded. "Go ahead, Mike."

"It's fair to say he wasn't thrilled when I laid the Uzbek report on the table," Underwood began. "My butt is still burning, and I left a sizable chunk of it on the Oval Office carpet. We all know the president's background in Eurasian studies, his personal friendship with many of the Russian leaders, especially President Milyutin. We know how he reacts to reports from this particular country. I think there's still a question as to the wisdom of briefing him on the report this morning."

Underwood stared straight into Cummings's eyes, then looked at the director, who gently shook his head. The DCI had broken up the tussle between his NESA chief and the presidential briefer, reluctantly overriding Underwood's objections. Better to bring it up now and take the presidential volley, the director had decided, than be accused later of holding back information on a potential threat. Underwood went on.

"In any event, we baited the man, and he came up out of the water and swallowed hook, line, sinker, and fisherman. The president truly did a superb job of shooting the messenger and then stomping on the corpse. Now it's suggested I go back to the White House and brief the world's greatest skeptic that this time we're really, really serious about the Uzbeki source, and here's why."

There was a touch of anger in Cummings's voice, and he continued as if chastising an impertinent subordinate. "I'm not sure why we're questioning a decision made by the director. Suffice it to say NESA deemed it a valid report worth bringing to the president's attention. This one merits the same treatment, especially since it tends to confirm the previous report."

Underwood did not retreat. He knew the NESA chief seriously outranked him in the formal scheme of things, but he also knew he didn't work for Cummings. "The DCI now has the advantage of knowing what the president's reaction was to this morning's report. Although it may, in theory, be a wonderful idea to bring this report to his attention, I want to be able to tell the president just why this particular source is so credible and so wonderful."

"Meaning?" Cummings asked warily.

"Meaning I want to be able to tell the president about the source's background and access."

Cummings slapped his hands on the arms of the chair in frustration. "Good God Almighty, Colonel Underwood! How many bloody times do we have to go through this? You're not going to get that information. Even the DCI and

I have trouble prying it out of our friends down the hall, and for very good reasons, I might add. We don't want some White House staffer compromising a source. The president simply needs to know the source is solid and reliable."

"May I quote you to President Noonan on that, Mr. Cummings? If you had ever briefed the president, sir, you would have experienced firsthand his legendary suspicions concerning intelligence."

Cummings turned crimson. Everyone in the room knew he had tried repeatedly, and unsuccessfully, to garner an invitation to the White House. When the president wanted an expert opinion on the situation in the Middle East, he called in one of the directors from the National Security Council, or he rang up his old friend, Secretary of State Madison. He had never called on Cummings, and for one who had built much of his career on an ability to garner face time with the Washington heavy hitters, the rebuff was especially painful. Underwood's shot had unerringly found its mark, and he smiled inwardly, reveling in his success at perforating Cummings's well-known ego.

The DCI intervened. "Gentlemen, I think we're starting to go off the tracks a bit here. Walt, I understand the problems with information on sources. I've already had many long discussions with the DO about this, and he always makes a valid point. At some point, we invariably end up in a situation where we just have to say to the man in the Oval Office, 'Trust us.' That's difficult to do when the occupant harbors an abiding distrust of intelligence, as Colonel Underwood points out."

The DCI directed his attention to Cummings. "If we're going to convince a skeptical president, we're going to have to provide him additional facts. I'll talk with Bob one more time after our meeting to see what we can safely break loose on this one. I don't want to put Mike in a situation where he's simply a target for the president, but there *will* be a limit to how much we can share. I'll call Noonan's chief of staff and see if we can clear the room tomorrow of everyone except the president and the briefers. This president has an aversion to these little executive sessions, but maybe he'll buy off this time. If not, we probably should hold off until there's another corroborating source or we have more detailed information. If necessary, I'll brief the president on this issue."

Underwood had his head down in his notebook, but he cast his eyes upward toward Cummings to see if the NESA chief would offer to accompany the DCI. Surprisingly, he said nothing.

The DCI continued, "Before I do that, Walt, you need to convince me the president has to know about this latest report tomorrow morning."

"In light of everything that's been said, I would agree it's probably best to hold off." Cummings grimaced and looked at Underwood. "I stand by my comments on how to handle sources, however. Sometimes we just have to tell the president what he doesn't want to hear."

Brave words coming from someone who's never been in the foxhole, Underwood thought as he stifled a derisive snort.

Underwood turned to the DCI. "What does this do to the plans to brief the veep? We probably don't want to brief Terryfield on something we're not going to tell the president."

"We'll postpone, Mike. I'll have the staff square it with the White House. In case the issue comes up tomorrow morning during the briefing, tell them the report has been pulled back for further evaluation. Knowing Terryfield, however, the question probably won't arise."

The DCI stood up and started toward his desk. He stopped, turned his head, and asked Cummings, "Was there anything else in the report we didn't cover in this session that Colonel Underwood needs to know? Nothing comes to mind from our earlier conversation."

Cummings responded quickly, "Nothing important. Some minor details on possible means of attack, but given your guidance, we can hold off on that. Our analysts will provide the information to Underwood if anything else comes up."

Underwood noted the NESA chief hadn't said *Colonel* Underwood. And, he concluded, it was clear Cummings's analysts would tell him squat.

As he left the DCI's office, Underwood could hear footsteps hurrying to catch up with him. All at once, there was a ferocious whisper in his ear as Cummings fell even with him.

"Briefing the president or not, Underwood, one should remember one's place. Remember your position, and mine. Don't cross me again or embarrass me again in front of the director. Believe me, I can make your job very, very difficult."

Underwood stopped. He looked down at the floor for a moment, a smile flickering across his face. He knew what he really wanted to say, but realized that even the director, whom he considered a patron, would come down hard on him. He looked up, fixed the most benign smile on his face he could muster, and said, "Whatever, *Walt*." He then turned abruptly and walked away, leaving Cummings fuming in the hallway.

Underwood returned to his office, where Josh Evans had been on standby, waiting to see what would have to be done to get ready to brief the vice president. Evans stopped pacing about as Underwood walked in, and relaxed visibly when he was told the briefing was off. In time he'll get used to this being yanked around. At least Underwood hoped so, because he was driving him nuts.

"Okay, Josh. Let's work on tomorrow morning's briefing. We've got lots of time now, thanks to the DCI."

Evans stared and was tapping his pen on his desk.

"What?" Underwood asked.

"You going to tell me what this was all about?"

"Some other time, maybe. It's not important. Just be on the lookout for Walt Cummings. I have a feeling he's taking no prisoners."

"Terrific." Evans sighed as his boss laughed quietly. "You know, Colonel, losing friends inside this building won't make it any easier to keep track of what's going on."

"Thanks for pointing that out, Mr. Evans. I'll be sure to keep that advice in mind the next time Cummings ambushes me."

"Sorry, Colonel, I didn't mean to sound like I was lecturing you on how to do your job. That's certainly not my place. But after your comments this morning, and now this, I hope I can be forgiven for a little bit of concern."

"Noted, Josh. Now, if you'll concern yourself with the briefing, please."

Although Evans lacked the seasoning that many years in the intelligence community would eventually bring about, Underwood liked this energetic young man. He was dedicated, loyal, and would do whatever Underwood asked. Underwood had never been accused of not speaking his mind, but he had to confess that periodically he would deliberately let his comments stray well into the heretical just to watch Evans's predictable reaction.

There were times when Evans mannerisms drove him crazy, however. Josh had the physique of Ichabod Crane, save the unfortunate visage. He made a point of running every day, a practice Underwood had abandoned many years before. Evans's lunch consisted of two candy bars. He washed those down with a Coke and consumed many more in the course of a workday. And he constantly snacked. Underwood was convinced Evans's measure of nutritional value was based on a food's sugar content.

They were sitting at the conference table, working on the briefing text, when Underwood noticed a vibration. He looked up, but Josh was busily scribbling away on his legal pad. The vibration continued. Underwood placed his hands flat on the table; the vibration grew stronger. He pushed back his chair and peered under the table. Evans's feet were dangling over the feet of the chair, and his right foot was tapping madly away.

"Josh."

No answer.

"Josh!"

Evans looked up, startled.

"Josh, starting tomorrow, Cokes and candy bars are no longer allowed in this office."

Evans sat still, clearly perplexed by Underwood's decree. The vibration had stopped. He waited a moment, decided no explanation was forthcoming, and started writing again.

The vibration resumed. Underwood gathered up his materials and moved to his desk.

First he eats like a hummingbird, now he flutters like one, Underwood mused. *He'll need to develop the instincts of a raptor to survive in this town.*

Chapter Seven

Empire Air Express was a small venture. Five years old, it had started out with five aircraft, aging Boeing 737s, to handle the intended cargo flights from La Guardia to National Airport. As it turned out, these five were more than enough to handle the air freight business Empire was able to generate during the first few years of its existence. The company was still very much awash in red ink.

In a frantic effort to avoid bankruptcy, the company's president, Andrew Jackson Malloy, decided to diversify. He convinced a number of struggling resorts up and down the East Coast to allow Empire to provide charter flights. The very basic accommodations on the aircraft were well-matched to those offered by the second-rate resorts. Malloy had his crews reinstall the seats in three of the 737s. Miraculously, the FAA had approved Empire for the new passenger service, and Malloy began his enterprise with great hopes, offering cut-rate package deals to weary New Yorkers living on meager budgets desperate for a break from the city.

And it worked. The charter service would never be

enough to ensure operating profits, but it made a serious dent in the company's deficit. Malloy had great expectations that the express freight and charter business would allow him to expand operations to the regularly scheduled passenger shuttle service into the lucrative Washington, D.C., market. But he needed a break.

The break had come during what seemed the darkest moments for his business. He had been seeking a loan for capital expansion and was turned down by several banks. He had once again begun to despair over the future of his airline. His usually jovial mood had been replaced by a very bitter humor.

As often happens in such situations, good news appeared at the bleakest time. Malloy received a call from Commerce Europa Bank, a financial institution that had escaped his attention during his unsuccessful foray into the world of high finance. The loan officer informed Malloy that he had been told by a colleague at another bank—one that had just recently turned down Malloy—of Empire's plight. According to the Commerce Europa officer, his colleague believed Empire had a promising future, but the other bank simply couldn't get around lending requirements and Empire's current balance sheets. Thanks to the tip, Commerce Europa had done some checking on Empire and liked what it saw, particularly Malloy's willingness to venture into previously untapped markets.

Malloy made an appointment. The loan was approved the next day. In exchange for Empire Air's assets as collateral, Commerce Europa paid off his existing debt and offered him a $50 million line of credit barely above the prime rate.

Malloy couldn't believe his good fortune. He barely had the line of credit in hand before he began upgrading Empire's facilities. He hired fifty new employees and, at Commerce Europa's suggestion, placed an order for Empire Air's newest aircraft, a refurbished Airbus A300-600 medium-haul jet transport. The Airbus would be a dream come true for Malloy: It could be rapidly converted to either freight or plush passenger service. He was convinced he would soon be able to order additional aircraft. It was only a matter of time before he could start offering his long-hoped-for shuttle service to Washington.

The Airbus Industries representative sat across the desk while Malloy went over the final paperwork for delivery of the aircraft. There were a few papers to sign, but everything had gone remarkably well, thanks in large part to Commerce Europa.

"As you can see, Mr. Malloy, everything is in order. The aircraft obtained its final certification. The import license is in order. You should be able to take delivery of the aircraft next week. As you are aware, your pilot has completed training with us. I am told he did very well. One of the best students we've ever had. One of our company pilots will accompany him on the delivery flight next Sunday. All that information is in your package."

"Wonderful, Mr. Michaud." Malloy had returned to his trademark effusiveness. "I can't say enough about your company's responsiveness. And your service. It's more than I ever thought possible. Between your company and Mr. Hanafin at Commerce Europa, I feel like a kid who got everything he ever wanted for Christmas. Instead of saddling up the pony, however, I'm looking forward to taking my first ride on Empire's Airbus."

Michaud smiled politely at Malloy's metaphor, and he began stuffing copies of the papers back into his briefcase. "We experienced a slight delay ensuring the aircraft met your somewhat unique specifications," he said. "The changes you requested in the forward cargo area, including the change to the port cargo door and the floor, posed a bit of a challenge, but our engineers came up with a solution which I am sure will make you happy."

Malloy smiled. "I can understand the difficulties, having worked a little on aircraft design myself while I was in the Air Force. I was really impressed with what your people came up with. It'll work great, I'm sure."

"We weren't entirely certain of the purpose behind the

configuration you requested, so it was a bit of a stab in the dark. We are pleased that you are happy."

"The changes in the cargo area configuration were the brainchild of one of the new employees we hired after Commerce Europa came to our rescue. We were lucky to find him. I think he's come up with ideas for cargo handling that'll revolutionize the commercial air freight industry. Although I can't personally take the credit for the idea, I'm happy to take the credit for Empire Air. It'll be quite a feat for a small outfit like ours."

"Not quite so small as before, Mr. Malloy." Michaud leaned forward, almost conspiratorially, in his chair. "And can you share any of Empire Air's secrets with me? I know my company would love to know what you have up your coat."

Malloy grinned. "I think you mean 'up your sleeve.' I understand your curiosity, but I'm afraid I can't say anything quite yet. I'm sure you understand. Proprietary information and all that stuff. We wouldn't want to run the risk that one of our competitors would get hold of this information. Sorry, I'm not suggesting you'd leak the information. It's just better we keep the information in-house right now."

"Of course, Mr. Malloy. We understand the importance of discretion in my country. We don't pry. What you do with the product after delivery is certainly none of our business. Our only concern is to make sure our customer, whoever he is, is happy with the product and the arrangements. I trust that you are satisfied with the arrangements we have made for you and Empire Air?"

Malloy stood up and extended his bear paw of a hand to the Frenchman. "Monsieur Michaud," he drawled, "rest assured that I couldn't be happier."

Malloy's joy was short-lived. A few weeks later he sat glaring across his desk at Marcus Kuhlmann. Kuhlmann had introduced himself as Vice President for Marketing of the American Office of Modern Digital Technologies, a French-German computer systems company looking—he said—to break into the American market "with panache." Malloy disliked Kuhlmann instantly.

Ken Currie

Perhaps it was Kuhlmann's condescending tone when he used the ten-dollar word. Or maybe it was the severely trimmed mustache that twitched as he spoke, or the dark eyes that peered without blinking through tiny wire-rimmed glasses. Whatever the reason, Malloy suddenly found himself wanting to back out of the offer he had made with Kuhlmann's office over the phone. He didn't want to do business with someone who made his skin crawl.

"Mr. Malloy, based on what I've seen, your company truly is a perfect match for what we have in mind. Although your rates seem a little on the high side, your ability to move our cargo on the date and in the manner we want outweigh that negative factor."

Malloy frowned. "Could I have a bit more detail on that last point? Just how many of your folks are going to come in here and *assist* with the operation?"

Kuhlmann leaned back in his chair and crossed one knee over the other. "Obviously, I haven't been precise enough," he said with the hint of a smile. "Our cargo is extremely sensitive. It requires very special handling. My company's crew won't be interacting with your personnel at all. The MDT personnel will deliver, ready, and load the cargo completely on their own."

Malloy bit down on his cigar. "Excuse me? Do you really expect me to allow guys who don't know jackshit about aircraft operations to come cruisin' in here and get free rein over my facilities? Just how crazy do you think I am? You'd better look for somebody else."

"Calm yourself," Kuhlmann said as he tried to wave the now-standing Malloy back into his chair.

"I'll stand, thank you, since you're leaving."

"Mr. Malloy, may I remind you that you made a verbal commitment with my company over the phone. Besides, we're throwing a substantial amount of money your way. This seems like a small price to pay to land such a lucrative contract."

"It isn't a small price, Kuhlmann. This is my damned company. I run the operations side of the house. No one else does. No one. Period. Got that? I'll get along without your

54

company's business just fine. And an agreement over the phone doesn't mean shit."

Kuhlmann crossed his arms and stared at Malloy for a moment. He shook his head. "How would it look if word circulated among the New York business community that Empire Air reneges on contractual agreements because it doesn't want to meet specific customer requirements? How much revenue do you think your cargo operations would generate if that happened? And we can let our lawyers resolve the issue of whether a phone call means 'shit,' as you so delicately put it. Do you really want to find yourself in an expensive court battle?"

"Are you threatening me?" Malloy said, straightening his large frame to its full height. He glared down at the slender Kuhlmann.

"I'm afraid this is just simple reality. I know you've had difficulty getting your Airbus cargo operations off the ground. I know you have a very expensive potential white elephant on your hands. I know that if you're not worried about all of that, you should be."

Malloy's shoulders sagged. "You want to tell me where you're getting your information?"

"Don't be obtuse, Mr. Malloy. The bank referred us to you. My company is one of Commerce Europa's biggest customers. They saw us as an ideal match. Do you blame them for wanting to protect their investment? You have a golden opportunity here. Why are you making it so difficult? We're only talking about a few hours. Besides, how do you think the bank would react if they found out you refused to honor a commitment which promises to meet your financial obligations on the loan?"

Malloy sat back down.

"I think you're beginning to understand the logic of the situation," Kuhlmann said. "Now, let's discuss particulars. I promise you that MDT wants to make this as painless for you as possible. You won't want us to come back if we don't."

Chapter Eight

19 August, 1945 hours Local

"*Constellation*, this is *Angel One*. We're in the area of the target but do not have visual. Repeat, we do not have visual. Negative radar returns. Weather over the search area is deteriorating rapidly. Estimate we can remain in this location about fifteen minutes. Over."

The search-and-rescue helicopter from the USS *Constellation* had been dispatched to search for the *Regulus* as soon as the order had been received from the National Military Command Center in Washington. The NMCC had remained in continuous contact with the *Constellation*, and with TRANSCOM's Mobility Control Center, as the helicopter made its way toward the missing ship's last reported position. The weather over the search site had started turning ugly as soon as the helo had lifted off from the *Constellation*'s deck. Sunset was also rapidly approaching; the bad weather meant that darkness would come earlier than usual. The prospects for locating the ship, even on radar, were diminishing quickly. Even assuming the *Regulus*'s transponder had been working properly right up to the moment she became missing in action, the ship could still be anywhere within a 100-nautical-mile-square search area. It was becoming clear that additional resources would be required to locate her, but time and weather were not cooperating. The search would have to be resumed in the morning, assuming better weather prevailed over the search area. Reluctantly, a joint decision was reached by all three parties in communication that it was best to postpone the search until conditions improved.

"Roger, *Angel One*. You are ordered to terminate the search and return. We will resume operations at first light, weather permitting. Over."

"*Constellation*, request permission to continue the search for another quarter hour. Over."

"Negative, *Angel One*. Return at once. Appreciate the gesture, guys, but we don't want to risk losing anybody else. Over."

"Roger, *Constellation*, terminating the search. See you in thirty. Over and out."

19 August, 1215 hours CDT

The last several hours had not been happy ones for Tom Mulkey. He had spent most of the time on the phone with MSC headquarters in Washington and the Military Traffic Management Command unit at the port on Charleston trying to find out how ammunition had found its way onto the *Regulus*'s cargo manifest. MSC denied responsibility, suggesting the decision must have been made at the port. MTMC authorities in Charleston admitted the ammunition and the JASSMs had been loaded on the *Regulus*, but insisted they wouldn't have made such a decision without authorization from TRANSCOM and coordination with MSC. Someone in Washington or Illinois must have been responsible. And so it went, through repeated phone calls, until Mulkey wanted to strangle everyone in MSC and MTMC.

Obviously, he wasn't going to get a straight answer through his contacts. It was time to bump the issue up the food chain. He walked over to Williams's desk and laid out his tale of woe. He would be more than happy to place the problem squarely in his boss's lap and was elated when Williams said he would take it on. He deflated a bit when Williams suggested he should have come to him sooner, given the CINC and DCINC interest in the matter, but a final thumbs-up from his boss made Mulkey feel better that he had busted his butt for the better part of a day in a verbal jousting match.

He stole a glance at his watch and was pleased to note that his relief would be coming in just a couple of hours. He would finally get a break from all this, unless someone decided additional bodies were needed in the Mobility Control Center to handle the growing crisis caused by the *Regulus*'s disappearance. In that event, he would be looking at days—perhaps weeks—without a break. He wasn't thrilled with the idea of spending all that time at work, especially with the Cardinals getting ready for a long home stand. He could only hope that his counterparts at MSC and MTMC—who he was convinced were responsible for the asinine decision on the ammunition and JASSMs—would be putting in equally long hours. At least that would create a symmetry of pain.

Blair Williams wasted no time in picking up the phone and calling the chief of MSC's Operations Center, knowing that if he didn't get the answers he wanted, he would instantly elevate the issue to his boss, General Lee. In turn, Lee—a three-star—would, if necessary, call the MSC commander—a two-star—and read him the riot act regarding MSC's lack of cooperation in uncovering what had happened to the *Regulus*.

A chief petty officer answered the phone at MSC and informed Williams that his boss was in a staff meeting and couldn't be disturbed. He asked if Williams would like to leave a message.

"Chief Andrews, is it?"

"Yes, sir."

"Chief, put down your donut, get up out of your chair, walk into the conference room, or snack bar, or wherever Captain Thatcher is having his meeting, and tell him I want to talk to him right now. The staff meeting can wait. What I have to discuss with him is just a little bit more important." By now, Williams's voice had become a wondrous bass bellow that would have frightened away a pride of lions. He barked out staccato-style, "Do you understand, Chief Andrews?"

"Yes, sir. Absolutely."

Williams could almost see the chief standing at attention, and he couldn't resist a smile as he heard the thump of the phone being put down and the sound of quickly retreating steps. The chief apparently had been so nonplussed he had forgotten to press the hold button, simply dropping the receiver in his haste. It was only a matter of moments before Williams heard the sound of returning steps.

"This is Captain Thatcher. What can I do for you?"

"Mac, this is Blair Williams. I know you folks at MSC are probably jumping through hoops right now for many of the same reasons we are, but I need some help ASAP on an issue that surfaced this morning regarding the *Regulus's* cargo."

"Blair, I'd love to help, but we're putting together a briefing for the admiral. If you can call me back in a couple of hours. Or better yet, if you can have your guys call mine, they can provide whatever help you need."

Williams continued in the most level voice he could muster. "Mac, we've tried that route. Tom Mulkey, my cell chief, has been on the phone the better part of the day with MSC and MTMC trying to sort this out. He got nowhere. Now, unhappily and unnecessarily, I've had to step in, and I'm coming to you directly for the answers. The CINC and DCINC want the information as soon as we can get it. I think you can understand that our first priority is meeting their requirements, the MSC commander notwithstanding."

"Blair, trust me, I understand your predicament, but I've got an admiral looking over my shoulder right now, and he wants answers, too."

Williams's patience had run its course.

"Okay, Captain Thatcher. Let's terminate the bullshit. I am now *telling* you to provide me the information I require.

Cancel that. The information the CINC requires. I am instructing you to take whatever action is required to find those answers, regardless of what briefings you might have on the docket for tomorrow."

Thatcher had tried to interrupt the verbal assault, but Williams pressed the attack.

"Frankly, Mac, I'm amazed you tried to blow me off without the courtesy of even asking me what I'm looking for. This is the same song and dance Lieutenant Colonel Mulkey was treated to earlier today. That crap won't work with me. So I suggest we discuss what we need here at the unified command and how you're going to get it to me quickly and in the format I require. And, oh, rest assured, you're not being singled out. I'm going to have this same discussion with MTMC as soon as you and I are through."

"Now, look, Colonel Williams, I don't have to take this from another 0–6. I've got my problems and priorities, too. And my priorities right now are to take care of my boss. If you've got a problem with—"

"Yes, I do. This is not just another 0-6. When I'm on this floor, sitting in this chair, I'm talking with the full authority of General Lee and the CINC. I'm speaking as the unified command to the component command. Your priorities have just been preempted by the unified command's. If you like, I will have General Lee call Admiral Jackson, and General Lee will make the point at that level as well. Now, unless you would like to have the admiral ripping you a new one for not responding to a direct tasking from TRANSCOM, I suggest we talk about the kind of information I need and the time frame in which you will deliver it. Any questions?"

Williams knew that Thatcher was furious, but he also knew the Navy officer was smart enough to know when to cave. After one last sputtering attempt to resist, Thatcher gave in and promised Williams he'd have an answer within the hour.

"Thanks, Mac. You have a great day, okay?" Williams hung up the phone and looked around the room. Work had stopped, everyone's attention captured by their boss's quintessential performance. All of them were looking at him, and all of them were smiling.

"So, what are you people looking at? Get your butts back to work."

A brief round of applause rippled around the room before Williams cut it off with a swipe of his hand across his neck. But he couldn't suppress his own smile as he picked up the phone to call MTMC.

19 August, 1605 hours CDT

Colonel Williams and General Lee walked into the DCINC's office. General Allen was still on the phone; he waved them into the seats in front of them as he finished up his conversation.

"That's all the information we have as of now, Mr. Secretary. I want to thank you and General Hannah for your time this afternoon. I know the NMCC is keeping you informed of events on the ground as the search for the *Regulus* continues, but the CINC wants to ensure that you're aware of the additional information we have gathered through TRANSCOM's operational channels. If we have any significant new developments, I'll pass them along directly. In any event, I'll see you during the teleconference tomorrow morning."

General Allen returned the secure phone to its cradle and signaled with a nod toward General Lee that he was ready for the update.

"General, Colonel Williams just got off the phone with Captain Thatcher at MSC and Colonel Gutierrez at MTMC," General Lee began. "Blair's people have done an excellent job of prodding the components in Washington during the day, in the face of some resistance. That problem has been solved. Everyone now appears to be on the same sheet of music; that is, everyone understands their primary focus for now is finding out for you and General Petersen what happened to the *Regulus*."

General Allen leaned forward and rested his chin on

Ken Currie

clasped hands. He raised his left eyebrow slightly. "I would think that would go without saying, Preston."

"Sometimes, it seems, you *do* have to say it, sir. But, as I said, the communication problem appears to have been solved. Blair can fill you in on the latest."

Williams leaned forward in his chair and placed a folder on the general's desk. "Sir, these are faxes from both MSC and MTMC that trace how the ammunition and JASSMs ended up on the *Regulus*. Suffice it to say, it appears to have been a tragicomedy of errors, and that is the charitable way of describing what happened. Clearly, the left hand was clueless as to what the right was up to."

Allen pulled the folder across the desk but did not open it. "I'll look at these later, if I get the time. Give me the gist, Colonel."

Williams sat back in his chair. He did not betray the fact that he was disappointed General Allen did not look at the faxes after the proverbial goat-rope he had gone through gathering the information. He pressed his fingertips together in front of his chest and began his summary of the events.

"The ammunition and JASSMs were originally manifested for another ship, an ammo carrier, but somehow got left behind. Yes, sir, I know that sounds perfectly incredible, but I guess these are incredible times we're living through."

Williams noted that his feeble attempt at humor went nowhere. The general continued looking at him without any hint of expression. Williams pressed on and stuck with a straight recitation.

"Anyway, when it was discovered that significant numbers of artillery rounds and the extra JASSMs had been behind, apparently inadvertently, somebody in MTMC at Charleston decided to rectify the error by remanifesting the items on the *Regulus*, contrary to all operating procedures. The change was authorized by the deputy commander of MTMC, according to the paperwork, but I have been assured by MTMC headquarters that such an authorization was never given. Somebody—we don't know who yet, but we will—seems to have forged the deputy commander's name to cover up his mistake. The ammo pallets and the crated

JASSM canisters were then loaded on board the *Regulus*, the next ship due out of Charleston. Since she was carrying the remainder of the 24th Division's equipment, there turned out to be some wiggle room. Whoever fouled this up shoved the other items, the proscribed cargo, into the available space."

General Allen's expression still had not changed. Williams began worrying he had done a poor job of filling in the details. He looked at General Lee, who was also sitting motionless, obviously waiting for Allen to respond.

General Allen placed both hands palm down on his desktop. His mouth slowly turned downward into a barely discernible frown. He closed his eyes for a moment. When he opened them, their expression was anything but pleasant.

"General Lee. Colonel Williams. It's bad enough we have some unethical moron at Charleston falsifying papers and thereby endangering people's lives. It's doubly bad that we have others at the port who apparently were willing to turn a blind eye to what was going on. After all, these folks loaded these items without asking any questions, without double-checking, right?"

Lee and Williams nodded.

"What's really troublesome is that such a thing could have occurred within this command, even in one of the components. The CINC set a strong ethical standard for everyone at the beginning of his tenure. That standard has been drilled into everyone since day one. Obviously, some have not been persuaded by the CINC's message. Right now, there's at least one individual at MTMC who will very much regret the day he ran afoul of our very clear-cut guidelines. I hold that person very much responsible if anything has happened to the *Regulus* and its good crew, and he *will* pay the price."

General Allen stood up and walked over to the windows, his back to Lee and Williams. He looked out over the circle in front of the headquarters building and quietly studied the American flag fluttering beneath the eagle-capped pole that stood at the center of the circle. He rested his hands on the windowsill and continued.

"But I also hold us responsible." He looked briefly over his shoulder at his audience. "No, don't worry, I don't mean you two personally, but all of us. It is unfathomable that someone in this command could have made a decision potentially so detrimental to the safety and welfare of its personnel. It displays a cavalier—no, an arrogant—disregard for the welfare of others. And that won't be tolerated."

General Allen walked back to his desk, stopping behind his leather executive chair. He rested his arms on its back as he looked directly at Lee and Williams.

"Everyone in the world will demand to be involved in an investigation of the 'Regulus incident.' That will be especially true if, God forbid, she has gone down with all hands. Given the fact that the initial search turned up nothing, that outcome is beginning to look increasingly likely. The SecDef is already involved to a degree. If misfeasance within the command was responsible, his involvement will increase exponentially. I've no problem with that. We just need to hold his staffers at bay while we discover the truth. The same holds true for the chairman. The Navy will want to do its own investigation, probably the Army. That's a nonstarter for General Petersen and me. The Regulus was, or rather is, a TRANSCOM asset. This command and the appropriate offices within the DoD will take care of the investigation. The CINC will make that very clear to the service chiefs. But Congress will want its turn. We'll have to make sure the CINC is prepared well when he gets called to the Hill."

"Sir," General Lee said, "you know we'll dig until we discover everything there is to know. General Petersen will have all the information he requires, every step of the way."

General Allen waved off Lee. "I know that, Preston. I know your folks will come through in that regard. You've got great people working for you, and this fellow's one of them." The general nodded his head toward Williams. "What we must guard against is a siege mentality. This command will hide nothing. We also have to guard against this becoming a TRANSCOM versus the components issue. What hurts MTMC, MSC, or the Air Mobility Command hurts us all. We will uncover and provide all the relevant facts to the appropriate authorities when called upon to do so. There will be no shifting of blame, no scapegoats. Those who are responsible for this will be rooted out and dealt with severely."

Allen clenched his fist in front of him, as if grabbing someone around the neck. "That's not going to be the end of it, however. We're going to make it very clear that after the *Regulus* matter is resolved, this command will undertake a thorough top-down review of its procedures. We *will* put our own house in order, before someone else decides to do it for us. Hopefully, one of the good things that comes out of this will be the final consolidation of control over component operations under your people, General Lee."

General Lee nodded vigorously. Reining in the divisive tendencies among the command's components had been a long-standing challenge. It was a battle continually fought by almost all of the unified commanders. The CINC, DCINC, and Lee were all agreed on the appropriate remedy, but they continued to encounter resistance from the components and the services. The end of that truculence now appeared on the horizon, a good outcome out of a very bad situation.

"Preston, I know this is a bit out of the ordinary. I know Colonel Williams has a job to do here, especially now. But our liaison at the Pentagon is not going to be able to do what has to be done with regard to the *Regulus*. Quite clearly, someone from the operations directorate needs to be involved. We also need someone on the scene who thoroughly understands all phases of mobility operations from soup to nuts. Also, someone who knows how to handle accident investigations, and someone who won't bend to intimidation."

At this point General Allen looked directly at Williams. "Blair, you're it. You probably guessed that. I know looking into possible ship sinkings is not quite the same as being on the inspector general's staff or doing accident investigations in the Air Force, but you have the experience in these areas, or at least that's what your bio tells me."

Williams wasn't sure how he should feel. He had to admit

that this much ego-stroking felt wonderful, and he was thrilled to have the CINC and DCINC placing this much responsibility on his shoulders. But he also knew the considerable cost that was about to be inflicted on his family life, beyond that already imposed by his working long hours in the MCC and countless temporary duty trips. But his life had ceased to be his own to control as soon as he pinned on the eagles. He knew it. He accepted it. He was in no position to protest.

"The bio's correct, of course, General Allen." He smiled weakly. "I knew the IG experience would catch up with me someday."

Allen returned the smile, but much more strongly and warmly. "I know what must be running through your mind, Blair. You're likely to be on the road quite a bit over the next few days and weeks. This isn't going to be easy for any of us, especially for you. The CINC and I are likely to run your legs off over the next several weeks. And it's going to extract a hell of a price from our families at a time when our operations tempo is already causing widespread geographic bachelorhood. But you know as well as I do that what you're about to do is absolutely essential."

"Yes, sir. Absolutely."

"Good man. I've already called Colonel Pettibone, the TRANSCOM liaison at the Pentagon. You'll be working out of his spaces. He's been instructed to render you all possible assistance. You'll want to pick a couple of folks from your staff to go with you. I've also arranged with the J-6 to have his people equip you with one of the new cellular secure phones. Keep that little gem with you at all times. In fact, don't let it out of your sight. Admiral James will draw and quarter both of us if anything happens to that little treasure."

Williams laughed along with General Allen and General Lee. Everyone knew the J-6's reputation for being a mother hen when it came to the computer and communications systems for which his directorate was responsible. James was especially protective when a new toy came along.

Allen pushed himself up from the back of his chair to his full height of six-four. Williams thought he'd like to see the admiral try to take on this very formidable Army three-star.

"Well, gentlemen, I guess that concludes our discussions. Blair, you're being given carte blanche by General Petersen to find out what the hell happened to the *Regulus*. Don't worry about stepping on any toes or offending any sensibilities at MSC and MTMC. I'm about to call the commanders to make it clear they and their staffs will cooperate fully with you. I expect you to call me immediately if you have any problems in that regard. General Petersen and I will expect daily updates, of course. I know you'll be talking to General Lee a lot more often than that, however. He can keep us informed of the latest developments, if necessary. Good luck to you, Colonel. Find the bastard."

General Allen shook Williams's hand heartily.

As Williams walked back to the third floor with his boss, he pondered what had just transpired. As they continued walking, he looked at General Lee.

"Sir, if you don't mind my asking, what the hell just happened? I thought I was laying the facts out for the DCINC for the first time, but I get the distinct impression he knew exactly what I was going to tell him. I mean, this team he wants me to head out to Washington. That didn't come off the top of his head. You don't make something like that up on the spot, even if you are the DCINC. That was a well-scripted plan, including the part about how he'd already told the TRANSCOM liaison to clear the decks for me."

Lee fixed Williams with a brief stare, then just shook his head. "Blair, how many years do you have in the Air Force?"

Williams gave Lee a puzzled look. "Close to twenty-six. It'll be twenty-six this November."

"Twenty-six years, all that experience, and you still haven't figured out why some guys make general."

Williams frowned as they continued walking. He felt like a fool and didn't know why, but he knew his boss was about to tell him.

"As soon as the DCINC heard about the manifest gaffe at this morning's briefing, he quickly figured things out. I think we all did. We knew someone had screwed up, or worse. Big time. The fact that none of us caught the mix-up until this late in the game indicated that someone tried their best to hide what they had done, and they were successful up to a point. But they were also stupid. You can't hide something like that in this command, for God's sake. You can't change manifests on a whim and expect to get away with it. The DCINC knows that whoever is responsible for this almost certainly has a record as a shady operator. He'd have to. In the process, he's undoubtedly left a trail. You're going to sniff him out, and any buddies he might have. And then the CINC and the DCINC are going to crucify him, or them, regardless of who they are."

Williams mentally kicked himself. Of course the DCINC had figured this out. It was obvious . . . now. "Thanks for the insight, sir. Still much to learn even after twenty-six years."

"Believe me, Blair, there's still a lot to learn after *thirty-six* years."

Williams looked at his boss, expecting to see a smile. There wasn't one.

Chapter Nine

"Colonel Underwood, it's your wife on line two."

He took a deep breath, cursed silently, and punched the button on the telephone.

"Colonel Underwood speaking." He made a point of answering formally, even though he knew who was on the other end of the line.

"Mike. Hi, this is Jennifer. How are things going?"

"Great. What's up? What do you need?" There. Just the right amount of brusqueness. Also the message that he knew the only reason she would be calling was that she wanted something. She always did.

"I don't need anything, Mike. I was just calling to say hello. It's been a couple of weeks since we talked. I wanted to know how you were doing."

"Things are going just fine. I'm awfully busy. You shouldn't be calling me at work." He was growing impatient and wanted to end the conversation as quickly as possible, but she persisted.

"I'm sorry. I was getting lonely up here. It looks like I'm going to be working on this case for another few weeks. I've been trying to call you at home, but all I get is the answering machine. Been working long hours, I guess?"

"Yeah, you could say that. I really have to go. I've got a briefing to go to this morning. In fact, I'm on my way out the door right now," he lied. "Then I'll be getting ready for the dinner tonight."

"Dinner?"

"Oh, yeah, I forgot to call you. We were invited to dinner at the White House tonight. In honor of the Hungarian prime minister. I don't really have the time, but—you know—it's one of those command performances. Even though I'll just be a small part of a large cast. I guess I must have impressed the president in some little way."

There was silence at the other end of the line. His shot had found its mark. He had kept the news of the invitation from her, knowing how disappointed she would be when she found out she had missed an opportunity to hobnob with Washington's elite.

"Mike, why do you do this?"

"What are you talking about?"

"Why do you play these stupid games? You know I'm upset you didn't tell me about the dinner. I don't know why you didn't call me. I would have loved to go. But I couldn't have gone anyway. This business really has me tied up in New York. So if you thought you were going to hurt me, forget it. Do me a favor, Mike."

"What kind of favor, Jennifer? Do you want me to drop dead?"

"Hold that thought, Mike. But for now, how about just growing up? We're not in a contest. We're supposed to be in a marriage."

"Thanks for the advice, Jennifer. I always treasure it so when it comes from you. Especially when it deals with the problems concerning our relationship."

"I give up, Mike. I don't understand you. I guess I never will."

"Nope, guess not. Goodbye." He quickly hung up the phone, hoping he had made the click as loud as possible.

If there had been a time when the relationship between them had been a good one, he had long since forgotten when that might have been. It now seemed as though he had been in this rut forever. The track had worn so deep he couldn't climb out if he wanted to, but he had never found himself willing to make the effort. Things had continued to just glide along, albeit in a continuously downward spiral. Better to stay with the devil he knew . . .

They had met while he was attending graduate school at the University of Michigan, a gift he had earned for excelling as a student at the Air Force Academy. He was completing a graduate program in international relations; she was putting the finishing touches on a law degree. He had never been fond of the legal profession and had never met a lawyer he had liked or trusted, but he quickly put those concerns aside after their first meeting.

He had rounded a corner in the library stacks, searching for a book on the Ottoman Empire, concentrating on the call numbers but not paying attention to where he was going. She had happened by at that precise instant, and their collision had sent the books and papers flying out of her hands. He was profoundly embarrassed, abjectly apologetic for what he had done, and unabashedly drawn to her soft brown eyes and incredibly long black hair. It had not been the first time he had been attracted to someone in this manner; it certainly would not be the last. But at least for the time being, he was convinced their running into each other this way was an act of karma, and he was not going to deny the twists and turns of fate. He immediately asked her to coffee as a first act of contrition for what he had done. She accepted. Six months later, right after graduation, they married. Six months longer, and he was convinced he had made the greatest mistake in his life. His attention began to drift elsewhere.

By then, he was packing his bags for an assignment to

71

Nellis Air Force Base. They had decided—he hadn't argued much—that she should accept the best offer, given all the time and effort and money she had devoted to her studies. She accepted a position with a law firm in Baltimore. She headed for the East Coast, and he headed for Las Vegas.

They would not see each other for two years. He wrote her nine times and called her a bit more often, but not much. By then, he had volunteered for an assignment to Guam. He hadn't discussed the decision with her. In fact, he presented the assignment as a *fait accompli*, telling her that the Air Force had made the decision to send him there. He had no choice but to comply. She believed him. Two more years passed, and he was no more attentive in his letter writing than he had been in Nevada.

He returned from Guam to an assignment at Langley Air Force Base in Virginia, and his mind remained fixed elsewhere. The location was perfect as far as he was concerned. They remained married, separated by seven hour's driving time. They got together when they felt like it, which wasn't often. Both let time slip by quickly, both passionately devoted to their jobs, although his passion was fed by different fires. He wandered into and out of several relationships with other women along the way. He assumed—and it certainly helped assuage his conscience—that she spent at least some of her spare time in the same way. He didn't know his assumptions were wrong, and he wouldn't have believed the contrary in any event.

Her passion for her work was real, however. She often wished they could spend more time together, and she often felt guilty about the fact they did not. But as far as she was concerned, he was the only man she would ever let get close to her in that way. Life was too short, and there was too much she wanted to accomplish. She couldn't afford to waste time on dalliances, even if she had wanted to.

And so their arrangement continued. He moved from assignment to assignment, first to Tampa, then back to Norfolk, and finally to Washington, where he remained for several years, finally ensconced in the very jobs he had once said he would never accept. All that time she remained with the law firm in Baltimore, finally rising to become a senior partner. Now, however, they at least lived together. In a manner of speaking. They had purchased a home in McLean, near Washington. Neither spent much time there. Her work kept her in Baltimore or on the road to New York. He let his work keep him in the office. By now he had become thoroughly addicted to the routine of long hours, late days, and lost weekends. There was no supervisor to throw him out of the office. As he rose in rank, no one was going to challenge the necessity for him to spend sixty to eighty hours per week in the office. He thrived on it. He couldn't imagine doing anything else.

There was never any time for children, of course, and neither of them ever regretted it. In any event, he hated kids.

On one of the rare occasions when they did get together— one night over dinner—she remarked on his workaholic ways—half jokingly, because she had also become a victim.

"Tell me, Mike, whatever happened to the man who once told me he would never, ever, not in a million years accept a job in Washington because he didn't want to be buried by the bureaucracy or be seduced by the closeness of all that power? What made you change your mind?"

She had eyed him closely after asking the question, slowly sipping her wine. She was convinced she knew the answer. Everyone succumbed to the fever once they were in Washington. Few ever broke free of its hold. He had landed an incredibly important job, with connections that would make many more serious aspirants for power salivate at the opportunities. She was convinced he had heard the Sirens of the Potomac.

His answer didn't confirm her suspicions, but it didn't surprise her either. Michael Underwood was not about to admit he was as weak as other men.

He hesitated a moment before he answered her. He recalled a similar conversation many years before. His resistance had begun to waver even then.

"Circumstances change, Jennifer. I'm not that young lieutenant anymore. He was immature, thought he knew it all.

I know better. The Air Force rewarded my hard work with promotions. With those came increased responsibility. You've experienced the same. With my background, they had to send me here. I think it's as simple as that. I didn't beg to come to Washington."

No, he hadn't begged. But he had to admit that he had been an active lobbyist. He had called several of his old bosses and other senior officers he had met during the course of his career. He contacted anyone he thought could pull the magic strings and assure him an assignment to Washington. He was convinced he could parlay the move to the capital city into at least one more promotion. After all, he saw the chairman of the Joint Chiefs of Staff on a regular basis at the White House, and the Deputy DCI was a four-star general. How could he fail to trade his eagles for the stars of a brigadier?

But that dinner had been months ago, and it seemed like decades now. Their conversations had become extremely rare and extremely difficult. Jennifer initiated all the calls and discussions, hoping that when Mike answered the phone or showed up at home, he would somehow be different. Somehow better.

He arrived at the White House, one of the few without an escort for the evening. Even though he and Jennifer were seldom together anymore, it would have been unseemly for him to appear in public with anyone else, no matter how innocent the relationship. Best not to give people any reason to wag their tongues. He had established a reputation above reproach in that regard. It didn't matter that the truth didn't always validate the reputation.

He passed through the reception line, shook President Noonan's and the First Lady's hands, and explained Jennifer's absence. Noonan spared a few words of praise about the briefing he had received that morning, but couldn't resist adding that it had been a marked improvement on the session he had had the day before. Underwood located his seat on the chart and made his way to the table, more convinced than ever of the rightness of his assessment of the president.

He introduced himself to his dinner companions, a few of their names registering some recognition, most not. But there was one individual who grabbed his interest immediately: F. Jordan Polk. Polk was of diminutive stature, with a face that looked for all the world like it belonged atop one of the parapets of Notre Dame. Despite his appearance, or perhaps because of it, Polk had a reputation as one of the shrewdest, most successful businessmen in the country. He had moved as CEO from failing company to failing company, wielding the downsizing scythe without mercy, cutting thousands of jobs and restoring his temporary corporate wards to vigorous financial health. In the process he garnered millions of dollars in salaries and bonuses. He was one of the darlings of Wall Street; the workers he displaced saw him as the devil incarnate. There was, after all, some resemblance.

Polk also had one other claim to notoriety. He was the head of Executives for a Responsible Defense, a group of CEOs and presidents from some of the country's leading corporations—none of whom had any defense contracts—who had been calling for sizable cuts in the military budget.

This would be an interesting evening. The temptations were too much to resist. The waiters had barely begun serving when he leaned toward Polk, excusing himself to the exquisite young woman seated between him and the secretary of commerce.

"Mr. Polk, I really am glad to have the opportunity to meet you. I've heard and read quite a bit about you, of course, even though the demands of my job don't leave me much spare time."

"Oh, Colonel . . . I'm sorry, what was your name again? I'm afraid I didn't catch it the first time around."

Even though he had told Polk his name twice during the introductions, he repeated it one more time. "Underwood. Just associate it with deadwood. I frequently use word association to remember things."

Polk stared at him for a split second, his eyebrows converging downward toward the bridge of his nose. It was obvious he was filling in a scorecard on Underwood, just as he did on the executives and managers at the companies he reorganized.

"Yes, of course," Polk said. "So tell me. What kind of job is it that you do that gets you invited to the White House? You're not carrying the football, are you?" Polk smiled, and everyone around the table laughed at his reference to the nuclear launch codes that were always close to the president. The commerce secretary's companion smiled, but it was obvious she had missed the humor.

Underwood smiled but did not laugh. He bristled slightly, because he saw Polk's comment as a challenge to his presence at the table. "No, I'm afraid nothing quite as exotic as that. I work for the director of Central Intelligence. I brief the president on the world's events every morning." As he summarized his importance, Underwood marveled at how the world had changed. In years past, one would never have made such a revelation. Now, it seemed, it was perfectly natural to admit one worked for the intelligence community and to describe in some detail one's place in it. How fortunate there was such openness. It gave him a weapon with which to prick at the edge of Polk's ego.

"Well, that is quite a responsibility. And how long have you been doing this?"

"A little over a year."

"And you haven't been fired yet? My goodness, what an enviable track record, Colonel."

"Not nearly as enviable as yours, Mr. Polk."

Underwood watched as Polk involuntarily swelled up a bit in his chair. He had thrown out the bait. He was certain Polk would rise to it.

"Well, I must admit, fortune has smiled on me. But when one is good at one what does, as you certainly appear to be, Colonel, then the rewards just naturally come, don't you think?"

"Mr. Polk, I would say that fortune has done more than smile on you—she has showered you. Tell me, sir, are the reports true? Have you really made several hundred million dollars in bonuses?"

"Colonel, I hardly think this is the time and the place to discuss such a thing."

"But, sir, the stories are all over the business press. I'm just trying to confirm what's widely reported."

"I really don't think I want to talk about this, Colonel."

"Sorry, sir. No offense intended." Underwood felt exhilarated by the boldness of that lie. He pressed ahead. "I was just curious how one justifies such substantial sums while thousands of workers are told they no longer have jobs. Especially after those workers have devoted a substantial portion of their lives to that company. I noted one story where a senior manager was laid off five days before he was eligible for retirement benefits. That's a bit crass, don't you think?"

Polk was fuming. His normally ruddy complexion had taken on the hue of a sugar beet. His lips had become fine lines as he strained to keep his anger in check. He had obviously come to the White House expecting an evening of conviviality and rubbing shoulders with the President of the United States, and here was some upstart Air Force officer trying to lecture him on business ethics.

"Tell me, Colonel, just what business is it of yours how I run these companies and how much money I make? I would suggest you drop the subject. The president is a very good friend of mine. I'm not sure he'd react very favorably to his briefer attacking one of his friends."

Underwood looked around the table, a mock expression of shock upon his face. "Mr. Polk, I assure you, I'm not attacking you. Again, I meant no offense. I'm just engaging in conversation. Seeking information. But since you ask, I suppose I'm concerned that you propose to run the military the same way you've run your businesses."

"Excuse me?" Polk asked, befuddled. "What on earth are you talking about?"

"Sir, your Executives for a Responsible Defense is proposing the same type of downsizing that has cost thousands of civilian workers their jobs. You seem to be asking everyone else to pay a price except yourself."

"So that's what this is all about. Another disgruntled member of the pampered officer caste."

Ken Currie

Now it was Underwood's turn to fume, but he forced himself to calm down before he answered. By this time, the others seated at the table were absolutely spellbound that such a conversation could be taking place at a state dinner. Indeed, the table next to theirs was beginning to grow quiet as others in the room began picking up bits of the conversation, although both men had done their best to keep their voices down. There were several tables to go before the verbal battle could reach the president's ears, but at this point Underwood no longer cared.

"The evidence, sir? The evidence that we're pampered?"

"Give me a break, Colonel." Polk had obviously dropped his well-rehearsed veil of pomposity. "You guys travel all about the world at taxpayers' expense in gold-plated airplanes. You're accountable to no one except yourselves. You investigate yourselves. There are far too many of you. You're a continual drain on the budget. You take away money that should be going for other programs. You folks haven't a clue about sound fiscal practices. Special stores, hospitals, schools, golf courses. Such incredible waste. It's time the military sacrificed like everyone else, wouldn't you agree?"

"Mr. Polk, I can only guess whether your song would be the same if your company had any defense contracts. Yes, sir, I do read the business page, even though I'm a member of the fiscal management *illiterati* you just attacked. I know what your company does, what it produces, where it spends its money. You've opened plants everywhere except in this country. You've laid off workers everywhere except at those new plants. All in the name of the so-called bottom line. Just what exactly does your company contribute to the welfare of the United States, other than to a few well-heeled shareholders who are profiting mightily from your savaging of American workers?"

Polk narrowed his eyes but said nothing.

"As for doing our fair share," Underwood continued, "let me remind you, sir, that the defense budget has declined sixty percent in real terms over the past fifteen years while spending on all those other programs has continued to increase. Military manpower has declined by over forty percent. We continue to have enlisted people on food stamps. That certainly sounds like a fair share to me. We're sharing in the economic depression that you and your friends seem to be intent on imposing on the rest of this country."

Underwood paused for a drink. Polk started to respond, but Underwood cut him off. There was no stopping him now.

"As far as traveling about at taxpayers' expense. Yes, we have some problems. There are still a few bad apples, but we've done a damned good job weeding them out. Tell me, how's that corporate jet doing that you fly around in? I wish our equipment was gold-plated, that our forces hadn't been cut, that we had more money. Then perhaps we might have been able to give the last president some options when the Chinese moved into Taiwan, instead of just sitting stupidly by and lecturing Beijing on its naughty ways."

Underwood picked up his dinner knife and started stabbing the air with it, emphasizing his points.

"Special stores, hospitals, schools? We call those things factors in the military quality of life. They're meant to compensate the soldiers, sailors, and airmen, and their families, for the sacrifices we call on them to make every day. But you wouldn't know anything about that kind of sacrifice, would you? Damned few people in Washington do these days. But let me tell you, Mr. Polk, our quality of life stinks. You owe us, sir, you owe us a hell of a lot. But you'd rather sit up there with your millions asking guys who make a few hundred bucks a week to sacrifice. If that's your definition of fair, then you'd sure as hell better buy a Webster's, because there's been a fundamental flaw in your education."

Underwood delivered the last sentence, punctuated with the knife pointed squarely at the middle of Polk's face, with a vehemence that startled even him. There was absolute silence in the middle of the room; the discussion had carried well beyond the table. Underwood realized that his last comments had been heard two tables away, where General Hannah sat watching him, his salad fork suspended in midair.

Ken Currie

Hannah shook his head, but then he put down his fork, smiled ever so slightly, and gave Underwood a discreet thumbs-up.

Meanwhile, Underwood's table companions had started moving again, the breathing of some having been interrupted during the last sixty seconds. At that point, the secretary of commerce picked up his water glass, turned toward Underwood, winked, and said in a loud voice, "How about those Redskins?"

The middle of the room erupted in laughter. The president looked across from the head table, visibly leaning forward, hoping someone would repeat what surely must have been a wonderful story.

Underwood spent the rest of the dinner in silence, then took his leave as the music started, pleading the necessity of returning to the office to prepare for the next day's briefing. That part, at least, was true. He shook hands with General Hannah, who put his hand on Underwood's shoulder and whispered in his ear, "They're dragging on the floor, Mike, just be careful someone doesn't come along and snip them off." Then he added, "I think it's probably safe to say that this was the first and last time you'll be invited to dine with the president."

As he left the White House grounds, Underwood's feeling of pleasure was mixed with equal amounts of gloom and regret. What had started out as sport had turned into what quite probably would be the worst night of his life. He dreaded the thought of facing the president the next morning.

Chapter Ten

The rest of Blair Williams's day after the meeting with the DCINC had been a circus. The administrative section had broken all records and prepared his blanket travel orders within an hour. With a little help from the CINC's office, a C-20 from the airlift wing at Andrews Air Force Base in Maryland had been placed at his disposal, so the problem of transportation had been mostly resolved. The aircraft was already on its way to Illinois. A staff car would be waiting for his group when they arrived at Andrews that evening.

He had dragooned Tom Mulkey onto the team, although Mulkey didn't require much coercion. Mulkey was looking forward to finding out firsthand what had happened to the *Regulus* and why. He was also pleased by the prospect of getting a little payback for the runaround he had received during his calls to Washington that first day. He relished the thought of nailing the individual responsible for rigging the cargo manifests.

The other member of the team Williams picked was Lieutenant Commander Wayne Johanssen, who worked on the logistics side of General Lee's large directorate. Johanssen was intimately familiar with the fast sealift ships; his expertise would come in handy once the *Regulus* was located.

Williams had called the TRANSCOM liaison at the Pentagon as soon as he returned to the office. He wanted to ensure the liaison officer, or LO, also a colonel, that he would make every effort to minimize the disruption to his Pentagon routine and to thank him in advance for the use of his facilities. The colonel said he was pleased to help and would make his staff available as required to help in the investigative effort. Williams knew there was no other answer the LO could have given him, but he wanted to avoid any ruffled feathers. He had visited the LO's office once before; they would be working in very cramped quarters for the foreseeable future.

General Lee's executive officer had made the trek to the J6 to pick up the cellular secure phone. He passed it on to Williams, good-naturedly asking the colonel to protect the device with his life since he'd just had to sign his away to pick up the damned thing. Williams assured the major that he would keep it with him at all times.

"I'd prefer you left it outside the shower, sir," the exec pleaded with a smile, "but all other times would be good, thank you."

Williams completed his preparations, locked his safe, told Mulkey and Johanssen he would meet them at base operations in an hour, and headed toward home. Since he lived on base, he had only a very short walk across Scott Drive to his quarters. Organizing things carefully in his mind, he failed to notice the oncoming motorcycle as he stepped into the crosswalk. He was startled by the motorcycle's shrill horn and he stopped just as the rider swerved his bike around him. Williams made a mental note of the license number, vowing to take care of the matter when he returned. He missed the not-so-old days when people understood and practiced simple military courtesies on and off base. There was no time for such concerns now, however, as he pressed on home.

He hadn't had a chance to tell his wife about his imminent departure. He hadn't had time to make a phone call. He called out to her as he unlocked the front door. He insisted she keep the door locked when he wasn't home, even though they lived on the base.

"Erica, hello, I'm home. Where are you?"

"Upstairs, hon, I'm in Justin's room. I'll be right down. What are you doing home so early?" she teased, since he usually didn't make it out of the office until it was nearly dark. "Did you miss me? Justin's just out in the backyard with his friends if you've got something in mind."

Williams smiled. Erica was the treasure of his life. She had put up with everything service life had thrown at her, even the separations, with minimal complaint. When things didn't go right, she just smiled and said, "Hey, I knew it would be like this when the Air Force issued me to you," her endearing reference to the old saw that if the military wanted one to have a spouse, it would have provided one. She had been indispensable. He couldn't have made it without her, and he told her that every chance he could. She was not the woman he had married, she was better. She flirted with him constantly, and he was convinced she was the sexiest woman on the face of the earth.

He bounded up the stairs, walked into the bedroom, grabbed her around the waist, twirled her about, and kissed her passionately. After a moment, she reluctantly pulled away.

"Well, either you *did* come home for *that*, or else you're getting ready to go TDY again. And since I'm standing here in a worn-out pair of blue jeans and a faded sweatshirt, I'll put my money on the temporary duty, right?"

"My love, you see right through me every time. There's no deceiving you. That's why I could never have an affair. You'd know in an instant." He continued holding her hand and smiled warmly at her, losing himself for just a moment in her wonderful blue eyes.

"Even when I'm old and gray and my boobs are down to my belly button, you're still going to love me, right?"

"More than ever. Besides, I like belly buttons." He gave her a kiss on the forehead.

"Okay, enough of this foolishness. When? And for how long?"

"One hour. I don't know. Weeks, maybe longer."

She frowned. "You know, I love the Air Force almost as much as you, Blair, but it does seem a little short on specifics at times, don't you think?"

"Sometimes. But we've got a very messy situation on our hands, and it could take a little time to clear it up."

"I assume I need to pack the usual. You go say goodbye to your son while I throw things together for you." She rubbed his cheek with the palm of her hand as she walked out the door and headed toward their bedroom. She had perfected the art form of getting him ready for his many official trips. An extra uniform and several shirts were always ready; she had even prepared a special travel bag filled with all the personal items he would require. She spoiled him rotten, and he knew it.

Williams walked out into the backyard, where Justin was playing touch football with three of his friends in the growing twilight. Justin waved at his dad and jogged over.

"Don't tell me, Pop, you're getting ready to abandon us again, aren't you?"

"Lord, you take after your mother, Justin. I think you've inherited all her instincts, as well as her looks." Williams pulled on his largish ears, thankful he had not passed those along to his son. One guy having to put up with the adolescent nickname of Beagle was enough.

"You going to be gone long?"

"Could be. I'll try to wrap things up as quickly as I can, but it could be a few weeks, maybe a little longer this time."

Justin whistled softly. "I guess that shoots Labor Day in the shorts, huh, Dad? So much for our trip to the Lake of the Ozarks. I guess I'll just have to hang around here and watch the air show with the rest of the guys." Justin hung his head low between his shoulders, attempting to look distraught, but there was a wrinkle at the corner of his mouth that his father hadn't missed.

"Oh, you poor, poor boy. Such hell we put you through. You know the last time *I* saw the Thunderbirds? *I'm* the one who should be disappointed."

"Poor, poor Dad. Okay, you're forgiven. Just be home by Thanksgiving, all right? Mom's going to be really pissed off if you stay away so long you miss Turkey Day."

"Justin, how many times have I told you—"

"Sorry. Forgot. It just slipped out." Justin feigned chagrin.

"Well, I suppose I should be thankful your language isn't worse, given the crap they keep putting put on television and the radio. Just watch it, okay?"

"Sure, Dad," Justin replied, turning to roll his eyes at his friends.

"Anyway, don't worry, I'm going to bust my rear so I can get back here as soon as I can. I wouldn't want to miss Halloween and your next great act of makeup wizardry."

Justin smiled broadly. He had dressed up as Dr. Jekyll and Mr. Hyde the previous year—one half of his body made up as the dapper physician, the other half a grotesque vision straight out of a Lovecraft novel. He had scared several of the neighborhood children half to death, but his creation had won him a local contest.

"Last year *was* pretty great, wasn't it, Dad?"

"Well, I did think I was going to have to cart Mrs. Jensen over to the hospital. She either came close to cardiac arrest or put on one of the finest acting jobs I've ever seen. You may be too good at your hobby."

They laughed together.

"On a more serious note, Justin. Look after things around here while I'm gone. I'm going to do my best to call you and your mom every night. I want to know how things are going with my favorite son."

"I'm your only son, Dad." Justin sighed and looked at his father with a pitying expression.

"Oh, yeah. That's right. Good point." Williams smiled as he snapped his fingers. "Well, you'd better give me a hug, buddy."

As they embraced, Justin patted his father on the back and said, "Don't worry, Dad, I'll take care of Mom."

Williams squeezed his son a little harder.

Ken Currie

Williams looked back toward the center of the base as the C-20 lifted off the runway. He looked down at the sprawling but nearly vacant Mid-America Airport adjacent to the base, then looked back toward Scott. He pretended he could see his house. He closed his eyes for a moment, fixed Erica's face firmly in his mind, and smiled. Finally, he turned toward Mulkey.

"Well, Tom, are you ready for this adventure?"

"Yes, sir. You bet I am. I still can't believe we all got ready for a trip this fast. I'm used to it taking weeks to get my orders and tickets. Doors open magically when the CINC puts his weight against them, don't they?"

"Absolutely. That's why he's the CINC."

Mulkey gazed out the window, his angular nose and wire-rimmed glasses accentuating his thoughtful expression. "You know, Colonel, this is going to be very interesting. A couple of Air Force guys trying to find out what happened to a ship. Think the Navy will make us honorary members after all this is over?"

Williams leaned forward and called across the aisle to Johanssen. "What do you think, Wayne? Will Tom and I qualify as a couple of old sea dogs when we get back from this TDY?"

"I doubt it, Colonel," the slightly rotund Navy officer responded. "From what I hear, you Air Force guys are awfully boring on these trips. Besides, sir, we call it TAD."

"I'll try to remember that." Williams sat back in his seat and resumed his conversation with Mulkey. "I don't have to tell you we're breaking new ground here, Tom. TRANS-COM's never lost a ship before, and we sure as hell seem to have misplaced this one. General Petersen's expecting a lot of us, especially yours truly. I'm not too worried about doing the job we have to do at MTMC and MSC. We have, as they say, one of the nine-hundred-pound gorillas supporting our effort. General Petersen will make sure we have the component cooperation we require. We'll have to wait and see

86

how much assistance we get from elsewhere in the DoD, including the Services."

Williams sat silently for a moment, remembering the times the command had supposedly been counted out in the budgetary battles in the corridors of the Pentagon and the Hill. General Petersen had prevailed almost every time. His logic had been compelling: *Our forces are here in the States, the problems are across the big blue waters. You can't get there from here without this command, gentlemen. We need this aircraft, this ship, this equipment. Any questions?*

And now that the unified command CINCs had wrestled substantial control over the Pentagon budgeting process away from the individual Services, they had become very powerful forces to contend with indeed. To many observers in Washington, Petersen was seen as the absolute first among equals.

Williams looked at Mulkey once again. "I understand a staff car will meet us on the ramp at Andrews?"

"Yes, sir. Wayne has graciously volunteered to drive." Mulkey grinned. The junior person always volunteered for chauffeur duty. "Then we're on our way to the hotel. Reservations are confirmed for us at the Ritz-Carlton."

"You're kidding. We're at the Ritz?"

"Well, they do offer a government rate, and we got lucky. They actually had some rooms available. We'll have all of Pentagon City at our disposal. Not that we'll have the time to enjoy it, of course. And we'll be nice and close to the Pentagon. The LO's office has already arranged reserved parking for us at the River Entrance."

"Sounds like we've really lucked out. So far, so good. You know, Tom, I'm going to leave you in charge of all my TDY arrangements from now on. I'm very impressed."

"Oh, thank you, sir. May I have another, please, sir?"

Williams laughed. He was glad Mulkey was along for this ride: Good people always made the tough job easier and more bearable. He spoke loudly enough that both Mulkey and Johanssen could hear him over the whine of the jet's engines. "We're going to be arriving much too late to check in with the LO, of course. We need to be in his office by 0700 tomorrow. So I'll meet both you guys in the lobby for breakfast at 0600. We have a teleconference scheduled at 0800 in the NMCC. The LO will take care of getting our tickets for access to the NMCC. I'm assuming our clearances were sent?"

"Yes, sir. Checked on it again before I left," Mulkey responded. "All taken care of. There should be no problems." He tapped his forehead. "Knock on wood."

"General Allen and General Lee will be on line at the Scott end for the teleconference. There'll be somebody there from JCS/J4. I don't know which of their loggie guys it'll be. We'll see tomorrow. The vice chairman and someone from the SecDef's office will also be attending. The primary purpose is to review the latest information available at Scott and the Pentagon. I'll be calling the MCC from my room tonight. Oh, hell! Where *did* I put that cellular phone?" Williams started searching frantically through his pockets.

"Very funny, sir. You want me to have the crew call General Lee's exec and tell him you left it in the snack bar at base ops? That should make his whole day."

"No, I'll pass this time. The poor guy already has the world's highest pucker factor. Have you ever seen anybody worry about every little detail like him?"

"I don't think so."

"Well, good. Because General Lee needs someone like him to keep things straight. Especially now."

Williams sat back in his seat and closed his eyes. He wanted to rest a little before they arrived at Andrews. He had no idea how well he would sleep this night. Events had been happening so fast, he had little time to think about taking a breath or grabbing something to eat.

"I just realized I'm starving." He turned toward Mulkey and Johanssen. "You guys hungry?"

Both nodded emphatically.

"Tom, see if you can get one of the crew to dig out the lunches—that is, if Wayne remembered to order them."

"That I did, Colonel. Only the best for the boss."

"Right. I'll tell you what, I know this place in Old Town

Alexandria, a great little restaurant called Scotland Yard. If Wayne can get us there without killing us some night when we have some downtime, I can promise you guys an excellent meal. And they've got some great single malts on the menu. Sorry, Wayne, you'll have to pass, but I'll give you a raincheck."

"That's all right, sir. Appreciate the offer, but I don't much care for Scotch whisky."

"You're a peasant, Wayne."

Johanssen smiled. "Ah, yes sir, but I am in the Navy, sir."

Chapter Eleven

The Russian looked down from the high walls onto the city. He had been here once before, long ago. In a different age. He had forgotten how beautiful the view had been.

"Absolutely spectacular, wouldn't you say?"

The heavily accented voice disturbed his reverie. He turned toward the sound and saw the familiar, thin face crowned in perfectly coiffed grayish-black hair. *The French-man certainly has style,* he thought, *especially for someone in this deadly business but—after all—he is French.*

"Indeed," the Russian responded.

"Mark Twain once visited here. He was captivated by this place as well. If I remember correctly, he wrote 'A ruin must be rightly situated to be effective. This one could not have been better placed. Nature knows how to garnish a ruin to the best effect.' Interesting that a man with such a dim view of humankind would be held in such awe of its creations."

"Perhaps it was mankind's creations that caused him to take such a dim view."

"A possibility I hadn't considered, Dmitriy. It was, after all, my countrymen who helped make this a ruin."

Dmitriy took one last look at Heidelberg from the heights of the castle that towered majestically over it. A fine haze covered the city as the sun was setting off to his left. He looked down at the twin towers of the Karl-Theodor Bridge and imagined the view of the castle from that point: By now the *schloss* would be bathed in golden late-afternoon light. From left to right, the Neckar River cut a solid dark line through the middle of the city, as if emphasizing the difference between the old city, now slightly seedy, and the elegant homes across the water. He turned away.

"Let's walk, Anatole. I need something to drink. I've been waiting too long. The wind is cutting into me."

"Forgive me for being late, Dmitriy. The streets were still a bit slippery from this morning's rain, and I lost my way. Heidelberg is not an easy city to drive in."

They made their way along the path toward the castle entrance. Outside the gate stood a small snack bar. Inside sat an older woman bundled up against the cold and the damp.

"*Guten Tag. Eine Tasse Kaffee, bitte.*"

Dmitriy left a Euro on the counter and gratefully took the cup of coffee, taking his first wonderfully warming sip of the strong brew. It was unusually cold for this time of year. He turned again toward the newcomer. "I'm sorry, forgive my manners. Did you want something?"

Anatole waved him off. "A Russian who can't stand the cold. Absolutely amazing, Dmitriy."

"Ten years in Central Asia made me soft, Anatole."

Dmitriy drank a bit more, savoring the restorative effect the coffee was having while glancing at the castle walls. Feeling warmer at last, he motioned to Anatole to follow him to a park bench near the castle entrance but far enough away from the few visitors still strolling the area to ensure that they would not be disturbed. Dmitriy sighed contentedly as he sat down.

"That's much better. Thank you for indulging me. Now that we have discussed American literature, the wonders of man, and the weather, I assume you are wanting to know if I have anything to tell you?"

Anatole nodded. "I'm looking forward to positive news. You are going to give me such news, aren't you?"

"Good news, indeed, Anatole. The merchandise has been secured and is being prepared for shipment to the location you specified. Your representative has seen the shipment and is awaiting your call. Once you take care of the first payment, I'll fly back to Moscow and personally arrange for the transfer of the merchandise."

"Very good news, if true. Verification?"

"Again, as agreed." Dmitriy reached into his briefcase and pulled out a letter-sized brown envelope. He pulled off the tape holding down the flap, pulled out three photographs, and handed them over to await the reaction.

Anatole took the photos with slightly trembling hands. He smiled broadly as he examined them closely.

"Dmitriy, I can feel the hair tingling on the back of my neck. This is incredible. I'd hoped but never thought this would succeed. I assume you want these back? And I assume you will destroy them as soon as you leave here?"

"Of course. These would cause me a great deal of embarrassment if they were discovered." Dmitriy put the photos back in the envelope and closed and locked his briefcase. He tapped his fingers on the outside of the case, then asked, "And now I assume you will make the agreed-upon phone calls."

Anatole nodded as he reached into his inside coat pocket and retrieved his cellular phone. He punched in the number. He smiled at Dmitriy, shook his head, then spoke into the phone. "I've seen the photos. Are the items in as good a condition as they appear to be?" His smile broadened at the response.

"They tell me they're in absolutely pristine condition," Anatole said as he flipped shut his phone. "It appears you have more than satisfied your end of the bargain. Now comes the part you've been waiting for. Do you have the number?"

Dmitriy handed him a slip of paper. Anatole punched a new set of numbers into the phone. He waited for the tone, then began entering the appropriate codes. Finished, he slid the phone back into his coat. The money has been transferred. You should be able to verify."

Dmitriy activated his own phone. In a moment, a familiar female voice answered. Dmitriy turned away from the Frenchman and spoke softly into the receiver. "They've sent the funds. Can you confirm it? Excellent. See you back in Moscow in a few days." As he tossed the phone back into the briefcase and carefully secured the case's locks, he said, "Everything is in order." He stood up, lifted his collar up around his neck, and quickly walked away, calling a hasty *"Wiedersehen"* to Anatole over his shoulder.

Anatole scrambled up from his seat. "My greetings to your father, Dmitriy."

But Dmitriy had already disappeared down the steps.

Chapter Twelve

The briefing went well. Despite his lack of sleep and the sense of dread that had haunted him since the night before, Underwood's delivery had been crisp, expert. It had helped that the topics he briefed were straightforward, noncontroversial items the president couldn't pick apart without going to a great deal of trouble to find fault, not that such an obstacle had stopped him in the past. Underwood was packing his briefing materials away in his briefcase, listening as the president surveyed the room, asking for comments and questions on the briefing they had just heard. He was poised to stand up in anticipation of Noonan's dismissal.

"Well, I guess that's everything, then," Noonan said as he stood up behind his desk, an obviously very expensive replica of the one that used to grace Teddy Roosevelt's presidential office a century before. Everyone else in the room took Noonan's cue and arose immediately.

Before excusing the others, Noonan turned toward Underwood. "Colonel, if you could stay behind for a few minutes, I'd like to have a brief chat with you. The rest of you are free to leave."

Noonan's chief of staff hesitated near the door. "Mr. President, I really think I should—"

"Jeff, I believe I can handle this. You go on about your business. Senator Chatsworth is due here in a half hour. Let's make sure we're ready for his visit. Right?" Noonan waved Farley out the door as if batting away a pesky fly, then directed Underwood to sit down.

As the door closed behind the chief of staff, Noonan walked around to the front of his desk. He folded his arms across his chest and leaned back against the desk. He stared into Underwood's eyes for a moment, his face devoid of any expression. Neither friendly nor hostile, much to Underwood's discomfort. He wished desperately he could fathom what was going through the president's mind. At least he could anticipate the president's questions during an intelligence briefing. This was entirely new terrain, and he didn't like it. He tried to sit still, but found himself shifting involuntarily in the chair. It took great effort not to look away from the president's face, but he decided that was the last thing he should do.

"Well, Colonel," the president began, "what do you have to say in your defense?"

"Mr. President?"

Noonan's expression grew stern. "I strongly suspect you know what I'm talking about. I had a most interesting conversation with Jordan Polk last night, after you left the White House. He cornered me to complain about how a certain military officer had the temerity to question his business ethics. He's a hard man to shake when he's angry. I doubt the Secret Service could have pried him away from me. The First Lady was not at all happy that he was delaying our taking a few turns around the dance floor. And the First Lady can be very difficult to deal with when she's displeased."

Underwood had a momentary image of Frances Noonan

berating her husband in their White House bedroom. He decided Mrs. Noonan must indeed be a formidable sight when her ire was aroused.

"Sir, I assure you I had no intention of engaging in personal attacks on Mr. Polk. I certainly had no desire to disrupt a state dinner. I'm afraid my words got away from me. Mr. Polk's well-known dislike for the military seemed to have inspired me, although I admit the timing was unfortunate. That's an explanation, sir, not an excuse. I have no excuse for what happened. I hope you will forgive me for my unseemly behavior."

Noonan listened patiently, then, quite unexpectedly, he smiled. "Colonel, rest easy. Forgive me. I couldn't resist the opportunity." Noonan noticed Underwood's bemused expression and continued. "My anger at you was very short-lived. And I assure you, it had more to do with my being trapped by Polk than with anything you may have said last night. Jordan Polk is an insufferable boor and an overbearing bastard. I'm sure you would agree with my characterization of him, wouldn't you?"

Before Underwood had a chance to respond, Noonan continued.

"Despite that, he's also a Republican and a big contributor to the party. So we put up with him. That's the burden I have to bear as a chief executive running for reelection. No, your contretemps with Polk is not the reason I asked you to stay behind. Although I trust the episode will never have occasion to be repeated."

"I am relieved, Mr. President, and it won't, you have my word," Underwood said softly, and sank back in the chair. He relaxed visibly.

"That goes without saying. I thought you might be relieved to know you're off the hook for now. But after torturing you repeatedly during briefings for the past year, I couldn't pass up the chance to pull your chain again. Please forgive your commander in chief."

Underwood studied the president's face. This was not the conversation he had expected. Now that Noonan had told him he had received a presidential pardon for disrupting a state dinner, he was positively confused why the president had asked him to stay. He flinched slightly at Noonan's use of the phrase "commander in chief," but his discomfort was quickly displaced by confusion.

The president finally unfolded his arms, a sign the discussion of Underwood's social behavior was finished. He remained leaning against the desk, which he now grabbed hold of with both hands, as if to steady himself.

"Mike, I need a military assistant."

"I thought you had one, Mr. President."

"Pat Callaghan is leaving the White House at the end of the month. In fact, he's really already departed, what with all the preparations he has to take care of. You see, his wife is dying of cancer. He wanted a job where he could spend more time with her. Not a request I could refuse."

"Jesus," Underwood said softly.

"Indeed," the president agreed. "A very sad situation. The result of all this is a vacancy at the White House, one which I can't afford. Pat has been an indispensable part of my staff. I need a replacement. Mike, you're it."

Underwood was stunned. Here was a president he loathed asking him to come to work for him. He started to protest, but he had already begun rationalizing in his mind why he should take the job.

"Mr. President, I really don't think I'm—"

"I don't want to hear it, Colonel Underwood. Everyone who knows you, including Phil Hannah, says you are the consummate military professional. I'm not entirely certain what that entails, but I'm counting on their assessment. And I trust their judgment, especially regarding your willingness to put in whatever effort and however many hours it takes to get the job done. But I've formed my own opinion of you as well. Don't forget, I've had a chance to evaluate you closely over the past year. I've been as cantankerous as a president possibly can be during your briefings. I think you'll probably agree I've exercised my presidential prerogative and abused you mercilessly. You never blinked once. The DCI tells me you're absolutely fearless, especially when it comes to his senior staff. I need that kind of backbone in this position. Especially now."

The president paused for a moment. Underwood assumed he was talking about the crisis in the Middle East.

"It's no secret, Colonel, that I never served in the military," Noonan said. "My only exposure to the military world was during my Pentagon days. That exposure was from a very high, disconnected perch. I consider myself an expert on defense policy, but certainly not on the military. Pat Callaghan and General Hannah have been a great help to me in that regard, but now I'm losing Pat, and Phil Hannah is leaving early next year when his second term as chairman expires."

Underwood couldn't resist silent disagreement with Noonan's self-assessment of his defense expertise. He was still trying to come up with reasons for not accepting the job Noonan had offered, but the pros were rapidly outweighing the cons.

Noonan paused for a moment. He walked over to a credenza and poured two cups of coffee. Walking back to the center of the room, he placed both cups on the table in front of Underwood and took the chair beside him. Underwood found himself totally disarmed by the president's easy informality. His dislike for the man was being replaced by twinges of sympathy. He debated in his mind whether those feelings and his ongoing change of heart were the result of his being mistaken about Noonan, or the thought of accepting a job next to the world's most powerful man. The president interrupted his musings.

"Quite frankly, Colonel Underwood, I don't want to commit the same mistakes made by other occupants of this office. They seem to have thought they could compensate for their personal lack of military experience either by playing soldier or making empty gestures to the people in uniform. I'm not going to pretend I'm a general by returning salutes when I board *Air Force One*. I'm not going to stuff the gallery with soldiers during State of the Union addresses. I think the military wants something more than theatrics, something a bit more tangible. General Hannah has been a valuable source of advice in this regard. But I'm looking for the perspective from the folks at the lower levels. Both the General and I think you're a lot closer to those folks, Mike."

Underwood wanted to feel gratified by the president's apparent concern for the welfare of the common soldier, but he couldn't help sensing there was something very artificial about Noonan's sudden interest in what the average person in uniform thought of his administration, especially since the elections were only a few months away and there was the threat of a serious military conflict halfway around the world.

"Mr. President, I appreciate your and General Hannah's vote of confidence in me, I really do. But, quite frankly, I've been in Washington for a long time. I don't know how much I really reflect the concerns of the average soldier. I probably reflect more of an inside-the-Beltway mentality. I'm not sure I completely understand what service I can be to you."

"Don't sell yourself short, Colonel. I think you'll do a fine job of telling me how my policies are playing in the military, even if you have to do a little research to find out. I want you to be my eyes and ears."

Bingo, Underwood thought. He was still the same old Noonan, worried about how his actions were going to play in Peoria—or in this case, Camp Lejeune.

"Mr. President, it seems to me you have a press secretary and staff to sort out that kind of information. I've very little experience as a political pollster."

Noonan coughed slightly and set down his coffee cup. He looked at Underwood, but his expression was considerably less friendly than before. He spoke very precisely, in a tone that betrayed his anger. "I'm not asking you to be my press secretary. If you think I'm asking you to be my front man at the Pentagon, you're very, very wrong. I don't expect you to make my case to the average soldier in the trench." Then his tone softened. "Tell me, Colonel, do you have any opinions of the Noonan presidency? Give me the Underwood view of my policies."

Underwood realized Noonan was giving him the opportunity to cut his own throat. Should he kiss Noonan's butt, or tell him what he really thought? What in the hell did Noonan care *what* he thought?

"Mr. President, it doesn't really matter what I think of your policies. I'm bound by my oath as an officer to execute them. I don't think you're asking me to be a policy adviser. That is clearly the chairman's position, and I wouldn't dream of offering counsel in his stead. If I understand Colonel Callaghan's position correctly, the job is pretty much nuts-and-bolts kind of work. I'm a go-between for the White House and the Pentagon. I'll do the job. I'm not about to question the actions of the president, regardless of what my personal feelings may be."

Noonan looked at him for a moment, then stood up and extended his hand.

"Excellent answer, Colonel. Whether or not you really believe it is immaterial. Some might have thought I was looking for brutal honesty and told me how my policies were leading the country to ruin. I would have shown them the door. Others might have told me how wonderful I was doing, thinking that's what I wanted to hear. They also would have been shown the way out. You chose the judicious course, as I expected. However, I conclude from the way you phrased your response that you probably think I'm farther off course than on. That doesn't matter. You start next Monday. Farley and his staff will get you settled and go over your responsibilities. Welcome to the White House."

"Thank you, Mr. President. I assure you I'll do my best."

"I'm counting on that."

Josh Evans had been waiting outside the White House, and was relieved to see his boss finally appear.

"I thought you'd been kidnapped by the president for a minute, Colonel."

"Shanghaied would be more accurate, Josh," Underwood responded, then decided by Evans's perplexed look that an explanation was in order, especially since his young subordinate would be affected by what had just happened in the Oval Office.

"I'm about to undergo a career change of sorts. The president just asked me to be his military assistant."

Evans's face was a blank, as if he was pondering what he had just heard. Suddenly, he grinned and extended his hand. "That's fantastic, Colonel! No, wait a minute . . . starting when? Besides, I thought you couldn't stand the president. What's the military assistant do? And now that I think about it, who's going to do the morning briefings?"

Underwood smiled. "So many questions. Starting next Monday, Josh. And I'm still not fond of him, but I had the distinct impression I didn't have a whole lot of choice on this one. It sounded as though the chairman and the DCI were intimately involved. Hard to turn down such an offer, wouldn't you say? I'll tell you about the job later. And in response to your last question, you are. You feel like having some coffee and talking things over?"

"Actually, I feel like having an early drink. I think we should celebrate your good fortune, while mourning my descent into the pit."

Underwood placed his hand on Evans's shoulder, pretending to console him. "Now, now, Josh, I'm sure Walt Cummings will be more than happy to offer you advice in your new position. He's such a caring individual."

Underwood sent the staff car back to Langley, calling his office to tell them that he and Evans had an unexpected appointment and would return after lunch. They caught a cab to Alexandria, a place Underwood loved to visit whenever the opportunity arose. He made a point of stopping into an Irish pub in the Old Town near the Courthouse, especially when its owner scheduled one of the many Irish folk groups that passed through the area. He would order a Black and Tan and lounge away in the booth, listening to the lyrics and letting his mind wander wherever it wanted to go. It was a relaxation he truly cherished, but it came all too seldom. And it was something he insisted on doing alone.

The cab dropped them off along the waterfront at the end of King Street. They grabbed a sandwich from a nearby deli and found a bench near the pier. They sat there quietly for a few minutes, watching the sailboats passing by and the seagulls diving for the periodic bread crumbs tossed into the water by a departing diner. It was peaceful. Underwood was reluctant to say anything for fear of disturbing the wonderful tranquillity of the moment as the water lapped against the pier and the birds squawked overhead. The Washington humidity had abated momentarily, miraculously, and there was a cool, refreshing breeze blowing up the river. Evans sensed his boss's mood and kept quiet, despite an almost overwhelming urge to talk about what had happened barely thirty minutes before.

Underwood finished his sandwich and threw a few remaining crusts of bread into the river, sending a swarm of gulls nearly crashing into one another as they scrambled for the meager banquet. He took a final drink from his soda, stood up, and tossed his trash into a nearby garbage can. He started walking northward along the waterfront, forgetting that Evans was still eating. Evans had been watching the traffic wend its way across the Woodrow Wilson Bridge. When he noticed his boss had moved on unannounced, he quickly threw the remainder of his sandwich into the trash and hurried to catch up.

This was not the first time he had been temporarily stranded on one of these outings. Underwood would frequently grow very pensive and wander off without a word. Evans caught up, slightly out of breath from the effort. Underwood heard his approach and turned to him with an embarrassed smile.

"Did it again, didn't I? Sorry, Josh. I seem to get lost in a world of my own. Especially in this place. I expect you want to talk about what's going to happen, don't you? Thanks for indulging this selfish little habit of mine once again."

"Quite all right, Colonel. I'll forgive you, if you just tell me what's going on."

"I'm not completely sure myself. Last night I was at the White House insulting one of the friends of Richard, and the next thing I know I'm working directly for the president."

Evans stared openmouthed at Underwood. "You did what at the White House?"

"No big deal, although I thought it was afterwards. Turns out the president doesn't like the jerk either. Dodged a bullet that time."

Evans shook his head. "Colonel, nobody's fast enough to dodge all the bullets that seem to come flying your direction. I'm convinced you've got a Kevlar vest under that uniform."

Underwood grinned. "Does it show?" he asked as he looked down at the front of his uniform. "All right. Let me fill you in."

Underwood described his meeting with the president. He told Evans he wasn't completely sure what the new position would entail, but he anticipated he would be sitting in on the morning briefings as his predecessor, Callaghan, had done.

"The president likes having Hannah there to provide a Pentagon perspective on the briefing, since the chairman gets briefed by the folks from the Defense Intelligence Agency. However, the chairman and the vice chairman are not always available. So the military assistant acts as the surrogate. So, Josh, it looks like you'll continue to see quite a bit of me."

"That's what I wanted to discuss. Are you sure the DCI is going to let me take over the briefings? I'm not sure about this. I'm not convinced I'm ready for this," Evans replied, a look of distress on his face.

"I'm sure the DCI will want to bring someone in to replace me as soon as possible, Josh, but in the meantime I suspect you're going to be the guy in the barrel. What are you afraid of, fella? You've done the briefing before."

"Sure, but you've always been there to help field the questions and to run interference for me. This won't be the same. I've watched the president on the prowl during the briefings. The next time he pounces, I'm going to be the poor water buffalo he brings down."

Underwood chuckled gently at the image Evans conjured up. For a moment he visualized Noonan dressed up as the cowardly lion in *The Wizard of Oz*, growling fecklessly at the Iranians. The idea amused him enormously, and he guffawed so hard he began choking. Evans quickly patted him on the back.

"Thanks, Colonel, but I didn't think it was that funny."

"No, no, I was thinking of something else," Underwood said. "But you did paint a wonderful picture. Anyway, stop worrying. You're going to do a fine job. You wouldn't have been picked for the briefing team if you didn't have what it takes to brief the president. So relax."

Evans smiled, and Underwood was pleased that his stroking of Evans's ego was producing the desired effect. Underwood could almost see him puff up.

"So tell me, what did you say when the president asked you what you thought of his policies as president?"

"You would have been proud. I was very diplomatic. I didn't call him a son of a bitch once."

They continued walking a little farther. They had almost reached the Torpedo Factory art gallery when a dog bounded in their direction, his leash flapping wildly behind him. The animal stopped at Underwood's feet, then rubbed against his leg, finally bounding up and placing its paws firmly on the front of his uniform. A young man in cutoffs ran up, a rottweiler reluctantly in tow. He apologized profusely for his pet's behavior, explaining that the dog had broken away from his grasp at the sound of the seagulls. He pulled the animal away with some difficulty. Underwood brushed the dust from his coat, thankful it wasn't raining.

"It's all right. I don't think there's any harm done. Friendly fellow, isn't he?" Underwood reached down to pat the springer spaniel on the head.

"Yes, yes, that he is. Too friendly, I'm afraid. I'm truly sorry."

They exchanged a few more words, Underwood reassuring the young man once again that there was no damage and no need to worry. Finally, the young man walked on down the waterfront, gripping the spaniel's leash firmly in his hand, bumping into Evans as he departed. He apologized, then looked back and gave Underwood a small wave before disappearing completely into the crowd.

Underwood watched as the dog followed its owner, bouncing about and periodically trying to dart toward the water to scare the birds. *Nice young man*, Underwood thought. *All too rare these days.* He turned to Evans and clapped his companion gently on the shoulder.

"Well, Josh, at least dogs love me."

Chapter Thirteen

Williams was sitting at the conference table waiting for the meeting to begin, making some notes to himself on the latest information regarding the search for the *Regulus*. Most of the principals had assembled. The MSC commander, Rear Admiral Furst, could be seen on one of the screens leaning across his table talking to Captain Thatcher. Thatcher looked toward the camera for a moment. Williams waved; there was no response. Williams leaned over to Mulkey and whispered.

"Would you say he's still upset, Tom?"

"Good bet, Colonel. Some guys just have no sense of humor."

Williams's smile grew broader as he continued, "Thatcher always looks like he's just smelled something unpleasant. Maybe the aroma from Blue Plains is getting to him."

Williams had once been assigned to Bolling Air Force Base. The proximity of Washington, D.C.'s, sewage-treatment plant had been the source of many jokes, and

106

many complaints, by local residents. One of Williams's co-workers at Bolling had opined that Blue Plains's future was secure, despite accidents and setbacks, because Congress would always provide a guaranteed source of raw materials.

General Lee was visible at the TRANSCOM conference site. The chair at the head of the table was still vacant; everyone, including Major General Price, the director of operations for the National Military Command Center, was awaiting the arrival of General Petersen.

Williams completed his note-taking. He pushed his notebook forward on the table and did a quick survey of the room. He recognized most of the individuals, both civilian and military, who had flowed into the NMCC conference room to take part in the meeting. He would try to remember the names of the rest during the introductions he knew Petersen would insist upon.

While he was still trying to put names with faces, a squat rear admiral walked into the room, a tall but stooped Navy lieutenant in tow, and quickly took the seat to Williams's left, close to the head of the table. The admiral nodded to General Price, set his planning book in front of him, and leaned back in his chair so he could whisper something to the lieutenant, who had taken a seat in the row of chairs along the wall.

Williams found himself eavesdropping, in hopes of identifying the newcomer, but he could make out only a few words. As far as Williams knew, every organization that needed to be concerned about the fate of the *Regulus* was represented at the table. His curiosity finally prompted him to turn to the admiral and introduce himself.

"Excuse me, sir. I don't believe we've met. I'm Blair Williams from the Transportation Command at Scott."

The admiral raised his index finger while he continued talking to his subordinate. Finally, he brought his chair forward and turned his attention to Williams. "Good morning, Colonel. Jim Dunleavy. I'm the head of OP-33 in the Chief of Naval Operations office."

Williams studied Dunleavy's face for a second before he responded. The presence of someone from the CNO's office was not expected. To his knowledge, that office had not been invited to the meeting. He was more than interested in how they had found out and why Dunleavy was there.

"Admiral, pardon me for asking, but what interest does the CNO have in this matter?"

"We're always interested when we lose one of our ships, Colonel."

Before Williams could respond, General Petersen appeared on the screen and called the meeting to order. He exchanged pleasantries with General Price, and then, as Williams had anticipated, the CINC asked everyone to introduce themselves. But Williams was only half listening. He was still pondering his neighbor's last comment. *Wonderful, a pissing contest first thing in the morning. Welcome back to the Pentagon, Blair.*

If the CINC was perplexed by Dunleavy's presence, he didn't betray it. Perhaps he had not even noticed it. He opened the proceedings by asking Williams and his NMCC counterpart to summarize the status of the search for the *Regulus*. Williams leaned forward, preparing to speak, when Dunleavy spoke up.

"General Petersen, OP-33 can provide the latest information on the search since ships from the Sixth Fleet are involved in the rescue effort and we're monitoring their operations. I'm prepared to give you an update on where things stand at this moment."

Even though Petersen's familiar square face was very small on the screen, Williams could clearly discern a sharp narrowing of the space between the CINC's bushy eyebrows. A frown formed on his face as soon as Dunleavy began speaking.

"Admiral, we certainly appreciate the offer, but General Price and I have already set the agenda. That's why we've asked Colonel Williams to go first, followed by Captain Swain from the NMCC."

Dunleavy was undeterred. "General, the CNO's office didn't have a chance to comment on the agenda. In fact, we only found out about this meeting a half hour ago."

Williams was asking himself how they had found out at all when Dunleavy provided the answer.

"Captain Thatcher alerted me to this meeting, and the CNO decided it was in our best interests to attend."

Williams could sense the growing tension and confusion in the room. He knew the CINC expected events to adhere to a tight agenda. He didn't have time to waste, and he didn't expect his staff to waste its time in attending meetings for meetings' sake. Williams knew Peterson was probably fuming by this time, but he also knew the CINC would hold his legendary temper in check, at least until his patience ran out. Determining when that would occur, however, was always the problem. General Lee had a keen understanding of the CINC's limits, and he made sure the people in his directorate were also aware of them. Admiral Dunleavy obviously was unaware that he was now treading on quicksand.

"Admiral," Petersen said, "it was my understanding the CNO's interests were to be represented by the NMCC, which has operational control through the Central Command over all of the forces involved in the search-and-rescue effort for the *Regulus*. Frankly, I'm a little uncertain about this last-minute interest in this session. You're going to have to explain to me where your office fits into this picture. If you could keep it as brief as possible, please. We have to move forward. There's a lot of ground we have to cover."

"General Petersen, the CNO feels strongly that the Navy should take the lead in determining what happened to the *Regulus*. Investigating accidents affecting Navy ships has always fallen within our purview. The CNO has asked me to ensure that's the case in this situation. Consequently, we've been following events on a daily basis and working closely with the MSC Operations Center."

Williams was dumbfounded. Dunleavy's comments following their brief introduction had signaled the possibility of a turf war, but Williams had expected a minor skirmish at most. This was not the forum in which to take on such heady issues. The admiral was either very brave or very stupid. Williams's assessment leaned toward the latter. He found it difficult to believe that the chief of Naval Operations, a most astute practitioner of military politics by all accounts, had sanctioned such an open challenge to Petersen's prerogatives as a CINC. Williams was now convinced that Dunleavy was a loose cannon. No matter; the CINC would lash him down very quickly.

Williams looked across the table at Swain, who almost imperceptibly shook his head. Williams understood the gesture: It meant Dunleavy's intercession was completely unexpected and as unwelcome for the NMCC as it undoubtedly was for the CINC. Williams looked at the screen, trying to read Petersen's face. He noticed the CINC's fingers tapping on the table. Williams calmly sat back in his chair, prepared to watch the fireworks. Dunleavy had dared to bring up the issue, and now Petersen would dispose of it.

Williams was uncertain what antagonized the CINC more: the overtness of the challenge to his authority in this matter, or the unseemliness of airing the dirty laundry of inter-Service rivalries in a forum dedicated to finding out what had happened to a ship and its crew. In the final analysis, it didn't really matter. Petersen's heavy guns would blow Dunleavy out of the water in any case. And the CNO would get a phone call from a very angry CINC.

"Admiral Dunleavy. Let me explain the procedures we have all agreed to follow in finding out what happened to the *Regulus*. I've already outlined these procedures to the secretary of defense, whose interest in these matters is increasing by the hour. It goes without saying these are the procedures we've worked out with our counterparts in the NMCC, as General Price can attest."

"Absolutely, General Petersen," General Price interjected, and gave Dunleavy a very sharp look, which the admiral missed completely.

Petersen briefly touched two fingers to his right temple in a simple salute to acknowledge Price's support and continued. "We haven't discussed these procedures with the Services because, quite frankly, this is not a Service issue."

"It *is* a Navy ship, General Petersen," Dunleavy replied.

Williams felt an almost instinctive urge to duck for cover.

He slid down a little lower in his seat, waiting for the gale he now knew was coming. General Petersen had intertwined his fingers and placed his large hands upon the table. General Lee had coached his people well on the CINC's "Five Danger Signals." Petersen had gone from Number One directly to Number Five. The clasped hands were a way of holding his anger in check, but they also resembled a club ready to be wielded on the unwitting victim. Petersen gently tapped the table. He leaned toward the screen and unclasped his hands, reached up to his left shoulder with his right hand, slid his fingers under the epaulet, and tilted the fabric forward to clearly reveal the four silver stars glistening under the camera lights.

"Admiral, the last time I checked I was still the commander in chief of the United States Transportation Command. Neither the secretary of defense nor the president has informed me otherwise. Perhaps you've heard something different from your sources."

Dunleavy did not respond. *Silence is very wise.* Williams thought.

Petersen shifted the direction of his gaze slightly, and Williams surmised he was looking at the monitor showing MSC headquarters. Williams looked at the screen to see if Thatcher was displaying any emotion. He could see Thatcher's hands resting on the table, but his face was out of view. Williams directed his attention back to General Petersen, who had dropped the epaulet and clasped his hands together once again.

"A reminder, for your benefit and for anyone else who may be confused on this score. I oversee a unified command that has peacetime—as well as wartime—operational control over its components. The components do not report to the CNO or the Army and Air Force chiefs of staff. I believe we still teach that fact at the senior service schools, do we not? Perhaps you slept through that particular lecture?"

Williams peered sideways at Dunleavy.

"I have an admiral and two generals in charge of those components who are very much aware of this command-and-control relationship," Petersen continued. "They have no questions as to how it works. If you are still uncertain about these relationships, Admiral, or if you feel the CNO requires some additional information, I'd invite you both to come visit us. Better yet, visit all of the unified commands. I'm sure the other CINCs would be happy to make you aware of their perspectives, which I'm certain are similar to my own."

Williams looked in Dunleavy's direction once more. The admiral's lower jaw was slowly moving back and forth as he ground his teeth together. It was clear he was not enjoying this lecture from a four-star in an audience filled with lesser-ranking officers, especially those from his own service. Williams was certain Dunleavy wanted to say something in response, but—to his credit—the admiral continued to say nothing.

Petersen continued. "Admiral, my command—and I think I can speak for the NMCC here as well—would welcome whatever cooperation your office can offer in determining the causes of the *Regulus*'s disappearance. However, TRANSCOM and the NMCC, with the assistance of the Central Command, have the lead in this investigation. The officer sitting next to you, Colonel Williams, is my personal representative in Washington and, together with Captain Swain, is in charge of the investigation from that end. Please work through him if you have any information you can provide."

Dunleavy gave Williams a look of utter disdain. His expression told Williams he wasn't about to report to an Air Force colonel about a Navy ship, regardless of what this four-star had to say.

"Let me make one final comment," Petersen's voice boomed from the speaker once more. "I'm very unhappy that such matters came up here. This is not the appropriate forum for these issues, and I'm certain the CNO would agree. Now, I would very much like to get on with the agenda, starting with Colonel Williams's wrap-up of where we stand in the search-and-rescue effort."

Dunleavy pushed himself away from the table and hurriedly left the room, his aide scrambling to get through the conference room door before the admiral shut it in his face. The CINC made no effort to interfere with Dunleavy's departure. Instead, he unclasped his hands and sat back in his chair.

Williams hesitated for a moment, reviewing the events of the past few minutes, something he was convinced everyone else in the room was doing as well.

"Colonel Williams, you're on," Petersen prompted.

Williams nodded toward the computer operator and the first slide popped up on the screen, a somewhat grainy image of the ocean, with the silhouette of a ship in the background.

"General Petersen. What you're seeing is a direct feed via handheld camera and satellite link from one of the search-and-rescue helicopters. The quality of the image is poor. The weather in the area is still marginal, but conditions are significantly better than they have been for the last forty-eight hours. There's not a whole lot to see, but if you look closely, I believe you'll be able to spot a small amount of debris in the midst of a dark discoloration of the sea's surface. That darker area is the fuel slick from the *Regulus*. Fuel is still seeping from the wreckage."

Using an electronic pen, the computer operator highlighted the area of the slick. Williams continued his summary.

"As you are aware, the *Regulus* went down in fourteen hundred feet of water. Sonar and radar mapping of the bottom have determined her precise location. The *Carolyn Chouest* is en route from Kenya with DSV-14 on board. DSV-14 is equipped with a remotely operated vehicle. The *Chouest* should be over the site in about twelve hours. DSV-14 will make an initial reconnaissance of the wreckage, using the ROV for a closer look, including the inside of the *Regulus*. We're assuming we can at least access the ship through the aft cargo doors."

General Petersen and General Lee studied the television picture at their site. Williams could see Lee pointing to something on the screen.

"Anything significant in the debris field so far, Colonel?" the CINC asked.

"No, sir. And that's a problem. There's nothing that's come to the surface that can give us any real clues what might have happened. We're estimating the *Regulus* went down quickly, based on the pattern of the debris and her location on the bottom. That would indicate a catastrophic failure of the hull, probably due to an explosion. Whether the hull breach was caused by an internal or external explosion can't be determined until the DSV goes down for a look. Even then, the true cause may not be readily apparent. It may be several days before we start getting any answers."

Williams paused, swallowing, because the next portion of the briefing, although necessary, was unpleasant for him.

"One thing we haven't found so far is bodies. None have come to the surface. We have recovered some body fragments, but nothing large enough to enable rapid identification. Follow-up DNA analysis will be required, at least until we can recover the rest of the remains. It appears the crew was trapped inside the ship when she sank."

"There's no indication of any effort to abandon the ship? No lifeboats? No beacons?" Petersen asked. "Does that strike anyone as odd? It does me."

"Yes, sir, it does seem strange. If an explosion sank the *Regulus*, there still should have been time for at least some of the crew to get away. But there's been no sign of lifeboats, no rescue beacons, nothing to indicate anyone survived. Even with no survivors, some of the bodies should have come to the surface. Nothing, however."

Williams signaled for the next slide.

"Sir, Captain Swain of the NMCC will talk about the next two slides."

Williams sat back as the lanky Navy officer arose and stood next to the screen as he discussed the ships and aircraft involved in the search effort and their plan of action for the next twenty-four hours. The change in briefers provided a welcome break in the discussion. Williams felt great distress every time the subject of the *Regulus*'s crew came up, because it was now very clear there were no survivors. He had dealt with the loss of life before, in the numerous aircraft accidents he had been called upon to investigate, but countless investigations didn't make the reality of death any easier to accept. At least he could accept the fact that aircraft accidents were likely to happen: mechanical failure, weather, pilot error. So many factors could conspire to bring down an aircraft and its crew. This was different. This was a ship out on a cruise. She wasn't supposed to sink. He had hoped, even expected, the search would turn up some survivors, perhaps most of the crew. The loss of so many lives, in what should have been a routine mission for the ship, filled Williams with pain and anger.

It would be a few days yet before he could visit Charleston and talk to the people responsible for the cargo flap, but he was already looking forward to his mini-inquisition of the personnel at the port. He wanted nothing more than to nail the culprits who had put the JASSMs aboard the *Regulus*, because he was now convinced the forbidden cargo was the reason the ship was lying at the bottom of the Indian Ocean. He would make it his goal to guarantee that a similar fate befell those responsible for this disaster.

His attention drifted back to the briefing as Swain described the upcoming DSV operations.

"As Colonel Williams mentioned earlier, General Petersen, the *Carolyn Chouest* will be over the *Regulus* site in about twelve hours. It will take several hours to prepare the DSV for the dive. They'll want to wait for daylight in any event. We will establish a direct feed to the NMCC from the DSV's cameras. You'll be able to see everything the crew of the DSV and their ROV is seeing. We're coordinating everyone's schedules. Initial contact with the *Regulus* takes place during tomorrow morning's briefing, barring any last-minute mechanical glitches. This is the first time we've ever attempted this, so we're not quite certain how well it will work or what we can expect in the way of the quality of the transmission. But we're optimistic. Sir, that concludes my portion of the briefing. Do you have any questions?"

"Good briefing, Captain Swain. We'll all be here in the morning. No questions for you, but I do have one for Colonel Williams."

Williams leaned closer to the microphone sitting in the center of the table. "Yes, sir?"

"What's the latest on the reports we had about unknown aircraft activity near the *Regulus* prior to the loss of contact?"

"We've spoken with the Defense Intelligence Agency. In fact, one of their analysts is present if you want to ask any other questions. Anyway, to sum up, DIA has reviewed everything they have, and they've polled the other intelligence organizations. The best they can come up with is this: There were some aircraft in the general vicinity of the *Regulus*. At one point, they appeared to be heading in the direction of the ship. However, the last information they have indicated the aircraft turned away from the *Regulus*. We don't know if the message fragment we have from the ship reflects the flight activity before the aircraft changed course, or whether it suggests the aircraft resumed a flight path toward the *Regulus*. We simply don't know at this time. But I'm assured by the intelligence folks they are continuing their review in-depth. If they uncover anything new, they'll let us know immediately."

Williams looked across the room at the DIA analyst, who nodded her agreement.

"I don't think I have any other intelligence questions," Petersen said, looking around his conference room. Everyone else visible on the TRANSCOM screen shook their heads. "Thanks for the update. We all know what we have to do for the rest of the day. See you all tomorrow morning."

The technicians cut off the microphones at all the conference sites. At last everyone could relax and contemplate the morning's events. A few individuals lagged behind in the NMCC conference room to discuss Petersen's dressing-down of Dunleavy. Williams had no time for gossip, and he pushed out the door with Mulkey and Johanssen close behind. He paused for a moment to thank Swain for his help, telling him he would see him in a couple of hours.

Williams and his small entourage snaked their way up the stairs and through the Pentagon corridors back to their temporary offices on the fourth floor. He spent the next two hours talking to various offices in the Military Traffic Management Command headquarters, identifying points of contact at Charleston and ensuring MTMC would send someone down to Charleston for that portion of the investigation. In between his conversations with MTMC, he received a call from General Lee.

"Blair, great job this morning. You guys had your act together and the CINC appreciated it. However, next time he wants a heads-up before he's ambushed."

"General, I assure you Dunleavy's entrance was as much a surprise to me as it was to the CINC. If I had known he was going to be there, I would have done some legwork and found out why. You and the CINC would have been the first to know."

"Well, no great harm done, except perhaps to Dunleavy. Do keep your eyes and ears open in the future, though. The CINC really doesn't like surprises. Something I want to pass along—for your ears only. I did speak to the MSC commander. He had just gotten off the phone with the CNO."

Williams smiled. That procedure had in itself sent a clear message. The fact that neither the CINC nor the DCINC called the commander, leaving that task to the director of Operations, signaled to the MSC staff that it was now occupying temporary quarters in Petersen's doghouse.

"The admiral was most apologetic and said he had already talked to his errant 0-6. Thatcher's next duty may be as a signal buoy in the middle of the Chesapeake. That's b-u-o-y, lest there be any confusion."

Williams chuckled out loud and said goodbye to his boss. Events had turned out exactly as he expected. He turned to Mulkey and Johanssen. "Gentlemen, I would say this has been a most interesting day so far. Which reminds me of the old Chinese curse. Let's hope for fewer such interesting days in the future. Since Admiral Dunleavy hasn't called and invited us to join him at dinner this evening, let me suggest we get together after work and do some serious relaxing. Does anyone like Cajun food?"

"Does the Pope eat fish?" Johanssen asked.

"I'll take that as a yes. We'll get out of here by 1800 and head toward this place I know on King Street. Wayne—"

"Yes, sir, I know. I'll do the driving. But what about all that Scotch you were talking about on the plane? I thought you had your heart set on Alexandria and me as the designated driver."

"Some other time. This place is closer, especially to our hotel. Now, let's go over what we need to take care of this afternoon. You two need to complete the arrangements to get us down to Charleston."

"Already working on it, Colonel," Mulkey responded. "Here's the preliminary itinerary. MTMC has been very cooperative so far. And I have friends at Charleston Air Force Base."

"Tom, I wish I had five more like you."

"Oh, please no, sir," Johanssen spoke up. "One of him already keeps me plenty busy."

Chapter Fourteen

20 August, 1945 hours EDT

The restaurant Williams picked turned out to be a mob scene. The receptionist handed them a paging device, explaining it would vibrate when their table was ready.

"I'll take that, sir, if you don't mind," Johanssen spoke up, and grabbed the pager. "I've always wanted to see how one of these works. I have a theory that if you juiced the power up on one of these things, it'd make a great marital aid."

Williams and Mulkey groaned. Williams rolled his eyes and frowned at Johanssen. "Wayne, are you sure that under that logistician's exterior there doesn't lurk a soul yearning to be a Navy aviator?"

Johanssen blushed ever so slightly, quickly looking around the room to see if anyone else had heard him. There were a few smiles, and one young woman, noticing Johanssen's uniform, leaned over to her companion and whispered something in his ear. They both chuckled, looked at Johanssen for a second, then resumed their conversation as if nothing had happened.

"Sorry, boss. Just ask Tom. In the office I'm a real straight arrow. In fact, I'm so well-behaved, it's disgusting. Get me out in public and you have to put a leash on me." Johanssen paused, then grinned at Williams.

Williams could only wonder what was on Johanssen's mind now. He turned back toward Mulkey, shaking his head.

Mulkey smiled at him. "You'll get used to him, Colonel. He becomes a bit rambunctious when he gets his kitchen pass for one of these trips, but he's only mildly embarrassing. I've only had to lock him in his room a couple of times."

"Thanks, Tom," Johanssen replied. He'd taken a seat on the bench by the door and was studying the pager intently.

Williams scanned the restaurant. He had started toward the bench to join Johanssen when he spotted a vaguely familiar face. He studied the individual for a moment, then made the connection. "You two guys excuse me for a minute, will you? I see someone I recognize. Come and get me when the table's ready."

Mulkey and Johanssen watched Williams snake his way through the crowds, craning their necks to see where he was headed. Both were curious as to whether Williams's acquaintance was male or female. They lost interest immediately when they saw he was heading toward a man seated by himself near the window.

Williams reached the table just as its occupant looked up.

"Mike? Aren't you Mike Underwood?"

"Yes, I am." Underwood stared at Williams for a moment. "I'm sorry. I should know you, since you obviously remember me, but I've always been very bad with names."

Williams came around to the side of the table and tapped his name tag with his finger. "Blair Williams. We were stationed together at MacDill several years back."

"Of course! Please, sit down and join me. Have you eaten? The food is wonderful here."

"Yes, I know. I'll sit for just a minute, thanks. I've got two starving fellows waiting for a table, and I don't think we'd all fit around this one. You're welcome to join us if you'd like."

"Thanks, but I'm almost through and I need to get home. I've got a long day ahead of me tomorrow."

Williams studied Underwood's face for a moment. This wasn't the young major he had known in Florida. That officer had been tanned, energetic, even though he always seemed to be tied to his desk. Underwood had enjoyed a reputation as an intelligence officer who could always get you what you needed, and he didn't seem to care how long he had to stay in his office to get it. Williams would frequently encounter him in the headquarters building's corridors at some god-awful hour of the morning. He was convinced there were times when Underwood simply didn't bother to go home. The long hours had never seemed to slow him down. Now, as Williams looked at him, he was convinced Underwood's work routine had finally taken its toll.

"I know the feeling. So tell me, Mike, what've you been up to since MacDill?"

"Well, let me see. I went from MacDill to Air Combat Command at Langley. About seven years ago, I ended up in Washington. I was on the Air Staff for a while, working on joint issues for Air Force intelligence. One of the best jobs I ever had. We worked with you operations types and put together position papers for the chief of staff. We were constantly in the Joint Staff's knickers."

There was a wistful look on Underwood's face as he recounted his jobs for the past decade. Williams couldn't imagine anyone enjoying the paperwork and the bureaucratic battles of the Pentagon, but here was one who clearly seemed to love it. Underwood never seemed to have a life other than the office at MacDill. Williams was convinced he hadn't changed, and he began to understand the man's sallowness and the dark lines under his eyes. He felt a touch of pity for Underwood, but at the same time told himself here was someone made for a life inside the Washington Beltway. As Underwood continued his resume, Williams thanked God he had been on a different career path and had an obviously different approach to life.

"About a year ago, I went to work for the director of Central Intelligence."

Williams was intrigued—a leap from the Pentagon and the Air Force to the other Langley.

"That seems like quite a change. If I remember correctly, you had a great reputation with the operators. You were always able to track down the information we had to have, usually before anyone else could lay their hands on it. So you got out of the Air Force and went to work for the CIA?"

A look of discomfort crossed Underwood's face, and Williams realized he had said something wrong.

"Let me correct you, Blair. I don't work for the CIA. I'm not a believer in the philosophy that you 'can't inform anyone' that a lot of folks out there seem to have. I work strictly for the director in his capacity as the DCI. And, no, I didn't get out of the Air Force. I still wear the blue uniform, with the same rank as you."

"Sorry, Mike. Didn't mean to offend. Congratulations on the promotions."

"That's okay. Same to you. It's just that the business about where I work seems to be a common misperception, even among people in this city who should know better. Anyway, it's your turn. What have you been up to?"

Williams found himself wanting to rejoin Mulkey and Johanssen. He stole a glance in their direction, but they were still seated by the door. He had initially looked forward to saying hello to an old acquaintance, but this was not the same person he had met so many years ago. Although Underwood became animated when talking about his days in the Pentagon and his current job, there was something sullen in his demeanor, something that made Williams very uncomfortable. Quite clearly, they were in different Air Forces now. He felt as if they had nothing in common anymore. But he couldn't just stand up and leave. He gave Underwood the barest highlights of the past several years. He had just started talking about his job at the Transportation Command, careful not to divulge anything about the reason for his current stay in Washington, when Mulkey walked over to tell him their table was ready.

Williams quickly stood up. But not too quickly, he hoped. He shook Underwood's hand and wished him well, saying that perhaps they would run into one another again while he was in Washington, all the while fervently hoping they would not.

As they walked toward their table, Williams placed his hand on Mulkey's shoulder and said, "Thank you."

Mulkey looked questioningly at Williams.

"I'll tell you later. Right now, I need a beer."

Chapter Fifteen

They watched as the camera showed first the sky, then the rush of water across the lens as the DSV sank below the surface of the ocean. The room was deathly quiet, and everyone was left to form their own mental picture of what they would see on the ocean floor. It would be several minutes before the submersible reached the *Regulus*'s location, but no one attempted to disturb the solitude. It was as though all had agreed to observe a few moments of silence for the ship and her crew before the reality of what had actually happened became painfully clear. The only sound came from the submersible as its commander called out the passing depths.

"Six hundred feet."

Even though the submersible's searchlights were on, they revealed nothing except the uniform grayness of the water, growing darker as the DSV descended, and occasional glimpses of schools of fish, scattering as the strange vehicle disturbed their habitat.

"One thousand feet."

Chairs squeaked and clothes rustled as the audience shifted their positions, attempting to get a closer look at the images on the monitors. The anticipation in the room was now palpable; the DSV was within a few hundred feet of the sunken ship.

"Twelve hundred feet."

The image changed abruptly from an empty wall of water to a wall of steel, perforated by the outlines of windows. The center of the *Regulus*'s bridge had come into view, evoking a barely audible collective gasp in the conference room. The DSV commander's voice crackled over the speaker.

"We're moving astern to give you a wider view. We dropped in a lot closer to the superstructure than we expected. But I think you can already see something major happened to the bridge. There's a lot of twisted metal here, especially toward the central part of the bridge. Obviously, some sort of explosion at this location, from within the superstructure."

Williams looked at Johanssen and raised an eyebrow. An explosion near the bridge. This was unexpected. The ordnance should have been far belowdecks, a long way from the bridge. Johanssen shrugged slightly, but his interest had intensified. Williams sensed his colleague's excitement as the camera explored the ship's exterior.

"We're going to descend a bit toward the bow of the ship now and do a sweep along the starboard side of the hull. We'll work our way back to the stern, then up the port side. Then we'll head back to the cargo doors and send the little guy in for a look around."

The image of the bridge slowly faded as the DSV maneuvered toward its new location. In a few moments, the pictures of the tangled metal of the ship's superstructure had been replaced by the gently curving shape of the bow and the forward hull. The DSV started its cautious trek along the hull, the camera revealing the progress of the search for clues.

"Fantastic images," General Petersen said, breaking the silence, and his statement reflected the consensus of everyone watching the screens. The images *were* amazing, their clarity far greater than anyone had anticipated. Johanssen was positively captivated by now, intently watching the monitor.

"Hold on here," came the call from the submersible. "Something is coming into view. If you can see this as well as we can, you're getting quite an eyeful. We have the beginnings a major break in the hull. In fact, the hull bends at a very sharp angle at this point, as if the ship broke in the middle. There appears to have been major outward pressure at this point. The metal is bent back in several places."

Williams studied the image. Indeed, the hull resembled the petals of an opening flower, with enormous shards of metal sloping backward in majestic curves that filled the monitor screen. A black trail was visible creeping eerily through the center of the flower—fuel escaping from the ruptured tanks.

"There's fuel escaping at this point," the submersible captain confirmed.

Johanssen turned to Williams. "That's the area of the forward hold, boss, and I'd be more than willing to wager that's where the idiots stored the ammunition. It would take a lot of explosive to cause that much damage to the hull of a ship like the *Regulus*. She was a tough old girl."

Williams leaned forward and spoke into the microphone.

"General Petersen. Commander Johanssen tells me what we're seeing is the area around the forward cargo hold, the most likely location for the ammunition. That would explain the size of the rupture in the hull. I think it may also explain the damage to the bridge. A projectile from the exploding hold could have penetrated the decks and detonated in the bridge area."

"Roger that, Colonel."

The room fell silent again, but the quiet was broken almost immediately by the submersible commander.

"We have a proposal here that should speed things along. It will make things easier for us, since it's going to get a little sticky maneuvering around this mess. We all want to find out as quickly as possible what really happened here. The break in the hull gives us an opportunity now to take a look inside the ship. We can do the more complete external examination later. For now, judging from what we're seeing and what you all are saying back there, we've probably found the location of what sank *Regulus*. The hole we're looking at is big enough to fit two DSVs through. We'd like to go ahead and send the ROV through the breach. It should be able to work its way through the interior of the ship from this location. If not, we'll head back to the stern and go from there."

"Sounds like an excellent plan from here, Commander," Petersen responded. "Please, proceed."

"Roger, sir. We're deploying the ROV now and switching cameras. Your screens will go blank for a second, but don't worry. We'll be right back at you."

A new image popped into view as the ROV switched on its video camera and its strobe lights pierced the blackness of the water around the wreck. As the ROV detached itself from the DSV, the image bobbled briefly, then stabilized quickly as the ROV operator inside the larger submersible guided it toward the *Regulus*. In a few moments, the twisted metal around the hull breach passed from view as the ROV penetrated the fractured hull. Dark, shadowy images of the interior replaced the clearer shots of the outside of the ship. As things came into focus, the viewers realized they were looking at more shredded steel. At first glance, it would have been difficult to say what they were seeing inside the ship, so devastating had the explosion been.

"Not much to see here, I'm afraid," came the voice from the submersible as the ROV threaded its way carefully through the maze of sharp-edged steel. "We're going to steer him toward the stern now, and hope our access isn't blocked."

The ROV passed through two more huge compartments, the damage becoming far less noticeable the farther the craft moved away from the *Regulus*'s forward area. The image became very confused, with strange shapes lying at odd angles.

Williams moved closer to the monitor, and he instantly became aware of what he was looking at. "It's the division's combat equipment," he said. "If you look closely, General, you can make out a Bradley and what looks like the rear end of a Humvee."

The camera moved in for a closer look. It was, in fact, what Williams had guessed. Beyond there were faint shadows of other pieces of equipment, tossed and turned by the violence of the explosion and the sudden onslaught of seawater filling the decks.

The ROV moved gingerly around the Humvee and ascended slowly until its camera lens came even with the vehicle's still-intact windshield. This time there was a loud gasp in the room, and almost everyone simultaneously jumped in their seats. There was a human face, a very lifeless human face, staring back at them from the other side of the glass.

"Good God Almighty," Williams blurted out as soon as he was able to take a breath.

"Padrillo," Johanssen whispered.

"What?" Williams asked, startled.

"Not what, sir, who. The person on the screen, or what's left of him. It's Padrillo. I mean, the face is badly distorted, but still recognizable. Jim or Tom, or something like that. He was the engineer's mate on the *Regulus*. I met him when I was down at the course at Fort Eustis. We went out to the *Regulus* as part of the course orientation. Hell of a nice guy. Great storyteller. He was the highlight of the trip." Johanssen had been smiling as he recounted the story but then grimaced. "Damn."

Williams turned back to the monitor and studied the face. It was almost as if the eyes could see into the conference room. Williams wondered what they had seen before the *Regulus* was swallowed by the ocean. Johanssen's brief meeting with this man had resulted in the first casualty identification. Life was full of such chance encounters, or so it seemed.

As Williams continued staring at the face, he realized there was something very wrong with this picture. It made no sense. He turned back to Johanssen. "So tell me, Wayne.

What the hell is the engineer's mate doing sitting in the cab of a Humvee in the middle of the ship? Why isn't he closer to his duty station, or just floating about somewhere?"

"Good question, sir. I haven't a clue. Maybe he was hiding out, taking a nap."

"And slept through the whole thing until it was too late to push open the door or crawl out the window? I don't think so."

Williams decided it was time to pass this latest revelation along to the CINC. He leaned forward once again.

Peterson spotted his movement. "Yes, Colonel Williams?"

"Sir, my font of information here, Commander Johanssen, has identified the body. He says it's the engineer's mate. General Petersen, you may be asking the same question I just posed to the commander. I have no idea why the mate would be sitting in a Humvee while the wreckage of his ship is lying all about."

Petersen said nothing. Williams sat quietly for a moment, contemplating the discovery. He ran through all the possible explanations for Padrillo's strange location, eliminating each one as too bizarre. He felt he was approaching his wit's end, and he was frustrated. He forced himself to relax, closed his eyes, and took a couple of deep breaths. He opened his eyes and once again stared into Padrillo's face. It was almost as if the dead mate were speaking to him. He slapped his forehead with the palm of his hand. The sound startled everyone at the table. Suddenly, twenty pairs of eyes were trained on him, and General Petersen was staring out of the monitor trying to figure out what had just happened.

"Of course," Williams almost shouted out. "He was put there!" Then he realized the excitement he had caused. He gave a sheepish grin. "I'm sorry. Got a little excited there, I guess."

"You want to explain that, Colonel Williams?" the CINC asked. "Who put him there?"

"Yes, sir. Padrillo certainly wouldn't have been taking a nap or stealing a smoke in a Humvee with all the windows rolled up while all hell was breaking loose on his ship. He would have been at his duty station. Quite simply, he was put there. And I would say that in all probability after he was already dead."

"The second part of my question?" Petersen prompted.

"It all makes sense now, General. Those weren't bogus aircraft contacts. The *Regulus*'s captain did see something on his radar. The aircraft, whatever they were, did close on the ship. The damage to the bridge wasn't caused by exploding ammunition. That was a stupid theory, now that I think about it. I should have realized that immediately. The bridge was hit by something from the *outside*. It penetrated the bridge and then exploded. That explains the damage pattern. The *Regulus* was attacked. The bridge was the target. Take out the bridge and you stop the ship in its tracks. A risky move, because they could have blown up the ship on the spot and scattered bodies all over the Indian Ocean."

Williams paused to take a breath. He was on a roll, and he knew it.

"After the attack, they stuffed the mate's body into the cab in an effort to cover up the whole affair. I suspect we'll find the rest of the crew stashed elsewhere, either in other vehicles or in one of the compartments. If the bodies don't reach the surface, if the ship goes down, we don't find out what happened to her. At least not right away, not until they've accomplished their purpose."

"You're weaving quite a scenario there, Colonel Williams," Petersen said. "So who attacked and why?"

"General, I don't know, but I think we can all make an informed guess, given who we're up against in the Gulf right now."

"All right, you're making an interesting if not completely compelling argument. But why go after the *Regulus*? She's not the only ship carrying important cargo to the theater."

Williams realized the CINC was leading him along for the benefit of the others. He remembered General Lee's brief lesson from the day they had briefed General Allen: Petersen already knew the answer to the question. The CINC, of course, had seen the contents of the briefing from that first morning when contact with the *Regulus* had been lost. Suddenly, that briefing seemed a memory from long ago.

Williams responded, as if on cue. "Because she was relatively slow, unprotected, and sailing precariously close to potentially hostile shores. She was a target of opportunity."

"That seems likely. But wouldn't this suggest somebody knew her schedule and perhaps even what she was carrying?"

"Sir, right now, I'd be willing to bet that's the case. The way the cargo manifest was handled suggests two possibilities. Neither is very comforting. Either there was gross incompetence and an effort to cover up the mistake."

"Or?" Petersen asked.

"Or there was an effort to ensure ammunition was mixed with combat equipment badly needed by our units in Kuwait, so that when the attack on the ship came, the perpetrators got an added bonus. They could scrounge around a ship now dead in the water, taking everything useful they could haul away in their . . ." Williams paused for a moment, then continued, very deliberately. "Could haul away in their helicopters."

He realized he was suggesting something far more serious than an ill-trained, dishonest employee at an American port. He was implying a conspiracy in which members of his command may have been involved. TRANSCOM civilian—and possibly military—personnel conspiring with countries with whom the United States was virtually at war.

There was nothing new about such a betrayal, of course. People had sold out their country before for a few bucks or a commission in a foreign army. Loners, or misfits, looking for a thrill. But like so many others, Williams had never believed it could happen in *his* unit, *his* command. The people there surely were too honest, too loyal.

Sitting there pondering these possibilities, Williams realized the naïveté of holding such a view. His anger quickly flamed up. He envisaged someone at Charleston port, or somewhere else in the command, taking money for a cowardly act that resulted in the murder of so many brave men and women. He wanted to choke the life out of the guilty ones, extracting some small measure of retribution. He knew he could never fulfill this passion, but he could use his rage, control it, and direct it in a way that would motivate his search for the killers.

The ROV had moved well past the disjointed rows of combat equipment and entered yet another area farther aft in the ship. Williams glanced up just as the camera's lights shone on objects looking vaguely familiar. *What the hell is that?* he wondered, then realized almost immediately what he was seeing. JASSM crates. At least somebody had displayed a little common sense. Apparently, an attempt had been made to break up the hazardous cargo. The ROV's cameras panned around the room, and as it did so, Williams's unease resurfaced.

He leaned over to Mulkey. "Let me tax your memory, Tom. Remember the figures you dug out on the *Regulus*'s manifest?"

"Vaguely, sir," Mulkey joked.

"Do you remember how many JASSMs she was supposed to be carrying?"

"Twenty-four, Colonel, if memory serves me correctly."

"It serves you very correctly. General Petersen, I wonder if we could have the DSV crew pan the camera around this area of the ship once again, paying special attention to those crates I think you can see scattered about."

"Did you hear that, Commander?" Petersen asked.

"Roger, sir. Starting the sweep."

Williams watched closely as the camera lens wheeled slowly around the room, the ROV's umbilical cable drifting lazily into view, then out again as the craft completed its circle. He had counted silently.

"There are only twelve," he said to Mulkey. "How many did you see?"

"I counted eleven, but your eyes are sharper than mine, Colonel."

"Now, they could be elsewhere, jostled about by the ship's descent. But I'm willing to bet we're not going to find them."

The ROV had stopped its rotation, its lens pointing steadily at one of the ship's bulkheads. Williams's attention was momentarily diverted elsewhere as he prepared to tell the CINC about the latest bad news.

"General Petersen, what you just saw were the JASSM crates. There were supposed to be twenty-four canisters on board the *Regulus*. Tom Mulkey and I just counted about a dozen. I think the ship not only had some unwelcome visitors, I think they found what they were looking for. They took some prizes with them when they left."

The room was now filled with several muffled conversations as the participants discussed Williams's latest speculation. Williams looked at the monitor; Petersen was resting his chin on clasped hands, his eyes closed.

"Colonel, this is one bit of news I hadn't expected. What you're suggesting is that one of our latest, most advanced weapons may have fallen into the hands of an enemy."

"I don't think there's any 'may' about it, General. I would say it's a certainty. As far as the JASSM's technology, I'd say we're looking at a huge compromise of one of our key weapons systems here, if the Iranians can figure it out. I'd be willing to bet they can find the necessary help if they have trouble doing it on their own."

"I read you loud and clear, Colonel."

Captain Swain spoke up at this point, directing a question toward Williams. "What else could they do with the JASSMs, Blair?"

Williams looked at him quizzically. "What do you mean?"

"Could they use them against us?"

Williams thought for a moment, then said, "I don't really think so, Pete. I doubt they would know how to program the guidance system. They'd have to have some sort of launch platform adaptable to the JASSM. I think they were after the technology, so they could try and defeat the system." Williams spoke with certainty, but Swain didn't look entirely convinced.

"What's that?" The question had come from the back of the NMCC conference room.

Williams looked up and noticed everyone's attention was directed toward the television monitor.

Ken Currie

Visible on the screen were some strange markings on the bulkhead that became clearer as the ROV slowly drifted toward the wall. The markings looked like writing, but the salt water was eroding the inscription. Whoever had written the message probably hadn't planned on there being any witnesses to their handiwork, especially at fourteen hundred feet under the ocean. But even without an audience, they hadn't been able to resist the temptation of advertising their presence by leaving a makeshift calling card.

Williams studied the writing. There was something familiar about it.

"It's Arabic."

Williams didn't bother to turn around. He knew the comment had come from Johanssen. A wry smile crossed Williams's lips as he craned his neck around just far enough to see the Navy officer out of the corner of his eye. "You are a constant source of amazement, Commander."

"So my wife tells me, Colonel," Johanssen responded, beaming.

"I don't suppose you know what it says?"

"Well, sir, it just so happens I do. I took Arabic at Naval Postgraduate School. Top of my class. Amazed the hell out of my instructor, since I was pretty miserable at the rest of my courses."

Williams shook his head with a small smile. "Well, this time you can speak to the general directly. No go-between. The floor, as they say, is yours."

Johanssen got up from his chair and leaned over the table toward the microphone. "General, Lieutenant Commander Johanssen. I can read the inscription. It says 'Fist of God.' "

General Petersen looked around the table in his conference room and turned back toward the camera. "Any idea what that's supposed to mean, Commander?"

"No, sir. I don't. I understand the language, but I'm afraid I fall short when it comes to understanding the culture behind it."

Williams listened to the brief exchange, then realized he had to step in. Someone had to state the obvious.

134

"General Petersen, Colonel Williams again. I'm not a world affairs analyst. I'll leave that to the intelligence folks. But it does seem clear that we've now gone beyond the simple accident investigation we all hoped this would be. What we have now is an act of terrorism, if not an act of war. It's too early to affix clear blame for what appears to have happened here, but I think we're all smart enough to realize that the trail probably leads to Teheran. Only an inscription written in Persian would have made it clearer. The timing of the attack on the *Regulus* with events in the Gulf is not a simple coincidence."

"Go on, Colonel. I know you're taking us somewhere with this."

"Yes, sir. This now goes well beyond the organizations represented in this room. If someone in our command was somehow involved in the planning of a foreign attack on the *Regulus*, other agencies are now de facto involved. I don't want this to turn into a cast of thousands any more than you, sir, but the FBI, at least, is going to have to be included. In fact, I think you'll agree they have the lead now in tracking down those responsible, even if it includes personnel within the command. I'm positive other agencies will insist on being part of this effort, once word of this gets out."

Williams leaned back, waiting with everyone else for Petersen's guidance. He knew Swain would go to his bosses in the JCS/J3 as soon as this was over, especially since General Price had been unable to sit in on this session. He would have to try and tag along; he was sure Petersen would expect him to be there when Swain broke the news to the high rollers in the Joint Staff. He suspected Swain would also want his folks to take the lead in notifying the secretary of defense, but he was certain General Petersen would reserve that task for himself. His assets, his people, his organization's discovery. The CINC would want to make sure the SecDef was aware that the command was on top of the situation and knew where to take this thing.

Petersen coughed lightly and then scratched his temple, as if trying to figure out what to say next. Williams knew this was a ruse; Petersen was way ahead of everyone else in the room, now that he knew the full scope of what had happened in the Indian Ocean.

"Colonel Williams, please work with Captain Swain to handle the notifications within the NMCC and the rest of the Joint Staff. Make certain they understand that I will personally notify the secretary of defense and Chairman Hannah of our findings. General Price can call me directly if he has any questions about that. I'll make the necessary calls as soon as we're done here."

"Yes, sir," Williams responded. He was getting to know his CINC very well, he thought.

"I'll also leave it to you two to handle the notification of the FBI and other law-enforcement agencies as appropriate," Petersen continued. "I'm certain the NMCC has procedures for handling that, correct, Captain Swain?"

"Yes, sir. We'll take care of it. We'll ensure someone from the Bureau is present at the next meeting, although I'm certain they'll move out on this long before then."

"Agreed, and there's nothing we can do to stop the attorney general or the director once they're notified. But we can stay right on top of things here as well. I'd like to step up the frequency of these meetings to twice a day until further notice. Everyone should expect more crowded quarters after I phone the secretary and General Hannah. I want Colonel Williams and Captain Swain to continue playing the leading roles on the military side of the house. The wiring diagram you two provided yesterday for how you're going to operate there is still valid, as far as I'm concerned. The cast members may change a little bit, and there'll probably be a couple of extra lines that have to be drawn in. The SecDef and the chairman may overrule me, but I'll push for that arrangement. The last thing we want is twenty different agencies yelling they're in charge. You can also rest assured the White House will get involved once the SecDef phones the president, as I know he will."

Petersen paused, put his hand over his microphone, and leaned over to General Lee. He came back on the line, speaking in very distinct, almost sepulchral tones. The participants in the NMCC conference room could tell he was looking at someone in the room, but it was impossible to tell who at this point.

"I have to tell you all that there's something about this whole affair that troubles me deeply," he said. "Colonel Williams has just drawn a very compelling scenario of what happened to the *Regulus*. Judging from what we've seen on the monitors, I'd say his suppositions are right on target. I'd like to ask the representative from the Defense Intelligence Agency how we missed this one. Has the intelligence community been sitting on its hands again while I have a ship sitting on the bottom of the ocean? We have an entire crew who's dead. We have missing JASSMs."

Petersen's voice now filled the room. The legendary temper was about to be unleashed, Williams knew, and he thanked God he was not the target.

"This has all the hallmarks of a goddamned disaster! Yet the intelligence folks provided no warning. Zero, zip, none." Petersen turned toward his intelligence director.

"What the hell happened, Hank? Who dropped the ball?"

"General, we had some information, but it came in after the first indication there was a problem with the *Regulus* and it was incomplete. It wasn't much to go on."

Petersen waved him off impatiently. "I don't want to hear excuses about how bad the info was. I want to know why nobody acted on it. And I want to know if there was anything else available that could have tipped us off. If there was, I'd going to hand someone their head. I want some goddamned answers, Hank, and I want them fast."

The director of intelligence stared down at the table.

Petersen stabbed his finger at the camera. "There's someone sitting right there in Washington who should be able to help. Maybe you two can convince her agency and the rest of the intelligence crew to get off their butts."

Petersen paused, but absolutely no one in the conference room moved. They were collectively holding their breath, wondering if the CINC would rake the room with fire one more time.

"A word of warning to you all. I can't tell the secretary

of defense, the chairman, or the president what to say in public, but for damned sure none of you will talk to anyone who's not directly involved. The last thing we want to do is tip these bastards and flush them out too early, or have the press causing a bureaucratic panic by misstating the facts. We need to find out what these terrorists are up to, why they stole a boatload of cruise missiles, and how many people supposedly working for our side were involved. If someone speaks out of school, it will not be anyone sitting here today, because I guarantee they will not be sitting here tomorrow. Understood?"

There was a chorus of "yes, sir" in response to Petersen's admonition. All knew the CINC would grant no mercy if anyone from this small group leaked information.

"Excuse me, General Petersen."

Everyone looked at the screen. The voice had a disembodied quality to it. Williams realized it was the skipper of the DSV reminding the CINC he was still floating about the *Regulus*'s hull, his ROV marking time while Petersen was issuing marching orders to his troops.

"Sorry, Captain," Petersen responded. "Didn't mean to forget about you. Thanks for the great work. I assume you heard everything that went on here."

"Most of it, sir. Some of it faded in and out, but we caught the gist. Don't worry about us. Our lips are zipped. With your permission, sir, we'll continue with the examination of the *Regulus*. Sounds like your experts have most of what they need, plus their marching orders. If we uncover anything else new and exciting, we'll pass it along to the NMCC. Everything will be on tape in any event."

"That's super, Commander. Thanks for the excellent work."

"Anytime, sir. DSV-14 over and out, for now."

Petersen stood up from his chair, waved at the screen, and told the audience he would see them all at 1700.

Williams quickly stood up and made his way toward Captain Swain, who was already on his way out the conference room door at flank speed.

Chapter Sixteen

"Damn, Colonel, it's a real shame we won't be able to sit in on the meeting with you."

Williams looked up at Johanssen's smiling face. They had just found out the conference that morning had been changed to a session in the Tank. The chairman and all the chiefs would attend; General Petersen would participate by satellite link, as he had done all week. In addition, General Kingston, commander in chief of the Central Command, would take part by means of another satellite hookup, this one from his deployed headquarters in Kuwait. Williams had grabbed an empty desk in the NMCC while waiting for the meeting to begin.

"Don't worry, Wayne, you'll be busy," Williams said, and grinned back. He removed the sheet of notepaper from his planner and handed it to Mulkey. "Here, Tom. You and Wayne work on these while I'm tied up in the Tank. Make sure you give the comedian plenty to do."

"With pleasure, sir. Come on, Navy, let's go."

139

* * *

Williams followed the crowd of joint staffers into the Tank. He drew a few stares from officers wondering who this stranger was in their midst. Once they spotted the TRANS-COM badge on his coat pocket and the eagles on his shoulders, they smiled and nodded. A few walked over and introduced themselves, curious whether he had ever attended a session of the Joint Chiefs before. When he said no, they promised him he was in for one hell of an adventure, especially now that it looked like a U.S. military ship had been hit by terrorists. Williams winced at the comment. Already word was spreading beyond the NMCC to the foot soldiers in the Joint Staff. He knew it was impossible to keep a lid on such information inside the Pentagon, but he had not expected the news to make the rounds quite so quickly.

He was also warned that response options would undoubtedly be a topic. Consequently, this morning's session would probably get a bit dicey. He was cautioned to make sure he had on his flak vest.

He laughed with them but felt uneasy. He wondered how events would play out as the chiefs, their chairman, and the two CINCs attempted to fix responsibility for what had happened. He had watched Petersen in admiration during the preceding few days, but he had never seen the CINC interact with his peers. But now, here he was, the proverbial fly on the wall. He sensed this was a heady atmosphere for the other people gathering in the Tank. It just made him nervous. He was certain he would end up preferring the meetings of the past few days.

One by one the service chiefs walked into the room, taking their designated places around the table. Williams looked at the television screens; Petersen and Kingston were staring back into the Tank. Everyone was awaiting the arrival of General Hannah.

Finally, someone appeared in the doorway and intoned, "Ladies and gentlemen, the chairman."

Williams promptly stood up with the rest of the group, including the chiefs, and watched as the short, stocky Hannah—exuding the look of the F-16 fighter pilot he had been in his younger days—strode to his chair at the head of the table.

"Good morning," he announced to the room, and then bid a special welcome to the two CINCs. Having exchanged pleasantries, the chairman nodded toward the Army major standing at the podium. At the same time a slide bearing the logo of the Defense Intelligence Agency appeared on the screen, followed almost immediately by another slide, a map, showing the location of the *Regulus*. Another slide, this one covered with so many bulleted lines of text as to be almost unintelligible, popped up on the adjacent screen.

Williams supposed he was meant to be dazzled by this display of technical wizardry. In reality, he found himself desperately trying to match the briefer's words with those on the screen. He reflected on the old days of the cold war when critics of America's enormous nuclear arsenal asked how many warheads were required to make the rubble bounce. Now, it seemed, the proper question was how many words it took to make the eyes glaze over. He tried to pay attention as the speaker spewed out information Williams was convinced everyone in this room already knew. Virtually all of it had been the subject of intense discussion during the previous twenty-four hours. He was incredulous at the idea any sane person could enjoy, let alone understand, the briefer's oral onslaught.

He found himself impatiently waiting for the major to cut to the chase. Finally, a new slide appeared on the screen, this one showing what obviously were flight tracks originating in Yemen and reaching out toward the spot identified as the *Regulus*. The tracks didn't stop, they reached all the way to the lost ship. This was interesting. Williams sat up straight in his chair and began paying close attention.

"Sir, in response to General Petersen's question at yesterday's session," the briefer said, "we have gone back and done a complete reanalysis of information available at the approximate time contact was lost with the *Regulus*. The aircraft, probably helicopters, were tracked from the point of origin highlighted on the map, beginning at 1321 Local, 0321 Eastern Daylight Time. Earlier reports were in error.

Tracking was in fact continuous throughout the unidentified flight activity, except for a period of fifty minutes when all contact was lost with the targets. Loss of contact occurred at 1351 Local, 0351 Eastern. This suggests the aircraft dropped to a very low altitude while in the immediate vicinity of the ship, perhaps hovering over the *Regulus*. We cannot rule out the possibility the aircraft may have landed on the ship."

Exactly. How else to get the cruise missiles off?

"The site tracking the aircraft issued a message at 0340," the intelligence briefer continued, "once it became apparent the aircraft were heading southwest toward an area where U.S. ships were operating, including the *Regulus*, in support of Operation Resolute Eagle."

Williams was perplexed. This didn't sound right. There weren't any U.S. Navy combatants within two hundred nautical miles of the *Regulus* at the time of the incident. Where was he getting his information?

"The National Military Joint Intelligence Center retransmitted the message to a number of addressees, including US-CENTCOM and USTRANSCOM."

Williams was stunned, and stared first at the briefer, then at the screen. *What message to TRANSCOM? What the hell is this clown talking about?* Williams jerked his head toward Petersen's screen. The CINC was leaning over to his director of intelligence, their heads almost touching. No doubt asking him the same question, Williams surmised. The TRANSCOM intelligence chief disappeared from view almost immediately. Williams was certain he had been dispatched to check on the alleged message.

The briefer left the subject of the *Regulus* and the unknown helicopters, at least for the moment, and moved on to current Iranian moves in the Gulf. Another series of maps and complicated word slides showed recent redeployments of Iranian Army divisions, forward movement of attack aircraft, and the occupation of yet another Silkworm site near the straits. Despite this activity, the briefer concluded, there were no indications of an imminent Iranian attack on U.S. and allied forces.

Williams stared first at the briefer, then at the slides, and finally back at the briefer. He wondered whether he had stepped through a time warp. Certainly he had heard that wrong. He looked around the room. He noticed some wry smiles, a few shaking heads. Obviously, he hadn't misunderstood the assessment. Everyone in the room had just heard the intelligence officer describe substantial movements of Iranian forces toward friendly forces operating in the Persian Gulf, yet conclude there was no increased threat.

"I assume this is the assessment of your director as well?" General Hannah asked. "I only ask because what you are telling me, Major, is diametrically opposed to what you briefed me last week. I assume something has happened to cause a reassessment."

"Yes, sir, this is the director's assessment."

Hannah looked at the service chiefs. All except one were smiling. The exception was the Marine Corps Commandant. He was holding the end of a clenched fist over his mouth, his body shaking gently from repressed laughter.

"You're probably aware CIA disagrees, at least judging by what I've been hearing at the White House over the past few days. The folks at Langley are painting a much more alarming picture of Iranian troop activity. State seems to agree with you, however. As does the president. You picked good company, it would seem. But, of course, I wouldn't want to suggest that's the reason for your agency's reassessment."

The briefer looked flustered for a moment, and muttered something about CIA's tendency to overstate Iranian capabilities. Hannah let the comment pass and told the major to continue the presentation. Williams expected to hear more on developments in the Gulf; instead, the major jumped back to the *Regulus* to discuss possible identities of the attackers. Hannah broke in one more time.

"I judge from the last comment that your analysts don't believe Teheran could have mounted such an operation?"

"No, sir. Iranian involvement is certainly one of the possibilities, if for no other reason than events in the Gulf. However, we believe such a step carries great risks for Teheran. We're certain the Iranian leadership is aware of

143

those risks. They would have to calculate such an act of terrorism would carry a significant risk of a sharp U.S. reaction."

"You're assuming the current Iranian leaders are capable of making such a reasoned calculation?" Hannah prompted. "Or that they know they would get caught in the act?"

"Yes, sir. They would have to judge they would be the first we would suspect and that we would do our best to find the connection. Overall, they have shown a good deal of restraint in response to actions by U.S. and allied forces. We judge they are extremely wary of doing anything that would further escalate the crisis."

Williams could only shake his head, trying to keep the gesture as discreet as possible. He marveled at the major's ability to overlook the obvious and ignore the Iranian military movements he had just covered in detail. For his part, the major appeared convinced he was back on safe ground. His voice settled into the strong, deep tones with which he had started the presentation, the sign of a well-rehearsed practitioner of the military briefing arts.

"The other options are an attack carried out strictly by the Yemenis, possibly with Iranian support, or an attack by an as yet unidentified terrorist group. The Yemeni and Iranian governments may or may not have supported an independent terrorist operation."

Williams waited for the briefer to say something about the "Fist of God" inscription discovered the day before in the *Regulus* cargo hold. DIA analysts had been present in the room. They had heard Johanssen. Amazingly, the major said nothing. Instead, he changed subjects once again, this time to cover briefly two other potential crises brewing in Africa and the Balkans. At that point, Williams stopped listening, distracted by the subject hopping and totally perplexed by the failure to mention anything about the evidence found on the sunken ship. He barely noticed as the briefer wrapped up his presentation and departed the room. A number of the joint staffers followed him out the door.

Williams drew a few questioning looks from those walking out and some of those remaining behind. They obviously wondered why this outsider remained behind. He settled back into his chair, knowing his presence bore Petersen's stamp of approval.

"Well, gentlemen," Hannah said softly, as if afraid to spoil a moment of contemplation, "once again we've got the latest and the best from our intelligence folks. I know everyone feels better, having been told the Iranians aren't going to do a damned thing while we cruise all over the Gulf dropping a potful of cruise missiles on their heads."

The chiefs began laughing. Most of those seated around the edge of the room immediately joined the mirthful chorus. Williams only smiled, but he was gratified the chairman shared his skepticism about what he had just heard.

"Tell us what we need to know," the Marine Corps commandant responded, "just make sure it tracks with what the administration wants to hear."

"Hennessey must be angling for a job on Pennsylvania Avenue after he retires." The reference to the DIA director had come from the chief of Naval Operations.

Williams studied the CNO's face for a moment, wondering what comments he would offer when the subject of the *Regulus* resurfaced. The encounter with Dunleavy was still very much on Williams's mind.

"I thought you were very easy on the major, General Hannah," the Air Force chief of staff offered.

"No good jumping down *his* throat," Hannah responded. "He's just one of Hennessey's talking dogs. His boss is the real problem. There was a time when the DIA director and his staff told us what *we* wanted to hear. I'm not sure which is worse. In any event, he'll only be around for three more months."

"By that time, General," the CNO answered, "the war in the Gulf may be over and he'll have missed the whole thing."

"Unfortunately," Hannah replied, "the Oval Office academic also refuses to see it coming."

Hannah's gibe at the president made Williams feel very uneasy, as if he had just been part of a conspiracy. He forced the feeling aside, reassuring himself that this was just the way the chiefs talked when they secluded themselves in the

Tank or their E-ring offices. But he still felt uneasy, strangely vulnerable.

He had heard and read about the Joint Chiefs and how they could be disarmingly blunt in their assessment of the civilian leadership. He thought many of the accounts were simply inventions of hyperactive imaginations, fictions dreamed up by ambitious journalists. Yet here he was, witnessing just such a display during his first and probably only visit to a session of the joint chiefs. Williams shared many of their misgivings about Noonan, but he had always carefully refrained from offering any judgments on the subject to anyone except his wife and a very few close friends. He couldn't imagine himself making such comments in the office in front of either superiors or subordinates. It wasn't his style.

He wasn't naive. He had let his guard down, a few years before, when he was still a lieutenant colonel. He was having a beer with his boss, a colonel, who was ranting about the "sonuvabitchin' civilians" in the White House and the Pentagon. Williams had sought to calm down the colonel's beer-induced invective, pointing out he didn't always like what the civilians did either, but they were in control. His boss had sobered up instantly, fixed him with an angry stare, and bellowed, "I believe in civilian control of the military, too, Williams, but tell me, who's going to control these goddamned civilians?" Since that time, Williams had adhered strictly to a personal rule of avoiding discussions about politics. One way or another, he had concluded, such discussions always ended up getting one in trouble.

Williams was suddenly aware he had been reminiscing instead of listening. He glanced around, feeling a bit sheepish about letting his mind wander. He relaxed when he noticed everyone's attention was still focused on the chiefs and the screens over their heads. He caught the tail end of a discussion among Petersen, Hannah, and Kingston. They were trying to sort out current shortfalls in airlift to Kuwait and Saudi Arabia. He was relieved they had been talking about a familiar issue. He couldn't have missed much he didn't already know, and the operations staff at Scott was busy working the problem in any event. He decided the chiefs were clearing the decks before returning their full attention to the problem of the *Regulus*.

"I think we can conclude," Hannah was saying, "based on General Petersen's comments, that the airlift shortage is temporary. I thought as much, but it's reassuring to hear that's actually the case. The completion of the noncombatant evacuation operation in Algeria should resolve most of the current difficulties. Once the NEO is over, our friends in Paris can worry about the rest of the mess in Algiers. The aircraft committed to the NEO will be redirected to support Resolute Eagle."

Williams saw Petersen and Kingston nodding in agreement. This was a rare moment, Williams knew. Kingston was a perpetual critic of the support he received from Petersen's command. Even before the latest turn of events in the Gulf, he had complained on a weekly basis about how TRANSCOM was shortchanging his mission requirements. Kingston wasn't unique, however.

The supported CINCs of the regional commands like Central Command were invariably perturbed about the level of assistance they felt they should be receiving from the "supporting" commands. TRANSCOM was the most important of the latter group, because it provided strategic lift for all U.S. forces, regardless of their operating theater. Every supported CINC insisted his command should have the highest priority. The only time they would refrain from asserting such claims was when large numbers of U.S. forces were engaged in potential or real hostilities in another CINC's area of responsibility. Obviously, support would have to flow to the engaged command. Even in those situations, however, the other CINCs would search for some way to get in on the action. The effect on the supported commands, especially TRANSCOM, would be the same in either case: Requirements would far outweigh available resources.

Fortunately, Williams knew, Petersen also wore four stars, making him one of the legendary nine hundred-pound gorillas—indeed, it was often suggested he looked the part— in charge of the unified commands. Petersen had waged an

147

aggressive and successful campaign to assert his coequal status with the other CINCs. General Hannah had also made it clear he recognized the importance of Petersen's command to the overall ability of U.S. forces to perform their mission. Petersen was able to use his success and Hannah's patronage to fend off excessive demands. He never turned the other CINCs down flat; that simply wasn't an option. While giving the CINCs less than they demanded or insisted they had to have, he skillfully convinced some of them they were receiving TRANSCOM's special attention.

Some refused to be stroked in this way. General Kingston was one of those who continued to spar with Petersen on an almost daily basis. Williams knew, as did everyone else, that there was a strong element of rivalry in their relationship. Petersen and Kingston were leading contenders for the chairmanship when General Hannah's term expired in the coming spring.

Hannah turned in his chair to speak to a one-star Army general seated in the row of chairs immediately behind him. Williams didn't recognize the brigadier general, but that didn't surprise him. He didn't know seventy-five percent of the people in the room.

"Kurt, what does the J2 have on the site in Yemen? I can trust you guys to give me the straight skinny, can't I?"

So this was General Norbert. The DIA analyst at the previous day's meeting had referred to difficulties she was having passing analysis on the *Regulus* through Norbert's office. The general apparently saw himself as the gatekeeper, or filter, for information flowing from the rest of DIA to Hannah's office. Williams found himself thankful that Norbert was performing such a role, if the analysis being passed was anything like what he had heard during the intelligence briefing. He did find it interesting that Norbert had remained silent during Hannah's assault on the agency's quality of analysis, as well as its director.

"Absolutely, General Hannah. Unfortunately, I'm afraid there's not much to tell. Nothing conclusive, in any case. There is a base that corresponds to the coordinates where the aircraft were first picked up. It's an old fighter base. The

Yemenis have some ancient MiG-21s stationed there, but most are nonoperational. The base was covered yesterday. No sign of any helicopters, other than an equally decrepit Mi-8. If the helicopters originated there, they came and went. We've requested coverage of the other known bases in Yemen. We should have photos within the next twenty-four hours. We'll make sure the readouts are passed along to General Price's folks as soon as they're available."

"Bottom line, Kurt?"

"I don't think we're going to find anything, General. We've never carried anything in the Yemeni inventory that would match the capabilities these helicopters obviously had. On the other hand, it would have been hard for the Iranians to move the helos into Yemen undetected, and then back out again. Frankly, we couldn't say where the damned choppers are right now. But we'll keep looking."

"Thanks, Kurt, please continue the search. And keep pinging on CIA and NSA to see if they can give us anything tangible."

"We have that covered, sir. I talked to both this morning. Nothing definite there either, at least that they're willing to share at this point. The counterterrorism center is also drawing a blank, except for the very tenuous report on the Fist of God. They're skeptical, even though the group's name was spotted on the *Regulus*. There's no record of such an organization, according to the terrorism folks. No information at all."

"Obviously we're not going to find the smoking gun," Hannah observed, "but the president's the monkey on my back. He's convinced the Iranians did this. I'm also pretty positive they were involved somehow. But he wants us to take out something in Teheran in response. I don't want to risk putting a JASSM down the minaret of the city's main mosque unless I have something more tangible to go on, but frankly, I don't know if I can hold off Noonan or the secretary for very long. In any event, Price is working on options in case we can identify the responsible group and their assumed state sponsor. He'll brief those options in executive session."

Ken Currie

Norbert left the room as Hannah directed his attention toward the screens. "General Petersen, General Kingston, I know your commands are working together on the *Regulus* recovery effort. I understand bodies of about half the crew have been recovered."

"That's correct, General Hannah," Petersen responded. "Their condition confirms our initial speculation about the attack, at least the basics. No surprise there. Some of the crew members were badly disfigured, apparently from the explosion on the bridge. Others were shot, repeatedly. One of the female crew members was recovered. The autopsy suggests she was raped before being killed. The overall brutality of the attackers was extraordinary. Apparently, they took time from the principal objectives of stealing part of the cargo and sinking the ship to terrorize the crew. This was a ruthless bunch, unlike anything we've seen before."

"Damn it all to hell!" Hannah thundered. "If the press gets hold of that story, they'll be piling on the president to do something before we can gather all the facts. I can just see what's-her-name gravely claiming growing public sentiment for Noonan to retaliate."

"Only a few people know about the medical results, General Hannah," Petersen replied. "There's no need for that information to be made public, and I've warned people about the consequences of speaking out of school."

Hannah surveyed the faces in the room. He leaned an elbow on the table, his forefinger sweeping back and forth.

"General Petersen just made an excellent point. What you've just heard stays in this room. I'll decide when and to who else it should be released. Clear to all?"

Satisfied everyone understood his order, Hannah turned back to Petersen. "I spoke to the director of the FBI last night. They've assigned a number of people to the case. They've already started their investigation. He made it clear he wants to work with us. That means with your command, General Petersen, since the heart of what we know so far comes from assets under your control. I understand there was some confusion on that point earlier, but it's been resolved to everyone's satisfaction."

"That's correct, sir," Petersen acknowledged.

Williams shot a glance at the CNO. There was no response. It looked as if the CINC's phone call to the admiral had the intended effect.

"The director made it clear, however, that the bureau would be taking charge of the investigation of all criminal activity, since there clearly is an international terrorist connection and U.S. citizens appear to have been involved. I told him I had no objection to that arrangement. I also assured him we would cooperate in whatever way we could. I know you want TRANSCOM to stay deeply involved in this whole matter, General Petersen. That's my wish as well. I don't want the Bureau running around the Pentagon and the commands without our being aware of what's going on. We help, they share."

"That's our intent," Petersen said. He turned away from the camera for a second as the TRANSCOM intelligence director returned. "General Hannah, if you'll give us just a moment. Hank MacBride, our J2, has some information regarding a point in this morning's briefing."

"Yes, sir. Good morning, General Hannah. I had our joint intelligence center do a quick bit of research. We did indeed receive a message, but it was very sketchy and provided only partial tracking of the aircraft, not the complete coverage the briefer implied. If there were additional messages sent, TRANSCOM didn't receive them."

"General, if I may?" General Kingston asked. "CENTCOM can confirm only one message as well. We were also troubled by the implication that we had all the information we needed. None of my intelligence staff—either here or back at MacDill—felt there was sufficient data in that one message to justify pulling assets away from the Gulf to investigate. With twenty-twenty hindsight it would be easy to say we should have. If there was subsequent reporting, we, like TRANSCOM, didn't receive it."

General Hannah looked around the room. "Kurt's gone, isn't he?" He looked back at Petersen and Kingston. "We'll look into this. If we had information in this building, and it didn't get passed, we'll deal with the problem. Very quickly.

If the DIA director is blowing smoke in our faces again, I'll deal with it even more quickly." Hannah sat quietly for a moment, then muttered, "I should've fired that goddamned Hennessey a year ago."

Williams was certain the room wasn't intended to hear the comment, at once a condemnation of Hennessey and a self-indictment by Hannah. Hannah looked up with a rueful smile. "Any opinions on what the terrorists, or whoever the hell took the cruise missiles, is going to do with them?" he asked, looking at no one in particular.

General Petersen was the first to answer. "General Hannah, we talked about that briefly yesterday. The general consensus was they would disassemble the JASSMs and exploit the technology, first to defeat it, then perhaps to replicate it."

"Why take so many, if that's the case? If they'd only taken one or two, we might not have immediately noticed the missing JASSMs. By the way, I want to commend your staff for picking up on that."

"You can thank Colonel Williams for that astute observation, General. He's sitting there with you."

Hannah looked around the room, spotted the stranger in their midst, and nodded at Williams. "Good job, Colonel."

"Thank you, sir," Williams quietly responded, embarrassed by the sudden attention.

"Back to my question," Hannah continued. "Why take so many?"

"It gives them an insurance policy if they screw up during disassembly," Petersen answered. "In any event, we doubt they planned on us getting down to the *Regulus* so fast, and they almost certainly figured we wouldn't quickly discover the cargo loss."

"Okay, then," the CNO asked, "why not take more?"

"No room. They took all the helicopters could carry," Petersen responded without hesitation.

"Why couldn't they use them against us? Couldn't they just program one of the things and use it against one of our facilities?" the Army chief asked.

"Very difficult to do, Ted," the CNO quickly said. In this

case, the JASSMs were his responsibility; he was going to handle the technical questions. "To use the JASSM, you have to know where you are, where the target is, and how to program it to get from point A to point B. Figuring out where the points are is relatively easy. Programming the missile isn't, especially with the GPS advances we've made with the guidance system. The JASSM, being an advanced weapon system, has an advanced inertial as well as an updated terrain contouring matching—TERCOM—system. You have to know how the guidance systems operate. Plus, you have to have the right equipment to do the programming."

"You'd have to have a fancy launch system, too, wouldn't you?" the Air Force chief asked.

"Not really. You could basically prop the canister up and pop off the JASSM, if you could figure out the launch circuitry. They probably could do that. But the problem is, as I've just stated, guiding the missile to the target."

"How about using the warhead as an explosive device?" General Kingston asked. "They could use them to mount terrorist attacks against our sites in the Gulf."

"Not really practical," the CNO countered. "The warhead does pack a good wallop, but so does a truck bomb. There are better ways to blow up barracks or headquarters buildings. No, I really agree with General Petersen. They wanted these so they could take them apart and figure out a way to defeat them. There's almost no chance they can use the JASSMs against us."

"I'm not sure I share your optimism, Admiral," the Air Force chief said, shaking his head slowly. "If these guys can figure out a way to defeat the missile, then I'm willing to bet they can figure out a way to reprogram the guidance system to make the JASSMs go where they want them to."

"I appreciate your concern, General, but there's really very little chance of that happening. There are other features, security features, that we added to the JASSM. I doubt they could get past those."

"They could if they had inside information," the Air Force chief argued. "If someone told them how to do it."

"You're talking about a fairly significant security breach on one of our top programs at one of our most secure production facilities."

"Not that such a thing has ever happened before, right?" Hannah said. "How good is security at the contractor's plant? No, no, don't answer. That's meant as a rhetorical question, Brad. But how about doing a little checking just to make sure? A review of procedures? Maybe we can make sure to slam the barn door shut before all the cows run away."

"Yes, sir, will do," the CNO replied as he scribbled in his notebook.

"Well, I think we've gone over what we need to in this forum. If the OPSDEPS will remain, the rest of you may leave."

Everyone arose on cue. Only the chiefs and their operations deputies would be allowed to stay behind. Williams gave General Petersen a subtle wave, unsure if the CINC could see him on camera. To his surprise, the CINC smiled back and gave a quick thumbs-up. The gesture revived Williams's flagging spirits; he had felt mentally and physically drained by the session in the Tank.

Tom Mulkey was waiting outside the door. Behind him stood an attractive woman wearing a Navy captain's uniform.

"Colonel Williams," Mulkey said immediately in response to Williams's raised eyebrows. "I'd like you to meet Special Agent—aka Captain—Carolyn Younghart of the FBI."

Williams extended his hand. "A pleasure. I wasn't aware the FBI was now wearing Navy uniforms."

Younghart laughed. "This is the attire for my part-time job. I'm in the Navy Reserve. I pull my duty here in the NMCC. General Price and my director decided I was the logical person to take charge of the investigation within TRANSCOM."

Williams caught himself wondering whether this was the CNO's and Dunleavy's revenge for Petersen's drawing the jurisdictional line in the sand. He studied Younghart's face and manner, looking for clues as to where her loyalties really lay.

As if reading his mind, Younghart added, "At the end of the day, I will, as you Air Force types love to say, segue back into my real job in the Bureau. The Navy whites go back in the closet. Lieutenant Colonel Mulkey has been kind enough to get me onto your flight down to Charleston on Monday. I look forward to whatever help you can offer the investigation. We'll want to discuss some ground rules on the way down. Right now, I've got to get back to my desk and wrap things up here. Good talking to you, Colonel. See you Monday morning at Andrews."

Well, this is going to be fun, Williams thought as she walked away, anything but reassured by her comments. She had made it clear his group would be strictly a supporting cast. He put his hands on his hips and watched her depart.

"I know what you're thinking, Colonel," Mulkey said. "She certainly comes across as the take-no-prisoners type, doesn't she?"

"Yeah, well, we're not her prisoners. Damned right we'll be talking ground rules." Williams grabbed Mulkey's arm. "How about some coffee? I need something to drink and some painkillers. For some reason, I feel a very large headache coming on."

Chapter Seventeen

"Good morning, Michael," the voice came over the phone.

"Good morning, Valery."

Underwood had recognized the voice immediately as that of Valery Akhmetov. Valery spoke with the clipped, precise English of someone who had learned the language in the British schools. In fact, he had graduated with honors from Cambridge University, a distinction of which he was justifiably proud, although he had the grating habit of starting his sentences with "When I was matriculating at Cambridge . . ." He could be on the pompous side on occasion, but many found his affectations endearing, particularly some of the Washington women. His various claims of being descended from the Cossacks or distantly related to the Romanovs only added to his charm. Of course, it didn't hurt that Akhmetov was also tall, muscular, and very handsome. He reminded one of a Russian gymnast. But when he spoke, he spoke with the polished grace of a diplomat.

Underwood was fond of the Russian. They had met while

Underwood was a student at the National War College. His class had been on a field trip to Moscow, and he had encountered Akhmetov while his class was touring the Ministry of Foreign Affairs. Akhmetov was one of the ministry's press spokesmen. He left the job a short time later, fed up, he said, with the dead souls who continued to haunt the Russian bureaucracy.

There was no doubt in Underwood's mind that Akhmetov was very well-connected in Moscow, but he did have doubts about who really paid his salary. Akhmetov had begun his journalistic career with the old Soviet news agency, Novosti, just before the collapse of the USSR. Consequently, there was a strong possibility he worked for the KGB, as so many of his agency colleagues did. Whether or not he continued to work for the Russian security services after the dissolution of the USSR was an open question, but Underwood didn't let it bother him. He was always careful to report his contacts with Akhmetov as required, confident Valery was doing the same. Neither had ever passed significant information to the other. Instead, they engaged in friendly banter about their respective countries and their mutual problem of contending with Washington traffic.

"And how is my old American friend on this wonderful summer day?"

"Feeling very old and very harried, Valery."

Underwood was preoccupied with clearing up last-minute details with Josh Evans prior to reporting to his new assignment, but he was intrigued by Akhmetov's phone call. Valery rarely called him at work. He feigned concern about someone eavesdropping on their conversation, but both knew it was better to limit their contacts to after hours. Obviously, Valery had an important reason for breaking their unspoken rule.

"I take it this is not a social call, Valery."

"Am I that transparent, Michael? No, you're quite right, this is not a social call. I did want to call you up and wish you the best in your new job, however."

Underwood had learned not to be surprised by anything Akhmetov said, but this caused him to stop fiddling with the papers on his desk and sit down. "Could you tell me, please, how the hell you knew about that?"

"Ah, my friend, Washington's a small town with very large ears. There are few secrets in this city. Anyway, President Noonan's White House isn't known for its ability to keep a secret."

Very true, Underwood silently agreed. When it came to protecting information, the executive mansion was more than a sieve, it was a bloody colander.

"Well then, Valery, I guess I should thank you, although I'm not completely certain what I'm getting myself into."

"I would say you're getting yourself into the center of power, Michael. I know you better than you think. Probably better than your wife. For certain better than she. You couldn't resist the temptation, could you, Michael? Even if it means working for a man you truly dislike."

Underwood didn't like the direction the conversation was taking. Valery could be a real pain in the ass, especially when he started playing amateur psychologist with Underwood as his patient. "Let's just say the president made me an offer I couldn't refuse and forget about the psychoanalytic bullshit, okay, Valery? I trust you'll keep the information to yourself until it's made public?"

"Sorry, Michael, and of course. I wouldn't want to embarrass the president's staff now, would I? We'll discuss the other over a pint sometime, old chum. There was another reason I called."

Underwood grew attentive once again. "And that is?"

"Is there a problem in the Gulf, Michael? I've heard reports of a lot of naval activity south of Yemen. There's a rumor you may have lost a ship in the area."

Underwood hesitated. He had heard the news about the *Regulus* just that morning. The information available at the Agency was very sketchy. Obviously, the Pentagon was playing this one very close to its chest. He knew very little. But if he answered Valery too quickly, the Russian would see through it. The same if he answered too slowly. It was part of the game they played. He hoped he timed it right.

"Valery, even if I knew what you were talking about, you

know I couldn't talk to you about it. Besides, I thought you had all the answers."

"Only part of the time, Michael. Only when people are willing to talk, and I'm finding very few who are willing to talk this time around."

"Then how can you be sure anything is going on? There is a crisis in that part of the world. All kinds of crazy rumors are going to fly, particularly when certain countries are involved." He realized he was babbling and caught himself.

"Don't protest too much, Michael. I'm not going to press you. I do want to provide you with some information before I ring off. This is the real reason I called, although my congratulations on your new job were sincere. What have you heard concerning an organization called Voskreshennaya Rossiya?"

"Red Russia?" Underwood responded.

"No, Michael, not Krasnaya Rossiya. Your Russian was always execrable, a very affront to my sensitive ears. Pushkin and Dostoevsky are turning in their graves. Please, don't try to speak my native tongue any more until you've learned it."

Valery laughed gently as he delivered the reprimand, but Underwood could tell it was an uneasy laugh. There was clearly something on his mind.

"This is Voskreshennaya Rossiya. It means 'Resurrected Russia.' It is one of our many patriotic organizations, as they love to call themselves. This particular group is a real band of fascists, however. It draws its support from industrial workers and former members of the Russian Army. Unfortunately, its message appears to have considerable resonance among some of our *serving* soldiers and officers. It's an ugly beast with the capability to do some very ugly things."

"Valery, this is interesting, but why are you telling me this? Russia has a lot of these fringe groups."

"Michael, this is much more than a fringe group. Voskreshennaya Rossiya is populated by some lunatics, but most of its members are quite lucid, and their message can be compelling. They have proved very adept at proselytizing. Many of my countrymen want to believe all our problems can be blamed on outsiders, or forces beyond their control.

Ken Currie

The VR also appears to have considerable sums of money. Significant sums are deposited in foreign banks. There are people in the Russian government who suspect the VR has very strong ties to the Russian mafia. I believe it also has some supporters within the government as well."

"I still don't see anything new about—"

"Michael, listen to me, damn it!"

Underwood was startled. Valery never became this agitated. Something *was* troubling him, deeply. "Sorry, sorry. I won't interrupt. Go ahead."

"The VR is planning some type of operation. Unfortunately, we—I—don't think the operation is limited just to Russia. There are other targets and other countries involved. And they are receiving assistance."

Underwood realized he was swallowing hard. He felt frightened. First the report from the Uzbeks, now this. He had dismissed the report Cummings insisted be briefed to the president. Surely there was no connection. It was simply a coincidence of baseless rumors. But he couldn't dismiss Valery or the alarm apparent in his friend's voice. Valery was scared.

"What kind of targets are we talking about here, Valery?"

"Very important targets, my friend. Very big targets."

"Valery, you and I both know I'm not the right person to talk to about this. There must be people in your country who will listen."

"No one at the Russian Embassy will listen to me, Michael. They refuse to believe it. They say they've heard it all before. When I try to explain how excellent my sources are for this story, they just laugh. I've even spoken to some old colleagues at the Foreign Ministry. I've hit a dead end. The people I've talked to don't want to accept something like this as possible. They're trapped, Michael, trapped by their own simple minds. Or worse, my friend, but I refuse to consider that other option. I've known these people too long."

"Valery, I'm not entirely certain what it is you think this group, this VR, is going to do. You haven't given me a whole lot of particulars to go on, other than a vague reference to big targets."

"I don't have many particulars, Michael. But the VR is a bloody group. What they're planning is certainly a bloody affair. This is not a small group, Michael. I believe they're quite capable of causing much pain. I've been told what they're planning will make the IRA look positively amateurish."

That seemed a bit melodramatic, but Underwood couldn't voice that opinion to his overwrought friend, nor could he tell him he was scaring the hell out of him. "Valery, there are other people you can talk to."

"I've tried that, Michael. I called the 'people.' I was told they weren't interested either. In fact, they dealt rather abruptly with me. Perhaps you can do something?"

"Maybe. I'll look into it. How about I meet you later? We'll do a little pub-crawling. Tip a pint or two to Mother England, Mother Russia, and the mothers in Washington."

Akhmetov started laughing. "An excellent idea, old friend. Ring me up when you get home. I'll be the chauffeur tonight, and the first round is my treat. And, Michael, thank you for listening."

"Anytime, Valery, but please don't call me at the White House about this kind of stuff, all right?"

"Of course not. We have to have some secrets, don't we?"

Underwood's hands were shaking. He poured himself a cup of coffee and then placed the call he had promised Valery.

"Hello."

"Todd, this is Mike Underwood." God, he hated how they answered their phones. You had to guess who was on the other end. They both worked for the same boss and he was on a secure line, so Todd *could* tell him who he was talking to.

"Oh, hello, Mike. What can I do you for?"

"Todd, do you know Valery Akhmetov?"

There was silence on the other end of the line.

"Todd, did you hear the question?"

"Yes, Mike. Yeah, I know of him."

"Did he call you?"

"Not me personally. He talked to one of my people."

Like pulling teeth, Underwood thought, his anger growing. "Did he tell you about a group called Resurrected Russia?"

"Yes."

"And?"

"And what, Mike?"

"And what did you think about it? What are you going to do with the information?"

"We hadn't planned on doing anything. You've got to understand, we've talked to Akhmetov before. He's a bit of a flake. He drives us nuts with his ersatz British accent and name-dropping."

"Todd, he studied in Britain for several years. He learned English there. It's no surprise he speaks with a British accent. As far as the name-dropping, he knows the Russian Foreign Minister and he's interviewed Milyutin several times. You do know that, don't you?"

Silence again.

"Todd?"

"Yes. I hear you. Let me tell you again. He's a flake. We don't think his information is reliable. He just comes across as weird. Not to be trusted."

"So you ignored the message because you didn't like the messenger," Underwood replied.

"It's a judgment call. We have to make those all the time over here."

"Fine. I guess I'll have to handle this myself. By the way, how's the view from that angle?"

"What are you talking about?"

"I mean, you have your head buried so far up your ass, I was just curious what it looked like from that vantage point. You have one hell of a nice day, Todd."

Underwood slammed down the phone to the sounds of sputtering protest.

Crisis Point

Underwood crawled into the passenger seat of Akhmetov's Jaguar and gave his Russian friend a broad smile. "And how was the rest of your day, Valery?"

"Apparently not as enjoyable as the rest of yours, Michael. Why the happy face?"

"Because, comrade, today was my last day of having to put up with the bozos down the road."

Akhmetov looked at him intently. "I gather from that you made your phone call."

"Yes, I did, and a most cordial conversation it was, too. I commended them on their unique perspective on the situation."

"You had no success either, if I understand you correctly?"

"Absolutely none."

Akhmetov frowned. Underwood caught the expression and patted him on the arm. "Not to worry, Valery."

"I am worried, Michael. Very worried. Now what do we do?"

"You seem to have forgotten about where I'm going on Monday."

Akhmetov looked at Underwood, his face a mixture of surprise and delight.

"Are you serious?"

"You bet your ass I am. Maybe the *president* will listen. By the way, there's no Uzbek blood in that ancient and noble lineage of yours, is there?" Underwood teased.

Akhmetov's expression changed instantly, his strong jaw squarer than usual, his Carolina blue eyes a shade darker. "Absolutely not! I am one hundred percent Russian," he said defiantly. "Why do you ask such a thing?"

"Some other time, after this is all over. Right now, there's an ale waiting for me somewhere around Tyson's Corner, and it has my name all over it. Drive."

Chapter Eighteen

As Williams stepped through the door of the C-20 and started down the ramp to the tarmac at Charleston Air Force Base, he involuntarily shielded his eyes from the bright morning sun. He instinctively reached for his sunglasses, only to discover they were not in his pocket. He couldn't remember how many pairs of sunglasses he had lost in the last year. He was forever leaving them on a plane or at some far-off destination. He no longer told Erica when he misplaced a pair; too embarrassed to mention the losses and ask her to pick up replacements, he now quietly slipped into the clothing sales store on base. His frequent trips had become a standing joke among the sales staff. And if Erica wasn't fooled by the amazingly pristine condition of his glasses, she never let on.

Finally, he remembered: He had left them on his desk in the last-minute scramble. He grimaced, squinted harder, and mumbled to himself about his forgetfulness. There would be no relief from the unrelenting brightness of the South Carolina sky.

There certainly had been no need for sunglasses when they left Washington. It had been one of those dreary, overcast days that seemed to haunt the capital for days and weeks on end. The sky couldn't quite decide whether it just wanted to glower at the Washingtonians or pummel them with a steady downpour. In the end, it decided on the latter—the raindrops had started pelting the runway at Andrews as their plane departed. Although his eyes were still hurting from the burning southern sun, Williams welcomed the transition in the weather. The humidity was nearly as stifling as what they had left behind in D.C., but at least it wasn't falling on their heads.

As he stepped onto the concrete, he turned to wait for his fellow passengers. They were better prepared: All were wearing aviator-style sunglasses, the universally fashionable style of government employees, both military and civilian. Frowning at this reminder of his forgetfulness, he vainly tried using his hand to shield his eyes from the glare off the concrete. As they clustered at the bottom of the ramp, Younghart surveyed the sprawling air base and offered her assessment of military travel.

"Very nice, Colonel Williams. This is what I really call door-to-door service. You Air Force guys know how to travel. I usually end up flying coach on Useless Air or some puddle-jumper. This is a most welcome change. And you even made sure the weather was perfect."

Williams managed a slight smile. "Charleston's one of our bases. The C-17 wing here belongs to Air Mobility Command, one of our components. The arrangement helps makes travel like this fairly easy to set up. It also didn't hurt that General Petersen has more than a passing interest in what we're able to find out while we're down here. As far as the weather is concerned, I'm afraid I can't take credit for it. I guarantee you I would have ordered up less humidity."

"Ah, but this makes it a bit more like home, don't you think?" Younghart replied with a grin.

Johanssen had ambled over to the waiting staff car. The technical sergeant standing between the open passenger doors gave him a snappy salute and handed him the keys.

"You're gassed and ready to go, sir. I'll help you folks load your stuff into the trunk."

Johanssen returned the salute and glanced at the name patch on the noncommissioned officer's battle dress uniform.

"Thanks, Sergeant Taylor. Appreciate the help in setting this up so quickly. You've got a good crew. Now, if I can trouble you for one more bit of help, how do I get us to North Charleston?"

"There's a map in the car, sir. It's fairly easy to get to from here. The only tricky part will be finding your way around the port. We prepared a schematic with the buildings you want highlighted. If you have any problems, you can give me a call at the number written at the top of the sheet. Just ask for the chief dispatcher. Or you can call the other number. That'll hook you up with the transportation brigade at the port. Good luck, sir."

"Thanks. Appreciate you making the trip out here yourself," Johanssen responded.

"Not a problem, Commander. When the call came in from the wing commander's exec, we were only too happy to oblige. We don't get a whole lotta calls like that one. Let's just say Brigadier General Emerson's office conveyed a sense of urgency about the whole thing."

Johanssen responded with a knowing smile. The command's flag officer network could clear away roadblocks very quickly, a power a lieutenant commander simply didn't have, especially on an Air Force base.

Williams, suitcase in hand, walked over to the car. Taylor saluted, grabbed the suitcase out of his hand, and stowed it in the trunk. He hurried back to help Mulkey and Younghart with their bags. Williams watched as the sergeant finished loading their belongings in the car, marveling at how well travel arrangements had gone on this trip.

He would have to commend Johanssen on his ability to get things done. He wanted to find out how a Navy officer managed to set up the arrangements so quickly. Obviously, for once in his life, Johanssen had reined in his penchant for taking digs at Williams's service. He had many times overheard Johanssen grumbling about the "goddamn Air Force" as he tried to coordinate among the command's components. Williams could only chuckle and empathize. He had himself dealt with the same intransigence, a legacy of the days before TRANSCOM's formation, when the Air Mobility Command enjoyed the pride and prestige of a specified command. Those halcyon days were long gone, but, as Williams knew, the tail sometimes still thought it wagged the dog.

Williams wasn't always this lucky in getting to his official destinations. Being a duty passenger wasn't usually this enjoyable. He had to endure many long, tedious flights where the aircraft seemed to visit every base in the Air Force before it finally arrived where he wanted to go. Through all his travels, however, there had always been a constant: people like Taylor who kept things humming. They were everywhere in the command, wearing every shade of uniform. That made the events of the past few days all the more difficult to accept. If someone in the command was part of this, it wouldn't be one of these troops.

They had no trouble finding the gate to the complex. They were quickly waved through by the civilian security guard, who gave their identification cards and travel orders a perfunctory examination. He had immediately recognized Williams's name. The guard looked at the port diagram Johanssen handed him and reaffirmed the directions to the transportation brigade's headquarters. Johanssen drove slowly, guiding the car through the maze of buildings and cargo containers crowding the several hundred acres of the busy defense port.

Williams had visited one of these port facilities before, but not during an international crisis. The operations tempo was significantly greater than anything he had seen before. Numbers on a planning sheet couldn't convey the real scope of activity. The port had a half-dozen intermodal cranes and almost a score of container handlers, and all seemed to be in operation, removing twenty-foot and forty-foot containers from arriving train flatcars and trucks, stacking the containers in clusters, then moving them again toward the waiting ships of the Military Sealift Command. It reflected a level of preparation that belied the temporary lull in events in the Persian Gulf. The pier could accommodate three cargo ships easily. Today, there were only two tied up alongside.

"That's the *Bellatrix*," Johanssen said as he pointed out the first ship. "She's a sister ship to the *Regulus*. I'm sure the stevedores and the crew feel like they're up to their asses in alligators, but if we can get on board for a little bit, I think it would be worthwhile for all of us."

"Agreed," Williams said. "We'll see what the brigade commander can do for us. Something tells me he'll cooperate with just about any request I might make on General Petersen's behalf."

He smiled at Younghart. Her presence was obligatory given the nature of the possible offenses they would be investigating. Her expertise and status would also be mandatory if they actually uncovered any conspirators, since Williams had no authority to detain anyone. He had been concerned, however, that the military and civilians working at the port might well be leery of her prowling about a Department of Defense facility asking all kinds of questions. She wasn't, after all, one of them.

Williams told her of his concerns on the flight to Charleston, and she dismissed them out of hand, telling him in so many words that all she would have to do was flash her credentials and resistance would melt away. He didn't share her certainty, and his reference to the CINC's authority had been a reminder she was in a different world, where not even her Navy reserve rank would count for much.

Williams had spoken briefly to Lieutenant Colonel Timmons, the North Charleston transportation brigade commander, by secure phone before they left Washington. The Army officer almost gushed with enthusiasm as he promised whatever help Williams required, and more.

Williams had been reluctant to convey too much information, but he knew he had to give some reason why a delegation from Scott was suddenly descending upon the lieutenant colonel's command in the midst of crisis operations. He had also been reassured by talking to Army officers at Scott who knew Timmons and had strongly vouched for his character. Even so, there was still a risk—albeit minimal—that Timmons had been involved, and Williams had been as circumspect as possible during the phone conversation.

"Colonel Timmons, there's been a serious accident aboard the *Regulus*, one involving loss of life. We have evidence there may have been involvement by command personnel. The CINC has asked us to conduct a preliminary investigation, so I'll need to talk with as many of the brigade's personnel as possible."

"Absolutely, sir. I'll make sure everyone is available."

"We don't want to disrupt your schedule or activities, but this has to be done."

"Don't worry, Colonel, we can work around it. Folks here are used to having their routines disrupted. You'll blend right in."

Williams smiled, then grew serious again. "I have to ask you not to share the purpose of our visit, or even the fact of our arrival. We don't want anyone destroying incriminating evidence or perhaps even fleeing."

"Understood. You have my word." Williams instantly sensed that the promise would be kept.

Williams knew there was no guarantee that the lieutenant colonel would have a job after all this was over. Responsibility traveled upward. If the brigade commander had concerns in that regard, he didn't let on.

"Colonel, I want you to know I'll do whatever I can to help track down the bastards, especially if they're working for me. We've worked hard to make this the best transportation brigade in the Army. No lying little prick is going to spoil our good name."

"Appreciate the cooperation," Williams responded.

"Treason, Colonel. That's all it is. Pure and simple," Timmons had said emphatically at the end of their conversation.

Williams had to agree, but he knew the culprits, if caught, would probably end up charged with actions having a far less onerous label than the commander's pithy truth. Their punishment most certainly would not be pleasant, but Williams knew it would be much less than what they deserved.

After a couple of wrong turns, and good-natured questioning of Johanssen's navigational abilities ("I'm only a loggie, Colonel, somebody else has to tell me where to make the deliveries," Johanssen offered in his defense), they finally located the brigade headquarters. As Williams stepped through the front door, the brigade commander rushed breathlessly out of his office to greet them, clutching a huge, foul-smelling cigar in his left hand. He was short, stocky, and possessed a jaw that jutted challengingly forward. Williams thought he should have been commanding a tank battalion in the Saudi desert.

The commander grabbed Williams's hand, shaking it vigorously, and Williams winced slightly from the firmness of the grip. Maybe the commander did belong down here on the docks.

"Colonel Williams, very, very pleased to meet you at last. Mark Timmons. Welcome to the brigade. If you'll follow me, we'll all go into my office. There's some coffee and donuts set out. You can relax a bit while we discuss how the brigade can help you with the investigation."

Somehow they all managed to fit into the commander's small office in the corner of the building. Younghart looked out the windows for a moment before taking her seat, but there wasn't much to see. Rows of containers blocked one side, while adjoining buildings occupied the view from the other.

Timmons noted Younghart's wrinkled nose and promptly extinguished the cigar. "Sorry, it's one habit I can't break. And I haven't banned smoking in my office yet."

Williams surveyed the starkly furnished office. He decided the quarters reflected the spartan, utilitarian approach he had encountered at various Army bases throughout his career. The building was rather run-down, although the brigade obviously made an effort to keep its quarters tidy. The pale green walls had a sheen to them and there was the smell of fresh paint in the room. The combination of paint and cigar smoke was not pleasant, and for a moment he shared Younghart's disgust. Then he relaxed and decided the austere conditions and the acrid, slightly bluish atmosphere in the room complemented the commander.

Williams began the proceedings by introducing his colleagues.

"This is Special Agent Carolyn Younghart of the FBI. She'll be conducting the interviews with brigade personnel."

Timmons stood up partway behind his desk and extended his hand. Younghart took it warily, having noticed Williams's pained reaction earlier.

"Well, I guess I shouldn't be surprised the FBI's involved. I was wondering if perhaps the CID might be the first to pay us a visit."

"The Army's Criminal Investigation Division has no jurisdiction in this case, Colonel," Younghart said firmly. "This is a bit more than fraud, waste, and abuse, as you're well aware. This is a terrorist act, and the Bureau has responsibility in such instances."

Williams tried not to smirk, but he lost the battle. Younghart didn't notice his reaction. He had offered her the best advice he could think of on how to avoid antagonizing the brigade's personnel. The officious tone she had just used with Timmons was not one of the tips he had shared; given Timmons's cigar-chomping style, the transparent reference to her authority undoubtedly was tossed quickly into his mental wastebasket. Moreover, she had unceremoniously relegated the Army's CID to investigating falsified travel documents, a slight Williams was certain Timmons noticed. Finally, Williams had carefully avoided mentioning the terrorist connection in his earlier conversation with Timmons. It was an altogether inauspicious start.

Younghart pulled a planning book out of her briefcase and propped it open in her lap. She made a few notations with her pen, then turned her attention back to Timmons once more. "I want to start the interviews as quickly as possible. Who would you suggest we talk to first?"

Williams crossed his arms and watched the interchange.

Younghart stared directly into Timmons's eyes without blinking. A challenging stare. She wasn't wasting any time. Timmons stared back, his fixed smile a thin disguise for his obvious irritation.

"Terrorist act?" Timmons asked, retrieving his cigar from the ashtray. "Colonel, you didn't mention anything about terrorism. This puts things in a different perspective. You're suggesting one of my folks may have been cooperating with terrorists? It would appear I need to talk to our port security people, if that's the case."

Younghart glanced at Williams, who quickly responded. "Colonel Timmons, I think you can understand my previous caution. But now that you know the real situation," he said, briefly looking back at Younghart, "you should be aware there's nothing whatever to indicate that whoever pulled off the *Regulus* operation is targeting the port or your personnel."

Timmons looked skeptical, and Williams couldn't blame him. Timmons had just been blindsided, and his reaction was understandable—his first thought was for the safety of his people. Williams had to refocus his attention on the real reason they were invading Timmons's turf.

"Colonel Timmons, you mentioned the contracting and dispatching offices during our telephone conversation. Considering the nature of what happened, let me suggest we go with the personnel in dispatching. That seems a logical place to start."

Timmons looked at Williams quietly for a moment, then nodded. "Of course, Colonel Williams. I hope you and I will be able to talk again when you're through."

"You can bet on it, Colonel."

"Colonel Timmons," Younghart interrupted, "if you wouldn't mind, I'd like to use your office for the interviews. Colonel Williams mentioned on the way out here that he'd like to take a look at one of the ships at the pier. The *Bellatrix*, I believe. Do you think that can be arranged? You can do that while I start the interviews. It will give you both the opportunity to talk further."

Williams shot a glance at Younghart, then shook his head

at Timmons. "Special Agent Younghart, I appreciate your efforts to speed things along, but as I've said all along, I plan on sitting in on these interviews."

"Colonel, I understand your interest in these matters, but I've tried to tell *you* that I can't allow that. This is bureau business. I have to conduct these interviews on my own. Your presence would not be appropriate. It certainly isn't required."

"I'm not sure as to the appropriateness, but I assure you General Petersen believes my presence *is* required. I would partially agree with your suggestion, however. Tom, you and Lieutenant Commander Johanssen go with Colonel Timmons and see what can be done about taking a look around the *Bellatrix*. Colonel, forgive us for confiscating your office space, but I think Special Agent Younghart is right. This is probably the best place to talk to your people. I'm sorry for the inconvenience. We'll try to make this as painless as possible otherwise."

Younghart was clearly not happy with this turn of events. "Colonel, I thought I made myself clear. You cannot sit in on these interviews."

"And Special Agent Younghart, at the risk of jeopardizing a cordial working relationship among the Joint Chiefs of Staff, my command, and the FBI, let me repeat—I will be sitting in on these interviews. If you continue to have a problem with that, the CINC can discuss the issue with your director. Or, if you'd like, I'm sure General Petersen could arrange for the chairman to talk with him to clear things up. Would the rest of you please excuse us for a moment while we straighten this out? Colonel Timmons, if you can get my folks aboard *Bellatrix*, I'd really appreciate it. Could you all excuse Special Agent Younghart and me for just a little bit?"

The others almost fell over one another in their haste to leave the room. Timmons quickly agreed to do whatever had to be done to get Mulkey and Johanssen onto the ship. Johanssen jumped to his feet and sped through the office door, not waiting for Timmons and Mulkey. Williams noticed that Johanssen had put his hat on backwards. He repressed a smile; he knew exactly how Johanssen felt. There were times to make an exit, and this was clearly one of them.

Williams stood up from his chair and walked over to the office wall, briefly looking at a photograph of an Army locomotive in a prominent place over the bookcase. He could never understand the fascination with trains some guys had. So slow and ponderous in comparison to something like the C-17. He could sense Younghart's eyes drilling into the back of his head. He suspected she wanted to drill something else there if she could.

He turned around and gave her a crooked smile. "What in the hell is going on, Carolyn? We discussed this on the way down. I thought I had made it very clear why I needed to take part in these interviews. I have no intention of asking any questions. I'm just going to be an observer. If I think of something that needs to be asked, I'll pass you a note. The show is yours. I'm not about to interfere in the Bureau's business, as you put it. I might be able to offer some suggestions along the way. This is, after all, part of my command. For example, you might benefit from warnings about what and what not to say. I think you saw Timmons's reaction to the news about terrorists."

She started to protest, but he cut her off.

"Let me finish. My command has got to know what's going on. I hope that whatever happened is restricted to this port, but if there's anything to suggest this god-awful mess involves personnel elsewhere in the Transportation Command, General Petersen is going to want to know immediately. We don't have time for your agency to clear the information through channels. The CINC is not going to want to hear it secondhand. And you can be assured the CINC won't be sharing it with more than a couple of other flag officers."

Younghart was shaking her head vigorously, but Williams wasn't deterred.

"Believe me, Carolyn, I wasn't kidding. Petersen will raise holy hell with whoever he has to keep our hand in this. You have to trust me on that. That's a nonnegotiable point. So you and I can agree now to cooperate and forget about bureau formalities, or we can bump this up the chain and delay a critical investigation. I think you know what'll happen to the two of us if we take the latter route. Agreed?"

Younghart stopped scowling as Williams made his last point. The remark had the desired effect. There wasn't time to screw around with territorial games. The CINC had just a few days before shot down in flames a Navy admiral who had tried to play such a game. He wasn't about to brook opposition from a simple FBI agent. Williams hoped he had convinced her of realities.

She shook her head one last time before she responded. "Colonel . . . Blair, I'm not happy about this. This is not the way we do things, but I can see I've run into a brick wall here." She smiled. "And I think it lies between your ears. You're not going to back down, are you?"

He returned the smile, enjoying what he took as a backhanded compliment about his stubbornness. It was a trait that drove Erica crazy at times, but his obstinacy had usually served him well. "Nope."

"All right, then. Let's get on with it. But if the director gets on my case later, I'm going to give *you* an earful."

"Fair enough, Special Agent *in Charge* Younghart." He walked over and extended his hand.

Younghart looked at it for a moment before asking Williams whether he shook hands like Timmons.

"Ah, so you did notice? I thought he'd lightened up for your benefit."

"Are you kidding? I thought my hand was going to fall off. I wasn't about to let him know, however." She rubbed the fingers of her right hand as if she could still feel the pain.

"I promise to be a bit more gentle."

"That's what all you guys say."

Williams blushed immediately. He had intended no innuendo. He'd have to be more careful with future word choices around Younghart. She obviously believed in showing no mercy.

She stood up, straightened her skirt, and shot Williams one final challenging look. "Just let me ask the questions, as agreed, okay?"

"As agreed. Now, let's go find the sons of bitches, shall we?"

*   *   *

They had questioned three employees. All had denied any knowledge of the particulars regarding the loading of the *Regulus*. All were a bit nervous, but Williams attributed that more to their being interrogated by someone from the FBI. He believed Younghart's intimidating demeanor had more to do with their unease than any secrets they might be hiding.

One of those interviewed had asked if the interview was prompted by the time he experimented with marijuana in high school. He had admitted to this adolescent indiscretion on his security questionnaire when he was first hired, he said, and no one had ever brought up the subject again. Had someone had second thoughts? Was he going to be sent to jail? Younghart emphatically assured him that this was not in the least related to anything he had done as a teenager. He was not going to be sent up the river for taking a few puffs of weed, she said.

"Just make sure you never, ever do it again, or I'll be back," she had warned him as he left. The young man still appeared skeptical despite her assurances, but clearly was grateful when told he could leave. Williams and Younghart laughed raucously after he left the room.

"Well, that was certainly interesting," Williams said as he fought back tears. "Maybe you should have put your pistol on the desk for added emphasis."

"Are you kidding? With that deer-in-the-headlight look he gave me? I don't think we have to worry about him. But we don't seem to be getting anywhere. Obviously, we're not talking to the right people."

"Relax. We're just getting started," Williams replied. "Wait a minute, you're the seasoned expert. I'm supposed to be the impatient one."

She chuckled. "Okay, okay. You made your point. Who's next?"

The chief of the dispatching section sat in front of them. He was a large man with a stomach that refused to be confined by the thin belt he wore. Thick black-framed glasses perched on top of his bulbous nose. He had a pasty complexion that was crowned by strands of thinning reddish hair, combed across the scalp to give the illusion of volume. His nicotine-stained fingers drummed nervously on the arms of the chair.

Williams had recoiled when the section chief had entered the room, then chastised himself for giving in to stereotypes. He had glanced at Younghart to gauge her reaction. There had been none, and that made him feel even more embarrassed by his first impression.

As with the others, Timmons had called the section chief into the office, telling him only that individuals from command headquarters were interviewing brigade personnel about problems encountered on the *Regulus*. Younghart introduced herself and Colonel Williams. Williams simply nodded, then settled comfortably back into the easy chair beside Timmons's desk. There was no visible reaction from the section chief when Younghart identified herself as an FBI agent, although he confessed to being confused as to why he was being questioned by the FBI.

"Do I need to have a lawyer present? Are you going to read me my rights?"

"Only if you think I need to, sir," Younghart answered. "Right now, we're just gathering information. I just want to ask you a few questions. Colonel Williams is representing the TRANSCOM commander in chief. I'm sure you understand why he's here. I'm here because there's been an incident affecting one of the ships belonging to the Military Sealift Command, the *Regulus*."

Williams studied the section chief closely. The chief's eyes grew wide as he listened to the news. Williams thought he saw a hint of perspiration on his forehead, even though the room was quite chilly from the window air-conditioning unit. This was a different reaction from the others. All seemed curious about the fate of the ship, but none had been overly alarmed by the news. Their body language seemed to say, *So why am I here? This doesn't concern me.*

The section chief rubbed his forehead with the back of his hand. He looked down at the floor for a second, then

Ken Currie

cleared his throat and looked up at Younghart. "Can you tell me what happened?"

"All I can tell you is that there was an accident aboard the *Regulus*. There is evidence of foul play."

The section chief's eyes grew wider, and Williams now saw alarm in them. The chief began fidgeting in his chair.

"However, that's only part of the reason we're here. Somehow ammunition ended up on the *Regulus* while the ship was being loaded at North Charleston. Colonel Williams informs me such cargo should have been loaded on a different ship."

Williams looked admiringly at Younghart. It was a nice move. She had noticed the section chief's reaction. The reference to foul play had unnerved him. Now she was bringing up the cargo diversion, even though this was not the focus of her investigation. If this guy was involved, he'd understand she was linking the *Regulus*'s fate with whoever changed the cargo manifests. She was betting he would panic, and pressed ahead.

"In order for such a diversion to occur, someone had to violate your command's regulations, as well as federal law. We're trying to find out who was responsible for the change in the cargo documentation. Because of the falsification of the paperwork, and the improper loading of the ammunition aboard the *Regulus*, it appears to have suffered more damage than it would have otherwise."

She had a knack for understatement, Williams thought, but he understood perfectly why she was telling this part of the story.

"I know why I'm here, then," the section chief responded. "If something like that did happen, my office would have been involved."

"That's why we wanted to talk to you, Mr. Bilder. Let me show you something." Younghart pulled a paper from the folder lying in front of her and handed it to Bilder. He studied the document for a moment. "This is the final cargo manifest for the *Regulus*. You recognize the codes for the highlighted items?"

178

"Yes, of course," Bilder answered, placing the paper back on the desk, his hands trembling slightly.

"You also recognize the signature block at the bottom of the form, I assume? According to this, you approved the final manifest."

"That's my signature block, but I don't remember signing the form. I may have, but I could have been rushed with all the stuff we're shoving through the port. I may have just signed off without really paying attention. If I'm guilty of anything, it may be of not paying as much attention as I should have. Somebody may have deliberately changed the *Regulus* cargo, but I promise you it wasn't me. I would never have done such a thing."

"Again, no one's accusing you of anything, sir." Younghart paused, then asked, "Are you in the habit of signing things you don't read, Mr. Bilder?"

"I told you, if I signed it without paying attention, it probably was because we've been so overwhelmed."

"So there is a possibility an improper cargo may have been loaded on the *Regulus* with your permission but without your knowledge?"

"Like I said, it's a possibility. Things have been really hectic around here."

"So you've said. Would anyone else in your office have been aware of the change in manifest? Could someone have altered it without your knowledge?"

Bilder looked almost relieved at the question. He answered quickly. "Well, now that you mention it, that could have happened. The department staff prepares these forms ahead of time, then passes them to me for signature. Changes can occur right up until the last moment, so I don't normally get involved until the manifest is complete and ready for my signature. I usually get involved only if there's a problem the staff can't handle. Let me take another look at the form."

Bilder grabbed the form off the desk, studied it for about ten seconds, then laid it back down. "Yes, of course, if you look in this block, you'll see the form was prepared by another member of the staff. These initials belong to Ms. Samuels. Perhaps you should talk to her."

"We will, of course. One final question, then you can leave. How long have you been with the Military Traffic Management Command?"

"Let me see . . . it'll be sixteen years this January. Yes, that's right. Sixteen years. Doesn't seem like that long."

"You've spent all that time here at Charleston?"

"All but three years. The port's been my life. Every now and then they talk about closing down the port and moving us elsewhere. Talk like that makes all of us nervous."

Younghart studied Bilder's face for a moment before she responded. "There's been such talk?"

"Oh, yes, all the time. Especially over the last couple of years."

"I can understand how such gossip might make people nervous. It could also make them a little careless, perhaps?"

Bilder looked thoroughly chagrined. "Perhaps."

"All right, Mr. Bilder, you can go. I may want to talk to you again today. Please make sure you're available."

"Of course. I certainly hope you get to the bottom of this. I'd hate to think I was somehow responsible for any of this."

Bilder hurried out of the office. Younghart slumped back in the chair, then swiveled about to look at Williams, whose face was contorted by disgust over what he had just heard.

"Well, what do you think?" she asked.

"Interesting. He seemed willing enough to admit the manifest could have slipped by him. One can wonder whether he's trying to be honest or if he's just monumentally stupid. Regardless of which of those is operative here, I think it's about time Timmons fired his ass. 'Excuse me, I may have loaded high explosives on the wrong ship, but I didn't mean to, I wasn't paying attention to the paperwork.' How's that for an excuse?"

"I don't think it would fly past my boss."

"Exactly. Bilder's responsible. He can't dodge the bullet. Did you see how quickly he offered up someone else in his office to shoulder the blame? Samuels's signature is on that form, but I wonder how much she really knows. There's something about Bilder that makes me want to check to see if I still have my wallet."

Younghart laughed softly. "I know what you mean. I found myself tapping my purse with my foot to make sure it was still there."

Williams stood up. "I'll track down Timmons and see if he can get Ms. Samuels in here, if that's who you want to go with next."

"Might as well. But I want to talk to Bilder again soon. I assume you'll give Timmons an earful about the slimy bastard after this is all over."

"Absolutely," Williams answered as he started walking toward the door. He stopped dead in his tracks, his mouth gaping open. "What in the hell?" he mumbled.

Younghart looked up and saw him staring out the window. "What?"

"It's Bilder. He's leaving the building, and he's in a damned big hurry."

Younghart jumped up and ran to the window. "Son of a bitch!" she shouted. "Come on! Hurry!"

They ran down the hall and scrambled out the door just as Bilder started up his car. Williams ran past Younghart on an intercept course. She reached out to stop him as she pulled the gun out of its holster at the back of her waist.

"Blair, damn it, stop! Stay behind me!"

Williams ignored her warning and charged straight ahead. Bilder slammed the car into gear and headed directly toward his pursuer. Williams tried to jump out of the way, but the corner of the car caught him with a glancing blow in the thigh and sent him flying across the concrete. The tire of a container trailer stopped his tumbling.

"Shit!" He reached down and patted himself to make sure he still had all his body parts. "Shit, shit, shit! How frigging stupid!"

He heard the squeal of tires and looked up. Younghart had planted herself squarely in front of the oncoming car, her pistol pointed directly at Bilder's head. He had wisely decided to stop. The car had come to rest only a few feet from Younghart's outstretched arms. She was yelling at Bilder, the pistol in her hands rock steady.

Ken Currie

"Get out of the car! Now! Out of the car! Hands on the hood! Move it, you piece of shit!"

Bilder stumbled out of the car, hunched over. He whimpered as he spread himself on the car's hood, begging Younghart not to beat him.

Williams limped over, trying to dust off his uniform trousers, just as Younghart finished handcuffing Bilder.

"Blair, you idiot! I told you to stop, goddamn it! We don't need macho heroics."

She paused, having noticed the bloody abrasion on his thigh showing through a large rip in his pants.

"Oh?" Williams responded breathlessly. "What about you? Standing in the middle of the damned road in front of a speeding car! What the hell was that supposed to be, lady?"

"This jerk wasn't about to run me down. He wasn't brave enough to run the risk of having me ventilate his head." She looked at the excited Williams and shook her head gently. Then she wagged her finger in front of his face. "I'll tell you what. You can sit in on any interview you want. Just leave this part to me. Deal?"

"Deal. Damn! I'm impressed!" Williams was dancing from leg to leg, oblivious to the pain from his injury. "God, what a rush. It was like a scene from a movie!"

She looked at him as if she had suddenly found herself in the presence of a madman. She put a hand on his shoulder. "Are you okay? Just relax, Blair. It's the adrenaline talking. By the way, anything broken?"

Williams stopped hopping about and answered, "Just my pride from being nearly run over." Just then the excitement finally caught up with him. He bent over, placed his hands on his knees, and took several deep breaths.

"Don't worry, injuries to the male ego aren't usually terminal. You sure there's nothing else wrong?"

"Just a little dizzy," Williams replied, his head still down even with his waist. "I'll be better in a minute."

He turned his head sideways and looked at Bilder disdainfully. The dispatch chief was leaning over the hood of his car, sobbing uncontrollably.

"Nice car," Williams observed. "One of those BMW sports

jobs. Looks pretty impressive from this angle."

"Yeah, not bad head-on either. How do you suppose a GS-12 affords something like this? Must be really frugal. Remind me to get the name of his broker. Where do you suppose he banks? The Caymans?"

Williams stared at the car for a moment, then looked at their quarry with disgust. He rested his hand on top of the BMW's rear fender, fighting off the urge to kick in the driver's door. Shaking his head, he murmured, "What a stupid putz."

"Believe me, Blair, they usually are," Younghart agreed as she yanked Bilder up off the hood.

"Well, partner," Williams drawled, "to borrow a phrase from General Petersen's book, I think we've got one of the bastards."

"Just one, just one. But I have a sneaking suspicion this creep is going to help us find the rest. Let's get him inside. I think it's time for that second interview with Mr. Bilder. In the meantime, I'm going to have Johanssen take you to the hospital."

"Yes, Nurse Younghart." Williams's leg and head had started to throb, overcoming any objections he may have had to being carted off to an emergency room. He touched the back of his head and felt a lump. When he pulled his hand away, it was covered with blood.

"Well, I'll be damned," he said, then fainted.

Chapter Nineteen

26 August, 1030 hours EDT

"I'm sorry, Colonel Underwood, there's really no time on the president's schedule today. I might be able to get you five minutes tomorrow afternoon. You really need to try to arrange these meetings a lot farther in advance. I'm sure you're aware the president's a very busy man."

Underwood was making no headway with Noonan's secretary, and he could have lived without the gratuitous comment from a glorified receptionist about the president's activity level. At the same time, he hesitated to subvert the secretary's jealously guarded scheduling procedures and go directly to the chief of staff. No doubt he would find himself in need of a favor from the secretary sometime in the future.

He doubted Farley would be any help, and in any case he would insist on wanting to know why Underwood needed to talk to the president. Farley had made it quite clear after Underwood's session with Noonan the week before that all appointments would be cleared through him, all discussions would be approved by him before they were taken up with the president. Underwood hadn't been in a position to protest Farley's edicts; he didn't know the precise limits of his new job, and he certainly had no illusions about the kind of access he would have to the Oval Office. He had no desire to let Farley know why he needed to talk to the president. He knew he was taking a risk trying to set up an appointment through the secretary. Farley would blow a gasket when he reviewed Noonan's schedule and found an appointment he had not sanctioned.

"I really need more than five minutes, Ms. Morrow. It will take me that long just to fill the president in on what he needs to know. I do want to leave a few minutes for any questions he might have."

The secretary looked at him with an expression of matronly pity mixed with impatience. "Colonel, I've told you there's nothing I can do about the schedule. If something should open up, I'll give you a call. By the way, I assume you've cleared this with the chief of staff?"

"Mr. Farley knows all about it," Underwood lied, vainly hoping the subterfuge would persuade Morrow to move things along. But she didn't budge, even for the lie. She simply shrugged and went back to her keyboard. Underwood stood there quietly for a moment until he realized he had just been dismissed. He continued to linger at her desk, fending off a strong desire to comment on her rudeness. As much as it went against his instincts, he decided nothing would be gained. Morrow was an immovable object. He turned away and headed for his office. By the time he reached his door, he had reconsidered his course of action. He immediately called the secretary, adopting the most fawning tone he could muster.

"Ms. Morrow. Colonel Underwood. On second thought, don't worry about getting me any time on the schedule. I'll work this through Mr. Christoph. Thanks for your help and consideration."

Going through the national security adviser would be the wiser move anyway, Underwood realized. If he could convince Christoph to take Valery's information seriously, the national security adviser would be the key to tracking down additional information on Resurrected Russia's intentions. Christoph had a reputation for tenacity. Once he got his hooks into something that interested him deeply, he wouldn't let go until he found out everything there was to know. He drove the Pentagon and the intelligence agencies crazy with his insatiable appetite for information. To be sure, some of that appetite was driven by the desire to stay one step ahead of Noonan. But Christoph was a datamonger in his own right. His desire to keep on top of events was almost obsessive.

Underwood called Christoph's office and was hooked up with the national security adviser almost instantly. All he had to do was intimate that he had inside information on the activities of a hitherto unknown Russian terrorist group. Christoph promptly got on the phone and tried to milk Underwood for details. The inquisition ended suddenly when Christoph was called away for a meeting with Noonan, but not before Underwood was set up for a thirty-minute session that afternoon.

Smugly satisfied, Underwood poured himself a cup of coffee and settled into the love seat that graced one of the walls of his small office. He skimmed the *Early Bird*, marveling at the Pentagon's diligence in putting out this small tabloid containing defense-related items from the nation's principal newspapers. This unassuming little newspaper was one of the hottest publications in the Department of Defense, especially among the key decision makers populating the Pentagon's E-ring. Copies were also transmitted electronically to the commands so their leaders would be aware of the same issues generating interest among their counterparts in Washington. At times, the little paper could be a monumental pain in the ass, generating work for an already overtaxed staff who frequently had to respond to the stories, rumors, and disinformation that made their way with wild abandon into the nation's newspapers.

Underwood smiled as he tossed the *Early Bird* on his desk and unfolded the *Post*. He doubted he would see anything important not already covered in the Pentagon publication, but he wanted to check if the Washington paper had any new gossip on the comings and goings of the capital's elite. It always helped to know who was on the move; tomorrow they could be your boss, or your adversary.

His eyes immediately went to the bottom of the second page, to a brief item bearing the headline "Russian Reporter Killed in Auto Accident." A cold feeling seized his gut. He knew the reporter's identity even before he read the story. He had to force himself to continue breathing. His mind had stopped. He could think of nothing as he struggled through the words.

> *Fairfax County police are investigating a fatal traffic accident that occurred near the I-495/Route 50 interchange early Sunday evening. Police have identified the victim as Valery Akhmetov. Akhmetov, Washington correspondent for Moscow's International News Service, was traveling alone northbound on the Beltway when the accident occurred. According to a witness, Akhmetov's vehicle was forced off the road by a delivery truck. Police arrested the driver of the truck at the scene. Reckless driving charges have been filed and additional charges are pending, according to a police spokesman. Akhmetov, a highly respected journalist, had been stationed in Washington for almost two years.*

Underwood reread the article several times, as if hoping the facts would change. He had spoken to Akhmetov on the phone Sunday afternoon. Just yesterday, or was it only moments ago? Valery had sounded like an excited schoolboy, thrilled at the prospect that his information would find its way to the ears of the president. He wanted to make sure Underwood hadn't changed his mind, gone "weak in the legs," he had said. Underwood had reassured him his knees were fine, that he would somehow pass the information along to Noonan. Now he regretted not pressing Noonan's secretary a little harder.

He remembered the evenings spent verbally sparring with Valery—many enjoyable, some not so pleasant. They had debated many things, most often women and politics. Akhmetov had once accused him of being a misogynist and a pessimist. Underwood had parried that the two were inevitably intertwined. Undeterred, Valery had pressed his point: how else to explain Underwood's "abysmal failure" of a marriage to "one of the most fantastic women on the face of the earth" and his tendency to run down everybody and everything in Washington? Underwood at first tried to make light of Akhmetov's observation, deadpanning that he had tried very hard to make his marriage an "abysmal success."

As Valery continued to criticize his friend's shortsightedness, Underwood angrily replied that obviously Valery didn't know real women or the real Washington at all. He told Valery he could forgive his ignorance of the capital scene—although that was certainly a fatal flaw in a political journalist—but he thoroughly resented being psychoanalyzed about his marital problems, especially by an aspiring Russian playboy. He couldn't admit the real reason for his anger: the fear Valery was right. It had been a tense moment in their relationship, but it had passed, their friendship only momentarily diminished. Despite their different backgrounds, they had formed a unique bond. They had shared many confidences over the past two years. And now his confidant was gone, forever. Underwood felt as if he had been punched in the stomach.

He had no idea how long he had been sitting there, staring at the paper, remembering Valery, when he noticed the telephone buzzing. With much effort, he pulled himself up out of the overstuffed love seat and fumbled for the handset.

"Morning, Colonel. It's Josh Evans."

Underwood struggled momentarily to remember the name, his mind still clouded. "Yes, of course. Good morning, Josh. I wasn't expecting a call from you. I understand your briefing went well this morning. Sorry I couldn't be there. Maybe next time. In any event, congratulations."

"Thanks, Colonel, but that's not why I called. I saw the article in the paper this morning. I know Mr. Akhmetov was a friend of yours."

"How? I don't remember—"

188

"You mentioned him a couple of times in the office. I'm sorry to hear the news."

"Thanks," Underwood replied, struggling to remember when he had talked to Evans about Akhmetov.

"Colonel, we need to talk."

"Go ahead."

"No, sir, not now. I have some information on Akhmetov."

Underwood's daze vanished, but he wasn't sure he had heard the comment correctly.

"Would you mind repeating that, please?"

"There's something I need to tell you about him. Some information I picked up this morning after I heard the news. Something you didn't realize about your friend, something I'm sure you're going to want to hear."

"Tell me now," Underwood ordered, momentarily forgetting that his relationship with Evans had changed.

"Believe me, Colonel, I can't do that. What are you doing for lunch?"

"Whatever it was, it's now off my schedule. Where do you—"

"Roosevelt Island. Twelve-fifteen. Okay?"

"Fine. See you then. I hope you'll have some good reason for this secrecy," Underwood said sternly, but Evans had already hung up.

"Impressive, isn't it?"

Underwood had been staring at the massive statue of Teddy Roosevelt, periodically glancing at the former president's words inscribed on the surrounding stone monoliths. Roosevelt had been one of Underwood's favorite chief executives, and he loved visiting this spot. He looked up, startled out of his contemplation, and saw Evans approaching, his hand extended.

"Very," Underwood replied distractedly, quickly shaking Evans's hand. "Okay, Josh, what's the big mystery? I just lost a very close friend. If, as you say, you have some information about him, I'd really like to know what it is."

Evans didn't respond. Instead, he walked up to the statue and studied the presidential face. Finally, he turned, smiling strangely. "Akhmetov was a good reporter, wasn't he?" he asked Underwood, the smile disappearing.

"Yes, he was. One of the best. There's a point to this?"

Evans ignored the question. "Awfully good, even for a Russian. In fact, he was too good, one might say."

Underwood stared blankly at Evans. "I'm afraid you've lost me, Josh."

"He knew quite a bit about a group called Resurrected Russia, from what I understand. I believe he mentioned something about it to you, no?"

Underwood was dumbfounded. He tried to sound nonchalant. "I don't know what in the hell you're talking about. Valery and I talked about a lot of things, but I don't recall that particular subject. Would you care to elaborate?"

Evans shook his head, his expression growing darker. He suddenly looked much older, and Underwood began wondering if this was the same person he had worked beside for the past several months.

"Colonel, there's no time to be coy or play games. I know exactly what Akhmetov told you about the group. You're going to forget you heard it."

"What in God's name are you talking about? I'm going to forget it? And who are you to give me orders? As far as I'm concerned, the conversation's over. Get the hell out of my way."

Underwood tried to push past, but Evans grabbed his arm and spun him around.

"Don't screw with me, Colonel. Shut up and listen." Evans squeezed Underwood's arm as if to underscore his warning, looking around to make sure no one was intruding upon their privacy. "You're going to do exactly as I tell you. Number one, you're going to forget everything you've been told about Resurrected Russia. Number two, you will mention *this* conversation to no one. And number three, you're going to provide my friends and me with some special information. Very special, indeed."

"Screw you, you son of a bitch, on all three counts. Let

go of my arm, unless you want to regret the remainder of your short life."

"The only regrets will be yours, if you don't do what you're told. Anyway, I think you already have a lot of things to regret, isn't that true?"

"Go fuck yourself."

Evans's boyish face became lean and hard. His eyes were now cold and lifeless. Underwood shivered involuntarily at the transformation that had taken place in front of him. Evans reached into his jacket pocket and retrieved a gold cigarette case. He idly removed a cigarette, tapping it gently on the case, all the while staring at Underwood as if he were a specimen on a dissecting table.

"My, my, Colonel. You're usually so articulate. What's happened to that polish and erudition I've come to admire? One morning on the job, and you're already sounding like the vice president. I'd be careful about the company I keep." Evans was wearing the smile of someone who knows he has the upper hand. "Please, let me tell you what you're going to provide us. Aren't you the least bit curious? Why don't we make ourselves more comfortable? Let's sit over here. And keep your voice down, Colonel. We don't want any visitors to think we're arguing, now, do we? That would be bad for me, but it would be even worse for you. Trust me."

Underwood sat on the bench, staring straight ahead. He turned his head and looked at Evans. He wanted to beat the hell out of him, but he also wanted to know what was going on. He forced back his anger, intent on finding out what was expected of him. He took a breath and suddenly felt strangely calm.

"I hate to bring you sad tidings, Josh, but I'm afraid some people at the White House already know about your Russian terrorist friends. You see, you didn't call me soon enough."

"I doubt very much Akhmetov could have told you very much during your meeting last week. No need to look so surprised, Colonel. I know quite a lot about your comings and goings. Regardless, Akhmetov didn't have a lot of details then. So, if you've passed that along to your new friends on Pennsylvania Avenue, that's not a crisis. Unfortunately for his sake, Akhmetov wasn't satisfied. He just had to keep on nosing about. One very stubborn Russian. So let me be very clear. You will pass along nothing more about Resurrected Russia. I trust that's understood completely."

Underwood fixed Evans with a cold stare. "You're not listening. I've already told people about this group, and I'm going to be telling them more this afternoon. There's nothing I can do to change that. They already know about your miserable little group. You're wasting your breath."

Evans stared at him coldly. "Colonel, this doesn't make me happy. You're obviously not listening."

"Excuse me if I don't apologize."

"You will do what I tell you!" Evans whispered ferociously. He smiled once more, then continued quietly. "The consequences will be very severe if you don't. I can't be any clearer than that, can I? I trust you understand I'm serious about this. *Deadly* serious."

Underwood turned away from Evans's threatening stare. "So, what kind of information are we talking about?" he asked, his voice subdued.

"Simple stuff, really. Sometime in the next several weeks, I'm going to give you a call. I'm going to ask you for some details about the president's schedule. Isn't it amazing how things work out? We've been trying to develop a contact in the White House for weeks. Hell, we've even approached some of the more congenial interns. But nothing was working. And then, out of the blue, the president taps you to be his military lapdog. Unbelievable. We couldn't have choreographed it better."

"You're kidding, right? I'm not the president's secretary. I don't keep his schedule."

"I know that. We just need to know his general whereabouts. Whether he's in his quarters, his office, wherever, during a particular period of time. I'll specify the period at a later date. To make things easier, I'll be providing you a short list of phrases, sort of signals between friends. You're going to commit these phrases to memory. When I call, you'll respond with the appropriate phrase."

"Give me a fucking break. Where did you get this shit?

From a book? Are we going to exchange briefcases and a secret handshake next?"

Evans laughed hollowly. "Oh, how droll! There's that wonderful Underwood wit! Colonel, let's forgo the bullshit, okay? I'm not sparring with you. I'm not playacting. You *will* do what you are told, or, quite simply, you will end up like your friend."

A chill shot through Underwood. Evans had said the words matter-of-factly. There was no veiled threat. Resistance drained out of him.

"And you expect me to pass this information to you over an open line from the White House?"

"Don't worry, the phrases you'll be using will confuse any caller. Besides, I'll be calling you on the secure line." Evans smiled. "Ironic, isn't it?"

Underwood pondered what he had just heard. This situation was insane. Evans was nuts. He was talking to a madman. Then he realized he wasn't, and he became even more frightened. "And when will you call me?"

Evans just smiled.

"Okay, then tell me, just exactly why should I do this? So you kill me. I'm dead. Then what?"

Evans smiled again. "I agree, Colonel. Death is easy. And, admittedly, you're of little value to us in a state of rigor mortis. But other options are not so comfortable. For example, you wouldn't want people to find out about your relationship with Akhmetov."

"Everyone that needed to know about Valery already knew. There's no secret there. And we certainly weren't gay."

"Ah, Colonel, I wasn't asking," Evans quickly responded with a grin. "I wasn't expecting you to tell. But there are facts about your friendship with Akhmetov you'd probably like to keep secret."

"Such as? You tell me, you seem to know it all anyway."

"Well, for one, does everyone know you and Akhmetov shared at least one night with a hostile intelligence agent?"

"Now I really don't know what the hell you're talking about," Underwood blurted out, astonished. He started laughing loudly as he looked into Evans's eyes. "You really are nuts, Josh. You know that?"

"Don't you remember Marika Korniesh?"

Underwood stopped laughing. He instantly remembered the dark-eyed, dark-haired, extraordinarily statuesque woman he and Valery had encountered at an M Street bar several months before. Valery had conned him into trolling Georgetown. It had been a most unusual evening.

"She was quite a treat, wasn't she? She's also very good at her other, full-time job, working for the Libyans, or whoever else wants to pay for her most excellent services. I think you'd agree she offers quite an array of services? I must confess to having sampled a few of them myself. But, then, I'm not married now, am I?"

The question was accompanied by a lecherous grin. Underwood once again resisted the urge to put his fist through Evans's face.

"And who employs your services, Josh? The highest bidder as well?"

"If that's your best shot, Colonel, you really are losing your touch. Some of us aren't in it for the money, right? Look at you. Are you getting rich on your military pay? Of course not, but that's not why you're in the game. You're hungry for something other than money. You whore after power. That makes you just as weak as the greedy man. You don't need to know who I work for. All you need to know is that *you* are now working for *us*."

"I don't think so, Josh, or whatever the hell your real name might be. I'm content with my present employer. Your threats don't scare me. I'm not a virgin, and I'm certainly no saint. One indiscretion isn't going to come as any great revelation to anyone."

"Colonel, you do yourself a disservice. A *single* indiscretion? You think you've been that careful?" Evans burst out laughing.

Underwood glared. "I'm not sure what you think you know, but threatening to blow the whistle on my exploits between the sheets isn't going to be sufficient to turn me into a traitor. I doubt I'll get fired for any extracurricular activities, especially if I blow your cover."

"Please, Colonel. Listen to yourself. Trying to sound brave, defiant. I know what your career means to you. You're not going to jeopardize any of that, despite your grand words. We're not just talking about your grabbing a little on the side, we're talking about you consorting with a foreign intelligence agent, or have you forgotten about that? Even if the military doesn't court-martial you for adultery under the Uniform Code of Military Justice—oh, yes, I know all about that—they're still going to crucify you for the espionage angle."

"So you think I'm screwed? The way I see it, if I don't tell anyone about this and then get caught, I've had it. If I do tell, I'll still get burned, whether by you or someone on my side, but I'll also have the pleasure of knowing I've taken you with me."

"And why would anyone believe you? Where's your proof?"

Underwood snickered. "Josh, I know where you work. I worked there, too, remember? They'll believe it, or want to. They won't quit with you until you confess to all the unsolved murders in the United States."

Evans smirked. "Colonel, if I could get through the security screening process to work where I am now, do you really think you can scare me?"

Underwood felt as though he had just fallen overboard in a storm without a life jacket. Surely they could find him out, couldn't they?

"How *did* you get through security?" Underwood asked, his voice barely audible.

"Simple. The fools get caught because they have an adolescent sense of guilt or traces of a conscience. Or else they do something very stupid. I assure you, I have neither guilt nor a conscience. And I shun stupid behavior, except when it's someone else's, as in your case, and it can be put to good use."

Evans's eyes were cold, dark, frightening. As he stared

silently at Underwood, a thin wreath of cigarette smoke curled disconcertingly over his head. Underwood was convinced Evans was telling the truth. Evans had said Valery knew too much, and now his eyes told Underwood what happened to those who suffered from too much truth. Underwood felt his legs turn to rubber.

"You fooled everyone, Josh. You fooled me. You always came across as eager, perfectly loyal. You even tried to dress me down when I criticized Noonan. I never would have taken you for the first-class slime you really are."

"I'll take that as a compliment," Evans said as he stood up, tossing away his cigarette. He buttoned his suit coat and tugged on his shirtsleeves, all the while smiling at Underwood. "Cheer up. What we're asking you to do is very simple. It requires very little effort. And you'll be a part of a very grand plan. That's what you always wanted anyway."

"Get screwed."

"There you go again. An excellent suggestion, but I'm afraid I lack your adeptness in that area."

Evans placed his hand on the colonel's shoulder, but Underwood quickly pulled away, a look of total disgust crossing his face.

"Relax. This is going to be easy. I'll be calling you. By the way, why don't you go ahead and keep whatever appointments you have for this afternoon. We wouldn't want to arouse any suspicions, would we? As I said, Akhmetov couldn't have told you much before he met his untimely fate. Just be brief, tell them that's all you know. You can drive home the point that your contact's present position precludes his providing you with any more tidbits about Resurrected Russia."

Evans paused, straightened his tie, and took another look around the park. "Besides, I'm sure your new friends will scurry around aimlessly trying to find out more. Just remember to keep your mouth shut about anything else you might hear. I'm confident you'll keep this conversation strictly confidential. If you don't, it'll feel like you've been hit by God's fist. Please, bid Teddy adieu for me." Evans waved at the statue as he started walking away.

He paused, as if forgetting something, and turned back around to face Underwood. All traces of the college-boy looks Underwood remembered had utterly disappeared. Evans's face betrayed no emotion as he said flatly, "Oh, and if you should think seriously about talking to someone you shouldn't, there's something else I want you to keep in mind. We have your wife."

Chapter Twenty

He watched Evans depart, continuing to stare at the trail through the woods long after this new enemy had disappeared among the summer foliage. The midday heat had suddenly become very oppressive. He sat there, conscious of the perspiration covering his forehead and crawling down his back, but unable to move. He wondered what he should feel, if he could feel anything other than the unbearable heat.

You have a wife? Valery would have joked if he were here. If only Valery were here. The thought depressed him even more. He stared up at the statue. *Walk softly and carry a big stick,* he thought. *If I'd had a big stick, I would have beaten Evans to death with it, as loudly as I could.*

Arrogant bastard. Underwood didn't know whether he was angrier at the imperious manner in which Evans had ordered him about, or at himself for being so completely fooled by Evans's charming, ingratiating demeanor while working by his side. He felt little consolation in the fact that Evans had taken in—continued to take in—so many. And now he was briefing the president. Underwood had even praised his abilities when the DCI asked if Evans was capable of handling the job. Underwood felt completely powerless.

He had no way of finding out what Evans was up to, no way of stopping him. Evans was right. Underwood had placed his own butt firmly in a sling. He knew Evans would make good on the threat to ruin him. It would be easy given the ammunition Underwood had provided. Other military careers, far more lofty than his, had been ruined by only a fraction of what filled Underwood's checkered personal history.

His mind wandered back to Jennifer. What did it matter if they did hurt her? After all these years, why should he care what happened to her? She wasn't really part of his life, hadn't been for a very long time. So what if she disappeared?

He was immediately seized by deep remorse. He had to confess that there had been nights when he wished Jennifer would go away, would leave him. Even disappear. But as his present predicament forced him to peel back the layers of long-hidden feelings, he realized he never wanted any harm to come to her. Yes, he had been guilty at the moments of his greatest depression of fantasizing what it would be like if she were dead. But, he reassured himself, he had never wished for anything to really happen to her. He could never wish for such a thing, could he? He convinced himself Jennifer would never wish such a fate for him, even if she thought he was a total ass, and he was convinced she did. After all, he had to admit, he had given her ample reason to reach such a judgment. But in the final analysis, he told himself, he wasn't a *total* ass. He had always been civil. Well, maybe not always and maybe not civil, but at least he had tried. Hadn't he?

As he sat there, he was overwhelmed by a simple truth. It had escaped him because he had convinced himself he was the embodiment of the professional, politically astute officer. The truth of the matter, he concluded, was that he was in fact a total, irredeemable jerk. How else to explain how he'd ended up in this mess? He was totally screwed. And so was Jennifer, thanks to him.

He wondered if he still loved Jennifer, and he knew the answer was no. Such feelings, if he ever really had them, had long since passed. There had been passion, but no love. Yet, somehow, he couldn't imagine life without Jennifer, even though he seldom imagined life with her. Other women filled those idylls of his mind. He wondered whether he was trapped, or just resigned.

Then he imagined Jennifer in pain. No, agony, she was in agony. She would be bound, gagged. They probably had blindfolded her and dumped her away somewhere in the dark, her only company the strange voices of her captors. He pictured them dragging her away, hitting her to stop her struggling, to make it clear who controlled her fate. She would no longer be the confident, strong, sometimes overbearing person he remembered; she would be terrified, weeping quietly, uncertain whether she would be alive the next morning. She was totally at their mercy.

He was being melodramatic, even morbid. It was nevertheless strangely exhilarating. The thoughts dashing through his overactive brain made him feel very alive. Strange he should feel this way now, of all times.

His mind now flooded with an image of him dashing to her rescue, bravely heaving Evans and his accomplices aside. As they lay in bleeding heaps, he took Jennifer in his arms and comforted her. He was in charge once again. He had beaten Evans. He had beaten them all. He sat quietly for a moment. He shook his head, trying to clear his mind. He ordered himself to get a grip. This wasn't a goddamned story. It was for real, and he was the one who'd been beaten.

He sat there somberly for a few more minutes, his forehead creased by sweaty furrows. His expression changed slowly, his eyes brightening, the corners of his mouth gently curving upward. He stood up, wiped his forehead with the back of his hand, and looked up one last time at the bespectacled Roosevelt. He rendered the statue a brief salute, spun about, and quickly made his way down the path to the footbridge and the parking lot. Maybe he wasn't beaten, he reassured himself as climbed into his car and turned the air-conditioning on full blast. First, though, there were some things he needed to do.

*   *   *

"Good afternoon. Riddley, Smith, and Perkins."

"Hello, this is Michael Underwood. May I speak to Jennifer Norton Underwood, please?"

"I'm sorry, Mr. Underwood, she's not in the office today. In fact, she hasn't been in since the day before yesterday. She called in sick. Said she has the flu. A terrible time of year to come down with the flu. You can try reaching her at home."

"I'll do that. I've been on a business trip. I wasn't aware she was ill. Thanks for the information. Would you leave her a message that I called, in case I can't get hold of her at the apartment? Knowing Jennifer, she'll be back at work very soon."

"I can take a message, sir, but it won't do much good, I'm afraid. She said she was taking some time off to drive up to the lakes for a couple of weeks. She said she wanted to relax and prepare for a major case she's handling for the firm. I could tell she was very tired and not feeling well at all. She sounded very weak. The poor dear. You won't be joining her?"

Underwood was put off by the secretary's unwelcome curiosity, but he searched for a suitable excuse. "No, no. I'm afraid I'm tied up with my new job. How stupid of me anyway, to forget she was taking a break. Thanks for your help. I'll track her down. Goodbye."

He punched the button for the dial tone and quickly dialed Jennifer's apartment. He felt reassured when he heard her voice, then realized it was the answering machine. He put the phone back in its cradle.

Even though they were miserable at keeping track of each other's schedule, Jennifer usually let him know when she was taking time off from work. She always urged him to do the same, stubbornly insistent and vainly hopeful he wouldn't find yet one more excuse to avoid spending some time with her.

He sat pensively at his desk, tapping his pen on the polished surface, marveling at Jennifer's tenacity. He knew there would be no stubbornness this time, however. He was certain Evans had told the truth.

Ken Currie

He weighed his alternatives one last time. If he cooperated, Evans and his partners would follow through on their very grand plan, a plan that almost certainly involved physical harm to the president and probably many others. Why else would they want to know about Noonan's whereabouts? If he did what he was told, Jennifer might be spared, but he doubted Evans's generosity. There had been no promises made, just threats. More likely he and Jennifer would be viewed as unnecessary baggage once they had served their purpose. He shuddered at the image of Evans calmly putting a gun to the back of his head.

On the other hand, Jennifer would almost certainly be killed if he disobeyed Evans's instructions. He probably was going to be a big loser in any event. Either his life or career would be over, and he still wasn't entirely certain which would be worse. But as far as Jennifer was concerned, there was a slight chance for her if he divulged Evans's little secret. But he knew he couldn't tell just anyone at the White House. There would be no way the president's staff would keep this quiet, especially Farley. Farley would go flapping wildly down the White House corridors. Everyone in Washington would know by the end of the day, and Jennifer would pay the price for his mistake. No, this had to be done very carefully. Even then, he knew he would be taking a huge risk.

He had decided. His mind kept racing back and forth over the possible outcomes. He remembered Valery once more, and an almost forgotten barroom conversation about Russia. Their discussions of history always seemed so much more profound after they had tipped a few. Valery pointedly reminded him that 1917 was a Bolshevik coup d'état, not a real revolution. Some American scholars, Valery slurred, still seem to forget the Communists usurped power and turned the country into a living hell for the next seventy-five years.

Underwood had nodded vigorously, noting that even the Bolsheviks were amazed by their success. In an irresistible bit of grandstanding, he had quoted Lenin's comment to Trotsky. *"Es schwindelt,"* or "It is dizzying." Underwood spoke the phrase with his best German accent, the beer enhancing his pronunciation of the second word.

"My friend, you, like Lenin, are totally full of *govno*," Valery had responded, using the wonderfully descriptive Russian word for bullshit.

Lenin's little quote now flashed repeatedly through Underwood's mind as he walked out of the White House, zigzagged for a few blocks to make certain he wasn't being followed, and made his way to a pay phone in the lobby of the Willard Hotel.

He had nowhere else to turn. It was a risky step. He nervously dialed the Air Force Office of Special Investigations. He had met with one of their agents several times to provide information on his meetings with Valery. The cold war had ended, but suspicions about the Russians had not, and old procedures remained in place, one of the many continuing incongruities associated with his line of work. The interviews were always short; he had never discussed sensitive issues with Akhmetov, at least not until last week, so there was little to pass along to the OSI.

He had to wait for a few minutes while they tracked down the agent. The delay caused him momentary doubt and panic. He had started to hang up when he heard the voice at the other end of the line. Somehow, that familiar voice was strangely reassuring. He pushed the receiver firmly against his ear, gripping the phone as though afraid to let go.

"This is Mr. Harper."

"Good afternoon, Mr. Harper. This is Mike Underwood."

"Ah, yes, Colonel. I haven't spoken to you in quite some time. How can I be of help?"

"Mr. Harper, we need to talk, but I can't come into your office. It would be best if we met someplace off base."

"Colonel, you don't need to say another word. I saw the paper this morning. I was wondering if you would call. Do you have a location and time in mind?"

"Would Fort Washington be a problem?"

"Not at all. I appreciate the short drive. It's quite a trek for you, though."

"Actually, it isn't. You see, I'm no longer working up the

parkway. My job's a little closer to downtown now."

"I see. When do you want to get together? Tomorrow?"

"Today. It's imperative I talk to you today. This can't wait. I have a very tricky situation on my hands. Would 1700 be all right? I would press for doing this even a little sooner, but I have an appointment I can't miss."

"I'll have to do some reshuffling, but I think I can manage it. Yes, 1700 will be fine. See you then."

"Thank you, Mr. Harper. I really appreciate this. I'll meet you in the parking lot."

His meeting with Christoph went better than he expected. He had been uncertain how successful he would be in tap-dancing around the subject of the Russian terrorists. He had to tell the national security adviser something. He knew that, but Evans's warnings were persistent shadows in the back of his mind.

Christoph told Underwood he wished there were more on Resurrected Russia, but he clearly was intrigued. Underwood left out much of what Valery had told him, saying only that the group apparently was planning some sort of terrorist operation in the West, probably Europe, but possibly also the United States. As Evans had bluntly suggested, he had a ready-made excuse for the dearth of details: Valery had been killed before he could learn anything new or pass it along to Underwood.

Christoph's disappointment over the lack of data was more than offset by the tantalizing outline Underwood had provided. Here was a previously unknown group, with ties to Russian organized crime. The president would feast on this story. Christoph had speculated that Noonan would view the news, albeit sketchy, as reason enough to call Russian president Milyutin as soon as possible.

Underwood listened quietly but uncomfortably, cringing as Christoph excitedly described the need to inform the president. Underwood wanted to raise a red flag, to argue against such premature high-level contact on the basis of his very limited information. Underwood viewed himself as anything but a foreign policy wonk, but he thought tentative State

Department overtures to the Russian Embassy or Foreign Ministry would have been more appropriate. More important, such lower-level contacts would be much safer from the standpoint of not tipping Evans's hand. And in all probability, Milyutin would end up telling Noonan, "Thank you very much, but the Russian security services have the situation well in hand." There was nothing he could do now to stop Christoph from passing the information along to the president. There was one thing he could do, however, something he was sure Christoph would endorse, and something that he hoped would keep him out of trouble with Evans.

Underwood told Christoph he clearly understood the president's desire to call his Russian counterpart with this information, but perhaps it would be best to keep the CIA out of the loop at this point. He recounted his conversation with Todd and the skepticism of some parts of the agency regarding Valery. Christoph responded as Underwood had expected, nodding in agreement at the proposal to cut the agency out of the picture.

The national security adviser shared Noonan's disdain for most of the intelligence community. He had periodically joined Noonan in tag team attacks on selected intelligence agencies during Underwood's morning briefings. Moreover, Christoph despised the current DCI, feelings Underwood knew the director reciprocated to the fullest. Underwood was aware he was betraying the loyalty he still felt toward the DCI. Given the stakes, however, it was a betrayal he would have to live with.

"I see your point," Christoph had said. "Why bring this up with the Agency when they're going to discount it? We'll work this within the NSC staff and quietly through the FBI. I'm sure the president will agree."

Underwood had almost sighed with relief. So far, events were adhering closely to the design he had hurriedly worked out. He hoped to keep Christoph and the others busy chasing after Resurrected Russia while he dealt with his own problem. Just maybe, by examining the elephant from the other end, they could come up with something useful for his purposes. If he succeeded in getting Jennifer back, he didn't give a damn who was told what, as long as it didn't get back to Evans.

"Colonel, I want to thank you for bringing this information to me. Please let me know if you hear anything else, although I know you've lost your source."

Underwood grimaced at Christoph's coldhearted description of Akhmetov's role in the whole situation. Valery had been much more than a source. The national security adviser's detached comment reaffirmed Underwood's dislike for the man. He and Noonan were cut from the same mold—simple human gestures of kindness obviously were alien to the president and his men. Underwood gazed out Christoph's window, thinking about Valery's misplaced optimism in the American system of government. *We get the leadership we deserve*, he thought morosely. How else to explain the current set of characters in the White House? And then he recalled how quickly he had decided to join that cast. He marveled at his willingness to throw in his lot with the devils on Pennsylvania Avenue.

"I'm sorry about Akhmetov's death. It's clear he was your friend. Did he leave family behind?"

The question, so unexpected, startled Underwood, and he turned quickly back toward Christoph. He hesitated before answering, his mind laboring to remember what should have been the simplest of facts.

"No. No, he didn't," he answered. Christoph was not as predictable as Underwood thought, and that could be a problem. "He has a sister in Moscow, but no other family. His parents died several years ago. Valery was very much the confirmed bachelor."

As Underwood left Christoph's office, Jeff Farley burst past him, obviously in a hurry to see the national security adviser. Farley gave Underwood a quizzical glance. Underwood answered with a forced grin, a gesture that distracted the chief of staff's attention just enough to cause him to bump into the door frame. Farley swore softly and continued on. Underwood walked contentedly down the hall, his grin becoming quite genuine. He knew Christoph would say nothing to Farley about their conversation. In a White House rife with personal competition, the contest between Farley and Christoph was the most bitter, and the most public.

Dark gray clouds quickly swept away the afternoon sun, and a light rain began as Underwood left the White House. He frowned as he hunched his shoulders in a wasted effort to ward off the warm drops. He did not welcome the change, which would provide no relief from the August heat. Instead, it would generate that most unpleasant of Washington phenomena, an outdoor steam bath. He hoped the rain would stop by the time he reached Fort Washington.

The rain did not stop. It began to pour, slowing the rush-hour traffic considerably as he fought his way down the interstate past Bolling Air Force Base. Perhaps he should have seen Harper in the agent's office. He would be there now. He watched the base disappear from view in his rearview mirror. He would be late, but he knew Harper would wait. He was certain the urgency in his voice had been enough to convince the OSI agent to stick around.

He felt drained as he pulled into the nearly empty parking lot at Fort Washington. The park was normally busy this time of year, but the rain had obviously driven the usual crowd of visitors away. There was a car parked by itself near the end of the parking lot. As he steered in that direction, Underwood was able to recognize Harper through the swipes of the windshield wipers.

He now welcomed the miserable weather. He had watched to make sure he wasn't being followed. The highway congestion caused by the steady rain made it unlikely anyone could have kept pace with him. Now the heavy downpour would provide concealment for their meeting. He parked as close to Harper as he could and then quickly ducked into the agent's car after a momentary struggle with the slippery door handle.

"You picked a hell of a day, Colonel," Harper said with a smile. Even wearing a suit, Harper would stand out from the Washington crowd. The closely cropped hair, squared jaw, and ramrod-straight posture—even while sitting in a car— said he was military. Underwood found that comforting.

Ken Currie

"I would say the weather matches my mood, but days like this in Washington make the mood. I'm glad you waited."

"Not a problem, sir. You're only a few minutes late, and I certainly had nowhere to go in this mess. Sitting here out of traffic is probably one of the safer places to be."

"Right now I'd settle for any place that's safe," Underwood said somberly. He wiped a few drops of rain from his face as he looked at Harper. "I don't feel very safe at the moment."

The leather of the seat creaked as Harper swiveled to face Underwood more directly. "This is serious, isn't it, Colonel? What's going on?"

Even in the gloom, Underwood could see Harper's piercing gray eyes. He had always felt the Air Force agent knew what he was going to tell him before he opened his mouth.

"Can we drop the rank?" Underwood responded wearily. "I know we're probably violating military protocol here, but please call me Mike. I have a feeling that after today you and I are going to be very close, whether we like it or not."

"If you don't mind, sir, I'd prefer to continue calling you by your rank. I appreciate the gesture, but I'm afraid my discomfort level would be a bit high. I don't mind, however, if you call me Marty."

Underwood nodded. "I understand. Not a problem. By the way, is that your real name? I never know with you guys from OSI."

"That's my real name. You've been hanging out at Langley too long, sir. We use our own names in the Air Force."

Underwood returned Harper's warm smile. "You're absolutely right, Marty. I have spent too much time out there. Truth be told, I've been in this town too damned long. But enough of that. Here's the bottom line. Someone is trying to blackmail me into providing information on the whereabouts of the president. And they've kidnapped my wife to ensure my cooperation."

The rain pelting on the rooftop, the gentle hum of the car's air conditioner, and the flip-flop of the wiper blades merged in a strange melody as both men sat quietly.

Harper stared, slightly openmouthed, at Underwood. He whistled softly. "Jesus Christ, Colonel," he said, "I thought you were going to pass along some little tidbit Akhmetov told you before he was killed. I sure as hell wasn't expecting something like this. Why on earth are you coming to me with this?"

"Well, Marty," Underwood replied dryly, "they are asking me to spy, and according to Air Force regulations, I'm supposed to report such contacts to you."

Harper shook his head as he stared out the windshield. "Under normal circumstances, that's right. If someone is suborning an Air Force member to commit espionage—"

"Marty, I'm kidding. I'm sorry. I have to make these silly little jokes. It helps break the tension. And believe me, I'm incredibly tense."

Harper rubbed his chin with his hand. "I understand, sir. So can you tell me the real reason why you came to me rather than going to the security folks at CIA or to the FBI? They're used to dealing with situations like this, and clearly this lies within their jurisdiction. You have me confused, Colonel."

"Because I need someone I can trust," Underwood answered, "and I'm pretty sure I can trust you. I couldn't go to CIA security for two reasons. One, I don't work there anymore. I'm working at the White House as of today. Two, the guy who threatened me works for the Agency, and I don't know how many more out there might be working with him on this."

Harper's eyes widened. "God Almighty, are you serious?"

Underwood nodded. "Dead serious. That's probably a bad choice of words, now that I think about it."

"Then we need to get you to the FBI and let them handle this."

"No!" Underwood shouted, then took a deep breath. "No. I'm sorry, I didn't mean to yell. No, we can't do that. I'm taking a damned big risk even talking to you, Marty, but I didn't know where else to go. This has to be handled very, very quietly, or quite simply my wife is going to die, and quite likely yours truly as well."

"Colonel, let's start from the beginning, shall we? I need to know all you know."

Underwood described the meeting with Evans, including the instructions and the warnings. He then recounted his unsuccessful attempts to contact Jennifer, leading to his conviction that Evans was telling the truth about how far his group was willing to go to ensure Underwood's cooperation. Finally, reluctantly, he explained Evans's threat to reveal his sexual exploits.

"Colonel, I'm not going to BS you. The business with the foreign intelligence agent, if that's what she is, could be a serious problem. I believe you when you say you had no idea she was working for an enemy intelligence service. I'll check and see if we have anything on her. That name doesn't trip any alarm bells with me, but she may be in the files under a pseudonym. Before we leave here, I'll want you to give me as complete a description of her as you can."

"How complete?" Underwood asked lamely.

"I don't need the gory details, sir. But if you did notice anything unusual, such as tattoos or birthmarks, that would help a lot."

"I don't think tattoos were her style, Marty. I didn't pick her up in a biker bar."

"No, sir, I know that. Please, don't misunderstand me. Besides, you'd be amazed at the number of women who wear tattoos nowadays. My wife has one. But that's another story."

Underwood noticed Harper's gentle grin and relaxed.

"Anyway, Colonel, as long as you didn't tell her anything or pass her anything, the only thing you're guilty of is an overactive libido."

Harper paused, and it was obvious to Underwood he had thought of something else, but he appeared hesitant to say what was on his mind.

"There's something else?" Underwood prompted.

"Well, there is the adultery factor here. Normally, the Air Force doesn't go after somebody unless they've been messing around with the wife of another service member or someone in their chain of command. Fortunately, you didn't do anything that stupid." Harper looked at him carefully. "You didn't, did you, sir?"

Underwood shook his head vigorously. "Absolutely not."

Then he remembered Carolyn. "Unless you want to count something that happened almost fifteen years ago."

Harper smiled. "We don't need to go that far back, Colonel, unless you're about to confess you slept with the chief of staff's wife." Harper paused a moment, as if silently asking, *You didn't, did you, sir?*, then continued. "Having said all that, I can't make any promises. Once this all comes out, and at some point it will, regardless of what happens, someone higher than me in the hierarchy will have to decide what, if anything, to do about it. But if I were you, I wouldn't lose any sleep over this. There are more important things to worry about. You've told me about it, and I'll make a note of it. The million-dollar question now is. Where do we go from here?"

The rain had stopped. The sun suddenly burst through an opening in the clouds, then vanished almost as quickly. Harper turned on the defroster to clear away the fog that covered the windshield. Underwood shivered and crossed his arms; the car's air conditioner was working too well. Or maybe it was something else.

"You cold, sir? Want me to turn it down a bit?"

"If you don't mind. Maybe I'm just tired. It's been a hell of a day."

"We need to get you out of here. It's almost seven."

"I'll be okay. Anyway, I need to know what you want me to do."

Harper nodded. "I was just coming to that. Sir, I'm going to have to tell my boss about this." He raised his hand as Underwood started to protest. "Sir, I have to. That's all there is to it. But I know he'll understand the need for discretion. The fewer who know, the better for all of us, including Mrs. Underwood. You were absolutely right on that score. We don't want to do anything that would jeopardize her life. So please, don't worry, we're going to do whatever's necessary to guarantee her safety."

Underwood stopped grinding his teeth momentarily. He was wondering whether he should have told Harper after all, then realized the agent had little choice. He had broken the rules repeatedly, but he couldn't expect Harper to

Ken Currie

do the same, no matter what he said. He chided himself for his earlier fantasy of dashing to Jennifer's rescue. Harper was right: They didn't need a bunch of cowboys running around screwing this up.

"So tell me, Marty. How many people will end up knowing about this?"

"Colonel, at this point, I would say two people in OSI will know. My boss may decide I need some help. He doesn't like us to go it alone in investigations, especially ones that could be hazardous to our health. So there could be a total of three. You can live with that?"

Underwood shrugged. "Do I have much choice?"

"Colonel, that's the minimum, for safety's sake. But there are others who need to know."

Underwood started grinding his teeth again and waited for the explanation.

"I know what you're thinking, Colonel. This guy's going to dink things up big time. But please hear me out. I have a contact in the Bureau, the FBI, who may be able to help out on this. And considering what's happened to your wife, and what these guys may be planning, the feds need to be involved." Harper noticed Underwood's raised eyebrows and slightly crooked mouth. "Yeah, I know, sir, that sounds a bit corny, but we do call 'em feds."

"And how do you know the FBI won't send out a small army looking for Evans and his cronies? I watch the news, I know how the government operates. Something like this, and the FBI, or the ATF, or someone, leaps on it like a frenzied animal. How can you promise me that won't happen here? I've gotta tell you, Marty, I'm not liking this at all. I'm beginning to wonder if I haven't made one hell of a big mistake here."

"Calm down, Colonel. You didn't make a mistake. We're not going to blow this."

"You're damned right nobody's going to screw this up, because if I get the feeling that this is becoming a mob activity, I'll shut up tighter than Cheyenne Mountain. And if it blows up in your face and anything happens to my wife, I'll be screaming about this to whoever I can at the *Post*.

And I don't give a good goddamn who I piss off in the process, including that son of a bitch Evans." Underwood clamped his mouth tightly shut and continued to fume quietly.

"Colonel, please. Relax. Look, I know you have the advantage here. You're the only person who knows about all this, or at least we have to assume that's the case. We're going to do all that we can to keep your wife safe. But I'd be lying if I said you're calling the shots. This is really out of your hands now, and you know that. Otherwise, you wouldn't be here talking to me right now. Think about it. I know where your first priority lies. I assure you it's also mine, but there are other priorities as well, including the safety of the government. You can't deny that. Your wife's life is not the only reason you came to me, is it? You understand these other priorities as well, don't you?"

Underwood remained silent, but he was visibly less agitated. "Of course I understand them. I know you have a job to do. I know I lost control of the situation as soon as I told you about all this. Hell, Harper, I lost control of the situation at twelve-thirty this afternoon. But I'm telling you again—damn those other considerations if they endanger Jennifer. Period. And you'd better keep that in mind and make damned sure your boss understands that as well."

Harper nodded. "I'll do my utmost, sir. Believe me. And that brings me back to my friend at the Bureau. I'm pretty certain she has the clout to keep things clamped down. I've worked with her before. Yours is not the first situation where things have had to be done on the quiet side. Can you just trust me on this one, okay? I know what I'm doing."

Her? Underwood's antennae were tingling. He hadn't considered this. He was curious, or maybe his hormones were talking again. It frustrated him that he couldn't decide which it was. The friendly tone returned to his voice. "So, Marty, who is this associate of yours at the FBI? Will I have the opportunity to talk to her?"

Harper smiled broadly. "Colonel, given everything that's going on, I don't see how you can avoid it. She's going to want to hear everything you've told me, and then some.

She's good, sir, damned good at what she does. She comes across as a bit intense, but I think you'll feel better once you've met her."

"I'm looking forward to it, Marty. What's her name?" He smiled. "You can tell me that, can't you?"

"Younghart. Carolyn Younghart."

Chapter Twenty-one

27 August, 0005 hours Local

The Russian freighter slowly rose and fell with the gentle swells of the ocean, plodding relentlessly toward the rendezvous. Its running lights were the only clue to its presence in the moonless darkness. It was nearly midnight.

Two crewmen manned the bridge, also dark save for the soft glow of the instruments, while the rest slept soundly, waiting to be awakened in a few hours. Only two others were awake at that hour: the captain and a passenger. They had left the bridge only moments before, after the captain had made one last check on the status of his ship before retiring to his quarters.

"Frankly, I don't know why I agreed to this. If it turns out badly, I can lose my job, or worse, although being unemployed in the new democratic, capitalist Russia is bad enough."

"Captain, you're being paid well for this. All you have to do is keep your back turned and your mouth shut. We'll handle everything else. If all goes as we have planned, you

Ken Currie

will never have to fret again about whether the ministry is going to pay you or your crew. And Russia will take care of herself, with the appropriate assistance."

"And if someone finds out this crew is not legitimate?"

"Can you tell me who's going to find out? Their paperwork is in order, the best that money can buy. There will be no questions, no suspicions, even if we are stopped. To all appearances, you have one of the most legitimate crews around. Everyone with a Russian or Byelorussian surname. Who could ask for a more orthodox group of men, Captain?"

The captain refilled his glass with tea, then motioned toward his guest with the teapot. The lanky guest shook his head, instead reaching into his coat pocket to retrieve a silver case. He removed an expensive English cigarette, snapped the case shut, and tapped the cigarette gently on the cover.

"Please, don't. I dislike that habit, and cigarette smoke makes me nauseous, especially smoke from the American and English brands. Sometimes I think their tobacco companies are trying to poison us."

The guest stared at the captain for a moment, as if trying to decide whether to honor the request. Finally, he put the cigarette back in its case. "Perhaps I'll have some tea after all."

Three hours later, on the signal of his passenger, the captain ordered an all stop to the ship's progress. He then extinguished the ship's running lights and switched on a directional beacon. A moment later, there was the sound of chains and twin splashes as the ship dropped anchor. Then all was silent save for the gentle chirping of the beacon and the sound of footsteps as members of the crew prepared for the meeting. The almost total darkness was occasionally pierced by the beams of small flashlights, the crew's only concession to safety as they went about their preparations. The captain and his companion stepped outside the bridge, looked eastward, and waited.

In a few moments, they could hear the sound of approaching jet engines. The captain grew increasingly agitated; he had not expected the aircraft to make this much noise. He searched the horizon anxiously, even though the ship's radar had revealed nothing as they reached the rendezvous point.

"Over the side," the passenger shouted down the ladder from the bridge.

The scuffling of footsteps grew louder as the designated crew members hurried into the boat and began lowering themselves to the ocean's surface.

The captain peered into the darkness, his eyes growing accustomed to the starlight. At last, he could discern the dark silhouette of the transport aircraft in the remaining few seconds before it passed over the ship. Below the approaching aircraft, he could barely make out the silver-white billows of deploying parachutes.

This was going to be very close, almost too close. In a moment, the IL-76 flashed over the top of the freighter, the closeness of its passage vibrating the deck, then did a slow turn back toward the ship. The passenger flicked on an odd-looking flashlight that emitted an intense, highly directional bluish green beam. He aimed the dagger of light in the direction of the transport aircraft, acquired his visual target, and flipped another switch on the side of the lamp. The lantern emitted a series of light pulses for a few seconds, then shut itself off. The passenger then heaved the device as hard as he could over the ship's railing.

"You've heard of disposable lighters? One less item to be asked about," he said to the captain.

The skipper looked at his passenger in stunned silence, wondering why he worried about being caught with a flashlight when they were about to pick up contraband.

The aircraft completed another pass over the ship, its pilot waggling the wings before the transport disappeared once and for all into the blackness. The sound of its engines rapidly receded, and the captain was able to loosen his tight grip on the rail.

"Impressive flight skills, Captain. Very much like finding a needle in a haystack, but they found it perfectly. We have found only the best. Now it's time to pick up our airmail."

The ship's crane lumbered into action, and the crane operator gingerly lowered the cargo hook toward the water. Meanwhile, the crew members who had earlier lowered themselves and the powered launch over the side maneuvered their boat toward their prize. The tightly wrapped cargo pallet bobbed gently on the ocean, its location broadcast by a small flashing strobe light. They secured a line to the floating pallet, then towed the package back to the freighter and the waiting crane. The crane plucked the cargo from the water and lowered it into the hold, where it took the place of another pallet, identical in appearance. That pallet was dumped over the side, where, having served its purpose, it sank ingloriously to the bottom of the ocean. The entire operation took fifteen minutes.

The captain gave the signal, and the *Nizhniy Novgorod* resumed its course toward the Virginia coast. As the captain ambled down the ladder to make his way back to his cabin for a few hours of sleep, he noticed his hands were trembling. He paused for a moment, gripping the railing tightly to force his nervousness to pass. He assured himself the worst was over. Everything had gone as his passenger had predicted. In less than twenty-four hours, they would be in port. The cargo would be removed, and his life would return to normal.

Meanwhile, the passenger was making sure the special-delivery cargo was properly secured in the cargo hold. Satisfied everything was in order, he turned to the leader of the recovery team. "Once the cargo is secure in port, I promised the captain he would be taken care of. I entrust you with that responsibility. Kill him, but accidentally, of course. That should be fairly easy in Washington."

27 August, 0700 hours Local

It was early morning in Moscow, and the streets were already clogged with traffic. Modern delivery trucks, imported from Europe, Japan, and America, made their way to the still-burgeoning numbers of fast-food restaurants and Western-owned department stores. Less glamorous Russian-manufactured trucks, their exhausts spitting out plumes of black smoke, struggled to the city's markets and other Russian-owned private businesses. Decrepit Russian and rusting, older European cars filled with sullen government workers competed for space with the trucks, darting in and out among the behemoths. Taxis, their drivers oblivious to all the other vehicles on the road while on the lookout for foreign tourists, zoomed back and forth without regard for their own safety or that of the city's countless pedestrians. Every now and then, the latest Mercedes, BMW, or Jaguar sedan would glide by, its occupants members of either the city's new homegrown business elite or one of the flourishing organized crime syndicates; according to many Muscovites, it was difficult at times to tell the two apart.

In the Ministry of Defense building across the river from Gorky Park, a young Russian Army major, tugging on his uniform jacket, which bore the insignia of the Airborne Troops, hurried down the corridor, ignoring other officers trudging back and forth in the execution of their duties as he made his way to the office of the first deputy minister of defense. In the outer office, he walked directly by a colonel, who looked up briefly from his paperwork and then, having recognized the visitor, returned immediately to his reading. Both knew the airborne officer's status within these walls.

The major tapped on the door and, barely waiting for a response from the other side, pushed his way into the room. The first deputy minister looked up, breaking off his conversation with his current visitor, the commander of Russian Airborne Troops. Both men smiled at the major as he entered the room, for he was the son of the minister and the aide-de-camp to the commander. The major saluted the two generals.

"You have news for us, Dmitriy?" the first deputy minister asked.

"It's done," the major said. He then smiled broadly, spun about, and left the room as rapidly as he had come.

The first deputy minister turned around to a safe behind his desk, unlocked the top drawer, and pulled out a red folder. He tucked the folder into his briefcase, secured its lock, and quickly stood up.

"Good. Very good. It's time to go see Arkadiy Mikhailo-vich."

Arkadiy Mikhailovich Gromov had been Russian defense minister for six months. He was President Milyutin's third defense chief in as many years. Milyutin had unceremoni-ously dumped the first one, a holdover from the previous administration, for corruption, including the lining of his pockets with funds intended for the construction of military housing. The sacked general continued to live in his country dacha outside Moscow while the investigation into the charges dragged on. Milyutin suspected that other members of the Russian high command had closed ranks to protect their former boss and their share of the profits from the di-version of scarce state funds.

Milyutin's second defense minister had been enormously popular with the public, but was viewed with deep suspicion by the Russian officer corps. He had been the first true ci-vilian ever to hold the post, not a retired general. It was a move Milyutin's advisers insisted was long overdue. Al-though extremely knowledgeable of military affairs, at least according to his supporters within the administration, he had worn a uniform only briefly, many years before, as a common soldier. He had fought in the Caucasus, where he developed a deep loathing for most of the officers above him and for Russia's foreign adventures under her previous president. He carried the dislike of the military with him into the new post. Bent on reforming the military apparatus, he succeed-ing only in alienating most of the generals and admirals. Having come from a technical background, his focus had been on upgrading the Russian defense ministry. In the pro-cess, he did little to alleviate the plight of the common sol-dier. Although well-meaning, or so it was said, his inattention to the military's social problems turned out to have as much of a negative impact as the corrupt practices of his predecessor. When his aircraft crashed en route to a meeting of NATO defense ministers, there were few tears shed in the high command.

Gromov had not been an obvious choice as defense minister, although it had become patently clear Milyutin was looking for a military man to fill the post. There were no other civilians who possessed the qualifications held by the former incumbent, and Milyutin was under intense pressure from the generals and admirals to appoint one of their own. They had starkly warned that another civilian would be an unmitigated disaster in terms of military morale, and darkly hinted of a reaction among the rank and file. Milyutin had assumed that the high command would urge the appointment of one of the first deputy defense ministers, the most senior officers within the Russian military. He was surprised when they put forward Gromov's name, a nomination Milyutin's national security adviser, himself a former general officer, strongly endorsed.

Gromov's nomination flew through the Russian parliament in a matter of days, a welcome change to the resistance the Russian president normally encountered in his dealings with this "incorrigible group of reactionary recalcitrants," a label he routinely pinned on the hostile legislature. So it was that within two weeks of the death of Russia's first civilian defense minister, Gromov moved from his position as commander of Airborne Troops—the VDV, one of the last remaining bastions of Russian military power and prowess—to the country's highest military post.

The first deputy minister of defense and the new VDV commander announced themselves to Gromov and took chairs on either side of the large conference table that sat in front of the defense minister's desk. Army General Artem Leonidovich Pankratov, Gromov's first deputy and his chief of the General Staff, removed the red folder from his briefcase. He fished out a sheaf of papers and handed them over to his boss. As Gromov reviewed the materials, Pankratov stared stolidly across the table at Colonel General Petr Vissarionovich Grishin. They were certain this would be a very quick meeting; Gromov had only to give the thumbs-up or thumbs-down.

Gromov handed the papers back to Pankratov and leaned back in his chair, pretending to study the ornate ceiling in his office. "I assume that both deliveries are proceeding as planned; otherwise, you two wouldn't be here, correct, Artem Leonidovich?"

Pankratov nodded. "Yes, Defense Minister, we received confirmation only moments ago. The first package will be ready for delivery in three days. The second package, as you know, is already secured. Its escort is awaiting the final order. Its delivery will coincide with that of the first package."

"And all other preparations are complete, in accordance with the document I just read?"

"Yes, Defense Minister."

"Then I will talk to President Milyutin as planned. We will execute in three days, on my command. Agreed?"

Pankratov glanced at Grishin and turned toward Gromov as if to say something. He slowly nodded, then voiced his concurrence along with Grishin. They arose from their chairs and quickly left the room.

Gromov stood up and walked over to one of the large windows. He gazed pensively across the river at the park, its sidewalks teeming with Russians enjoying the morning sun. Why weren't these people working? They milled about in that heavenly oasis, enjoying their dalliances, while all about them Russia was treading a path to hell.

He walked back to his desk and picked up one of the many special telephones that connected him with the Russian political and military leadership. He was still looking out the window, watching the activity in the park, when a voice came on the line.

"This is Minister of Defense Gromov. I need to speak to the president immediately."

Chapter Twenty-two

Underwood had left his meeting with Harper in a daze. The rain had stopped and the heavy cloud cover had broken open to create a spectacular sunset, but he barely noticed. He was on autopilot as he steered the car toward home, only vaguely aware of the other automobiles passing him by. He ignored the rude gestures of those perturbed by someone going the speed limit on the Beltway this time of the evening. Normally, he would have returned the insults in kind; Washington traffic seemed to have a unique way of bringing out the best in people.

Awareness returned temporarily as he passed the spot on the highway where Valery had been killed. He slowed even more and caught a glimpse of the deep gouges in the median left by the tires of his friend's car, long since removed from the scene. The evening sun bounced off bits of debris left in the grass. The sight depressed him, and his eyes were drawn to the scattered reflections. He felt a sudden surge of nausea that forced him to turn his attention back to the highway. He continued on the path toward McLean.

His mind became preoccupied once again with Harper's

revelation. He had to ask the OSI agent to repeat her name, convinced he couldn't possibly have heard him correctly the first time. The reaction had prompted Harper to ask if Underwood knew her.

"I don't think so. No, I don't know her. The name just sounded familiar for a moment, I guess," Underwood said in a barely audible whisper. He wondered if Harper had been fooled, but the lie was the best he could muster under the circumstances.

He sorted through how he could avoid contact with her, but realized events had now gone too far. Harper had come up with a plan, the only possible plan, for nailing Evans and getting Jennifer back in the process. He had in the main agreed with Underwood's demand for confidentiality. He wasn't about to blow what had been a major concession because he was afraid to say hello to a woman he hadn't seen in years.

Nevertheless, he found himself becoming anxious once again as he thought about the coming meeting. *Be strictly professional*, he told himself. *Simply tell her the facts about Valery and your present situation. There's no need to bring up any garbage from the past. Let her mention it if she wants to. Anyway, all the rest is over and done with.* But then he had to ask himself why he continued to think about her, dream about her, if all was past and no longer mattered. There were strange stirrings inside he could not—or did not—want to understand.

Somehow he reached his house safely. He pressed the garage door opener and nearly missed the manila envelope lying in the middle of the concrete floor just beyond the sill. He drove over the parcel, then sat quietly in the car for a minute, certain he knew what was inside the envelope. He pressed the button once more, closing the door as he continued to sit in the car.

He got out of the car and slammed the door shut as hard as he could, perhaps thinking this would provide some relief from the tension rebuilding inside him. It did not, and he grimaced as the sound of his futile gesture echoed off the walls of the nearly empty three-car garage. All in all, he concluded, it had been a miserable damned day.

He picked up the package and walked into the very dark, very empty house. He assumed a direct course to the liquor cabinet and his beloved Tennessee whiskey, but then noticed the light flashing on the answering machine. He thought, hoped, even prayed for a moment that it would be a message from Jennifer.

"Hello, this is Sergeant Dunkel of the Fairfax County Police. I'm calling in regard to the traffic accident involving Mr. Actmeetoff, if I'm pronouncing the name correctly. There was a sealed envelope in his car addressed to Michael Underwood. Sir, if you'll give me a call, we can arrange a time for you to pick it up."

Underwood instantly dialed the number left on the machine. Dunkel had long since departed the station, and several frustrating minutes passed before Underwood could locate someone who knew what he was talking about. Underwood told the surprised policeman he was on his way. The whiskey would just have to wait.

Underwood locked the car doors and flipped on the map light. He turned the envelope over several times, examining the exterior. There was no evidence it had been opened, as he had been assured by the desk officer who handed him the package. Valery had been the victim of a simple traffic accident, or so the police had assumed since they still had the driver of the other vehicle in custody. No suggestion of foul play, and therefore no need to look inside the envelope. Even if they had, Underwood was convinced they wouldn't have understood Valery's message. Still, he was relieved the envelope was still sealed.

Underwood checked outside the car, then tore open the envelope. Inside was a typewritten letter Valery had signed in his wonderfully florid manner. Underwood smiled sadly. Yes, this was definitely from his friend. He glanced around one more time, then began reading.

Ken Currie

My Dear Michael,

I imagine you will have read this by the time I call you tomorrow, at least I hope you will have done so. As you will see from what follows, it is important you have this information as soon as possible. That's why I have left it at your house. I would recommend you include this when you talk to your president. I wish I could be there to see the expression on his face, but I will await your account of your meeting. A vicarious thrill is better than none at all, but I still prefer more tangible forms of excitement. I will be very distressed if you don't keep perfect mental notes of your session.

Enough humor, Michael, because, quite frankly, what I have discovered is not humorous, not in the very least. I am more than a little concerned that I have become embroiled in something better left alone. First, I am certain I am being followed. No, that's not paranoia talking. Don't forget, I grew up in the decaying old Soviet Union, where everything was falling apart except the KGB, even though you would say even the KGB was collapsing. I know when I'm being followed. As you Americans are fond of saying: it's not paranoia if they're really after you. Second, I believe my telephone is tapped, although I wonder whether it's being done by the people I've been investigating or your FBI. Perhaps even the CIA; maybe they were interested in me after all? Given all the static I hear on the telephone line, I would guess it's your people rather than mine (ha!).

I have found out more about Voskreshennaya Rossiya, Michael, and what I've found out scares the hell out of me, and I think it will have the same effect upon you and your president. Please ensure he knows about this, my friend, because he is an integral part of their plan. These are very dangerous people, Michael. They are capable of doing anything, and my source has told me that is exactly what they intend.

They plan to steal American missiles of an unknown type and then use those weapons to destroy several key targets in the United States, including the White House. They would, of course, blame all this on Iranian-backed terrorists. At the same time, similar attacks, again using stolen American missiles, would be mounted against Russian targets, including President Milyutin. Terrorists would be blamed for these attacks as well. Their objective? Simple revenge, nothing more, according to my source. They desire to punish Milyutin for turning his back on Russia's real friends while kowtowing to the Americans.

My source speculated they might even be planning to modify the missiles so they would carry stolen Russian tactical nuclear warheads, but he couldn't produce any concrete evidence to support this wild conjecture. I would be amazed if they were to take such a drastic step. These people are dangerous, but not crazy, Michael. For all the madness of their plan, I doubt even they are capable of taking such an insane step. Yet I wonder what type of missile could destroy the White House and a substantial portion of the Kremlin. Perhaps you can tell me? I am not a military expert, thank God.

I have no particulars on when and how they plan to steal the missiles, what type of missile they have in mind, or when they plan to attack. I wish I did for your sake. My source believes he may be able to gain additional information. We shall see. I did ask him if any of this information had been passed to the right people in Moscow. He told me not to worry, those who needed to know understood and were working on the problem. When I asked him whether this information had been passed to anyone in the American government, he was somewhat evasive. I don't know who on your side knows about this, if anyone. If no one else does know, I have to ask why he chose to entrust such information to me. That is another of the answers I must find.

I know all of this sounds simply fantastic, but you must believe me when I tell you my source is in a position to know all this. I cannot tell you his identity, not because I don't trust you, but because I don't trust these people. I am convinced he is taking a terrible chance by telling me even this much. As I noted, there are parts of the story I still find perplexing. I have much to do on Monday. I do have some other sources who may be of help. I will let you know what I find out. You owe me a Guinness, Michael. Until we talk. *Do zavtra.*

Valery

Underwood touched his cheeks, then wiped away the tears that had started trickling down his face. He glanced around nervously to see if anyone had noticed his emotional display.

He was now certain of one thing: Valery's death was not accidental. He trembled with rage and then pounded the dashboard until the heel of his hand began to sting. He looked furtively out the window once more. He had to get it all out of his system now—there could be no more lapses of self-control, no more tantrums. Too much was hanging on his ability to remain calm. He took several deep breaths and massaged his temples with his fingertips.

Valery was absolutely correct in one of his suppositions. The plot he outlined in his letter did indeed sound incredible. Underwood would have discounted it save for one fact that he suddenly recalled: the American ship that had disappeared on its way to the Gulf. He didn't even know the ship's name or what it had been carrying, but he knew there was a connection. He would have to do some checking up of his own tomorrow. Valery wasn't the only one with reliable sources. Some of his resided at the Pentagon. Certainly one of them knew what was going on and could provide him with the latest on the missing ship. Someone at the Pentagon had to know what the hell was going on.

Russians plotting to blow up the White House and then casting the blame on terrorists? That did sound more than a little far-fetched. The Iranians had reasons of their own for wanting to punish the American president; they didn't need any Russian help. Underwood was convinced they had the wherewithal, the motive, and the will to do something like this, while at the same time carefully trying to cover their tracks as they had done so many times before.

But Russians killing the American president? That sounded very strange. He desperately wished he knew the identity of Valery's source. There were too many loose ends here. He would pass the information along to Harper, of course. He didn't know who Evans was working for, and he didn't really care, as long as this information could take him one step closer to bringing Evans down. And saving Jennifer.

He would be providing all this to Carolyn Younghart as well. He felt anxious once more as he thought about the impending encounter, but he was able to shove the emotion aside and return to his more immediate task of dissecting the remainder of Valery's letter.

He concurred with Valery's assessment regarding the use of stolen nuclear warheads. A wonderfully terrifying idea, one that made a policy maker's heart pump faster and a novelist's mouth water, but not very realistic. The Russians, or Iranian-backed terrorists, or whoever was cooking up this plot, didn't need to destroy half of Washington to take out the president.

It was one thing to risk American retribution for assassinating the president; it was quite another to flirt with national suicide. While the Iranians might be able to fool some into believing their lack of culpability for terrorist bombings in the American capital, no protestations about their innocence in nuclear-related terror would be sufficient to stave off their own destruction. Teheran would keep a tight rein on its bloody agents, even those who with a pronounced bent toward insanity. Madness could serve a purpose, but only so long as it could be controlled.

The dangers of nuclear terrorism were overblown in any event, Underwood believed. The Russians had done a far better job accounting for and controlling their nuclear arsenal than many had thought them capable of following the collapse of the Soviet Union. While large numbers of Russian military personnel suffered from their profession's and their country's declining fortunes, those charged with safeguarding the nuclear weapons continued to be carefully watched over and cared for. There was no mercy shown to the soldier or his commander who demonstrated laxness in their duties of protecting these weapons. Occasional thefts of nuclear materials had taken place, but not from the military's reactors or facilities, and when the pilferage was discovered, the perpetrators were dealt with ruthlessly. Not even the Russian mafia had proved able, despite plentiful threats and ample supplies of money, to break into this presumably lucrative international market.

There was only one group in Russia with its hand on nuclear weapons, and that was the military. No warhead would move without their knowledge or approval. Claims by leaders of several of the former Soviet republics after the breakup of the USSR that they, too, controlled nuclear weapons had all proved to be nothing more than empty attempts to gain international prestige. Much to their chagrin, these leaders discovered their claims of membership in the nuclear club managed to generate only questions about their credibility and their sanity.

The Iranians, the Iraqis, and others still feverishly pursued the acquisition of their own nuclear weapons, and the Western countries tenaciously fought to thwart the realization of these ambitions. But did Teheran, as many in the West feared, really foresee using such weapons at the first sign of trouble with the West or passing them along to the terrorist groups they sponsored? It was one thing to sacrifice a few martyrs in the name of Allah to advance a country's interests. It was quite another to offer up an entire country—

including a leadership grown comfortably accustomed to exercising power—to martyrdom. No, if the weapons were used, they would not be carrying nuclear warheads. Still, even a conventional warhead could blow a hell of a large hole in the White House, and that was threat enough.

Chapter Twenty-three

"How are you doing, sport?"

"Carolyn, please get me out of here."

Williams was standing in the middle of the hospital room, hands on his hips in a defiant posture, still attired in a hospital gown. Squared off opposite Williams was an Air Force staff sergeant in hospital dress, her hands also on her hips.

"By the way, Blair, nice tush," Younghart said, grinning as she slid into the visitor's chair by the bed.

Williams reached around and grabbed the back of his gown, then glowered at the sergeant.

"Will you please get me my uniform, Sergeant? I have work to do. I can't be sitting on my butt in here while you people run around trying to decide what to do with me."

"Colonel, I understand your desire to leave the hospital," the sergeant replied, "but only the doctor can release you, and I'm afraid he hasn't done that yet. It shouldn't be too much longer, however. But let me remind you, sir, you came in here unaware of what planet you were on, let alone what base you're on. You had a concussion, and it took eight stitches to close the back of your scalp. Your injuries weren't minor. Please rest assured, sir, I share your desire to get you out of here as soon as possible."

Williams, nonplussed, dropped his hands from his hips. He smiled and replied, "I deserved that, Sergeant. But would you please see what you can do to expedite things?"

"Yes, sir, I'll go talk to the doctor." The sergeant glanced at Younghart, rolled her eyes, and left the room.

"Well, Blair, you've just reaffirmed the wisdom of my decision not to go to medical school," Younghart said. Then, in response to Williams's questioning look, she continued. "I never would have been able to handle patients like you. So, tell me, how long had you been subjecting the good sergeant to your petulant behavior before I walked in?"

"Oh, it wasn't that bad. I'm not an ogre, but I am starting to climb the walls. I have a feeling I'm missing all the fun."

Younghart frowned.

"So why the sour face, Carolyn? Bilder not cooperating? I was convinced the little weasel was going to spill his guts, or something, all over the floor."

"No, it's not that. He actually said quite a bit. Not as much as I had hoped, but enough to keep us going. It's something else."

Williams waited as patiently as he could. Younghart was in a different world, however. He would have to nudge her back. "Carolyn, I was never very good at guessing games. You're going to have to tell me what's bothering you."

"What? Oh. Sorry. Just thinking."

"More like drifting, I would say. So talk to me, please. I'm certainly not going anywhere, and I'm told I'm a fairly good listener."

"Except when you're arguing with the hospital staff," Younghart replied as she forced a smile. "Okay, so listen."

She got up and closed the hospital door. Williams, taking her cue, took a seat on the edge of the bed next to the chair. Younghart softly cleared her throat and continued.

"Just before I came in here, I got a call from a colleague of mine, an agent from the OSI. We've helped one another out a few times with information. He told me he had been contacted by an Air Force colonel he had been debriefing for several years. Seems this colonel had connections with some interesting foreign types, including one prominent Russian journalist in Washington. The journalist was killed in a car accident this past weekend, but not before he told this colonel about some neofascist group in Russia. No, wait, don't interrupt. Here's the kicker. Up until last week, this colonel had been working at CIA, briefing the president. Monday, he went to work at the White House."

"Sounds like a fast burner."

" 'Flamer' is a better word." Younghart frowned once more and grew silent again, but only momentarily. She was warming to her subject. "Don't look so confused. I'll explain in a minute. Back to the story. The same day this guy shows up at the White House—yesterday, in fact—he gets a call from a former coworker at Langley. This new player, who it turns out has taken over the colonel's old job of briefing the president of the United States, threatens the Air Force colonel and tries to coerce him into providing information on the whereabouts of the president. Oh, yeah, and to seal the deal, he informs the colonel they're holding his wife hostage. Sounds unbelievable, doesn't it?"

She looked up into Williams's wide-eyed face. "I can tell from your expression you're somewhat interested in this," she teased.

"I know what you're thinking, Carolyn. They're connected, aren't they?"

"You think? My instincts tell me yes, of course they are. And most of the time my instincts serve me well. However, it doesn't take a leap of faith here to connect these."

"So where do we go from here? We hanging around to talk to Bilder again?"

Younghart stood up and languidly stretched from side to side. She slapped Williams on the knee and opened the door. "We need to get you some clothes and get you the hell out of here. We've got a plane back to Washington to catch."

"Excuse me? What about our key suspect?"

"The big cretin is done talking, at least for a while. While

Mulkey and Johanssen were hurrying you back to the base, I dragged Bilder's ass over to the Federal Building. He was a pliant little sack of putty for a while. He was so scared, he started babbling away before I'd even finished reminding him of his rights."

"And?"

"He said he was contacted several months ago. He had a habit of stopping into an exotic lounge on his way home from work. He said he was sitting by himself having a drink when a stranger sat down next to him and asked if he would like to make a lot of money for very little effort. Well, the question immediately intrigued Bilder, since the bastard was up to his eyeballs in debt, a little secret he had been trying to keep from his wife, apparently with some success. No one at his work realized his life was a financial disaster, either. I mean, no one noticed his fifty-thousand-dollar car, for God's sake, why would they notice anything else?"

"He told you all this?"

"I told you he was a talkative devil, Blair. Bilder couldn't resist the offer. The stranger said they'd pay him a hundred thousand for starters. All he had to do was divert a single cargo shipment and make sure the paperwork was in order to make it happen. If he did a good job, they promised him additional work. He thought he had landed in heaven."

"And it didn't bother Bilder he was breaking most of the rules and letting sensitive cargo potentially fall into the wrong hands?"

"Hey, Blair, money has a language all its own. Anyway, Bilder said he didn't concern himself with the precise nature of the cargo. He said for all that money, he would have diverted an ICBM if they'd asked him to."

"And he probably would have."

"Absolutely he would have. When they do it for money, they don't care. If you're going to reach down that low for profit, why not reach just a bit lower? Maybe there'll be more profit in it. I've seen it happen more times than I wish to remember." She paused for a breath, then hissed, "God, I wanted to beat the living hell out of the pasty-faced, scum-sucking little prick! No remorse for what he did. He was upset he got caught. He wanted to know what was going to happen to his car. Do you believe it?"

Williams cast his eyes down toward the floor. "Yes, unfortunately I do. So did he tell you who his contact was?"

"No, he claims he saw him only the one time in the bar. They spoke only on the phone after that, almost always pay phones."

"And he wasn't the least bit curious how this stranger apparently knew when the JASSMs would arrive at the port, what ship they were supposed to be on, and how one would go about putting them on another ship, undetected until it was too late?"

She shook her head. "I'd love to be able to give you those answers. I'm sure your CINC would love to hear the answers. But Bilder's a dud. All he wanted was the money. He didn't care about any of the rest. Anyway, by the time he had said all this, he suddenly realized he might be in a lot of trouble. I told you he's no genius. He suddenly said he wasn't going to answer any more questions without a lawyer, and then, as promised, he totally zipped his lip."

"So now what?"

"So now he's in custody awaiting arraignment. The field office will take over, in the event he wants to talk some more. They'll play the usual mind game, telling him things will go a lot easier if he helps us bring in the others. Frankly, I don't hold out a lot of hope we'll get anything useful. I think Bilder tapped out every one of his brain cells remembering and passing along what he did know. You want to tell me how a civilian like that ended up in such a critical job?"

Williams laughed and held up a hand. "Trust me, you don't want to get me started on that particular subject. Let's just say he probably made it by demonstrating an ability to breathe. By the way, where are Mulkey and Johanssen?"

Younghart gave him a strange look.

"No, no, that was a bad juxtaposition, wasn't it? I didn't mean to imply . . . those two actually know a lot more about breathing. Oh, screw it. Where are they?"

"They're waiting at base operations. Your bags are packed

and awaiting your arrival. All we have to do is talk the military doctors into letting you out of here. Unless you want to fly back dressed like that."

"This is a bit breezy for my taste," Williams replied as he tugged at the back of the gown once more.

"Well, Colonel," Younghart grinned mischievously, "at least it'll be easier for you to check your six."

Williams grabbed the newspaper from the bedside table, rolled it up, and waved it menacingly in Younghart's face. "Just go get the doctor, please."

Williams thankfully settled into the plane seat beside Younghart, then flinched from the pain as he leaned his head back into the cushion. He sat there, looking glum, forcing his head uncomfortably forward. "Well, this is certainly going to be a fun trip," he mumbled as he looked about fruitlessly for something to prop his neck away from the seat. Unfortunately, the Air Mobility Command didn't provide pillows.

"Damn it," he suddenly blurted out, leaning suddenly forward.

Younghart jumped in her seat. "What? What is it?"

"I just remembered I forgot to call Erica last night."

Younghart gently pushed him back. "You give me cardiac arrest because you're concerned about not making a phone call? I think she'll forgive you, Blair. You were pretty doped up. I doubt she would have enjoyed talking to you while you were sailing off somewhere in la-la land."

Williams looked at her. "And how would you know what my condition was last night, Younghart?"

"Let's just say I was protecting my equities. I had no intention of letting anything happen to my partner."

Williams grinned and settled back into the seat, gingerly positioning his head this time. "You owe me an explanation, Carolyn."

"Oh?"

"Yes, you mentioned something about a flamer back at the hospital."

"Oh."

"Well?"

"A moment, okay? This is not one of my favorite memories. Unfortunately, it was revived by this morning's phone call."

Williams jerked his head around, ignoring the pain caused by the sudden movement. He had just experienced another epiphany. "You know him, don't you? The colonel. You know him."

Younghart looked at him and shook her head. "You're amazing, my friend. Yes, I know him. I met him a long time ago. I really liked him. I mean, I *really* liked him. Until I discovered he was married. A little detail he neglected to mention until it was time for me to leave. One of those, 'Oh, by the way, Carolyn.' So I got involved with a jerk. I got used. I got dumped. It's not the first time, and I'm not the first. I had done a terrific job of forgetting all about the creep until today. Now, suddenly, he's back," she said, stretching out the final word.

"Different playing field, different rules this time around, lady. This time, you're in charge."

"What? Oh, no. You really think I care about extracting some cheap revenge? Please. I would be far happier if he'd just stayed lost on the other side of the world. I really don't care. Unfortunately, Colonel Underwood appears to hold some valuable information."

"Excuse me. Would you care to repeat what you just said? Colonel who?"

"Underwood. Why are you looking at me like that? Oh, for God's sake, you know him, too? So, you're going to tell me he's an old buddy from the Gulf? You cruised for chicks together?"

"You wound me deeply, Carolyn. I never went 'cruising' for chicks. I married my high school sweetheart. I've never cheated on my wife. I contribute religiously to the Combined Federal Campaign. I dress up for Halloween and take my kid trick-or-treating. I'm as boring as they come. Just look at me. But yes, I do know him from a previous assignment. I met him years ago in Florida. At MacDill. He had quite a reputation as a hard-charging intelligence officer."

"Yeah, that's Mike Underwood."

"I saw him last week."

She raised an eyebrow. "You what?"

"I saw him last week. In Alexandria. I dragged Mulkey and Johanssen off to this restaurant I knew, and Underwood was there by himself. So I went over and said hello. He had changed. A lot."

"What do you mean."

"He seemed sullen. Tense. I would characterize him as a candidate for burnout, if he isn't already. He was wound so tight, I was afraid he was going to pop his mainspring right there. I was glad when I had a chance to get away from him."

Younghart stared out the window. She reached over and grabbed Williams's forearm.

"Ow," he shouted. "What was that for? By the way, you've got a grip like a vise."

"I want to thank you for sharing this wonderful news, Blair. Now I'm really looking forward to seeing him again."

"You don't see an advantage in knowing this about him?"

"Do you?"

"Yes, I do. Wait a minute. Who's the FBI agent here? Do I get paid extra for helping you out?"

She smiled. "Don't push it, Blair. I know where you hurt. Go ahead. I'm listening."

Chapter Twenty-four

Milyutin studied the documents while Gromov sat quietly, waiting for the president's reaction. Gromov was a study in self-control; despite the momentous news contained in the reports, the defense minister was confident how Milyutin would respond. Once he understood the implications of what he was reading, the Russian president would have no options other than those Gromov was prepared to lay out.

Milyutin betrayed no emotion as he laid the papers gently on his desk, nudging them together into a neat pile. Gromov leaned forward to retrieve the papers, but Milyutin put his hand firmly on top of the stack. Gromov shrugged and sat back.

"You are convinced of the authenticity of these reports, General Gromov?" Milyutin asked, staring intently into the defense minister's eyes, as if seeking there the validation of what he had just read.

"I can vouch for them in their entirety, President Milyutin." Gromov emphasized Milyutin's title and surname. Although Gromov disagreed quietly with Milyutin on many fundamental policy issues, he did approve of the president's decision to emphasize formality and titles within the ranks of the government bureaucracy. The forced—and hypocritical—informality of the old Soviet system's emphasis on "comrade" and the use of the first name and patronymic had never sat well with the bulk of the new generation of military leaders from which Gromov had come. While these officers snubbed most Western cultural values, they willingly adopted Western—primarily American—military practices and customs. They had even adopted American-style uniforms.

"I have heard nothing about this movement from the state security services. Now you come to me with highly detailed reports from the Main Intelligence Directorate. How was it the GRU managed to come by information that somehow managed to elude our best intelligence operatives?" Milyutin continued to stare at Gromov, challenging him for the answer.

"President Milyutin, I would like to remind you that your best intelligence officers do, in fact, come from the GRU, not from the other services. Unlike the other bodies, my intelligence directorate is not populated with holdovers from the old days. They have no hidden agenda which they serve by telling the leadership what it wants to hear. The GRU gives me the unvarnished truth. And now I have presented it to you."

"The head of the state security services probably would not agree with you, but your judgment is not without merit." Milyutin accompanied the comment with a conspiratorial wink.

It was a gesture Gromov had noticed before when the president was trying to ingratiate himself with a subordinate. It was a gesture Gromov thoroughly detested.

"Mr. President," Gromov continued, his tone reflecting growing impatience, "can we return to the substance of the reports I have brought you? There are matters which need to be discussed in light of this information. There are steps that need to be taken as soon as possible."

"General Gromov, I'm afraid I'm not following you. What steps are you talking about?"

Gromov was exasperated. "President Milyutin, did you not understand what you read? If you have questions, I'll be happy to provide the answers."

There was an edge to Milyutin's voice as he replied. "Of course I understood the reports. They tell me we have yet another ultranationalist group spreading its propaganda about Russia's imminent peril. These Black Hundreds have sprung up before, General Gromov. They generate some support at first among the malcontented, and then their popularity rapidly evaporates. I don't see any greater danger in this Resurrected Russia than in any of the other groups which our citizens have rejected since the founding of the Russian republic. Russians have become much too sophisticated to fall prey to such nonsense. Our young democracy will withstand the challenge from these outcasts, as it always has. Trust me on that, General Gromov."

The president is an imbecile, Gromov thought. He had anticipated the possibility of presidential obstinacy, but in the form of resistance to Gromov's suggested measures. He never suspected Milyutin would simply discount the reports. His jaw tightened while he listened to Milyutin's glowing portrayal of the country's democratic political culture. *He thinks he's still campaigning for president*, he thought disdainfully.

Gromov responded slowly, carefully enunciating every word, as if speaking to a recalcitrant child. "President Milyutin, permit me to review briefly for you the measures we have had to take over the past several years, several times at your direction, if perhaps not awareness, to deal with these unpopular movements."

Milyutin's eyes narrowed in response to Gromov's barb, but he did not interrupt.

"First, the attempt to establish a Far East Republic. A good portion of Vladivostok was destroyed in the process of putting down this unpopular uprising. The cross-border operations into Ukraine of the Cossack Brotherhood, another nonsensical, obviously unpopular group that somehow nearly dragged us into war. Then there was the revival of the separatist movement in Yakutia. We had to commit two airborne divisions to root out that feckless bunch of malcontents. Russian soldiers are still patrolling the streets, but obviously they're wasting their time, because these disturbers of the public order will simply fade away."

"General Gromov," Milyutin interrupted angrily, "I don't need to be lectured by you. You come in here with some wild report—"

"Wild report! My God, Mr. President, the GRU has infiltrated this group. They know exactly what they're up to, but you refuse to believe it."

"Because it's absolutely outlandish! The very idea, stealing American missiles and arming them with nuclear warheads to attack Russian and American targets. Such rubbish!"

Gromov forced himself to calm down. "President Milyutin, I did not intend to lecture, but brave men are risking their lives to provide this information to you. I cannot be held responsible if Danilenko's crack security agents have failed to uncover this group, but I assure you Resurrected Russia is very real. They are planning to do this, and they have very important allies among the Russian mafia who are committed to providing them the help they need. You have many enemies, President Milyutin, even though you may choose to deny it. There are many people who are unhappy with how you have embraced the Americans. And I shouldn't have to tell you how the mafia regards your war against organized crime in this country. You are not safe, Mr. President, and these reports provide only the latest confirmation of what is unpleasant, but nevertheless a fact."

"And tell me, General Gromov, how do you, as my defense minister, feel about my policy toward the Americans?" Milyutin asked challengingly.

"Does my opinion matter, President Milyutin? It is a matter of Russian state policy. It is the direction you have ordered us to go. If we were still debating the issue, I would probably have urged greater caution, especially regarding association with NATO. But the issue has been settled, as far as the military is concerned."

"Bravo, General," Milyutin exclaimed, clapping slowly.

"An excellent, if well-rehearsed, answer. Exactly the answer I should expect. You weren't so circumspect during the last summit, however."

"I only spoke my mind when provoked by the American secretary of defense."

"As I recall, General, you accused the Americans of emasculating the Russian military."

Gromov sighed. "Mr. President, we can argue such things, or we can discuss the serious situation at hand. In any event, there should be no question of my loyalty to the Russian state, or to you. The simple fact is, I have an obligation to bring to your attention matters which have not been formalized into state policy. How to deal with the threat posed by this group is one of those matters." Milyutin stabbed the stack of papers with his index finger to emphasize the point.

"General Gromov—"

"Mr. President, I ask your indulgence. I have one more item to add to my list, and you cannot have forgotten it. The attempted rebellion by the Tobolsk division. If you recall, there was strong evidence of involvement by Russian criminal elements in that disturbance. Several hundred died on both sides before the division was subdued. You commuted the division commander's death sentence because you were afraid of the reaction in the military. Have you forgotten all this, Mr. President?"

Milyutin slammed his fist on the table. "Of course I haven't forgotten it, but that was almost three years ago. We've gone beyond that. The conditions don't exist anymore that would make such breakdowns in order possible."

"President Milyutin, if that's what you're being told by your advisers, then you have surrounded yourself with fools." Gromov ignored Milyutin's terrible scowl and pressed ahead. "I deal with these conditions every day, and the problems with which I must wrestle in the armed forces are merely a reflection of the ills of Russian society. The tsar may have been far away, Mr. President, but you cannot afford to be."

"If the president is encircled by fools, then he himself must be a fool—is that what you're saying?"

"No, Mr. President. A man is a fool only if he chooses to ignore reality. I am confident you will not follow the fool's path."

"General Gromov, no one has ever dared speak to me this way."

"I am quite certain of that, President Milyutin. My only objective, however, is to tell you the truth of the situation confronting you."

"I believe *you* believe that was your purpose, General," Milyutin said, half smiling, "but I still don't share your conviction about the seriousness of the situation."

"President Milyutin, we can sit here all afternoon chasing our tails, but before I leave, or before you dismiss me, I have an obligation to outline for you options the ministry has drawn up to deal with the threat posed by Resurrected Russia and its unsavory associates. Then, if you choose to accept my assessment of the threat, we will be able to execute these measures rapidly. If you reject the assessment, then at least I will have fulfilled my obligation."

And wash your hands of responsibility for what follows, Gromov thought. He continued out loud, "The longer we wait, the more serious the threat will become and the more likely the leaders of Resurrected Russia will discover our intelligence operatives. They will be dead, Mr. President, and you will be blind."

Milyutin sat silently. Gromov sensed that his final comments had begun to wear away the president's confidence. Milyutin drummed the desktop with his fingers and stared at the far wall. He had started to respond but was interrupted by the ringing of one of the telephones sitting on the table behind his desk. The president swiveled immediately in his chair and grabbed the receiver of the direct telephone link to the White House. Milyutin acknowledged the call and waited while the connection was completed. He turned back to Gromov momentarily. "General Gromov, if you would excuse me for a moment."

"Of course, Mr. President. I will await your summons from outside."

*   *   *

Gromov isolated himself in a corner of the anteroom and reviewed his notes, oblivious to the bustling presidential staff, positive he would be making a return trip to the president's office. He reflected on Milyutin's instantaneous response to the American president's phone call. *Noonan plays the tune while Milyutin dances.* He imagined Milyutin as a *matroshka*, a Russian nesting doll; however, when one opened the first figure, one discovered there was nothing else inside, just a hollow shell. Gromov smirked at the image, just as the door to the president's office burst open and a disturbingly pale Milyutin appeared. He spotted Gromov and motioned him in. Gromov hurried into the office as Milyutin shut the door.

"Please, General Gromov, take a seat. It appears we do have much to discuss."

Gromov repressed a smile. "I must assume, Mr. President, that this change in attitude has something to do with the phone call?"

Milyutin responded to the question with a dour expression. He studied Gromov's face, as if trying to figure out what the general was thinking.

"President Noonan wanted to make sure I was aware of a potential danger, as he put it. He just recently became aware of a Russian terrorist group allegedly plotting attacks against Russian and Western targets."

"Resurrected Russia?" Gromov asked.

Milyutin nodded, a look of resignation crossing his face. "Of course. He had no details, but he informed me he has directed their FBI to look into the matter and would provide me whatever additional information they uncover."

"President Milyutin, I think you now realize you have all the information you require on this group. The Americans can add nothing to what the GRU has already discovered."

"But how would the Americans know?"

"It is a small world, Mr. President. People talk, often carelessly. They sometimes like to boast. I wouldn't worry how the Americans came by the information. The point is, they have it. Are you now convinced about what I told you?"

"I was not completely convinced until Noonan informed me of events that apparently escaped the attention of even the GRU."

Gromov suddenly became very attentive. "Regarding the group?" he asked skeptically.

"No, not about the group. I advised him our sources were claiming there was a plot to attack American and Russian targets with stolen American missiles."

Gromov winced at Milyutin's revelation that he had shared GRU secrets with the U.S. president.

"I expected President Noonan to laugh," Milyutin said. "Instead, he told me he had just been advised by the Pentagon that an American military cargo ship was attacked on its way to the Persian Gulf. As a result, the Americans are missing several missiles."

Gromov's jaw dropped open ever so slightly. He was stunned the Americans were willing to share such sensitive information.

"President Noonan tried to assure me the missiles could not be launched without special codes and equipment. He said the greatest danger was advanced technology falling into hands unfriendly toward both our countries. I understood what he was saying, but I did not tell him that I did not share his optimism."

"A prudent move, Mr. President. Based on my own experience, there is no weapon system that can't be turned against its designer, given time and expertise. You are right to believe the Americans are much too sanguine about what the attackers may intend for such cruise missiles."

"General Gromov, in light of these facts, it would appear I have to rethink my position. I still cannot accept that this Resurrected Russia and its message of hate enjoys much resonance among our people. But, if these fanatics have somehow managed to steal highly accurate and destructive weapons and the nuclear warheads to mate with them, then I must reluctantly accept the credibility of at least part of the GRU's reports."

Gromov opened his folder in anticipation. Although his mind was still clouded by illusions, Milyutin appeared ready to accede to the inevitable.

"There is one thing that troubles me deeply, General Gromov."

Gromov stared at the president without raising his head, his steel-gray eyes fixed on their target, his thick eyebrows giving him the appearance of a wolf.

"And what might that be, President Milyutin?"

"You have always reassured me Russian nuclear weapons are firmly under the control of your ministry. I have relied on those promises during discussions with the Americans. Now it appears at least a few nuclear warheads have made their way into the hands of terrorists. Perhaps your security practices are not so strict after all."

"I can assure you these warheads are not ours. We maintain a strict accounting of our inventory. There has been no change."

"And no one from the mafia bribed one of your boys to hand over a weapon?"

"Of course not, Mr. President. Absolutely impossible. If they have nuclear warheads, they acquired them from another source, most likely Iran."

"Iran? Iran doesn't have nuclear weapons."

"We believe they do, Mr. President, and we believe they provided them to one of their terrorist organizations, who in turn passed at least some of them along to Resurrected Russia."

"This is absurd. No one believes Teheran has nuclear weapons."

"No one in the West. Their intelligence services naively believe the Iranians are years away from having a nuclear capability. We have suspected otherwise for quite some time. Our friends in Baku have confirmed our suspicions."

"Why wasn't I told?"

"We tried to tell you, Mr. President."

"I don't recall—"

"We tried to tell you. Your staff interfered."

Milyutin looked helplessly at Gromov. "But it would be

insane for the Iranians to give away these weapons. They couldn't control them."

"Mr. President, we are dealing with a fundamentalist Islamic regime. They are frequently given to irrational, illogical actions. They would be willing to do anything to advance the interests of their religion and state."

"Even if it means their own destruction?"

"Irrational people do not heed the dangers of self-destruction, Mr. President. They simply act. It appears the Iranians have simply acted."

"The Americans wouldn't accept such a judgment."

"I am not briefing the Americans, President Milyutin. They can ignore reality if they choose; you cannot. By the way, did you discuss the question of the nuclear warheads with the American president?"

"No, I did not."

"I would recommend you keep it that way, Mr. President. It is better that we do not reveal our sources and capabilities to them."

"But if there's a nuclear threat to the United States?"

"We have no indication of that. The GRU reports the nuclear weapons that Resurrected Russia now possesses are intended for use within this country, not against the West."

"But why not? I thought they intended to punish all of us."

"Apparently, Mr. President, they believe you are deserving of a greater degree of punishment than your American allies."

"Our American allies, General," Milyutin corrected.

"Of course, Mr. President."

Milyutin wilted into his chair, as if beaten down by the terrible news Gromov had brought him. He rested his forehead in his palm. "I would be criminally negligent if I ignored an imminent threat to the Russian government, General Gromov. I am ready to listen. What steps do you propose to deal with this danger?"

Gromov handed a paper to Milyutin. "We must act decisively. These are the steps we recommend. You need only give your approval at the bottom, and I will direct the execution of these measures immediately. They will enable us to stamp out Resurrected Russia's neofascists and their criminal collaborators."

Milyutin's eyes widened as he slowly read through the points on the paper in front of him. "General Gromov," he finally said through tightly clenched teeth, "are you out of your mind? A declaration of martial law in Moscow would generate instant panic. Has the entire Ministry of Defense suddenly gone as insane as the leaders in Teheran? I can't accept such a step. I will never accept such a step."

Gromov had expected Milyutin's reaction. He grimly replied, "President Milyutin, you do not have much choice if you wish to deal with the threat. Only the imposition of martial law will permit the Armed Forces to take the defensive measures required to protect the city from the type of attack being planned. These people are the maniacs, Mr. President. They, not the Army, are your enemy."

"I'm not so sure, General," Milyutin answered heatedly. "Even if they are totally insane, that does not justify such an action."

"Mr. President, you have declared martial law in the past when there was a threat to the republic."

"Not in Moscow, General Gromov! It's one thing to impose military rule in a distant province; it's quite another to enforce it upon Muscovites."

"I understand your hesitation. I can see you are adamantly opposed to such a step at this time."

"At this or any time."

"I would ask that you not rule out this option completely. Things may yet come to this, Mr. President, given the nature of the threat Moscow is facing. In the interim, I propose that you approve the other precautionary measures at a minimum. These will improve the city's defenses and our ability to handle any situation that might arise. These actions can be taken very quietly, without arousing the public. They will facilitate a transition to more extreme measures if you should decide that is eventually necessary."

"I won't, I promise you. I'm even reluctant to agree to any of the other moves you've suggested here. Moving additional airborne divisions closer to Moscow may generate the same level of anxiety as a declaration of martial law. However, if I fail to do anything and Moscow is attacked by these lunatics, I'm certain the Defense Ministry will be more than happy to point out my shortcomings. Is that a correct assumption on my part, General Gromov?"

Gromov did not respond. He simply stared into Milyutin's eyes until the president looked away.

"Just keep the airborne troops as far away from the city and as discreet as possible until they're needed."

"Of course, Mr. President."

Milyutin studied Gromov's face for a moment, then gently shook his head, picked up his pen, and drew a heavy line through the offending paragraph in Gromov's paper. He made a few other minor adjustments to the text, signed the paper with a flourish, and handed it back to Gromov.

"You will present this at the next meeting of the Security Council," Milyutin ordered. "There will be an uproar over the martial law proposal. The council will be as opposed to this idea as I am, even when it's presented as a last resort. There will quite likely be bitter disagreement with the other measures, but," Milyutin smiled, "my signature should be sufficient to overcome their opposition."

"I will be prepared for the meeting. With your approval, we will go ahead and issue the order to the affected units to prepare for deployment."

"Yes, yes, go ahead," Milyutin replied, eager to conclude the meeting. "But they are not to move to their new locations until the Security Council has approved. Understood?"

"Of course, Mr. President."

"God help us all, General. And if God is charitable, your GRU has its facts all wrong."

"Even God's charity cannot overcome the truth, Mr. President," Gromov responded as he stuffed his papers back into the folder. He made a little bow and walked quickly out of the office, permitting himself a smile as he closed the door behind him.

Chapter Twenty-five

"I'm not entirely certain I'm ready for this." Younghart looked at Williams somewhat plaintively, as if hoping he would tell her the meeting was unnecessary.

He stared straight ahead, guiding the car through the evening traffic of downtown Washington. "Listen, you're the big bad-ass FBI agent who's afraid of nothing, remember? You faced down a speeding car, for God's sake. I'm pretty sure you can handle one skittish Air Force intelligence colonel. Believe me, from what I've seen of him, he's not going to be a challenge."

"You, of course, have missed the point completely, Blair. I'm not concerned about how to handle the questions. I'm concerned about confronting someone with whom I was involved a long time ago. Someone in whom I invested a lot of time and emotion. Someone who walked out on me, you remember?"

"Oh."

"Oh. Looks like you forgot what I told you on the plane."

252

Williams grinned sheepishly and touched his forehead with his fingertips. "Must be this head injury. I'm having trouble staying focused."

"More likely you've been thinking about how soon you can get to a phone and call Erica."

"Well, yes, the thought had crossed my mind. Damn!" He slammed on the breaks to avoid a car that suddenly veered across two lanes and ended up right in front of them, waiting to make an illegal left-hand turn. He eased around the offending vehicle, giving the driver the dirtiest look he could muster, while trying to avoid being rear-ended by other traffic. Unfortunately, the errant driver was busy waiting for an opening so he could challenge the oncoming traffic at just the right moment.

"Give me St. Louis traffic any day. The drivers here are totally nuts."

"You want me to take over? You seem to be having problems."

"I'll manage, Agent Younghart, thank you very much. Anyway, you were saying about our upcoming session with Underwood? By the way, couldn't we have chosen a better rendezvous than the Pentagon parking lot?"

Younghart peeled her fingers off the dashboard and settled back into the seat. "It's where he insisted on meeting. According to Harper, he wanted to meet someplace where he could ensure he wasn't being followed or watched."

"So we're going to be sitting in the middle of North Parking? As if no one can see us from there."

"We'll stop just long enough to pick him up, then you're going to take us somewhere else."

Williams frowned and stole a sidelong glance at her. "And when were you going to tell me about this little detour?"

"I just did," she snapped. She shook her head and reached over and patted his arm. "I'm sorry, Blair. This whole business is really making me tense."

"Yeah, I know. You're thinking, 'Of all the terrorist plots in all of the world, why did Underwood have to walk into this one?' "

She smiled back. "You're right."

"Carolyn?"

"Yes."

"You'll do fine. You'll handle this like the professional you are. Trust me. Underwood's not worth all the turmoil you're putting yourself through."

She smiled. "Believe me, I know that better than anyone else. Thanks, Blair."

"For what?"

"For listening."

"You're welcome. We'll be there in five minutes. Time to make sure your gun's loaded."

"Don't tempt me."

"I'm not sure I'm ready for this."

Harper looked at Underwood, trying to make out his expression in the darkness. "Colonel?"

"I'm not sure this is a good idea. I'm just not comfortable with this, with telling someone else. I'm not sure this is worth the risk."

"Look, sir. We've been over this. You can't handle this situation by yourself. Where do you think you're going to go with this information? I've tried to make it clear that my organization can't handle this alone. This is a bit bigger than the OSI. Unless we get the FBI involved, there will be zero chance to get your wife back and nail these guys."

"If I'd kept my mouth shut and cooperated with them, she would have been safe."

"Colonel, you know and I know that's just plain crap. You were absolutely right to think you would both be dispensable after you'd served your purpose. This is the only way. I think you know that. You'll feel better about this once you meet Special Agent Younghart. The waiting is what's making you antsy. Trust me."

Harper looked up as a car pulled into their row in the parking lot. It made its way slowly down the aisle, then turned in two spaces away from them, its lights briefly illuminating Harper and Underwood. Underwood looked about nervously, wondering if they'd been spotted by anyone. *Stop being paranoid.* Then he told himself that he had every reason to be paranoid, given the circumstances. He froze in panic as he watched two figures emerge from the parked car.

"What the hell is going on here?" he asked, trying to keep his voice down and his sudden anger under control. "I expected *one* FBI agent, no more. Suddenly, I'm dealing with an army. You're really starting to piss me off, Harper."

"Colonel, I have no idea who's with her. I wasn't expecting anyone else either. But we've gone this far—let's find out what's going on before you jump to any conclusions."

"You want to tell me how I can reach any other conclusion when there's more than one person standing outside the damned car?"

"Colonel, please, relax. Wait here. I'll try to find out what's going on." Harper quickly climbed out and headed toward the other car.

Underwood fought the urge to bolt from the scene and head toward the Pentagon bus stop.

Harper held up his hand in a stop signal as he walked toward Younghart and Williams.

"Good evening, Marty," Younghart said softly, extending her hand. "Why the hasty exit from the car?"

"Evening, Carolyn," Harper responded as he shook her hand. "We need to talk. The first thing you need to do is introduce me to your companion, because right now I've got a very nervous individual on my hands. He was under the impression, and so was I, that you were coming alone. I thought we had discussed the need to keep the numbers down."

"We did, and I have. I'm sorry if you got the wrong idea, Marty, but I really had no intention of doing this on my own. I'm sorry if I misled you. Anyway, this is Colonel Blair Williams, from the U.S. Transportation Command."

Harper shook Williams's hand, but his face bore an expression of total incomprehension. He looked first at Williams, then at Younghart. "Colonel, I'm pleased to meet you, but I'm completely mystified as to why you're here and what business any of this is to your command."

Williams turned to Younghart. "Carolyn, it would appear this was a bad idea. If you want me to wait here while you talk to Underwood, I'll understand. I'll keep out of the way. I don't want to screw this up."

Younghart listened to the brief interchange, her agitation growing. Finally, frustrated, she rounded on Harper. "Look, Marty, you called me, as you and I know you should have. This is not a matter for just the OSI." She looked at Williams. "Oh, Lord, am I going to have to go through this again? What is it with you people?" Turning back to Harper, she continued in a loud whisper, while angrily pointing at the car bearing Underwood. "Who the hell does this guy think he is? He comes to you with a story of a terrorist threat to the United States, to the White House, and he's trying to make a deal over how much he's going to tell us and how many can be involved? Excuse me, he's still wearing a uniform, isn't he? He's damned well going to tell us everything he knows, or I'll make things extremely uncomfortable for him. He needs to understand he's not in a bargaining position. From this point on I'm calling the shots, understand? Colonel Williams is here because I invited him. He has a right to be here, for reasons which I'll explain later, but suffice it to say he's been working with me from the beginning on a related investigation, and I intend to involve him in this one. Now, if you'll wait here with the colonel, I'll go say hello to an old friend. And if you or the OSI have any more problems with that, I'll be happy to let you talk to the director."

Harper watched wide-eyed as she walked over to the car, yanked open the door, and climbed inside.

Williams chuckled as he looked at the stunned Harper. "She's a pip, ain't she? Looks like she got over her jitters about seeing this guy again."

Harper turned, confused. "She knows him?"

"You could say that. Would you like to join me in my car for a chat? This could take a while, knowing Agent Younghart. So tell me, how long have you worked for OSI?"

Totally flustered, Harper mumbled something in response as Williams guided him toward the open door.

*　　*　　*

Underwood had retreated into the corner formed by the passenger door and seat as soon as Carolyn yanked open the door. Their eyes met briefly in the moment the overhead light came on. Now she sat silhouetted by the parking lot lights, her eyes glaring back at him. Her clothes ruffled as she shifted in the seat, squaring herself in his direction. She could hear his rapid breathing, and she felt a momentary satisfaction from knowing she was the source of his apparent panic.

She had been prepared to jump down his throat, but she had gathered her wits and checked her anger as she sat down next to him. She thought about how good it would feel to pop him right in the face and smiled in the darkness. How about just punching him in the upper arm? She smiled again. Finally, she took several deep breaths and jumped in.

"So here we are. I understand you have something to tell me?"

"I don't understand," he replied.

"What don't you understand, Colonel Underwood? I was told some terrorists have kidnapped your wife and are planning some type of operation, probably in Washington. I'm here to find out what you know and see what the Bureau can do to get your wife out of danger and prevent the terrorists from carrying out their plans. Was I misinformed?"

"I really don't understand why you're acting this way."

"I'm not acting in any way. I'm here to ensure your cooperation in this investigation. The first step is for you to tell me what you know."

"Carolyn, can we please cut the tough-cop bullshit? Unless my memory has failed me altogether, I thought we were involved once. I haven't seen or talked to you in years. Suddenly, out of the blue, you drop back into my life at the worst possible moment. And all you can do is start interrogating me. No 'Hello, how are you?' Look, I know I was a total horse's ass for what I did, but can you at least talk to me as if you know me? What good does this do either one of us?"

She sat quietly for a moment, then replied, "Hello, Mike.

How have you been since Guam? I'd really like to hear what you've been up to since we last saw each other, but I'm afraid we've got more important issues to deal with. There. Does that make you feel better? What else would you like me to say? This is not a social call, Mike. I wasn't exactly elated to hear that you were the one involved in this."

"So why didn't you back out?"

"And why should I? What would you like me to tell you? That my life has been miserable since you left? That there's been no one else since you? Would that stroke your male ego the right way? Mike, you were a total shit, but I got over it. I doubt you ever will. Anyway, I'd already told Harper I'd work this matter before he dropped his little bombshell about your identity. As it turns out, your problems are related to a matter I'm already investigating."

"I wasn't thrilled either," he admitted. "I tried to talk Harper out of involving anybody else, any other agency. I feel very uncomfortable right now."

"I can understand that. You have every reason to feel uncomfortable." *You son of a bitch*, she added silently as she looked at the shadow of the Pentagon.

"I'm the first to admit I acted like a total son of a bitch." The comment made her turn back toward him. "I can only say I'm sorry. I should have told you my situation before we got involved."

"Your *situation*?" she blurted out, incredulous. "My God, Mike, you were married. That's a bit more than a *situation*, don't you think?"

"I was going through some tough times. I still am."

She rolled her eyes. "Tell me, Mike, do men always feel compelled to say this to justify their behavior? You ever heard of working out your problems before you decide to drag others into them?" She turned in her seat to face forward, resting her hands on the steering wheel as she continued. "Listen, I really don't want to talk about what went on between us. It's done. I made a mistake. You made an even bigger one. Your *situation* hasn't changed, and frankly, I really don't care if it has. You can deal with your personal problems on your own time, and maybe you'll fix them someday. Right now, you have some problems that affect others in a very real way, and like it or not, my job is to try and fix *those*. I trust we can both act like adults and get on with it, okay?"

Underwood started to say something, then stopped. He reached out and touched her arm. "You still look good, Carolyn. I've thought about you a lot since Guam."

She yanked her arm away. "Good God, what the hell's wrong with you? Christ Almighty! It was over years ago, you poor dumb bastard. Stuff it back in your pants. If you weren't up to your eyeballs in this mess, I wouldn't even be talking to you. So keep your goddamned hands to yourself, or I'll break your arms. Got it?"

Underwood had retreated once again into the corner. "Okay," he replied weakly. "Okay. I'll behave." Then he sat up straight and said, "Just to set the record straight, I still don't like the growing numbers of people involved. I'm taking a chance, because if anything goes wrong, they'll end up killing my wife."

She resisted the temptation to ask him if that really bothered him. "Listen," she said, her voice softening, "at this point, you have no choice. As soon as I became involved, the terms were no longer yours to dictate, if they ever were. Don't you know you have a responsibility, wearing that uniform, to cooperate as fully as you can? I know there's a very real risk to your wife, but let me be very blunt, there's no guarantee of her safety even if you do cooperate completely with them."

"Don't you think I know that? Why do you think I came here? If I thought I could protect her by shutting up, I wouldn't be here, and neither would you. You think about that."

"It's good you know the risks. Knowing the risks, however, should convince you more than ever of the need to help me out on this. I need to know everything—and I do mean everything—that you know. Believe me, I share your desire to limit the number of people involved. I can take care of the Bureau, but you have to assure me that you'll help in every way possible. I don't want you telling me, when the crunch comes, that there's something you won't do. This is my area of expertise. You have to trust my judgment and my instincts. Is that understood? Anything less than your full assistance can endanger your wife. And I don't think you'd find the results if you fail to cooperate very pleasant, either. Understood and agreed?"

Underwood frowned. "You're a tough bargainer, Carolyn. Do I have a choice?"

"You're damned right I am, and you don't," she replied firmly.

"So tell me. Who's the other guy? Do I have to worry about him and how much he's going to tell others?"

"You already know him. His name is Blair Williams. He works at TRANSCOM."

Underwood laughed softly. "God, it really is a small world. Any other blasts from the past going to be turning up? Why is he involved in this? What do those guys care about some fanatics trying to threaten the Russian and American governments?"

"Because those fanatics apparently stole some cruise missiles off a TRANSCOM ship. We think those missiles are the centerpiece of your new friends' scheme. That's what we have to find out. That's where your access to them becomes very important if we're to find out what they're up to."

"I doubt they're going to let me in on exactly what they're planning."

"Certainly not, unless they're stupid, and I doubt that very much. But they may pass you enough bits and pieces that, if we put them together with what we know, we can figure out the big picture. That's what we have to hope for, anyway. And maybe those bits and pieces will give us some clue to the whereabouts of your wife."

"That would be nice."

"Are you sure?" She knew she should regret the question, but she didn't.

"And what do you mean by that?" he asked, a touch of anger in his voice.

"Just curious, Mike, about why you're really in this. You mention you're still having troubles, and I assumed you meant with your wife. Just a moment ago, you tried to come on to me. I was just wondering—"

"Look, I may not be on the best of terms with Jennifer. By the way, that's her name. See, I do remember her name. We're not getting along all that great. We haven't in a long time. But that doesn't mean I don't care about what happens to her. Do you think I want to get her killed, for God's sake? Who the hell do you think you are, asking me a question like that?"

Younghart held up her hand in an effort to stop his tirade. "Sorry. Just checking."

"That's a hell of a way to check. Do you intend to do your best to piss me off during your little interrogation of me? If so, you're off to a great start."

"I'll do my best not to ask any more antagonistic questions. And I prefer to call it an interview, not an interrogation. You're not being accused of anything, Mike. But, like I said, I need to know everything."

"And I'll do my best to see that you do. Just back off, all right? My mind's already swarming with doubts about whether any of this is going to turn out the way I hoped. And believe me, you're not helping."

"I think we both understand each other's concerns. Having cleared the air, can we press on to the interview? If you and Harper will follow us, we'll take you to a secure location."

She reached out to shake his hand. He hesitated for a second, then grasped her hand in his.

"Let go, Mike," she said with irritation as she pulled her hand away. She quickly exited the car.

"So how did it go?" Williams asked her after she and Harper had exchanged places.

"Just peachy," she responded dryly. "We're fast friends again."

"Uh-huh."

Chapter Twenty-six

"So this is all he gave you? These are the codes you're supposed to use when he contacts you?"

"Yes," Underwood replied glumly. He was tired. They had been going at this for over three hours. It was long after midnight. He had told them everything he could possibly remember. "Don't you think we'd better call it a night? Aren't they going to get a little suspicious if I don't return home until very late? We don't want to blow this for something so stupid."

Younghart looked at Harper and Williams, who both nodded. She handed the papers back to Underwood. "You're probably right. I think we all lost track of the time. Before we go, however, tell me one more time—"

Underwood groaned and twisted in the chair.

"Tell me one more time," Younghart began again. "You've no idea when he will contact you?"

"That's what the man said, and that hasn't changed since the last time you asked me that question. But I'll call you as soon as possible once he does call me."

"Just make sure you do so from the White House."

"Yes, yes, of course. Please, can I go home now? I'm exhausted, and I don't want to show up for work tomorrow looking like I'm at death's door."

"You're clear on what to tell him when he does call."

"Again, yes, okay? If he calls, I tell him the truth, although I don't see how that's going to protect anyone."

"We'll take care of that when we need to."

Underwood's head cleared for a moment. Her answer had made him suspicious. "And how are you going to do that?"

"With the help of the Secret Service." She had answered very deliberately while staring straight into his eyes, as if anticipating another angry outburst.

Instead, he simply shrugged. "I give up. You people are going to do whatever you want, regardless of what I think." He turned to Harper. "It will truly be a cold day in hell before I come to you about anything again. And the rest of you, you can all *go* to hell as far as I'm concerned."

"You would propose we leave the president, or whoever, unprotected?" Williams asked.

"Of course not, but why can't I just lie about Noonan's schedule? How's Evans going to find out?"

Younghart shook her head. "And what if you're not their only contact in the White House? Have you considered that?"

"I doubt that. Evans clearly left the impression that I was their stroke of good fortune."

"Or so he wanted you to believe," Harper said.

Underwood shot him a look. "I doubt it. But have it your way. I just want to go home. Are you going to invite the Boy Scouts in before this is all over?"

"Only if necessary, Mike," Younghart answered with a sympathetic smile.

"And how are you going to locate Jennifer in the middle of all this?"

"I think it's safe to say we'll be following Mr. Evans's activities very closely over the next several days. And his home will be less of a haven than he thinks."

"Meaning you're going to have him followed and his phones tapped." Underwood dropped his head into his hands. "And if he gets suspicious, or finds out he's being watched?"

"Unlikely." Younghart said it with such self-assurance that Underwood was almost convinced. "But if we do nothing, I doubt we'll ever find out where they're keeping her. It's riskier for her if we do nothing. Trust me, Mike, I don't want anything to happen to her either. It's just as much my desire as yours to get her back safely."

"I'm done," Underwood announced as he pushed himself out of the chair. "Agent Harper, I would be most appreciative of a ride back to my car before the Alexandria police have it towed away. I bid the rest of you a good night. Blair, good seeing you again. Although I'm still not entirely certain what your role is in all of this, I appreciate your help and concern."

"Not a problem, Mike. And believe me, I'd be a lot happier if I weren't involved. Younghart just keeps dragging me along, though. Probably for the entertainment factor."

Underwood managed a weak smile as he shook Williams's hand. He turned, looked into Younghart's eyes for a moment, looking for something, and, not finding it, headed for the door. "Let's go, Harper. I hear a bed calling my name."

28 August, 0950 hours EDT

"Good morning, Colonel Underwood. This is Josh Evans. Hope you're having a good day. Sorry I missed you this morning."

Underwood had recognized the voice immediately. His only response was a barely audible grunt.

"I wanted to firm up our plans for our get-together, but I wanted to make certain everyone would be available. We need to ensure your uncle is included in the festivities, since he missed out the last time, and he's always been the life of the party. Tell me, will he be available next Wednesday, in the afternoon?"

Underwood glanced at the calendar lying on his desk.

"Looks like he'll be home all day, staying in his workshop."

"Excellent. Give him my best. We're looking forward to showing him a good time. I'll talk to you soon."

Underwood waited a few moments, then picked up the phone and dialed the number Younghart had given him. She answered after a few rings.

"He called. One week. The White House. The president. Details to follow."

"Thanks, Mike. The rest of what we discussed last night will be in place by the end of the day. As soon as I hear or know anything, I'll give you a call."

"Thanks." Underwood replaced the receiver, his hand trembling. He placed his other hand on top of it to steady it, then gazed out the window. Normally, he would appreciate the beauty and grandeur of the White House grounds, or at least the part he could see from his office. But not today. He had reached the pinnacle, and now circumstances forced him to be all but oblivious to the trappings of power he had fought so long to garner.

Chapter Twenty-seven

29 August, 1320 hours Local

A very excited Dmitriy Pankratov dashed up the stairs to the second-story flat. He rapped on the door, waiting impatiently for a response.

"Yes," the answer came after a seeming eternity.

"It's me, Tasha. Please let me in."

She opened the door wide, appearing naked before him. He stood there dumbly for a moment, startled by her display of openness, his throat suddenly dry. Her closely cropped jet-black hair framed a perfectly chiseled face. Her muscular body still dripped from the shower she had obviously just left. His eyes moved slowly up her body, coming to rest on eyes as black as the Chechen night that had spawned her.

He stepped through the door, kicking it shut with his boot. He grabbed both her arms and pulled her toward him, crushing his mouth against hers. As his lips then traced a path across her cheek to her ear, he whispered, "You were— no, you *are*—magnificent, my darling Amazon."

"And you *will* be," she murmured as she grabbed him by the tie and led him through the apartment.

Crisis Point

29 August, 0800 hours EDT

"Good morning, General Hannah."

The chairman of the Joint Chiefs nodded to the briefer to begin.

"Sir, our first item concerns the recent troop movements in and around Moscow. This briefing will present additional details to those the J2 provided you early this morning regarding the scope of activity."

The briefer signaled for the first set of slides. There were murmurs in the Tank as the first graphic displayed several divisions deployed around the Russian capital. An accompanying photograph showed an obviously large military unit at an airfield near Moscow. Rumors had been circulating inside the Pentagon all morning in the wake of a CNN item that first reported the ongoing activity by Russian airborne and armored forces.

"At this time, all Russian airborne divisions are at their highest state of alert. Three of these divisions, with all of their equipment, are now deployed at the military airfields surrounding the Moscow city center. These are the 76th, 103rd, and 105th Guards Airborne Divisions. In addition, the Tamanskaya Tank Division, shown in the next photo, is preparing to move out of garrison. We believe elements of this division will deploy to the center of Moscow. There has been no announcement by the Russian Ministry of Defense as to the reasons for these movements, but they are almost certainly related to the threats of terrorist activity by the group known as Resurrected Russia, which you were briefed about on Monday. There is no indication of any unusual activity by the Russian president and his staff. President Milyutin has scheduled a news conference for 1000 hours, Eastern Daylight Time, to be carried live by the U.S. news networks."

"Any indications that a declaration of martial law may be imminent?" Hannah asked.

"No, sir, not at this time. We have been talking to our counterparts at Langley and they do have some reporting on that issue. Members of Milyutin's personal staff have been adamant that martial law will not be declared in Moscow. However, when our attaché approached the Russian MOD on this question, Ministry of Defense staffers did not rule out the possibility."

"I would think that's to be expected," Hannah rejoined. "The Russian military is going to be much less sanguine about the threat posed by these whackos." The Service chiefs smiled at the chairman's characterization of the terrorists and nodded.

"Yes, sir, that's our read on the situation. Sir, I'll continue if you have no further comments or questions."

"Go ahead."

"While the bulk of the activity has been centered on Moscow, MOD communications nets have been very active. The Airborne, or VDV nets, have been continuously active for the past thirty-six hours, as have those of the VTA, or Military Transport Aviation. Given the level of airborne activity in Moscow, that's to be expected. What is unusual is the level of communications activity between the MOD and the headquarters of the military districts. In addition, most other units of the armed forces appear to be moving to a higher state of alert, probably as a precautionary move to deal with any expanded threat by the terrorists."

"You're telling me that in order to deal with a reported threat to the Russian capital, the entire Russian military is moving to a higher state of alert? What about the Strategic Rocket Forces?"

"Normal day-to-day status. No indication of an increased alert there at all. SRF communications have been routine throughout this period. The focus of all this activity is clearly on internal security to deal with the terrorist threat."

"You know, Major, in the bad old days, DIA and the rest of the community would be talking military coup. I don't see anyone suggesting that today. You're quite certain there's no hidden motive behind these troop movements?"

The briefer hesitated for a moment and glanced at the J2, General Norbert, as if looking for help. The general said nothing. Finally, the briefer continued.

"General Hannah, given the lack of alarm on the part of

the civil authorities and the CIA reporting, we believe that President Milyutin has given his full approval to the steps being undertaken. Relations between the Russian presidency and the MOD have been amazingly quiescent over the past few years. The transition toward Russian democracy has continued unabated, and the government has strongly asserted civilian control over the military at every opportunity, reversing the trend under Yeltsin. While problems remain, the two sides appear to have worked out an acceptable *modus vivendi*. We consider the possibility of a coup attempt to be extremely remote."

"Major, that was a most erudite response," Hannah said with the slightest hint of a smile. "Obviously, you folks anticipated the question. Commend Dr. Morehain for her splendid analysis. I think she'll be pleased to know that in this particular instance I happen to agree with her conclusions."

A look of relief passed across the major's face.

"However, let's keep looking, shall we? It's one thing to sit here convinced that nothing is going to happen. I don't want to be surprised, and I know the secretary doesn't want to be either. Keep looking." Hannah looked in the direction of Norbert, who nodded vigorously.

Hannah leaned back in his swivel chair. "For the benefit of all those here," he began, "we were briefed much the same situation at the White House yesterday afternoon. They also discounted the possibility of a coup attempt and stressed the terrorist threat as the reason for what's going on in Moscow. That was a good thing, because the president told everyone after the briefing that he had been in contact with Milyutin just a short time before. The Russian president wanted to assure our side that this activity was intended as a response to the terrorist threat, and in no way represented a threat to the rest of Europe or his country's solid relationship with the United States. Major, you can tuck that in your back pocket, and Kurt, you can pass that along to the DIA director. Otherwise, that information stays in this room until the White House decides otherwise."

"General Hannah, if I could ask a follow-up question to

that." The Army chief of staff leaned forward in his chair and rested his arms on the conference table. "Did President Milyutin offer any explanation why four divisions are necessary to deal with a reported terrorist attack? This many troops seems a bit of overkill."

"President Noonan conveyed nothing along those lines," Hannah answered. "You're right, however. This is an unusually large number of troops. The only thing I can offer, pending Milyutin's explanation later this morning, is uncertainty over the scope, direction, and precise nature of the attack. I would say Milyutin and Gromov are hedging their bets. More likely than not, Gromov pushed for deploying such overwhelming force. He strikes me as being extraordinarily cautious, unwilling to leave anything to chance."

"Better to err on the side of prudence than let a bunch of terrorists run amok in the middle of Moscow. I'd probably want to do the same if I had the numbers," the Marine Corps commandant said.

"General," Hannah responded immediately, "I don't know if that was a vote of endorsement for Gromov's action or a plea for more people for the Corps." Hannah's comment elicited a round of laughter. The commandant, his face reddening, gave the chairman a rueful smile.

Hannah directed his attention back toward the briefer. "Major, we've sort of left you hanging while we discussed the implications of everything you've just told us. I'm sure you have loads more of excruciating detail to pass along to us about all this military activity. You folks usually do. Why don't we press ahead so we can all get out of here in time to listen to the Russian president?"

29 August, 1415 hours Local

Pankratov gazed serenely at the ceiling as Tasha wove her fingers through the mat of hair on his chest.

"Are you sure you're not just a little bit of a Chechen?" she asked.

"Why? Would it make a difference?"

"Of course not, my love."

"Perhaps it would make a difference to your father."

She jumped up from the bed. "That reminds me. He wishes to meet with you regarding the delivery of the American merchandise."

Pankratov propped himself up on one elbow and watched her as she tugged on a top. "Is there a problem? I thought everything was agreed. Your father knows where to deliver the canisters, and the payment has been made. You confirmed that."

"You know my father. He doesn't want any loose ends," she grunted softly as she pulled on her expensive Western boots.

Pankratov's confusion grew. "Loose ends? I don't know what you mean."

"I can't explain it, my love. You'll have to talk with him. He wants you to meet him at the usual location this evening. At 1800 hours. You can be there?" She put her hands on her hips and stared at him, almost defiantly.

He flopped back in the bed and draped an arm across his forehead. "Of course I'll be there."

Tasha leaned over and gave him a peck on the forehead. "That's my good little Russian major. I must go. You can let yourself out. I'll see you later."

"Of course." He peered at her from under his arm, smiling uncertainly.

As she shut the apartment door, Pankratov put his hands over his eyes and slowly shook his head. *What kind of shit is Izrailov up to now?* he wondered.

29 August, 1700 hours Local

Gromov, smiling serenely, was waiting patiently with members of the presidential staff for Milyutin to make his appearance before the cameras. The Russian and international press corps were noisily assembling in the conference room, waiting for the cue to be quiet from Milyutin's press spokesman. Snatches of conversation could be heard as correspondents exchanged stories about the soldiers seen or reported to be moving about the capital city. The room was rife with rumors. Some clearly hoped the Russian president would confirm their speculations; others were determined to press ahead with their stories regardless of Milyutin's comments, convinced they were not about to hear the full story of what was going on. Their minds had already been made up in any event. The international cable news organizations were camped near the front of the auditorium, their equipment and numbers clearly intimidating to their Russian colleagues, who scrambled for priority seating to hear firsthand what was going on in their own country.

The door opened suddenly and Milyutin entered the room with a rush, accompanied by the sound of flashing cameras and the rustle of bodies trying to crowd yet closer to the stage. He quickly stepped behind the podium, cleared his throat, and began speaking without introduction.

"Ladies and gentlemen, my fellow citizens of Russia, I come before you this afternoon to inform you of measures your government is taking to deal with an unprecedented threat to our nation's security." His face, already a mask of extreme seriousness, grew even darker. "It is my desire to reassure all of you in regard to these measures, for there have been many erroneous reports in the Russian and particularly in the foreign press about what is going on in our country. There must be no misunderstanding regarding our intentions." Milyutin stabbed his finger at the camera lens for emphasis. He gripped the sides of the podium as he continued. "An extremist organization calling itself Resurrected Russia claims to have stolen missiles manufactured in a foreign country and warns it will use these weapons to conduct an attack upon Moscow unless we accede to its demands, demands which are outrageous and therefore totally unacceptable. Their attempt at blackmail amounts to nothing less than a reversal of your country's peaceful foreign policy, from a policy of cooperation to confrontation and distrust."

Milyutin's expression grew softer, more reassuring. "Unfortunately, we cannot dismiss the threat posed by this group. Our security services are actively engaged in tracking down these terrorists and thwarting their plans to hold your government hostage. In order to safeguard Moscow, I have instructed the minister of defense to move several military units closer to the city. These units will provide additional protection until these terrorists and their weapons are captured. I have informed Russia's friends and allies of these steps. They fully support our actions. Several have offered assistance in dealing with the terrorist threat, and we will gratefully accept these offers where appropriate. All necessary resources will be devoted to ending this threat to our security and to rooting out the members of Resurrected Russia and bringing them to swift justice."

He smiled gently and assumed the tone of a father trying to reassure his children. "I ask for your patience during this difficult period. I ask you as citizens to be especially vigilant and report any unusual activity to your local militia or the Ministry of Defense. Call the telephone numbers displayed on your television to contact either one of these organizations if you believe you have information that may assist them in their efforts to capture these criminals. I do not want to overstate the threat posed by this group. Neither do I wish to diminish it. But be assured that we are doing everything in our power to ensure the safety of our citizenry, and we will do all that is required to protect Moscow and the rest of Russia. May God watch over our homeland. Thank you and good night."

Milyutin left as abruptly as he entered, ignoring the chorus of shouted questions that erupted as soon as he had finished speaking.

Gromov stepped to the podium and signaled abruptly for quiet. "Ladies and gentlemen. The president has asked that the Ministry of Defense provide you additional information on the steps being taken to ensure Moscow's security. We will provide that information when appropriate." He wheeled and left.

The room was eerily quiet as reporters and cameramen looked at one another questioningly, almost in a daze. The false serenity quickly gave way to chaos as correspondents scrambled to offer their commentary and analysis on what had just transpired. Others surged toward the stage, hoping to wring additional information from the few presidential

Ken Currie

staff members who had made the mistake of lingering behind after Milyutin's departure. Milyutin's press spokesman made his escape through a side door, stunned. All he could do was mutter, "*Bozhe moy, bozhe moy.*" My God, my God.

In the Oval Office, National Security Adviser Christoph pronounced his judgment on Milyutin's news conference as the president switched off the monitor. "Well, I know if I were a Russian, I'd sleep a lot better tonight," he wise-cracked.

Noonan shook his head in response. "I've no idea what he was thinking. He's told the terrorists he's coming after them, and he's told the Muscovites they might have to bend over and kiss their butts goodbye. Naïveté, inexperience. Maybe both. Milyutin better hope God is watching over them, because he's just dared the terrorists to make good on their threat."

In the Pentagon, the secretary of defense switched off his television and turned toward General Hannah. "What do you think?"

"Strangest performance I've ever seen. I think Milyutin just guaranteed himself a very dicey situation. One thing, Gromov's made it very clear who's in charge of Moscow's security for the duration of this crisis. I think we're going to have to watch this very closely. This is not quite what I expected."

"Not at all," the secretary agreed. "I think I'd better call the president. While I'm doing that, please stick your head out the door and tell my exec to get the J2 up here. The three of us need to sit down together and try to sort this out."

Chapter Twenty-eight

29 August, 1030 hours EDT

"I still don't get the need for all this damned secrecy, Kuhl-mann," Malloy said. "My ground crews trained your personnel, no questions asked. I agreed to keep my people out of the cargo area during loading. The cargo compartment will be sealed until opened by your folks in Washington. I even gave you your choice of our flight crews." Malloy grimaced. "Some asshole at Commerce Europa insisted I grant even that request. You really should be using one of my crews, but I guess I don't have much say anymore."

Malloy stared out his office window. "All these conditions," he continued, "while I'm trying to prepare for the first flight of the charter service. You're jeopardizing the schedule. I've half a mind to cancel the passenger flight and let you haul your own goddamned cargo. That'd be difficult, however, since I don't seem to be in charge of my own airline."

Malloy puffed furiously on his cigar, as if gathering a head of steam to charge the individual seated in front of him.

275

Kuhlmann shifted in his chair, pushing it farther away from Malloy's desk, as if expecting just such a move. "I think you're exaggerating just a bit, Mr. Malloy. I've apologized repeatedly for the inconvenience, but I assure you this is the last request we'll make. We won't interfere with any of your other operations for the charter flight. We want the passenger portion of this flight to go as smoothly and successfully as you do. It's not our desire to cause you any problems in that regard. We know how important this flight is to you. But we must be certain that our cargo arrives in Washington in perfect operating condition, because it will be transported to the trade show almost immediately."

"All this fuss over a supercomputer. You'd think you'd discovered time travel," Malloy said impatiently, continuing to fume.

"I've asked you not to talk about the cargo. I trust you haven't told anyone else? This machine is revolutionary. It will create a sensation in Washington, and we don't want to spoil the big surprise. You should consider yourself part of a momentous occasion. In a very big way, you've made it possible for us to carry out our plans. I think once you've read about the impact our device will have, you'll be as excited as we are."

"I seriously doubt it. So tell me, when does this precious computer of yours arrive?"

"It's on its way as we speak. It should be here in a few hours. Once it arrives, our technicians will move very quickly. You'll be able to keep to your flight schedule. We guarantee it."

"We'll see."

"Besides, I think you would agree you've been paid very well indeed for your company's services? You did manage to extract a substantial surcharge from us, didn't you?"

Malloy pondered Kuhlmann's point for a moment. He slightly relaxed the scowl he had worn all morning. "There is that," he conceded. "That *has* helped." His frown deepened again. "However, one could argue the fees you paid are the least you could do for reducing me to a eunuch in my own company."

Kuhlmann laughed. "In a few days this will all be over. We'll be out of your hair forever. We won't cause you any more problems. No more disruptions of your routine. Listen, I know we've demanded a lot, but I want you to know how much my corporation appreciates the excellent assistance you've provided. I trust we can part on friendly terms as true business colleagues. Hopefully, we can send more business your way." Kuhlmann stood up and held out his hand.

"Please don't," Malloy replied as he grudgingly shook Kuhlmann's hand and bit down hard on his cigar. He promptly withdrew his hand, once again fighting the queasiness he felt every time he dealt with Kuhlmann.

Chapter Twenty-nine

29 August, 1800 hours Local

Major Pankratov waited impatiently for the other car to show. He had been sitting in his personal vehicle in Ostankino Park for twenty minutes, feeling very exposed, and becoming increasingly irritated at being made to wait. He found this part of his job extremely distasteful, for he detested the man with whom he was about to meet. With any luck, he hoped, this would be the last time he would have to deal with this particular vulture. Hard to believe such a creature could father a daughter like Tasha. He looked in his rearview mirror to make sure his security escort was still parked a discreet but comforting distance away. Reassured, he lit up another American cigarette.

At that moment, two black Mercedes sedans with heavily darkened windows turned into the road and headed slowly in his direction. They stopped several yards away. After a few minutes, the driver of the lead car—significantly larger and more opulent than the other sedan—rolled down his window and nodded toward Pankratov. Pankratov stubbed out his cigarette in the ashtray, put his side arm on the floor under his seat, climbed out, and walked quickly toward the waiting automobiles. The back door silently opened, as if on its own, revealing the blackened interior. Pankratov fought back the sensation that he was peering into the maw of hell. He crawled through the opening and was greeted by the smell of expensive leather, expensive cologne, and bodies stale from too much spice. He desperately wanted another cigarette, but knew his host would not permit it, for fear of corrupting the interior of his very expensive status symbol.

"Good morning, Major." The greeting was in heavily accented Russian, so much so that Pankratov was uncertain at first whether he had understood correctly.

Pankratov responded automatically, then remained silent as his eyes grew accustomed to the darkness. Finally, he could make out the features of Aslan Izrailov. The rugged Caucasian features—dark eyes, strong nose, and luxuriant mustache—seemed to be those of the quintessential ladies' man and gadabout. Pankratov had now met with this man several times, and each time had difficulty accepting the fact he was talking to the most important—and least well-known—leader of the Chechen mafia. Izrailov affected a certain grace and elegance that belied his brutality.

Seated across from Izrailov, in the jump seat, was another Chechen, Udugov, with far less pleasant features, most prominently a large scar running from the corner of his right eye all the way to his chin. He leaned over and patted down Pankratov, breathing heavily as he did so. Assured the Russian was carrying no weapon, he sat back and folded his arms, but continued to glare threateningly. One of Izrailov's enforcers, what others in Moscow would call *khuligani*, Udugov looked as though he could snap Pankratov in two with one hand. Pankratov shuddered involuntarily, hoping the two would not notice his discomfort and fear. Even in the openness of a place such as Ostankino, Pankratov still felt extremely vulnerable.

Each time he looked into Izrailov's face, Pankratov found himself wondering how many men this outlaw had murdered, how many Russian soldiers he had butchered while serving

Ken Currie

as one of the rebel military commanders during the war in Chechnya. The battles had ended years before, but they had left deep wounds that still festered for Pankratov and other Russian officers and soldiers who had shed their blood in a futile campaign. Now he was forced to deal with one of the malefactors from that conflict, and the thought made him ill. He tried to fight the feeling by reassuring himself that this was only a temporary unholy alliance in the pursuit of a larger, noble end. Then, of course, there was Tasha. But even these thoughts were not enough to overcome his discomfort as Izrailov stared at him with dark, unblinking, malevolent eyes.

"Thank you for coming, Major, especially with such short notice. I know you're terribly busy, as am I. So I'll make this short, so you can get back to your father and I can get back to my businesses."

Pankratov fought the temptation to smirk at Izrailov's reference to his businesses. Operating out of offices in the Moskva Hotel, Izrailov directed a criminal empire of extortion, real estate speculation (or simply larceny), black marketeering in weapons and high technology, prostitution, and drugs. All those things, Pankratov sneered inwardly, that made Russian capitalism great. And soon, he knew, they would be swept away. Izrailov had unwittingly served as the instrument of his own ruin. What a wonderfully delicious end to this despicable character and all he represented.

"I understand you have questions regarding the details of the transfer."

"Transfer, Comrade Major?" Izrailov grinned at his use of the Soviet-style form of address, knowing how it irritated Pankratov and his contemporaries.

"Please, I am not your comrade, and you know perfectly what I'm talking about."

"Oh, you mean the American missiles that we acquired at your request. What a splendid operation that was. And my daughter Tasha." Izrailov smiled knowingly. "You know my daughter, don't you, Major? Can you believe such a delicate creature could manage an enterprise like that? I must tell you the particulars someday. The Americans were caught totally unaware. They were so wonderfully confident nothing could happen to their vaunted forces. It made our job so very easy. I understand they're still out there scratching around in the ocean, searching for their lost ship. As agreed, we covered our tracks pretty well. They won't know what happened for a very long time."

"Not quite true, Izrailov. They know the cruise missiles are missing."

Izrailov's smug expression disappeared as he turned back toward Pankratov. "The devil you say. And how do you know that?"

"They told us."

"Aha!" Izrailov laughed boisterously. "So they found her already. No matter. I do find it intriguing that there are no secrets anymore between your president and his good friend Noonan. So tell me, Major, do the Americans have any idea what happened to their precious weapons?"

"They seem to think they do."

"I see, but they don't really, eh? Part of Gromov's clever plan?"

Pankratov was growing impatient with this pointless chatter. "Look, Izrailov, I'm not here to talk about the Americans. We need to conclude the arrangements for the transfer of the weapons. The minister wants the missiles on their way to the French as soon as possible, as securely as possible, as we agreed. I'm assuming that's what you wanted to talk about."

"And what makes you think I intend to hand the weapons over to you or anyone else? Do you have any idea how much they would command on the international market? I already have interested buyers in several countries who are willing to beat your client's price by a substantial margin."

"What in the hell are you talking about, Izrailov?" Pankratov spat out, leaning toward Izrailov as he did so.

Udugov immediately responded, roughly pushing the officer back into his seat.

Pankratov straightened his uniform. "Please leash your pit bull, Izrailov," he said in English, knowing the mafia leader would understand what his slow-witted lackey would not.

"You know I can pose no threat to you here."

Izrailov ordered Udugov to take a walk. The enforcer reluctantly climbed out of the car, cursing the Russian under his breath while fixing him with a murderous look.

"What are you trying to get away with?" Pankratov yelled once the door closed after Udugov. "You know our deal. You've been paid. Now you turn the missiles over to us."

"I said I have better offers, Major. Besides, I may want to keep the missiles as an insurance policy."

"Against what?"

"Against Gromov doing something that might jeopardize my interests. How can I be sure he won't turn on me now that I've served his purposes? How can I trust anyone who could come up with a plan this devious? What guarantees do I have?"

"You have the minister's word."

"Ha! That and a million rubles won't buy me a bottle of vodka. Your minister's no fool, and neither am I. I'm a constant reminder of what he's done."

"Precisely, Izrailov. And that's why he won't go back on his word."

The Chechen looked at Pankratov intently, then smiled. "Very good argument, Major. Very clever. I can see why Gromov likes you. I mean, besides the fact that your father is his first deputy. You've almost convinced me. Almost. But, unfortunately, I don't think I would be very smart to hand over the missiles without some very specific guarantees from your boss that he won't interfere with my business activities."

"What type of guarantees do you have in mind?"

"Oh, decrees, making sure the Duma votes down any unfavorable laws and otherwise behaves itself, calling off the security organs."

"You already have the security services in your hip pocket. There's no challenge to you from that quarter."

"I just want to make sure there's no change to what have been very convenient arrangements, Major. I wouldn't want the Army to suddenly find morality and make life difficult for me and my business associates."

Pankratov bristled. "Don't impugn the honor of the armed

forces, Izrailov. I'm warning you. We can't be bought like Klyuchev and his henchmen. What we're doing is for the good of Russia."

"Oh, really, Major, and that's why you chose to deal with me? For the good of Russia? I'm not impressed by your injured pride, so don't waste your time. Gromov and I really want the same thing. We just call it by different names. You keep on believing in your code, if it makes you feel less guilty. I doubt Gromov is troubled by pangs of conscience."

"You have nothing in common with the minister, Izrailov," Pankratov responded angrily. "He wants to give Russia back her dignity, her pride. He's going to wash away the sewage that's corrupting her. All of the sewage, even . . ."

"Even me, Major?" Izrailov was grinning.

He had been baiting him. Pankratov knew he had been baiting him, but he had leaped anyway. He wanted to bang his head against the window out of frustration.

"I know exactly what Gromov wants to do with me," Izrailov said. "He wants to make me disappear. I'm an embarrassment, an obstacle to his plans. That's precisely why I'm keeping the missiles, just to keep your minister the honest man I'm sure he is. But who am I to question the honorable intentions of a Russian general officer, eh?"

Pankratov fought his anger, struggling for lucidity. He squeezed his hands into tight fists, forcing his fingernails into his palms, hoping the pain would restore his sharpness. Finally calm, he began weaving what he thought was a convincing scenario.

"If you sell the missiles to another country, Izrailov, the imminent threat to Moscow disappears. The Americans—and Milyutin—will focus their attention on this new threat from a renegade state. The Russian terrorists will be forgotten, the Army will go back into the barracks, and you'll get nothing."

"Nothing except business as usual, Major."

"You don't want business as usual, you want something better. You expect us to give it to you. That's why you went along with this deal. You renege on your contract with us by passing the missiles along to someone else, and you have

Ken Currie

no guarantees whatsoever. You make enemies of both us and the French."

Izrailov stared at him intently. "To hell with the French. They're no threat to me. The French are your problem. Besides, I'm certain they can find some other way to screw the Americans."

"You still have us to deal with then, Izrailov."

"Oh, my poor boy, have you forgotten what I know?"

"Tell your story. It will be seen as a fairy tale. Who in Russia is going to believe a Chechen mafia leader who's stolen American missiles and sold them to the highest bidder? They might believe your story in Groznyy, but they won't believe it in Moscow. That seems to leave you holding the bag, or should I say missiles?"

"You *are* clever, Pankratov. I'm really very impressed. So I keep the missiles. What good will that do me, correct?"

Pankratov nodded. "Correct. You can't launch them. They're no threat to anyone, except perhaps to yourselves. Your leverage, as they say, just went poof."

"Not clever enough, Major. The weapons are operational. We knew how to program them before they even fell into our hands. You'd be amazed what you can purchase on the international market. People will sell anything. It truly is a global market, Pankratov. I love the modern world, don't you? Why suddenly so quiet, Major?"

"You couldn't possibly—"

"Oh, trust me, we could and we have." Izrailov smiled. "All those unemployed scientists and engineers created by Russian capitalism? Let me tell you, they learned the meaning of the phrase 'job market' very quickly. They go to the place where the jobs are available. Russians are very intelligent people. And can you guess who offered them jobs so they could feed their families and maybe even buy a nice car and apartment?"

"It's not possible," Pankratov muttered.

"So how do you think the Russians will respond when Russian extreme nationalist terrorists fire an American cruise missile at some national treasure in Moscow, or take out their precious television tower?" Izrailov emphasized his point by gesturing over his shoulder at the Ostankino tower. "They're going to be yelling for blood. How do you think they'd respond if they found out your top military leaders were involved? Do you believe they would be more willing to believe my fairy tale then?"

Pankratov suddenly felt very warm. The car seemed to close in upon him. The smells he had noticed earlier intensified and a wave of nausea flowed through him. He placed his hand over his mouth, struggling against the urge to vomit.

"Aren't you feeling well, Major? Wait, there's more. What if those missiles were more lethal than originally designed?"

Pankratov's head cleared briefly. "You don't have nuclear warheads."

"Of course not," Izrailov responded with a laugh. "We couldn't get our hands on those if we wanted to. Actually, we do want to. Believe me, Major, we've tried. Can you imagine what those would bring on the foreign market? Unfortunately for us, this is one area where you Russian military officers *should* take pride. Your soldiers are doing a superb job. We haven't been able to come close. Too bad. No, what I'm talking about is something much more accessible, and almost as frightening to the simple citizen. You would be absolutely amazed at how easy it is—no, was—to acquire chemical warheads. Performing the necessary modifications was no challenge at all to your wonderful Russian scientists. Can you imagine the effect if one of those altered cruise missiles exploded over Moscow? Do you suppose the citizens of that great city might hang Gromov from the Kremlin wall if they found out his role in all of this? Perhaps you'll end up right beside him."

Izrailov stretched out languidly in his seat, then reached up and slowly stroked his mustache with his index finger. As he tugged gently on the tip of his mustache, he smiled broadly and asked, "So what do you think of the hand I'm holding now, Major?"

Pankratov could say nothing. He felt trapped and near panic.

"You can go back to your minister and assure him that he

285

Ken Currie

faces a very real threat. An even greater one than he imagined. That should let him do what he wants. After that, if he fails to do what I want, then we'll see what happens. I really don't see any more need to talk further. I think we understand each other now. If Gromov wants to talk about this again, tell him I expect to talk to him directly. With all due respect, Major, I'm finished talking to messenger boys. You can go now."

Izrailov dismissed Pankratov with a wave of his hand, but Pankratov didn't stop to think about the slight. He tugged frantically on the door handle, then stumbled into the evening, taking huge gulps of air. He walked unsteadily to his automobile. As he did so, he could hear the escort car starting its engine. He quickly waved the security team off, then fell into the driver's seat of his car. He looked back toward Izrailov's sedan. Udugov had returned. He gave Pankratov an obscene gesture, laughed, and clambered into the Mercedes.

As Izrailov's cars drove by slowly, Pankratov noticed a familiar face in the window of the second vehicle. Tasha flashed him a big smile, blew him a kiss, and shrugged. He felt as if he had been kicked in the groin, his nausea returning with a vengeance.

29 August, 1910 hours Local

"That black-assed bastard!" Gromov shouted as he slammed his fist down on his desk. He glared up at Pankratov. "That double-crossing, black-assed bastard. I'll kill the son of a bitch." But they both knew Gromov could do no such thing, at least not yet.

"Maybe he's bluffing, Defense Minister," Pankratov suggested.

Gromov shook his head. "No. Izrailov has the missiles. We know that. And he probably has the chemical warheads. Good God, anybody can make or buy chemical weapons. I'm sure these Chechen bastards have their sources. No, he's not bluffing. Now, the question is, what do we do about it?"

"Hadn't we better inform Milyutin?"

"For what purpose? He's already given us the authority we need. Telling him about this will just complicate things. Besides, he'll just want to ask a lot of questions. No, we'll keep the president out of this one. Out of the way." Gromov, lost in deep thought for a moment, rubbed his chin with his forefinger. "Maybe Izrailov was right. Maybe he has handed me the perfect instrument." He looked back at Pankratov. "Contact the other Moscow members of the collegium. I want to meet here in thirty minutes. Right now, I want to talk with my intelligence chief. It's time to find out if the GRU has been doing its job."

Chapter Thirty

2 September, 1100 hours EDT

Labor Day had fallen upon the capital with a brilliant blue sky and a scorching sun. The sidewalks and the streets caught the sun and threw it back at the crowds of city dwellers and tourists who had decided to ignore the weather and swarm to the Mall to celebrate summer's last holiday. They crowded into the air-conditioned museums or hovered around the reflecting pool and fountains, mistakenly believing the water would provide some relief on this stifling, windless day. Tens of thousands more chose to desert the city, seeking relief at the beaches, instead ending up in miles-long traffic jams, hounded by irritable children and struggling with overheated cars.

Most government buildings stood deserted on this Monday. The bulk of the federal workforce had been given the day off to spend with their families or, if they chose to do so, fight the crowds along with everyone else. The less fortunate manned round-the-clock operations centers or tried to catch up on work too long neglected. Still others had been called back into work, their bosses having deemed their services essential to the running of the government or the handling of the latest international crisis. For them, this was a workday like any other.

For others, it was to be a most extraordinary day.

Michael Underwood sat in the Oval Office, facing an incredulous president and national security adviser. Underwood was bracketed by Carolyn Younghart on one side and Hal Schaffer, the head of the Secret Service, on the other. Next to Schaffer was Tim De Young, Schaffer's immediate subordinate in charge of presidential security. Bringing up the rear, as it were, seated on the far side of the room, feeling very much out of place, was Blair Williams. Williams studied the faces in the room, all the while wondering what in the hell he was doing here. At that moment, General Hannah walked into the room. Williams felt instantly relieved, but still wondered why Younghart insisted on dragging him along. He remained unconvinced by her rationale.

"Look," she had explained during the drive to the White House, "I know this is a little bit unorthodox. If it weren't you, I'd be making this drive all by myself. But you know as much about this as anybody at the Pentagon, probably more. Mulkey said if it hadn't been for you, we'd still be wondering why they attacked the ship. You sat in on the Tank session with the CINCs and the chairman, you know the capabilities of the systems, you helped debrief Underwood. Yadda, yadda, yadda. Do I need to add anything else to convince you you're not a fifth wheel?"

"All true, even the yadda yadda part. However, I came here to investigate a missing ship, not to get involved in tracking down terrorists and thwarting a plot to blow up the White House or whatever. Maybe I feel a bit like an interloper. Maybe—just maybe—I'm starting to think I'm in something that's way over my head." He looked at her, shaking his head. "This is really out of my league."

"Well, it's not and you're not. There are a lot of things I wouldn't have known or been able to sort out without your help. You've given me solid advice."

"Which, of course, you have in every situation followed meticulously to the letter, right?"

She chuckled. "All too true. But guess who's been there to remind me when I've screwed up and put me back on the straight and narrow. Not a bad record for an Air Force officer, especially an aviator." She saw him wince. "I meant pilot."

He grinned. "So you are trainable, after all. The Navy hasn't corrupted you completely."

She smiled. "I choose to ignore the last comment. Anyway, let me put it as simply as I can. I consider us a team until this is over. You, my good colonel, have become my confidant and partner, like it or not. I got stuck with you. Now you're stuck with me. Please, Blair, I honestly need your help. And if your CINC doesn't like it, why, I guess I'll just have to have the director give him a call."

Williams smiled at her twist on his threat from a few days before. "Touché," he said with a laugh. "Coopted by the Washington bureaucracy. What a tragic end to what was once a promising Air Force career."

Their friendly banter was quickly forgotten as they entered the White House grounds. They were promptly escorted to the Oval Office, where Williams instantly sensed the deep concern, even fear, among those gathered in the room. It didn't take long for that dread to be voiced by those present, especially Underwood. It was apparent he was still fuming about this latest turn in what had become an increasingly painful ordeal.

He had been informed of the meeting by Younghart only the night before, when she had also informed him she had passed his information along to the FBI director. The director had responded to the news by promptly calling his counterpart at the Secret Service. With these two directly involved, it didn't take very long to convince Christoph of the need to meet with the president.

Although she protested, arguing Underwood worked for the White House staff, Younghart was given the odious task of telling Underwood to forget about having a day off. The director explained that since he had been responsible for killing the president's plans for a quiet day at Camp David, his special agent in charge could deal with Underwood and any problems that might arise from that direction.

Williams had watched and listened as a clearly frustrated Younghart sprang the news. They knew what Underwood's reaction would be. She had yanked the phone away from her ear, and Williams had no trouble hearing Underwood's screams of protest and streams of obscenities.

Now in the Oval Office, Williams studied Underwood, who sat fidgeting in front of the president. Underwood gently wagged his head from side to side, silently disagreeing with everything. Williams knew what he was thinking: Once again, he had ceded control over events. No one was going to listen to his recommendations. He was an information source, nothing more. Williams found himself empathizing with a fellow officer he had dismissed as a human wreck only a few days before.

The presidential security chief had just finished making the argument that the president must change his schedule. Even if they couldn't prevent the attack, he contended, they could at least ensure the president was moved out of harm's way.

Underwood angrily interrupted. "Hasn't anyone listened to a goddamned thing I've said?"

Schaffer was the first to break the startled silence. "Of course we have, Colonel. Without your cooperation, these terrorists' plans would have gone undetected. We can't ignore the fact we're in your debt for this information. Although it would have been better if you had come forward a little sooner."

"Sir," Underwood replied, throwing up his hands, his voice rising nearly to a shout. "I don't know how I could have come forward any sooner than I did. I called the OSI the same day I talked to Evans. That's fairly prompt, don't you think, given the circumstances that my wife's life is hanging by a thread?"

Schaffer frowned and said nothing.

"This is exactly what I wanted to avoid," Underwood continued. "This damned circus. It's why right now I wish I had kept my mouth shut. It's why right now I sincerely wish some of you would go straight to hell, some more than others." He looked straight at Younghart, then continued.

"Mr. President, forgive my impudence. I mean no offense to you. As much as anyone else in the room, I have a keen interest in guaranteeing your personal safety, but if you change your schedule as Mr. Schaffer has just proposed, I guarantee you'll kill my wife and will probably only cause a delay in Evans's plans. With all due respect, sir, Jennifer is my number one concern right now, not you."

Noonan arched his eyebrows.

"Your safety can be taken care of rather simply," Underwood argued. "I would like to know what these people are planning to do to ensure hers. Just by being here, with this particular group right now, we're endangering her."

"I would think Milyutin's press conference provides ample reason for the president to get together with his national security advisers, in case anyone asks," Christoph responded huffily.

"What about him?" Underwood replied, pointing at Schaffer. "What does the head of the Secret Service have to do with political turmoil in Moscow?"

Christoph didn't answer.

"Precisely my point," Underwood stated.

"What would you propose, Colonel?" Schaffer asked.

"Isn't it obvious? Why am I the one that has to suggest this? But is anyone going to listen to my opinion anyway? Do you really give a damn what I think anymore?"

"Mike, take it easy," Noonan interceded. "Look, I understand your frustration. If I were in your shoes, I'd probably have reacted the same way. And I would very likely be just as defensive as you are right now. But getting your back up is not going to put the situation right, and it's not going to protect . . . Jennifer. If I had known all the particulars, perhaps I wouldn't have agreed to this circus, as you call it, quite so quickly." Noonan looked at Christoph, who quickly looked down at his notes. "But what's done is done. We can't rewind events. We have to do the best we can with a very bad situation. Now, I want to hear what you think we should do. Given the intensity of your involvement in this, I do value your opinion, perhaps more so than other people in this room. But I expect the others to pay heed to what you have to say. Isn't that right, everyone?" Noonan asked the others.

They all nodded gravely, as if on cue.

Underwood looked at Noonan and slowly smiled.

"We know," Underwood began, "that they're planning something for sometime tomorrow afternoon. They know any last-minute change in the president's schedule would suggest I've not followed their orders. If I blow their chances of success, they'll murder my wife. Does anyone disagree with that simple analysis of mine, or is what I have to say totally irrelevant to the situation?"

"Agreed, Mike," Noonan urged in soothing tones. "Please, continue."

"You have to keep your schedule, Mr. President."

Schaffer looked at Underwood as if he were a lunatic. "This is your plan for keeping the president safe? Excuse me, I think there's a better solution."

"Wait a minute, Hal," the president ordered, "I don't think the good colonel is finished. Go on, Mike."

"Thank you, sir. You keep to your published agenda, Mr. President. Your schedule has you going over papers for most of that day, as well as working on your speech for the Christian Coalition. You have two brief meetings with Mr. Christoph and the chief of staff. I believe you even have fifteen minutes with me," Underwood said with a slight smile, his first sign of good humor all morning. Noonan responded in kind.

"We maintain the appearance of the normal, scheduled routine. Evans and his group have made it a little easier for us by picking a quiet day in your schedule. It makes it easier for them to make sure you're at home. At the same time, I would argue it makes it easier for us to make certain you're not. We quietly evacuate the White House through the tunnel to the Executive Office Building well before noon."

"And what about the rest of the city?" Schaffer asked heatedly. "You still have thousands of people in office buildings, tourists wandering around the White House."

"Actually," the chief of presidential security replied, "that's less of a problem if the target is the White House, with Pennsylvania Avenue closed in front of the White House and the buffer offered by the area around the Ellipse. With a little help from D.C. public works, we might be able to schedule some maintenance to push the perimeter even farther back. Short of evacuating several city blocks around the White House and creating a general panic, Colonel Underwood's suggestion may be the best way to go."

"And how do we know the terrorists are going to limit their attack to the White House?" Hannah asked.

"We don't, sir," Underwood answered, "but Evans left me with the clear impression President Noonan is their primary—if not their only—target. They haven't asked me to try and get information on any place or anyone else in the city. If they were planning something against the Pentagon, say, I'm fairly certain they would be pressing me for information in that regard."

"Hell, Mr. President, they could be planning an attack against multiple targets in the city," Schaffer objected. "And Underwood may not be the only one who's been compromised. They could have other sources of information we don't know about. What if they have someone in the Pentagon? Seems to me that General Hannah's concerns are well-placed. They could have contacts all over the city by now."

"But we only know of one," Underwood rejoined. "And that's the one we have to worry about. I think Mr. DeYoung would agree that with the president safely and quietly out of the White House, the Secret Service should be capable of dealing with an isolated move against the Executive Mansion."

DeYoung nodded. "We can lay on additional surveillance and deploy a special-tactics team quietly around the perimeter. We'll be ready for them when they come. With our own surprise."

"Unless they've found some way to make the cruise missiles operational." The comment came from Williams, and he surprised even himself by opening his mouth. It had an immediate, sobering effect.

"Colonel Williams, isn't it?" Noonan asked.

"Yes, sir."

"Your comment seems to have captured our undivided attention," the president said as he surveyed the suddenly pensive, very worried faces in the room. "Please explain, Colonel. It's your nickel."

Williams quietly cleared his throat and swallowed hard. Would he ever learn to disengage his mouth from his sudden flashes of insight? He looked at Younghart, almost pleadingly. She gave him a look that told him he was on his own. They had discussed their speculations before, but neither seemed willing to raise the possibility with this crowd, until now, until he had remembered something Underwood had told them. It had been tucked in the back of his mind, nagging at him, until just this moment in the Oval Office.

"Mr. President," Williams began tentatively, "Special Agent Younghart and I are convinced the theft of the missiles from the *Regulus* is very much tied up with this Evans character. Colonel Underwood mentioned something the other night during his debriefing that I should have picked up on immediately, something Evans said to him earlier. He told Underwood that being slapped around by God would be a walk in the park compared to what Evans's friends would do to him. That's about right, isn't it, Mike?"

Underwood sat motionless for a moment, then nodded slowly.

"The group that stole the missiles left a calling card on the ship," Williams continued. "They painted the words 'Fist of God' on the bulkhead in the compartment where the missiles were stored. If they've made these missiles operational and are planning to use them against targets in Washington, you have a whole new ball game."

"Mr. President, I think the Joint Chiefs have pretty well eliminated that as a possibility," General Hannah offered reassuringly. "No disrespect to Colonel Williams or Agent Younghart, and their investigative talents, but I think it's just a bit of a stretch to connect these two events because of some offhand remark made by Underwood's friend."

"He isn't my friend, General Hannah," Underwood said heatedly. "I would like everyone to remember that."

"Sorry, Mike," Hannah responded quickly. "Just a slip of the tongue, a figure of speech. I meant nothing by it. I know this bastard's not your friend. I was only trying to make a point."

Underwood lowered his eyes and dropped his chin to his chest.

"My point is this," Hannah said. "The stolen missiles are protected by several security systems. There's no evidence any of these systems have been compromised. We've done a complete security audit. Hell, we even went back to the contractor and asked him to give their records a wire brush to see if there was any indication of a lapse in security. Nothing."

Williams pursed his lips in an effort to keep quiet. He badly wanted to burst the chairman's bubble of optimism. Williams had dealt with defense contractors before. Most of the time they told you only what they knew you wanted to hear. And when it came to security issues, they would have you believe they had erected an impenetrable barrier.

"We don't think the theft of the cruise missiles is related to these Russian extremists that Evans seems to be involved with," the chairman continued. "They've got something else in mind. I think you have a simple coincidence with this Fist of God business. I think we're really reaching if we try to argue there's some relationship. I just don't believe there's any connection."

Williams unpursed his lips. He knew he should keep his mouth shut. What good would it do to antagonize the chairman of the Joint Chiefs? But his hunches had been right before, and there was way too much at stake here to let Hannah's remarks go unchallenged. Younghart turned in her chair, gave him the slightest of nods, and mouthed the words "Go for it."

"Excuse me for respectfully disagreeing, General Hannah. Admittedly, I'm no expert on the JASSM, but my learning curve has been fairly steep over the last few days. I don't think we should rule out any possibility. Whoever organized and carried out the attack on the *Regulus* was well-informed and well-financed. They were able to enlist the cooperation of at least one member of my command. Who knows how many more within the Department of Defense they were able to persuade with promises of instant wealth? We never would have thought such a breach of security possible within my command, but it happened. And Colonel Underwood's made it clear the Russian group has somehow extended its reach into the heart of the CIA, apparently totally undetected."

"No surprise there," Christoph snorted. Noonan gave him a sharp look.

"I'm hesitant to rule out a connection between the two," Williams went on. "It just seems to be too much of a coincidence."

"Colonel," Hannah replied gruffly, "we all appreciate the input, but I think the idea that a bunch of Russian thugs is behind the theft of the cruise missiles and is planning to use them to attack the White House has no basis in reality. It's pure speculation."

"Then how do we explain what Milyutin is facing, General Hannah?" Noonan asked his senior military adviser. "Is he imagining that? How did Resurrected Russia suddenly come up with stolen American missiles and threaten Moscow if they haven't been able to figure out how to make these missiles work?"

"They're bluffing, Mr. President," Hannah replied confidently. "Just having the missiles is enough to scare Milyutin, as we've seen. They're using a nonexistent threat to extort the Russian leadership. Unfortunately, we've confirmed the theft of the missiles to Milyutin. That has only served to feed his fear."

Noonan ignored Hannah's implicit questioning of his decision to share the JASSM information with his Russian counterpart. "Are you suggesting I call Milyutin and tell him not to worry, because my military tells me there's absolutely no chance Resurrected Russia has been able to make these things operational? Are you willing to stake your retirement on that, General Hannah?"

Noonan suddenly grew very pensive and gently tapped the desktop with his fingers. He had obviously thought of something.

"This is becoming an uncontrollable mess. If they have operational cruise missiles, they could hit anywhere in Washington, couldn't they? They could take out the White House, a sizable chunk of the Capitol, and who knows what else. I've seen what the old Tomahawks could do to a large building and the people in it. We're talking about a major catastrophe in the making here, and I'll be damned if I know what to do about it. If I leave the White House, I'll be safe, but lots of innocent people will die if the damned thing misses its target. If we warn the city, we create panic, and do nothing to prevent an attack, and many more innocent people will die. They'll strike anyway, or simply choose another day. And they'll certainly kill Mrs. Underwood for our trouble." Noonan looked at Underwood. "Don't worry, Mike, I haven't forgotten that stake in this miserable god-damned game they're making us play."

"Mr. President, please. You're worrying about nothing," Hannah protested. "I can assure you we're not facing a threat from our own missiles. I don't know what these jokers are planning, but I seriously doubt they have anywhere near the capability to stage the kind of massive attack you're talking about. Even if they could make the missiles operational, that would require significant assistance from another country. And no country, not even Iran, is going to risk U.S. retaliation by aiding and abetting such an attack. It would be tantamount to suicide."

"Mr. President?" Underwood, forgotten in the debate over terrorist capabilities, was signaling for Noonan's attention.

"Yes, Mike."

Underwood motioned toward Williams. "As my colleague would say, I'm no expert, but I would vote for Colonel Williams's assessment. An old friend of mine passed along some information a while back that makes me think Evans, the

Russian nutcases, and the missiles are all related."

Williams caught Younghart glaring at Underwood, and he knew what she was thinking. The bastard had held out on them. Big time. He leaned over and whispered, "Better late than never."

Younghart now glared at Williams.

"In any event," Underwood said, "there's an option none of us have considered. I didn't think of it until now, probably because on the face of it, it seems very risky. But the risk may be worth taking, to protect you, my wife, and the rest of the city." Underwood turned toward Hannah. "General, I don't know anything about the JASSMs, but if there's a way of making the damned things operational, I don't think Evans and his friends would hesitate using them if it would accomplish their purpose. Having seen the type of creature he really is, I truly believe he's capable of anything. And I'm sure the same holds true for his accomplices. Consequently, I don't think we have a lot of time."

Underwood looked at Younghart. "I assume you haven't received anything useful from the phone taps and the surveillance, correct?"

"Nothing so far," Younghart answered, a quizzical look on her face.

"If we're to prevent an attack, or at least minimize its consequences, we have to go straight to the source. Look, I'm no dummy. I know that Jennifer is as good as dead once they've carried out their attack. There's no use for her after that. She will have served her purpose of holding me hostage. I pray to God she's not dead already." He tried not to choke on the words, but failed. He paused a moment, then continued. "I don't think Evans is going to be stupid enough to lead you right to Jennifer or the rest of his group. And I seriously doubt he'll be making any unguarded phone calls that could tip anyone off. He's probably convinced he has me under his thumb, but he's not going to take any chances. There's only one way left to get the information we need."

Younghart was vigorously shaking her head, but Underwood ignored her and pressed on.

"Evans will be here tomorrow morning to brief you. It's a

measure of how arrogantly confident he is that he's coming to the White House on the morning of the planned operation. There are others who can do the briefing. Evans could quietly bow out for some excuse, then simply disappear to the safety of his comrades, anticipating he's bound to be discovered anyway. But I think he's made a point of being on the schedule. In a sense, he's thumbing his nose at all of us."

"I think I know where this is leading, but I'm not sure I agree," Noonan said.

"Please, sir," Underwood responded, "I don't think there's much choice. As soon as Evans shows his face in the White House, we have to grab him and get the answers out of him, no matter what it takes."

"And if he's supposed to contact his friends after he leaves the White House," Schaffer asked, "then what do we do? They'll know something's wrong. They'll be watching. They may decide to move early, and for certain your wife will be killed. No. There has to be another way, another option."

"Believe me, sir," Underwood rebutted, "I wish there were. But right now, more than ever, if I'm ever to see Jennifer alive again, I'm convinced there isn't."

The orderly progression of speakers broke down as the participants began arguing among themselves. Noonan watched the group quietly for a moment, his hands folded like a steeple in front of his face, his chin resting on his thumbs. Finally, he pushed away from his desk and stood up. The room instantly went quiet.

"I think Colonel Underwood is right," the president began. "If we want answers, we have to go right to the source, and Evans is that source. But I share Hal's concern that we not tip off Evans's partners." Noonan smiled. "I have a plan, but it's going to require the close cooperation of the Secret Service, the FBI, and the District of Columbia."

Everyone looked around in confusion.

"Excuse me, Mr. President," Christoph asked, "but I'm confused about what role the city can play in any of this. If you get the D.C. government involved, this really will turn into a circus."

"I understand your skepticism," Noonan said, "so let me explain what I have in mind."

Chapter Thirty-one

The streets of Washington were jammed. The day after Labor Day marked the end of the annual summer exodus. The return of the flood of vacationers meant a return of the city's usual traffic nightmares. The screeching of tires, the clouds of exhaust from cars needing tuning, the wails of sirens, and the vulgar shouts and gestures of angry motorists had returned with a vengeance. The nation's capital was back to normal.

Taxis and delivery trucks fought their way through the crowded thoroughfares to deliver their cargo. Vehicles swerved in and out in a mad dash to keep to imagined schedules, narrowly missing pedestrians who had the temerity to venture into the path of livery drivers oblivious to the presence of anything without four or more wheels.

This cacophony of traffic streamed past the White House as well, with the attendant dangers threatening those trying to make their way around and to the president's home. Fender benders occurred frequently in the city, and few paid much attention when the characteristic thud of colliding vehicles echoed down the streets. But it was a surprise when a large delivery truck plowed into the side of a car that had just left the White House grounds with enough force to force the car off the road into a lamppost—a not-uncommon occurrence, but an uncommon location.

The response to the accident was also uncommon. Several city policemen and uniformed Secret Service guards dashed to the scene. Two of them pried open the door to the passenger compartment, and one quickly crawled inside to check on the occupant's status. Meanwhile, the driver was hustled away to one of the White House gates, so he was not present when the Secret Service officer who had climbed into the car slapped something against the arm of the struggling passenger.

A crowd tried to gather, convinced that someone very important must be in the car to have attracted so much attention, but the police and Secret Service personnel quickly set up a tight cordon around the scene and angrily ordered onlookers to keep their distance. The sounds of an ambulance quickly grew louder, the emergency vehicle appearing in what would have been a remarkably short time to anyone familiar with the city's paramedical services. Out-of-towners in the gathering crowd could only marvel at the efficiency of the whole operation, opining that it must be wonderful to live in a city where police and rescue units responded so quickly. City residents in the crowd simply smiled at the naïveté of the remarks, although they were at a loss to explain why this situation was so different from what they were used to.

Paramedics pulled the passenger from the car, placed him carelessly on a gurney, and rapidly loaded the stretcher into the back of the ambulance. Two of the Secret Service guards, one a tall, blond woman, climbed into the rescue vehicle and seated themselves next to the gurney as the doors were closed. The paramedics dashed to the cab, and the ambulance departed as quickly as it had arrived.

The crowd, understanding that the excitement was over, slowly dissipated. A few lingered to watch a wrecker tow

Ken Currie

away the badly damaged dark blue sedan; one of them was the driver, who was gesticulating wildly while talking to police and White House guards. He tried to walk toward the sedan but was promptly pulled away by a large Secret Service guard, who pointed emphatically toward the White House gatehouse. Evans's driver yelled something, inaudible over the din of the traffic and the sirens, then shrugged and trudged to the guard shack.

Across the street, a young man with two dogs watched the unfolding drama. As the ambulance drove away, he made his way to Pennsylvania Avenue and started walking toward the Capitol, holding the dogs' leashes with one hand and a cellular phone to his ear with the other.

"Good morning, Victor."

"Good morning, Ted," the DCI responded. "My secretary tells me there's some urgency to your call. What can we do for you?"

"Victor, I'm afraid I have some very bad news," Christoph responded. "A most unusual situation. We've never had anything like this happen before that I can recall."

The DCI sat up in his chair, immediately alert and alarmed at the tone in the national security adviser's voice. "Yes?" he asked tentatively.

"As your briefer, Josh Evans, was leaving the White House grounds this morning, his car was broadsided by a large truck. Your agency's driver is okay, but I'm afraid the passenger compartment took the brunt of the impact. Evans is in critical condition."

"My God," the DCI breathed. "Where? I mean, where is he?"

"My understanding is he was taken directly to George Washington University Hospital, where he was immediately moved into surgery. The president has taken a personal interest in this, since it happened so close to the White House. The president is also very fond of the young man, so he's asked the hospital to keep him posted on Evans's status. He's ordered us to take the necessary steps to ensure Evans's security, given the level of his access. Consequently, every-

304

thing is quite secure right now, and that should allay any concerns you might have. We'll be sure to pass along whatever information we get as soon as it's available."

Noonan's fondness for Evans was news to the DCI, but he let Christoph's remark pass. He was more concerned about the security implications of the news. Here was one of his staffers, with access to the most highly classified information available, undergoing emergency surgery in a public hospital, and this was the first he was hearing about it. What the hell had happened to the driver?

"I'll get some of our security people down there as quickly as possible."

"There's really no need for that, Victor. There are Secret Service and FBI personnel at the hospital. Rest assured that we share your concern, given Evans's security tickets. That's why, at the president's direction, we asked for help from the closest agencies. Your folks would only be wasting their time. The service and the Bureau have the situation well in hand, so you have no need to worry."

Alarm bells were going off in the DCI's head. He didn't like or trust Christoph, and here he was being essentially directed to stay away from one of his own people.

"Ted, Evans is an agency employee. Let me remind you that our directives are quite clear in circumstances like this. I *will* be sending some of our security personnel down, and I don't want there being any problems when they arrive on the scene."

"Well, you can do that if you want, but they won't be allowed into the area where Evans is being kept."

"I beg your pardon? You can't do that. I want to speak to the president about this."

"These instructions come from the president, Victor, so I would suggest you back off."

"What the hell is going on? Are you telling me that one of my staff members is being held incommunicado from his own agency?"

"Let's just say the president, for now, thinks the situation is best handled this way. Evans is getting the best possible treatment. He's well guarded. There's very little danger of any sort of security problem. We'll keep you posted on his condition. I would suspect by late today we'll have a very good sense of whether he'll make it. The medical personnel are doing everything they possibly can. We just don't need a lot of extra personnel parading around the hospital inviting questions and unwanted attention. Wouldn't you agree?"

"Not at all. If there's an issue of too many people, I'll be happy to have my security personnel replace the ones already there."

"And have a bunch of guys in dark suits with buttons on their lapels and earphones running around the hospital? I don't think so, Victor. The president's way is better. Let me reiterate. This *is* the *president's* way. We'll stay in touch."

The DCI resisted a strong desire to call Christoph a son of a bitch over the phone. Instead, he said simply, "You bet we will," and hung up. He immediately called the president's office. After he identified himself to Ms. Morrow and asked to speak to the president, she politely but firmly told him the president was in conference for the rest of the day and was not to be disturbed. Perhaps he could call back tomorrow? Christoph stood by her desk, smiling, as she delivered the message.

3 September, 0945 hours EDT

"Mr. Evans. Mr. Evans, can you hear me?" Younghart asked as she gently shook his arm.

Williams sat next to Underwood in a corner of the darkened room, the only illumination provided by a small floodlamp over the bed where Evans lay strapped down. The Kafkaesque scene unfolding before him made Williams strangely uneasy. He silently vowed never to do anything to cross the president or his staff.

Younghart was seated in a chair next to Evans, while a doctor stood motionless at the head of the bed. His presence seemed superfluous since the only evidence Evans bore of an accident was a small bruise above his left temple. Another FBI agent stood by the door.

Outside the room, a third FBI agent acted as guard for the

proceedings inside. Down the hall, two uniformed Secret Service men and a D.C. policeman, completely unaware of what was transpiring, prevented access to the private ward where Evans was being held. To all appearances, for anyone inclined to be curious, there was a patient of some importance staying in this isolated part of the hospital.

Younghart repeated her question, and Evans mumbled a reply. Younghart leaned closer to the bed. "What did you say, Mr. Evans? You have to speak more loudly. I can't make out what you're saying."

"Where . . . am I?" Evans forced out the words with great difficulty.

"You're in a hospital room, Mr. Evans. You've been in a serious car accident. You're out of danger, but you're being kept under observation. I'm here to ask you a few questions, if you feel up to it?"

"Accident? I don't remember . . . an accident," Evans replied raspily. "Could I have a drink of water? I'm very dry. I can't move."

"You're strapped down for your own safety, Mr. Evans. You're heavily sedated, and we didn't want you falling out of bed. I suspect the medication is also making you thirsty, isn't that right, Doctor?"

"Yes," came a disembodied reply.

Evans tried unsuccessfully to bend his head back to see where the new voice was coming from. "If he's the doctor, then who are you? And can you please give me some water?"

Younghart stood up and reached across Evans to retrieve a water bottle from the bedside table. She lifted Evans's head and pushed the bottle's plastic straw to his lips. Evans had barely taken a sip when she pulled the bottle away. "That's enough for now. You can have some more after we talk a little bit."

"I need more, please."

"Later," Younghart answered firmly.

"Who are you?" Evans asked again, a bit more insistently this time, increasing anxiety apparent in his voice.

"You don't need to know who I am, Mr. Evans. All you need to know is you're being taken care of, and you're going to answer my questions." Younghart leaned back in her chair and folded her arms.

"What kind of questions? And why won't you tell me who you are? I don't think my employer will be very happy with this."

"Your employer thinks you're undergoing surgery at this moment, and the outcome of that operation is very problematic right now. Quite frankly, we're very uncertain of your long-term prognosis. A lot will depend on how well you respond during the next few minutes."

Evans began wiggling from side to side on the table and tugging against his arm restraints. "You let me out of here right now! You can't do this. What right do you have to do something like this? Who the hell do you think you are? What have I done? Damn you, damn you, let me up!"

"Relax. Struggling like that is going to do you no good. You'll just chafe your arms. You could risk a serious infection, and we wouldn't want that to happen, would we? It could affect your recovery."

Evans grew still. "You can't get away with this, you know. I'm not going to tell you anything. I don't know who you're working for, but you'll get no information out of me. My government will see to that."

"I think you're slightly confused. You see, I'm the one who works for the government. You, sir, are nothing more than a traitor. We're here to discover who you really work for."

Evans laughed. "What in God's name are you talking about? Traitor? You've got to be kidding. Who says I'm a traitor?"

"I do, Josh," Underwood said softly from across the room.

Younghart swiveled instantly in her chair, furiously slashing her hand across her throat in an effort to tell Underwood to shut up.

Underwood shook his head as he stood up and moved toward the bed.

"Hello, Josh. I'm sure you didn't expect to see me again, did you? Especially in circumstances like these."

Evans lifted his head from the bed, staring in the direction of the voice. As Underwood stepped into the light, Evans reacted with a crooked smile. "Why, hello, Colonel. Good to see a friendly face. Can you tell me what's going on?"

"Colonel Underwood, will you please sit down and let me handle this?" Younghart's eyes were shooting daggers, but Underwood was undeterred.

"I don't think so," he responded, and there was anger in his eyes as well. "We're going to be here all day at this rate. Let's get to the point, okay?"

Younghart finally threw up her hands in mock despair. She gestured Underwood toward the bed, where he was headed in any event. Underwood moved next to the bed and then leaned in close to Evans's face.

"It's my turn, you worthless piece of shit," he whispered in Evans's ear. "Payback time." Underwood straightened up and looked down at Evans, who had renewed his struggle against the restraints. "You can cut the bullshit, Josh. Everyone here knows what you've been doing. They know all about your friends. They know all about me. I would say you've lost your advantage. The game belongs to me now."

"I haven't the slightest idea what you're talking about."

Underwood started reaching for Evans's throat, but Younghart pushed him away. Williams leaped up from his chair and grabbed Underwood from behind.

"Mike, for Christ's sake," Williams whispered loudly, "this certainly isn't going to work any better than her approach. Take it easy. Sit down."

Underwood relaxed in Williams's grip. "I'm okay. It's okay. You can let go."

Williams slowly released him, but stood poised to grab Underwood again if necessary.

"Colonel," Evans said calmly, "this is quite an elaborate little scheme you seem to have orchestrated to cover up your tracks. What are your friends here going to think when they find out about your association with foreign intelligence agencies? I'm certain you haven't told them about that, have you?" Evans asked with a sly smile. He dropped his head back on the pillow and said matter-of-factly, "They won't buy this little ruse of yours."

Evans visibly relaxed, his voice filled with confidence.

"You're just trying to shift the blame to me for something you've obviously gotten yourself into. Everyone at the Agency knows how erratic your behavior's been lately. It certainly was no secret. You ran off to the White House before anybody could do anything about it. Look at you. Now maybe people will listen to me."

Evans turned his head toward Younghart. "Listen, I don't know who you are or exactly what Underwood's told you, but we've been suspicious of him for some time. You should be asking your questions of him. In fact, if you'll let me up, I'll call the DCI's office. I'm sure our security personnel would be happy to help out."

Underwood snorted. "Give it up, Josh. I've told them everything, and I do mean everything, even the things you thought I would never want anyone to find out. You have no hold over me anymore. But everyone in this room knows about your tie-in with the Russian terrorists. We know about the stolen missiles. We want you to tell us the rest of the story."

"Oh, for God's sake, will you shut the hell up!" Younghart barked. "You can't reason with this son of a bitch. You'll get nothing out of him except a con. There's no more time for sparring. Doctor, please go ahead."

The doctor took hold of Evans's arm and readied a syringe.

"Ow! Damn it! What the hell was that?" Evans shouted.

"Just a little something to help you relax and talk," Younghart answered.

"I don't need any help, because I have nothing to say. Talk to that man right there. He says he has all the answers. Besides, I think . . . you're violating . . . my rights." Evans was fading quickly, the combination of medications working rapidly on his system.

Williams watched the doctor's movements, feeling strangely detached from events, as if watching a play. He marveled at how calmly Carolyn had ordered the injection and wondered how many times she might have done so before. Apparently, the job of protecting the nation's security could be a real bitch at times. He reassured himself that this wasn't a common procedure; it was made necessary by the urgency of the situation. But everyone played their part very well, including the "doctor."

"Now, Mr. Evans, let's get down to business, shall we?" Younghart began. "You can tell me all about who you really work for later."

"Work for . . . government," Evans sputtered.

"Yeah, right, which one?" Underwood asked contemptuously.

"Quiet, damn it," Younghart said sharply. She turned back to her patient. "Yes, Mr. Evans, we know you work for the government, but you seem to work for others as well. You can tell us about them later. Right now, we just want to know what your friends are planning."

"Friends?" Evans asked lazily.

"Yes, Josh, your friends in Resurrected Russia and Fist of God."

"Oh, no friends there. No Resurrected Russia. Not good friends. I have real good friends, but I can't tell you who they are."

"Okay, okay, you don't have to. Just tell us what your real good friends are planning."

"Planning? No planning. Going to do it, they are. Already doing it." Evans giggled. "Already doing it. And there's nothing you can do to stop them."

"Already doing what, Josh?" Younghart asked insistently. "You can tell us. You're among friends. We know we can't stop it. You fooled us. Just tell us what they're already doing, okay, and we'll let you walk out of here."

"Okay, friends. I'll tell, but shhh. Don't tell anybody I told you. They might get angry with me. What time is it?"

The question jarred Younghart, for Evans had asked it in what had seemed like a sudden burst of clarity. "What?"

"Josh wants to know what time it is, okay?"

"Okay, okay, Josh. It's ten o'clock."

"Ha, I thought so! They've already done it. Good job. You can't stop them now. Say goodbye, Mr. President. Say byebye White House. Boom!" Evans laughed idiotically.

"How much of that shit did you give him?" Underwood snapped at the doctor.

"Mike, will you back off?" Younghart shot back. "It's okay. He's doing fine. A little goofiness is to be expected."

"Goofiness? He sounds like a goddamned imbecile!"

"Stop it! We're okay here. Let me continue. Josh, why does the White House go boom? You can tell me. We really want to know. You and your friends have been so clever. We want to know how you've fooled us."

"Fooled you. Fooled you," Evans chanted, then grew strangely quiet. He burst out laughing, then was silent again. "Airplane will drop cruise missiles on its way to airport. Isn't that clever?" He again had uttered the comment in an amazingly coherent manner. "You have a friend at Empire Air!" he shouted. "Too late, too late. Airplane is already on its way. Left New York and her huddled masses . . . yearning to breathe free. Lift your lamp, lift your lamp," Evans sang softly. "Miss Liberty will see the glow. Bye-bye. I think I want to go to sleep now."

"Good God Almighty," Underwood said, turning to Williams, his face ashen. "You were right. They're going to use the damned things against Washington. A day earlier than this bastard said they would. How the hell did they know the president . . . ?" But the answer was obvious: There *was* somebody else in the White House working for Evans. "Shit!" Underwood exclaimed. "God knows if there's any time left. What the hell do we do now?"

Williams pulled the cellular secure phone out of his pocket and quickly punched in a number. "I have a friend at the Pentagon, in the NMCC. And you'd better be prepared to talk to General Hannah. He may not listen to me after yesterday."

"And you think he'll listen to me?" Underwood shot back.

Younghart grabbed her cellular phone. "I hope to God it's not too late to get Noonan out of the White House. How could this happen? How could somebody like this get that close to the president? What the hell ever happened to background checks?" She sighed. "I really thought I had seen it all. Now, I guess I have."

"He had everybody fooled, Carolyn. And I do mean everyone." Underwood slowly walked back to the table and knelt down, placing his lips close to Evans's ear. "Can you still hear me, Josh?"

"Of course I can, Mike, but I want to sleep, okay? Please, let me sleep."

"You can go to sleep, Josh. Just tell me where Jennifer is, then you can go to sleep."

"Jennifer's safe, Mike. No more troubles. No more cares. Nobody can bother her anymore." As he began drifting off to sleep, he slowly, softly added, with a disarmingly gentle smile, "Jennifer's . . . sleeping with the angels. We took good care of her, old friend. You'll be with her soon. Now I want to sleep too."

Chapter Thirty-two

Younghart, completing her call and putting away her phone, caught the sudden movement out of the corner of her eye and instantly leaped from her chair to stop the lunging Underwood. His weight pushed her back against the bed. The agent by the door vaulted across the room and roughly pulled Underwood away, twisting his arm behind his back.

Williams, secure cellular phone up to his ear, stood for a moment in stunned silence, then realized he had left a lieutenant colonel hanging on the other end. "Hold one, Colonel Alvarez, don't go away. We've a small problem here. In the meantime, please get General Price on the phone. Tell him there's an attack under way on the White House. I think that'll get his attention."

"Let me go, damn you! I'm going to kill the son of a bitch."

Younghart pushed off the bed and the somnolent Evans and grabbed Underwood by the shoulders. "No, you're not. You're not going to kill anyone. That's not going to do anything to bring Jennifer back. Evans isn't going anywhere.

When he comes around, he'll help us find the rest. We want everybody, understand?"

"I'm not listening to this," Underwood spat out. He struggled against the agent's grip until the pain forced him to settle down. "He's going to pay. The bastard's going to pay. I'm going to rip his goddamned lungs out through his throat." He struggled futilely once more, then stopped and dropped his head to Younghart's shoulder.

"Yes, he's going to pay. They all are. But let's make sure we get everybody. Especially the ones who killed Jennifer. Evans isn't the one, but he'll lead us to them. One way or another. I promise."

She wrapped her arm around Underwood and nodded to the other agent to let go. He cautiously released his grip on Underwood, standing poised to grab him again.

"I'm so sorry, Mike," she said softly. "I'm so sorry. It's okay, go ahead. Get it out now. You'll need to be clearheaded, so let it out. Let it out."

Underwood straightened up and looked at her, his eyes completely dry. He screwed his face into a perplexed frown, then shook his head and shoved his hands into his pockets. He studied Carolyn's face for a moment. "There's nothing there."

She shook her own head.

"There's nothing to let out, Carolyn. After all this, there should be something. But there isn't. I don't understand. This wasn't supposed to happen. Jennifer was supposed to be all right. I was supposed to get her out of this." Finally, he slumped into a chair. "I treated her like shit. I avoided her. I cheated on her. I just left her hanging. And now she's dead. And for some reason, I don't feel any sorrow."

"It's the shock, Michael."

"No, no," he protested as he shook his head even harder. "I half expected this to happen. I'm disappointed, but I feel a little relieved at the same time. Isn't that strange?" He dropped his head into his hands as if to cry, but still nothing came.

Younghart reached out to touch him on the shoulder and

comfort him, then pulled her hand back quickly. She didn't understand what drove this creature now lost in his thoughts, and this was not the time to start trying. In fact, she was now slightly repelled by his presence. He didn't require—or want—any comforting. If he was haunted by any demons, he was going to be wrestling with them alone. Now that they had Evans, Underwood's value was, thankfully, sharply diminished. She was now eager to hand this unpleasant reminder of the past over to another agent.

She looked toward Williams. She saw tears in his eyes and knew he was thinking of Erica, wishing he could be back in the boring safety of the Illinois cornfields. And suddenly Younghart envied the woman she had never met, for Erica's man was a stark contrast to the person sitting in front of her. She reached up and dabbed at the corners of her own eyes. She looked down at Underwood once again and studied his motionless, emotionless form. She was not certain he wanted to exorcise his demons; they had, perhaps, become his friends. When she had thought of Michael in the past, the recollections had filled her with anger and disgust. The anger was now gone.

"Hello, hello? Colonel Williams, are you there?"

Williams became aware of the impatient voice shouting in his ear. He thankfully turned away from the scene in front of him. "Sorry, General," he responded, his words catching in his throat. "Things have turned out very badly here. We've had our first casualty, but I'm afraid we're going to have a hell of a lot more unless we act quickly."

"Go ahead."

"General, I'm afraid we don't have time to argue about the reliability of the information I'm about to pass along. I know very well how the chairman feels about this, but we've just been told by someone who's damned well in a position to know that cruise missiles are aimed at Washington, and they're on their way. Just tell General Hannah the source is the individual we discussed at the White House yesterday. He'll know. The airplane that's carrying them belongs to something called Empire Air. You ever heard of it?"

There was a pause at the other end of the line. "Yeah," Price answered finally, breathlessly. "A small outfit in New York—or at least I thought it was—run by an old friend of mine. Amazing coincidence. Hold on. I'm going to put you on speaker so the other people in this room can hear."

"Roger. Amazing indeed, General. The cruise missiles are apparently on board an Empire Air flight that has already departed New York, according to our source. I have no flight number. I have no idea when or from where it might have departed. Sorry I can't be of more help, but I know your folks can figure it out. I don't know how much your old friend knows about this, but for sure he's in it up to his ears now."

Price had already signaled to one of his staffers, who instantly departed to check on the status of Empire Air flights. He scribbled a note to another to order the Atlantic Command to immediately scramble F-15s from Langley Air Force Base near Norfolk. Having done that, he picked up the red phone to talk to the chairman.

"Colonel Williams, I think we've got what we need to take action at this end. I'll pass you back to Colonel Alvarez. Get back to him immediately if there's anything else."

"One more thing, General."

"Yes."

"Is Empire Air a cargo or passenger carrier?"

"Both."

"That's what I was afraid you were going to say, General. There don't seem to be any simple answers today."

"I'm sorry, General, but Mr. Malloy is not in."

"Can you tell me where he is? It's absolutely imperative I get in touch with him."

"He's supposed to be in Washington today, to greet an incoming Empire Air Flight. I could tell you where's he staying, but I'm sure he's already left the hotel. You see, the plane's due into National in about forty-five minutes. I would imagine he's already at the airport waiting."

"So you can verify that Flight 003 departed at 0945 as planned?"

"You seem to have very good information, General."

"Your operations people were very helpful."

"Good. That's how we train them. Wait a moment while I check the status board. Yes, it did depart as planned."

"With passengers? Your ops people indicated there were passengers on board."

"Uh, no. Just cargo. I'm afraid the operations folks didn't have the latest information. Oh, well, I guess sometimes things do slip through the cracks despite our training. Actually, there *were* passengers scheduled to make the flight, but Mr. Malloy had to cancel out the excursion due to problems with the cargo-loading equipment. He's not a happy camper about it, either. There was a considerable loss of revenue involved."

"I can imagine," Price said, a bit relieved. "Please, if you hear from Mr. Malloy, I would very much appreciate it if you have him call me. He has my work number. I can't stress enough how important this is. Thanks for your help."

"That's quite all right, General. Glad to be of assistance to the Pentagon at any time."

As Price put down the phone, he wondered how the other party had known he was calling from the Pentagon. Then he shrugged. Everyone probably assumed all generals worked at the Pentagon.

In New York, the erstwhile Empire Air employee hung up the phone. He looked down, then kicked Malloy's lifeless body. He turned to his companion. "Get the truck. It's time to take out the rest of the garbage. And don't forget the parcel in the front office. You know where and how to dump it. We'll meet later as planned." Having said that, Kuhlmann unplugged the phone, sat down, put his feet on Malloy's desk, and lit up a cigarette.

Chapter Thirty-three

Colonel General Ryabkin, the head of the Main Intelligence Directorate, the GRU, shifted nervously in his chair as Gromov read the report, waiting for the inevitable questions. The defense minister would be merciless in his search for answers and would be most unhappy if there were none. Ryabkin was calmer today than most days; he had most of the answers, but still not all. It would be difficult to foresee how Gromov would react to the specific missing items in Ryabkin's information.

"So you were able to track his movements after the meeting?"

"Yes, Defense Minister. Izrailov returned directly to his dacha after the meeting at Ostankino. He's remained there ever since. There has been no activity by the other members of his organization at the hotel."

"No unusual communications?"

"No, sir," Ryabkin responded proudly. The GRU had been able to place taps on all the voice and fax communications

319

into and out of Izrailov's dacha and his hotel headquarters. The GRU's impressive communications intercept capabilities had also been enlisted in the battle: Izrailov's cellular phones were being monitored as well. They knew the mafia leader's every move, if not that of everyone else in his organization.

"So where are the missiles?"

Ryabkin had expected the question, but was still not entirely prepared for Gromov's asking it.

"At this point we're not precisely certain, Defense Minister."

Gromov smiled grimly. "Are you imprecisely certain, at least, General Ryabkin?"

"Because of our relationship with Izrailov in this enterprise, we were of course able to track the missiles' precise movement from Azerbaijan through Georgia to Chechnya. We've identified the facility outside of Groznyy where they were stored."

"Were?"

"Yes. The missiles have been moved. We're very certain of that. We noted a lot of activity at the site a few nights ago."

"What kind of activity?"

"A truck convoy left the facility. Enough trucks to carry all of the missiles, plus a security escort."

"Headed where?"

"This is where our information becomes less precise, Defense Minister."

Gromov's eyes narrowed, but his tone remained steady, even calm. "Are you trying to tell me that the GRU, with the assistance of the rest of the armed forces, lost track of a convoy moving at night through open terrain? And no effort was made to stop this convoy from leaving the facility, even though you suspected they were carrying our American cruise missiles?"

Ryabkin nodded and cleared his throat. "That is unfortunately true, Defense Minister. The trucks left the site very quickly. And, as you know, our ability to move forces around in Chechnya is now somewhat limited thanks to Milyutin's agreement with the Chechens."

Gromov grimaced. "You have no idea where the missiles are?"

"That's not exactly accurate, Defense Minister."

"General Ryabkin, is it your intention to make me play the American game of twenty questions before you give me the information I want? Do you or do you not know where the damned missiles are located?"

"We believe they are somewhere near Voronezh."

"The missiles are this close to Moscow, but you're not certain where they are?"

Ryabkin shifted in his chair. "That is correct, Defense Minister."

"How long will it take before you can be certain?"

"It depends on the movement of Izrailov and his henchmen, Defense Minister. The suspected site is, of course, under continuous surveillance. We're awaiting some activity by either him or his men that would confirm the presence of the missiles."

Gromov folded his hands on top of his desk and stared into Ryabkin's eyes. "So you lost track of the missiles from the time they left Chechnya until you think they may have shown up near Voronezh? Have you considered the possibility that Izrailov is decoying us?"

Ryabkin nodded slowly. "Of course, Defense Minister, but we don't believe that is the case."

"Why is that?"

"Because there was a theft from a chemical weapons storage facility near Voronezh a few nights ago."

Gromov slammed his fist on the desktop. "Son of a bitch! Can't anyone do anything right anymore? What is happening to us? And why wasn't I informed of this incident before now? Can you answer me that, General Ryabkin?"

Ryabkin quickly fumbled through some papers in his hand, then looked up pleadingly. "The report was sent to you two days ago, Defense Minister."

Gromov settled back into his chair. "I haven't seen it.

Obviously, I'll have to talk to General Pankratov about that. Is there anything else the Chief of the General Staff hasn't told me?"

"Not that I'm aware of, Defense Minister."

3 September, 1445 hours Local

The members of the Russian Military Collegium sat quietly as Gromov studied the faces of the most powerful military officers in Russia. Soon, they would become much more powerful than anyone dreamed, and Gromov wondered whether all would prove capable of exercising that power as he intended they should.

"As some of you are already aware," Gromov began, "there is a complication in our plans. Mr. Izrailov has decided on trying to blackmail us into granting concessions to his organization."

There was a stir around the table as the uninformed took in the news.

"He is threatening the capital with cruise missiles armed with chemical weapons. Some of you know that he can make good on the threat with the missiles. You all should know that, according to the GRU, he can also carry out that portion of his threat dealing with chemical weapons. I have been informed that the chemical weapons storage site near Voronezh has been broken into. As a result, several missile warheads and canisters filled with VX are now in the possession of the Chechen mafia."

The stir became a commotion, and Gromov had to shout above the general din to restore order.

"I am as surprised as most of you," Gromov said. "I only just found out about this theft a few moments ago." Gromov stared at Pankratov, who quickly looked away. "I will sort out that particular problem later. For now, we have a very concrete threat with which we must deal. Izrailov is asking for license for his organization to do anything it wants. In return, he promises not to poison the city. Before someone asks the obvious, let me say we are not certain at this time where Izrailov is hiding the missiles, but the GRU believes it has identified the probable location, also near Voronezh."

"So why don't we move against it immediately?" asked the head of the Russian ground forces.

"Because, General Pyatakov, if the GRU is wrong, we have every reason to believe Izrailov will make good on his threat. We need to be absolutely certain *all* the missiles are at the suspected site. And when we move it has to be swift, decisive. There can be no margin for error this time around, unlike some of our predecessors' previous operations. I believe everyone understands that?"

"What does this do for the timing for Operation Salvation?" Pankratov asked.

Gromov's eyes narrowed as he looked at the chief of the General Staff once again. Pankratov had broken a cardinal rule by mentioning the operation out loud at a meeting of the Military Collegium. But at this point, what did it really matter?

"Izrailov concedes he has given us a ready-made excuse to act," Gromov responded firmly. "I recommend we take advantage of the situation. If the GRU can confirm its information, we can roll everything up at once. If not, we'll implement all other phases of the operation according to the agreed-upon schedule and take care of Izrailov later. But let me assure everyone that one way or another, Izrailov's days are numbered in very small digits."

"What about the Americans?" Pankratov persisted.

"What about them?" Gromov answered impatiently.

"Can we count on their doing nothing?"

"General Pankratov, how many times are you going to ask me that question? How many times am I going to have to reassure you?" Gromov turned to address the group. "For the benefit of all of you, let me state what I have already told our chief of the General Staff on several occasions: The Americans will do nothing. The American president is going to be occupied with much larger, much more personal problems."

Gromov scanned the faces in the room one last time, then took a deep breath and looked at General Grishin. "The airborne units are ready?"

"Absolutely, Defense Minister."

"The Tamanskaya Division as well?"

"Ready for your orders, Defense Minister," General Yakovlev, the Commander of the Moscow Military District, answered in his trademark no-nonsense manner.

"And the other military district and theater commanders?"

"All ready and awaiting the orders, Defense Minister," Pankratov answered crisply.

"Then I recommend we execute at 0001 hours tonight." Gromov studied their faces intently. "All agreed?"

There was no dissension.

Chapter Thirty-four

The two F-15s had located their target. They pulled up in trailing formation behind and below the Airbus, their air intercept radars locked onto the aircraft as a precaution; the hostile action would go undetected by the civilian aircrew.

"Empire Air 003, this is Eagle One. I am an Air Combat Command F-15 flying at the direction of the National Military Command Center. You are ordered to alter your course and land at Baltimore Washington International Airport immediately. You are not to deviate from these instructions. Do you understand? Acknowledge receipt, over."

There was nothing but silence.

"NMCC, this is Eagle One. There is no response from the Airbus, on any channel. I'm pulling even with the aircraft. Now."

The two F-15s broke formation, with the lead pilot easing his Eagle nearly even with the Airbus's cockpit. The civilian captain looked out his window at the fighter, waved at its pilot, then pointed to his headset and shook his head.

"NMCC. Eagle One. Airbus captain is signaling problems with his radio. That would explain *our* communication problem. Does the FAA controller have him?"

"That's a negative, Eagle One. They have him on radar beginning his approach, but they report negative radio contact."

"Terrific. I'm going to waggle my wings at this guy and see if he understands the universal signal for get your ass on the ground, over."

The F-15 pilot performed his maneuver in full view of the civilian pilot, who responded by firmly shaking his head and pointing toward Washington. The fighter pilot gave the thumbs-down, waggled his plane again, and once more pointed down.

"NMCC, I just received a communication from the Airbus captain. The asshole just gave me the finger. Instructions?"

Meanwhile, the civilian pilot was now looking straight ahead, deliberately ignoring the fighter's presence.

"NMCC, this is Eagle One again. We're awaiting your orders, over."

There was a debate raging within the NMCC, with General Price arguing in a loud voice that it was time to take the Airbus out before it could launch the cruise missiles. General Hannah, in an even louder voice, told his subordinate he wasn't going to order the shoot-down of a civilian airliner because some joker claimed there were cruise missiles on board.

"First of all, General Price, there's no way those damned JASSMs are operational. I don't care what some damned airlifter says to the contrary. Secondly, even if they could hot-wire the missiles, they sure as hell couldn't shoot them out of an Airbus. Let's get serious, shall we?"

"And if you're wrong on both counts, General Hannah?"

"Then I'm wrong, damn it! The only person who's going to tell us to shoot down this plane is the president, and he's not about to do that, is he?"

"Have you asked him, General? Does he really want 1600

Pennsylvania Avenue reduced to a hole in the ground?"

"General Price, you're treading on very thin ice here."

"Goddamn it, General Hannah! The entire damned city may be on thinner ice. We've got an airplane on a direct course to Washington. In a minute it's going to be over heavily populated areas and then over the Potomac. By then, it'll be too damned late to do anything. They can't contact the pilot, and the bastard just gave one of your pilots the bird. Surely that tells you something is wrong?"

Price could see Hannah's jaw moving back and forth. The chairman was obviously furious, but his silence indicated that Price's arguments were generating second thoughts.

"Damn you, Price," Hannah said. "Get Noonan on the phone."

"NMCC, this is Eagle One. Eagle Two and I are patiently awaiting your instructions. Son of a bitch! What the hell was that?" A loud crack on the F-15's canopy instantly caused the pilot to flinch, and the Eagle wobbled for a moment. Swiftly regaining control of his aircraft, the Eagle driver looked back toward the airliner.

The cargo door of the Airbus had just blown away, barely missing the airliner's wing and the F-15's tail. Debris from the separation had apparently struck the F-15's windshield, but had caused no other damage. The Airbus bounced around violently for a few seconds from the turbulence, then steadied itself. The F-15 pilot eased his aircraft back to get a better look angle into the aircraft.

"NMCC, this is Eagle One. We have an emergency situation here. The airliner has just lost his cargo hatch, and there's an object sitting in the cargo bay that looks for all the world to me like a rotary launcher, and it's starting to move. I need your instructions, now! Over!"

There was a moment of silence, but to the F-15 pilot it seemed like an eternity. Finally, a weary voice came on the line.

"Eagle One, this is General Price. The chairman wants to know if you can confirm there are no passengers on the airliner." Price already knew the answer to the question, but

Hannah had been adamant about having the F-15 pilot confirm the decision he was about to make. Was Hannah looking for someone to share the blame? There would be more than enough to go around if this turned out wrong.

"Please tell General Hannah that if I try to get close enough to verify whether anyone else is on board, you won't need to worry about the airliner anymore. You'll be able to sort us all out on the ground."

Price forced back a smile. He knew Hannah had understood the pilot's underlying message: The request had been stupid. It was the NMCC's job to verify who was on the airplane, not that of some fighter pilot fighting the sun's glare while trying to get his aircraft close enough to a fast-moving, unstable target so he could sneak a peek through a small porthole. The pilots had done all they had been asked; they had provided visual confirmation of the danger Williams had passed along. Now it was time to act.

Price looked at Hannah. The chairman nodded slowly, then turned away. "I just hope the pilot knows the difference between a missile launcher and a cargo pallet," he mumbled as he made his way to a nearby chair.

"Eagle One. You have clearance to splash one Airbus. Repeat, splash the Airbus."

"NMCC, please repeat your instructions, over."

"Splash the Airbus, Major. Do it now."

"Roger, NMCC. Eagle Two, do you have the shot?"

"Roger, Eagle One. I am saddled. Break left."

The F-15 banked away from the Airbus, quickly falling back parallel with his wingman so the two fighters were trailing the airliner, one on either side.

"Fox One," the wingman called out as the missile sped toward its target.

The Sparrow missile rapidly covered the distance to the Airbus, its warhead exploding directly on the left wing. The airliner was enveloped in a huge fireball and slowly began disintegrating as it fell to earth.

"Splash one Airbus," the pilot of Eagle Two called out excitedly, then, "Oh God, oh God, Brad, did you see?" he yelled out to the pilot of the other F-15.

"Yeah," Eagle One responded. "Yeah, I saw it. NMCC, this is Eagle One. The Airbus had passengers. I have the chairman's confirmation now. Repeat, there were passengers. God forgive us."

"What the hell do you mean there were passengers?" Noonan yelled into the phone. "You told me this was a goddamned cargo plane. You told me you were able to confirm there were no civilian passengers on board. Now you're telling me you were wrong? Does someone want to tell me how many people I may have just ordered to their deaths because you advised me there were no passengers on board?"

"Depending on the cargo configuration, Mr. President, it could have been carrying almost a hundred and fifty passengers."

"Oh, Christ Almighty," the president groaned. "That's just wonderful, General Hannah. Would you like to tell me where you got your original information? From the tooth fairy?"

"We spoke to Empire Air directly and were informed there were no passengers on board this flight, just cargo and the crew." Hannah's face was flushed. He stared straight into Price's eyes as he drew his forefinger across his neck. Price understood the significance of the gesture all too well. Both their careers were rapidly evaporating in the smoke and debris of what was an unmitigated disaster.

"And what did Empire Air in Washington have to say? You did check with more than one person, did you not?"

"The manifest showed ninety-three passengers, but as I said, Mr. President, the Empire Air president's office told us the passenger complement was canceled out at the last minute due to cargo-loading problems." Hannah did not mention the airline's operations center had given them a different account.

"And we certainly know now what those problems were. So these bloody bastards sacrificed ninety-three Americans in some wild-eyed plot to blow up the White House?"

"So it would seem, Mr. President."

"Yes, wouldn't it, General? I want the evidence this plane

was carrying passengers and cruise missiles. I have to try to explain this one to the American people."

"I'm afraid the evidence is scattered over several square miles of Maryland countryside, Mr. President."

"General Hannah, I don't give a good rat's ass if the airplane is scattered over the entire goddamned Catoctin Mountains. You get somebody from the Pentagon out there with the FBI and the NTSB and bring me back the evidence missiles were on that plane. I don't care if you personally have to get down on all fours and pick up the pieces with tweezers and a teaspoon. You get this done and you get it done now. I don't want any more bad news, although I don't know how there could be any news worse than this. Is that understood?"

"Yes, Mr. President." Hannah gently placed the receiver in its cradle, as if afraid to offend the president even further by making too much noise. He turned to Price. "General, retirement is looking awfully good right now, assuming I get there. I would suggest you start making your transition plans as well. Where the hell is this TRANSCOM colonel?"

"I'm not certain where he is right now, sir, but I can track him down fairly quickly."

"You do that. I want him on the first helicopter out to the crash site. He's the one that passed along the information, now let him help us sort this thing out on the ground."

Price extended his hands palm outward toward Hannah. "General, Williams only passed along information from another source, one of the plotters. He didn't have any information on the presence of passengers. In fact, he wanted to know what this particular version of the Airbus was capable of carrying. I really don't see why we need him to go out with the investigation team. Besides, he's a TRANSCOM asset. He belongs to General Petersen."

Hannah glared. "When his ass is in Washington, he belongs to me. Find him and put him on the damned chopper. Is that clear, General Price?"

Price stood up straight. "Very clear, sir." He then spun on his heels and headed back toward his desk, the clenching and unclenching of his fists the only sign of his anger at the treatment he had just received from his boss. He had no intention of tracking down Williams. He wasn't going to be responsible for shooting the messenger. *Screw the chairman,* he thought, *I'm out the door anyway. Right behind Hannah.*

Chapter Thirty-five

"I agree the situation is terrible, Mr. President, but not un-salvageable." Chief of Staff Farley had just finished listening to his boss bewailing the fact that the shooting down of the Airbus would probably undo everything he was attempting to accomplish in foreign policy and would almost certainly lead to his defeat in November.

"Farley, you've been a good chief of staff, but I don't think your abilities will get us out of this one. I'm going to have a hundred families camped on the White House doorstep ready to hang me by my thumbs, or worse, and I'm sure they have a similar fate in mind for the rest of the White House staff."

"Mr. President, you seem to forget that the Airbus was carrying cruise missiles aimed at the heart of Washington. If you hadn't acted, there would be thousands dead, rather than a hundred."

Noonan massaged his temples with his fingertips. "I think

you may be exaggerating. People are going to think I was only trying to protect my own ass, not the rest of the city. A single cruise missile would've made a mess of the White House, but I doubt it would have laid waste to the rest of the capital."

"And how do you know they weren't going to launch all the missiles, Mr. President, and at what targets? These were terrorists. They don't give a damn about how many innocent civilians they might kill. In fact, as far as they're concerned, the higher the body count, the better. It makes it look as though we can't protect our citizens. And that's exactly what you did. There was a regrettable cost, but it was still far less than it could have been."

Christoph had been listening to Farley's argument, watching the president's face relax as the chief of staff tried his best to portray Noonan as the savior of the city. He had heard enough of Farley's unctuousness. It was time to inject a small dose of reality into the president's thought processes. He sat forward on the sofa and cleared his throat. "Farley makes a compelling argument, Mr. President. If the Airbus was carrying several cruise missiles, and they had been able to launch them all, who knows what a mess we'd be in now? But a hundred dead Americans are still a hundred dead Americans, regardless of the chain of events that led to their deaths."

Farley started to protest, but Christoph raised his hand to cut him off.

"You said *if*," Noonan said.

"Mr. President, we don't know for a fact that there were cruise missiles on that airplane. What if there weren't?"

Noonan sucked in his breath. "Oh, Lord, I don't even want to think about that possibility."

"You have to, Mr. President."

Noonan shook his head. "But we have a source, one of the plotters, who categorically stated the weapons were aboard the Airbus. Plus, we had visual confirmation from our fighter pilots."

"Sir, we had a comment from a doped-up individual, with

access to the Oval Office, alleged to be part of a conspiracy to blow up the White House. How do you think that will sound to anyone outside these walls?"

"But we have Underwood's testimony about his meetings with Evans," Farley said, ticking off the points with his fingers. "There's the note from the Russian reporter—that we practically had to squeeze out of Underwood, I might add. Then there's the hijacking of the cruise missiles. We have airline pilots who ignored warnings. It all fits together. What more do you want, Christoph?"

"I want to know there were cruise missiles on that son-of-a-bitchin' plane, Farley, that's what I want. Before we put the president in front of the cameras to defend his actions, we'd better have all the facts. We'd better have a piece of a goddamned missile in our hands."

"And if we don't?" Noonan asked.

"Then, Mr. President," Farley answered without hesitation, "we say the two fighter pilots made a bad call on what they saw."

"And then what?" Christoph challenged.

"And then we blame the pilots or someone else in the military chain of command. It's been done before."

"Yes, it has," Christoph responded, a look of utter disdain momentarily twisting his normally tranquil features. "Tell me, Farley," he asked, "you ever been in the military?"

"You know I haven't."

"Just wanted to make sure. Mr. President, before you hold up the military as a whipping boy, or scapegoat, as your chief of staff so blithely suggests, we still need to get all the facts. The Pentagon won't like it much if they take an unwarranted hit on this."

"They'll do what they're told, Christoph," Farley said firmly.

"Precisely the kind of response I'd expect from a martinet who's never worn the uniform, Farley."

"Gentlemen, please," Noonan shouted. "You're supposed to be advising me, not aggravating me."

"Sorry, Mr. President," both advisers responded in unison.

Christoph looked chagrined; Farley was still seething.

"If the blame lies with the military, that's where it will fall," Noonan said. "But I'm not looking for a scapegoat. Blame will be apportioned according to actual culpability, not to cover someone's tail. Jeff, you have a lot to learn. If I let you deal with the Pentagon, all the chiefs would no doubt resign. You let me worry about the generals." Turning to Christoph, he said, "And we need to get Underwood back here as quickly as possible. We'll need his help in this. Jeff, I do want you to be the point man on talking to the NTSB and the FBI and their investigative teams at the crash site. Find us that piece of cruise missile we need to make sure the terrorists don't walk away from this. Keep me informed."

Farley nodded enthusiastically. "It's there, Mr. President. I know it is. We'll find it."

"As for you," Noonan continued, looking at Christoph, "continue to keep me honest. Work closely with that FBI special agent . . ."

"Younghart."

"Yes, Younghart. Keep pressing her to find out what more Evans knows about all this."

"I'm not sure how much longer I can fend off the DCI, Mr. President, even by invoking your name."

"I'll take care of that as soon as we break up. I think a personal phone call from me should convince him the matter should be handled my way. Besides, he and I need to discuss his agency's procedures for vetting its personnel. He needs to know about some of the people he has on his payroll, don't you agree?"

"Absolutely, Mr. President." Christoph smiled.

"Anything else before you go?"

Christoph stared at Farley for a moment, but the chief of staff failed to take the hint. Christoph turned back to Noonan, tipping his head in Farley's direction.

"Jeff, why don't you go ahead and start working on the investigation?" Noonan said.

"But, Mr. President, don't you think I should be aware of—"

"Don't worry, Jeff, if there's something I think you should know, I'll call you back. Leave us alone, okay, and make sure we're not disturbed."

Farley scowled at Christoph as he left. Christoph pretended not to notice, which infuriated Farley even more; although he yanked at the knob, he wisely resisted the temptation to slam the door shut behind him.

"You obviously have something you want to pass along."

"Yes, Mr. President. The secretary of state contacted me this morning. The Iranian UN ambassador approached Ambassador Jacobs this afternoon with a request for a meeting with the secretary. Given the situation in the Gulf, she was not about to agree to that without consulting with the White House."

"Of course. Any idea what he wants to talk about? I would hope they want to discuss ways of defusing the crisis. The ball's been in their court for several days."

"I didn't get the impression he wanted to make a démarche. He suggested the Iranian government might have some information of value to us in our antiterrorist efforts."

Noonan stared hard at Christoph. "This is a joke, right? We're in the middle of a crisis with the Iranians, and they want to help us fight terrorists?"

"I know it sounds crazy, Mr. President, and I was extremely skeptical until the secretary told me the Iranians had specific information regarding a movement they've uncovered called the Fist of God."

"You just found out about this?"

"Just before the start of our meeting. I waited to bring it up because, quite frankly, dealing with the airliner seemed the much more pressing issue, although this could be related. And I felt it prudent not to involve Farley in what are likely to be very sensitive discussions, if in fact you decide to approve those discussions."

Noonan leaned back in his chair, cradling the back of his head in his clasped hands. It was a moment before he answered. "Tell the Secretary of State she has my approval to proceed. But the matter must be handled discreetly. I don't want word leaking out that we're talking to the Iranians directly. Our allies in the Gulf might misinterpret. I want the secretary to visit New York, ostensibly to meet with Jacobs and our allies' ambassadors. There's no way we'll get the Iranian into Washington without attracting attention. I want to hear what he has to say, but not if it's going to disrupt our policy in the Gulf. Are we clear on that?"

Christoph nodded. "Absolutely, Mr. President."

"I want to know when she departs and when and where the meeting will take place. And I want a complete debriefing from the secretary after the meeting. And no meeting unless the Iranians agree to our conditions. If they don't abide by our terms, then as far as the United States is concerned, this meeting will never have happened."

"Yes, sir."

Noonan took a deep breath. "Is there anything else you think I should know?"

Christoph grinned. "I thought that would be enough for today, Mr. President."

Chapter Thirty-six

3 September, 1145 hours EDT

Younghart had walked Williams down to the front door of the medical center to see him off to the Pentagon. He had been summoned to a meeting with General Price. But she had also gone along to get away from the intensity of the situation in the room with Evans and to grab a cup of coffee from the cafeteria. She had tried to grab a candy bar, but the vending machine had taken her money and given nothing in return. As she tugged unsuccessfully on the knob, she noticed a tag on the machine instructing her to call Underwood Vending for a refund.

"It figures," she muttered as she walked away, coffee in hand.

As she was about to make the turn to enter the corridor where Evans was being held, a tall, thin orderly nearly bumped into her as he rounded the corner pushing a hospital cart. She pressed herself against the wall as he uttered an emphatic apology and hurried on his way. She watched his departure around the next corner, shaking her head. She took a sip of the coffee to steady her nerves, then suddenly realized something wasn't quite right. This was a sealed area. No orderlies. She dropped the cup and started running down the hallway. The agent who was supposed to be standing at the door was missing. She ran toward Evans's room, pulling her pistol from its holster as she did so. She turned the knob and pushed, but the door, although not locked, was blocked by something on the other side. She pushed harder and the door gave way. And then she turned her head quickly away from the scene in front of her until the sudden wave of nausea from the sight and the smell of blood had passed.

The doctor was slumped in the corner, his body twisted, his head against the wall, his smock turning crimson from the pool of blood collecting around his shoulders. The obstacle at the door had been the other agent; although mortally wounded, he apparently had tried to pursue the killer but had fallen against the door.

Evans was quite clearly dead. He was lying on the hospital bed, his legs and arms still firmly secured. But there was a bullet hole under his chin, and the back wall was decorated with what had once been the top of his head.

After confirming that there was nothing she could do for the agent, Younghart ran back down the hall at full speed in pursuit of the orderly, in the process grabbing a D.C. cop who had been standing guard at the entrance to the ward. He had seen the orderly board the elevator just a few seconds before. The policeman radioed ahead as he and Younghart dashed down the nearest stairwell and made their way to the closest exit. They pushed through the door and stood in an empty parking lot.

Realizing the orderly had escaped, Younghart remembered that there was one person she had not noticed as she quickly surveyed the carnage in Evans's room. With the policeman in tow, she hustled back to the room, this time having to fight her way past hospital staff who were rushing to the scene. Pushing her way back into the room, she quickly looked around once more, and this time she saw Underwood. He was sitting on the floor, his back propped against the front wall. In the semidarkness, he had escaped her notice.

Now, with all the lights on, his presence and condition were painfully obvious.

He gave her a weak smile and a little wave. The front of his dark suit was drenched, and she knew immediately that it was blood. She knelt down and gently took hold of his arm. She searched for the right words, but could only force out a lie. "You're going to be okay, Mike. The doctors will take care of you."

Underwood smiled again. "I don't think so, Carolyn," he whispered. "The only help they can give me is to zip me up . . . in a plastic bag."

"Don't be ridiculous, Mike, you're going to be fine. Tell me, can you tell me, what happened?" She already knew the answer, but she hoped the question would help keep him conscious.

"Guess, Carolyn," he rasped, "you're the FBI agent. And a damned good one." He smiled one last time, then his head dropped to his chest.

She stared at him for a moment, then felt a chill rush through her body. She gently released his arm, then stood up. As the staff scurried fruitlessly around Underwood's now-lifeless form, Younghart's cellular phone started ringing. She thankfully stepped into the hall as she pulled the phone from her pocket. "Younghart."

"Carolyn, this is Frank Simmons. We have some good news. We've found Jennifer Underwood alive. She's a little dehydrated and suffering from exposure, but she's going to be fine. She was alone. No sign of her captors. I'll fill you in on the details later, but I figured you'd want to pass this along to her husband."

Younghart stared absently down the corridor, and slowly closed the phone as she let it drop to her side. "Thanks, Frank, I'll do that," she muttered softly. She leaned back against the wall, dropped her head, and silently wept.

Near the hospital's emergency entrance, a tall, thin man wearing a physician's coat walked slowly but purposefully down the sidewalk, pausing for a moment to drop a bundle into the trash. He donned sunglasses and walked a little faster toward a red BMW in the staff parking lot. Exiting the hospital grounds, he gave a friendly nod to a policeman entering the lot in a patrol car.

Chapter Thirty-seven

3 September, 1205 hours EDT

Williams had expected the now-familiar staff sergeant to greet him at the entrance to the NMCC, but instead he was met by General Price. Price grabbed him by the arm and escorted Williams to the Pentagon's River Entrance. They walked down the steps into the hot afternoon sun and strolled across the parking lot to the steps at the top of the parade ground. Price had said nothing. He stared at the flag fluttering at the far end, then across the river at the Jefferson Memorial. Williams waited patiently, wondering about the purpose of this little sojourn. He began recounting the day's events in his head but was jolted out of his reverie by the intensity of Price's voice.

" 'To seek out the best through the whole Union, we must resort to other information, which, from the best of men, acting disinterestedly and with the purest motives, is sometimes incorrect.' Do you know who said that, Colonel?"

"No, sir, I'm afraid I don't."

"He did," Price said, pointing to the memorial. "That man

we honor there." Price paused. "I assume you've heard what happened?" the general finally asked, continuing to gaze across the Potomac.

"No, sir, you still have me at a disadvantage."

Price turned toward Williams and stared at him for a moment, somewhat incredulously. "Colonel, I envy you that ignorance, which I, unfortunately, am about to end. The information you passed along was the precursor to a whole series of events that are about to turn this country on its head, I suspect. You see, the Empire Air flight you warned us about was shot down by our F-15s about an hour ago."

Williams jerked quickly around. The general now had his undivided attention.

"There's a search team on its way out to the site in Maryland as we speak," Price continued, "looking for evidence that the aircraft was carrying missiles. Unfortunately, the airliner was carrying something else—about a hundred passengers on their way to a Florida vacation."

Williams reached for the stone railing as if he'd been hit in the stomach. "Oh, my God. How, General? How could that have happened?"

"I was given some very erroneous information by . . . oh, hell, Blair, some frigging bastard at Empire Air lied to me when I called to verify the manifest. It's that simple. The president was an old buddy of mine, but he wasn't in when I called, so I spoke to someone who I thought worked in his office. Now, I haven't a clue who I talked to, but I sure as hell have some suspicions as to who they're working for."

Williams slowly nodded. "The same folks as Evans, no doubt."

"No doubt. But if I was lied to about the passengers, I have to wonder whether or not Evans lied to you about what the aircraft was carrying."

Williams shook his head. "I don't think that's possible. I watched the interrogation. I don't see how Evans could have evaded, given his condition. He was in a very cooperative mood. Agent Younghart is still with him. We can press on."

"Evans is dead, Blair."

Williams winced. "But I just left them—"

"Apparently right after you left, someone disguised as a hospital employee made his way to Evans's room."

"Is Younghart all right?" Williams quickly asked.

"She's fine, as nearly as I can tell. But Evans was killed, as was another FBI agent and a doctor, as well as the president's military assistant."

"Mike Underwood is dead?"

Price nodded.

Williams leaned against the railing, trying to catch his breath. "I need to get back over there."

The general vigorously shook his head. "Blair, you need to get the hell out of Dodge. The chairman is head-hunting, and I'm afraid yours is at the top of the list, even though you were just passing along information that anybody—and I mean anybody—would have considered valid, given the situation. You're going to be a lot safer fifteen hundred miles from here. Hannah will be consumed with salvaging what's left of *his* career, and he won't care who else he destroys in the process." Price paused momentarily. "I see you're surprised by my bluntness. Hell, Blair, you did a great job. The point is, you did your job, and I'll be damned if you'll be made a scapegoat for that on my watch."

Price put his hand on Williams's shoulder and pursed his lips. "At some point, you're going to be questioned, seriously, about this whole affair, but go home and wait for the call. If anybody asks, I gave you a direct order to get your ass out of here. You did what you came to do. The mystery of the missiles has been solved. Your command's equities have been taken care of."

"General Price. Sir. I'm up to my eyeballs in this. I can't just leave. I appreciate the offer and your concern, but—"

"Colonel, goddamn it, it's not a suggestion, or a request. I'm ordering you to get on the next available flight back to St. Louis. If I have to, I'll put you on the damned plane myself!"

Williams raised his hand in surrender. "All right, General. But can I ask you one more question? Why are you doing this?"

Price smiled. "Blair, there's more than enough blame to

be spread around. I'm going to take my share. Hell, I may take the brunt of it. If Hannah has his way, I will. That's okay. I've had thirty good years. I can resign for the honor of the country and the Air Force, if it comes to that. If they want another sacrificial lamb, I'm willing to play that role. It's a role we Air Force generals seem to get stuck with every now and then."

Williams smiled back at this superior. He felt proud to be taken into Price's confidence in a rare moment of camaraderie.

"So who do you think is going to take my place after I'm gone, Colonel?" Price asked, raising an eyebrow. "If you weather this—and I think you will—you've got what it takes, as far as I'm concerned, to be sitting where I am in a few years. Your boss thinks so, too, or you wouldn't be here. Petersen better hang on tight, because if my successor is smart, he'll steal you right out from under CINCTRANS's nose. At least, that's what I'm going to urge him to do. Out of Hannah's earshot, of course."

As Williams smiled, Price extended his hand. "So, now that I've thoroughly stroked your ego, Colonel, how about following orders and getting on the airplane? I don't want to see your ass around here again. Your staff has been ordered to pack their bags; I believe yours will be waiting for you at Andrews. Go home, Blair. Hug your kid. Make love to your wife. You don't want to be here when it hits the fan."

"I think it already has, General," Williams said as he took Price's proffered hand and shook it warmly.

"Oh, my good colonel, it hasn't even begun, especially for the gentleman sitting over there." Price gestured in the direction of the White House. "Mr. Jefferson trembled for his country. I imagine the current commander in chief is trembling for other reasons, perhaps the fate of his next four years."

Williams rendered the general a parting salute and headed for the parking lot. On the way, he called Mulkey on the cell phone to confirm that everyone had the same departure orders.

"Well, Colonel, it's not quite like we're being ridden out

of town on a rail, but damned close," Mulkey chortled. "However, I'll be perfectly content to sit at home watching CNN when the shit hits."

"Tom, contrary to recent reports I've had, I think it's safe to say it's already started. See you guys at Andrews. I have one more stop I have to make before I catch up with you at base ops."

"But, Colonel, I thought you said General Price gave strict orders."

"He did, and we're going to carry them out. I'm just making a slight detour."

Chapter Thirty-eight

"You understand that President Milyutin was very reluctant to agree to this meeting?"

"Of course, Pavel Vissarionovich," Izrailov replied. "But given the importance of what I have to pass along, I think he'll agree that consorting in this instance with undesirable elements is in his and Russia's very best interest."

"And when have you and your comrades ever given a damn about Russia's interests?"

"You offend me deeply, Pavel Vissarionovich. I consider myself a Russian patriot, even if I wasn't born a Russian. The Russian Federation is my adopted homeland."

"More like your adopted pasture, you mean."

"My dear Russian friend, we're going to get nowhere if all you want to do is trade insults. I have some very valuable information for your president. If you can refrain from scurrilous comments for a moment, I will be most happy to pass it along."

Pavel Vissarionovich Stepashin, President Milyutin's na-

Ken Currie

tional security adviser and head of the Presidential Security Council, frowned at the impertinent lecture but decided he would be quiet and listen to what Izrailov had to say. "Very well, but I warn you, if this is some kind of chess match you're trying to play with the Russian president, he's not interested."

"I never cared very much for chess," Izrailov countered.

"Get on with it, please. The president has appointments this evening, and if you expect me to get this information to him, you'd best get started."

"But I'm not the one causing the delay, my dear Pavel Vissarionovich," Izrailov pleaded.

"Enough!" Stepashin shouted, exasperated. He stood up to leave. "The devil with you. I've no time for games, and neither has Milyutin."

"Would the Russian president be interested in knowing his generals are plotting a coup d'état?" Izrailov asked calmly, examining the backs of his hands. "But if you prefer to leave, Pavel Vissarionovich, please, don't let me hold you back."

Stepashin promptly sat back down and tried to muster up a smile. "And just how would the head of the Chechen mafia be privy to such information?"

Izrailov's eyes opened wide. "Pavel Vissarionovich! You wound me! Head of the mafia? I'm just a poor, honest businessman trying to make a living while protecting his homeland."

"Businessman, perhaps. Poor and honest, I very much doubt."

"There you go again. Why must you engage in these personal attacks? What have I ever done to offend you?" Izrailov's deeply pockmarked face screwed itself into a mock expression of pain.

"Very well, I will refrain from any further such comments. But the president will very much want to know your sources of information."

Izrailov slid an envelope across the table. "You will find a list of all the major conspirators in that envelope, which I ask that you deliver to Milyutin. Suffice it to say, the head of the conspiracy is his *trusted* defense minister, Gromov,

348

who has been in prolonged contact with members of my—
how shall I say it—my business consortium."

Stepashin wasn't the least surprised to hear Gromov accused of treason. He had never trusted the general himself,
but his suspicions were raised when the accusations were
made by the head of the Chechen mafia. Izrailov could be
doing nothing more than playing to his and Milyutin's private fears, for the Russian president shared Stepashin's fear
of Gromov as a potential man on a white horse. If that was
the case, one could only guess as to Izrailov's underlying
motives.

Stepashin opened the envelope and read the list of names,
which included virtually every member of the Defense Ministry's collegium. "How did you come by this?"

"I told you. My consortium has been dealing with Gromov
and his allies for quite some time. But there are those within
the Ministry of Defense who disagree with Gromov's plans.
They are afraid of what might happen. And their fear has
made them loose-tongued. They tend to talk, but not always
to the *right* people. It was a very simple task to put together
the list."

"And when is all of this supposed to take place?"

Izrailov laughed unpleasantly. "My dear Pavel Vissarionovich. It's already happening. Right under your and Milyutin's very noses. What do you think is the purpose of the
security measures announced last night by your president?"

"Those were Milyutin's measures, not Gromov's."

"The Russian leadership truly has become naive, hasn't
it?"

Stepashin bristled at the insult, his necking turning bright
red, but he said nothing.

"Gromov came up with the justification for the plan, did
he not? Didn't he, in fact, push for stricter measures?"

Stepashin shifted uneasily in his chair. Izrailov had no
reason to know these details. "I couldn't comment on that."

"I'm certain you could, but I understand your hesitation
to do so. We wouldn't want to divulge any state secrets,
would we, especially to the Chechens?"

Stepashin once again ignored the barb. "President Milyutin will want something more tangible than a list of names that anyone could pull out of the newspapers. Do you have anything more than this?"

Izrailov smiled. "Who do you think procured the American cruise missiles and the chemical warheads that Gromov is touting as the justification for declaring martial law?"

Stepashin deflated instantly. He now knew for certain that Izrailov was telling the truth, at least as much as he wanted to tell. He obviously was deeply involved in the whole affair. But why turn on Gromov? "How much time do we have?" Stepashin asked, his voice barely a whisper.

"My friend, you have seven hours. Gromov and his friends plan on presenting Milyutin with a *fait accompli* at this evening's Defense Council meeting. I have given them the reason for moving forward with their plans. And I have given you the justification for stopping them."

"Justification!" Stepashin screamed. "You tell us a coup is imminent seven hours before it's to take place. Why didn't you come to us sooner?"

"But it wouldn't have made things as interesting if I had done that, Pavel Vissarionovich. It's much more entertaining and challenging this way, don't you think?"

Stepashin wanted to kill the man seated in front of him, but the rather large bodyguard sitting in the corner made him more circumspect. Instead, he slammed his fist into his palm. "This is wonderful, Izrailov! Do you get your amusement from watching Russian democracy go under?"

"Oh, spare me, please, Stepashin," Izrailov responded, dropping the familiarity. "*Russian democracy.* What is that, anyway? Your president presents himself as the great democrat, but he runs the country like all the autocrats before him. And now he's in the same danger confronted by all self-deluded autocrats. It would have served all of you right if I had said nothing. In fact, I may just keep you here until Gromov has made his move and is sleeping in Milyutin's Kremlin apartments."

"But you won't?" Stepashin asked, already knowing the answer.

"Of course I won't. You wouldn't be here if I took Milyutin and his democratic prattling seriously. I took the time and trouble of setting Gromov up. Now I want you and Milyutin to take him down. I know the Russian security services are very loyal to the president, and," Izrailov paused while he retrieved another envelope from his desk, "here's a list of the officers and units Milyutin can trust. Same sources as before. Same fearful people as before. If Gromov succeeds, they will have claimed to have supported him all along, for the sake of their careers. But they're afraid to say anything, to expose Gromov's plot, because they think they'll be acting alone. If they know the president is acting forcefully, and they have other allies, they'll throw their lot in with Milyutin."

Shaking his head, Stepashin glanced at the list, then gave Izrailov a steady look. "I don't understand why you're doing this, Izrailov. What do you expect to gain from all of this?"

"I expect to get rid of an enemy. Gromov is a Bonaparte. He always has been. My business activities don't need a Bonaparte. A Gromov regime wouldn't tolerate the independence exercised by my types of business. There is honor among thieves, but Gromov is no thief, and therefore he cannot be trusted. He's simply an aspiring dictator. I really don't give a damn whether Russia can survive a dictator. I just know my consortium cannot. Besides, Gromov would kill me at the first opportunity. By preempting him, I am only defending myself. That's a concept I'm sure your Russian generals would understand and appreciate. Now you have my reasons, Pavel Vissarionovich. I ask nothing in return. Your elimination of Gromov and his friends will be all the compensation I could possibly ask for."

"So you can have free rein to continue your criminal activities?" Stepashin challenged.

Izrailov smiled. "If you say so."

"There is one bit of unfinished business, Izrailov. What about the missiles and warheads? They're still a threat, just as Gromov has been arguing. Is President Milyutin supposed to sleep safely at night knowing the Chechen mafia has chemical weapons?"

Izrailov chuckled. "Do you really think, after all this, that

I would eliminate the source of the golden eggs by destroying the Russian goose? In any event, there are no longer any American cruise missiles in Russia. That's what Gromov had planned all along. He tried to play all of you for fools." Stepashin frowned as Izrailov continued. "Our arrangement with Gromov provided for transfer to a third party. That's been accomplished, just not to the third party Gromov expected." Izrailov waved his hand. "Oh, the missiles did accomplish one purpose Gromov wanted, a desire we shared. But now that the shell game is over, the missiles have a new mission, one that you and Milyutin will figure out in time. I think you'll be amazed at the clever use to which they have been put. And so will the Americans. Don't look so chagrined, Stepashin. The president's security adviser can't know everything."

Stepashin stared at him. "I don't understand your game, Izrailov."

"Quite simple, really. With Gromov out of the way, the Army in disarray because of his treason, and Milyutin occupied with the aftermath, we foresee the consolidation of a most favorable environment for our business activities, free of interference from Moscow. I'm sure you'll convey to the Russian president how important it is, given our assistance in this matter, that he not do anything that would constrict that environment."

"And if he doesn't?"

"That would be a very bad mistake. I need say no more than that. Milyutin is intelligent enough; he'll figure it out. In any event, we already have taken out an extra fee for our services to the Russian state: some missiles and a few chemical weapons we liberated from Gromov's army. It's amazing how expansive the military's supermarket can be if you're willing to pay the right price. Almost anything you want. Almost." Izrailov seemed almost wistful as he uttered the word.

"However," he continued, "our interests are much more pedestrian. We're simply the middlemen. These wares fetch a very handsome price on the world market. There's much profit to be made. You just have to sell to the right people, the reliable clients. Milyutin and his cronies in the IMF would be surprised how many members of his own government have financed their dachas and accumulated personal fortunes with the assistance of my consortium's financial acumen and its international banking connections. And then again, perhaps *Milyutin* wouldn't be so surprised, eh, Pavel Vissarionovich?"

Stepashin once again shifted uneasily in his chair.

"Now, I suggest you make your way quickly back to the Kremlin. My employees will ensure your safe conduct."

"I don't need your protection."

"Oh, but you do, Pavel Vissarionovich, you surely do."

And Stepashin knew he did.

Chapter Thirty-nine

3 September, 1805 Local

First Deputy Minister of Defense Pankratov stared out of Milyutin's Kremlin office window, nervously digging at his fingernails while waiting for the Russian president to finish a seemingly interminable phone call. He jumped slightly as Milyutin dropped the handset back into its cradle. He turned quickly, searching for some clue in Milyutin's expression as to why he had been summoned here so peremptorily.

Milyutin clasped his hands on the desk. "General Pankratov, I believe you are a true Russian patriot," he said evenly. "I believe you understand the irreparable damage it would cause Russian democracy—Russian society—if the military were to carry out a coup."

Pankratov's eyes grew wide. "Mr. President, I can assure you—"

Milyutin raised his hand. "Let me finish. I will be the first to admit we have made mistakes. We have not always protected the interests of the military and the needs of our soldiers as well as we should. The military has shown remarkable patience, and I believe that has been due to its profound sense of professional honor. Are you trying to tell me the Army has now turned its back on such honor?"

Pankratov immediately sat up straight. "President Milyutin, we would never turn our back on our honor, but sometimes it seems you have turned your back on the Army. You must understand the level of frustration that exists, the desire to do something to solve the problems."

"A coup will not solve those problems, General, it will only make them much worse. You will rip apart the Russian nation. Are you prepared to do that?"

"Mr. President, why do you accuse us of plotting a coup? The armed forces are only seeking to do what you have asked—no, ordered—to protect and heal the nation, not tear it apart."

Pankratov wilted as Milyutin looked at him skeptically. "General, your grandfather died in the Great Patriotic War," Milyutin said. "Your father died in Afghanistan, and you defended Yeltsin against a reactionary parliament. Your family has a tradition of defending the Russian state. Are you prepared to throw all of that away, simply to satisfy one man's desire to be the new Russian tsar?"

Pankratov felt his resistance crumbling away. "General Gromov has only Russia's interests at heart. There was never an intention of imposing a military dictatorship, only a provisional—" Pankratov stopped abruptly, aware he had now said too much. "Besides, something must be done to deal with the threat."

"There is no threat, General Pankratov. Only Gromov's schemes."

Pankratov stared at Milyutin in utter confusion.

Milyutin tossed a sheaf of papers on the table in front of him. "General, you need to read what your so-called Russian patriot has in mind. And what he's been up to, with help from other Russian officers, some of whom are *very* close to you. But I would recommend you read quickly. We don't have a whole lot of time to turn off this disaster."

Ken Currie

"General Gromov," Milyutin began, "I agreed to convene this meeting of the Defense Council to address the issue of what further measures might be necessary to thwart a terrorist attack on Moscow. Frankly, you didn't seem to give me much choice regarding the question of whether we even needed such a meeting at this time. It would appear you believe there is now some increased urgency to the situation. Am I correct in that assessment?"

Gromov cleared his throat and pushed his chair back from the table. He stood up deliberately, assuming a straight posture that highlighted the multiple rows of ribbons adorning his Russian Army officer's uniform. He was the quintessence of the new breed of Russian officers, or so he fervently believed. As such, he had special obligations he felt he must fulfill. The time had come to do so.

"President Milyutin, the Defense Council's military members commend your foresight for allowing us to implement steps that will ensure the security of the capital," Gromov began. "Your speech to the nation was concise, to the point. But together we have only taken the initial steps. To ensure the long-term safety of Moscow and its citizens, it will be necessary to introduce additional measures aimed at rooting out the threat and ensuring its total eradication."

Milyutin stared hard at his defense minister. "I am assuming that the military members of this body have prepared a list of the measures you would like to see implemented?"

"Yes, Mr. President, the Military Collegium met a short time ago and approved a number of recommendations we are prepared to present to you and the other members of the council at this time. We are confident, given the facts, that the council will endorse these steps. If the council does not do so, we cannot guarantee the security of the capital or the safety of its citizens."

"Would you provide a summary, please, General Gromov, of what you and the members of the collegium have in mind?"

Gromov nodded toward Major Pankratov, who was standing behind a podium at the side of the room. The lights dimmed and the first image appeared on the screen. It was a map of Moscow showing current Russian troop deployments. There was a murmur around the table as the scope of the recent military activity became apparent to the council's civilian members. Milyutin appeared unfazed by what he was seeing.

"As you can see, President Milyutin," Gromov said, "acting under your emergency orders, we have moved several troop units to the outskirts of Moscow and placed them on the highest state of alert to deal with the terrorist threat. The council has only to give the order, and these troops will move to implement martial law in Moscow. The collegium strongly believes that a martial law decree must be issued by you at this time. We have detected recent activities by the terrorists that, in our judgment, suggest an imminent threat against the city."

Milyutin looked at Gromov intently. "General Gromov, you and I discussed this issue, as you well recall, and I told you then that such a radical step would be extremely premature. My position has not changed. There has been nothing you have presented to me that would make me alter that judgment. Do you have anything new to add regarding the situation?"

Gromov moved back from the table, his voice rising as he spoke. "President Milyutin, the military members of the council feel that we cannot wait to introduce martial law. As I have just made clear, we have new information."

"Can you elaborate for my benefit and that of the other council members?"

"I cannot do that, Mr. President, given its sensitivity. I will be happy to brief you later after you have approved the decree."

"You ask me to direct the implementation of martial law, based on new information, but you refuse to provide me that information so that I can make a reasoned decision. Is that what you're saying, General Gromov? Either you provide the information now, or this meeting is at an end." Milyutin started to rise from his chair.

Gromov was undeterred. "We insist that you and the other members of the council endorse the introduction of martial law."

"This sounds very much like an ultimatum, General. And if we do not do as you insist?"

Gromov stared at the Russian president. "Then we are prepared to do so unilaterally."

Pandemonium erupted in the room. The council's civilian members leapt from their chairs, shaking their fists across the table and accusing the generals of treason. The generals responded by accusing their civilian counterparts of what they saw as the equally heinous crime of neglecting the country's needs, especially those of the military. Both Gromov and Milyutin shouted above the din in an attempt to restore order. The noise slowly subsided, but the tension did not.

Milyutin glared at Gromov. "Are you telling me that you and the other military members of the Defense Council are prepared to defy presidential authority and act alone? Are you aware of what you are suggesting, General Gromov, and what the consequences of such an action constitute?"

"Such action constitutes patriotism of the highest order, President Milyutin," Gromov quickly replied. "It is time to restore Russia's greatness. It is time to resurrect her from the slow death that you and your misguided notions of democracy have imposed upon her. It is time Russia had a leadership worthy of her greatness. We are prepared to provide that leadership, and we intend to do so. We are prepared to do so immediately."

Milyutin's face betrayed no emotion. "You mean *you* are prepared to provide that leadership, don't you, General Gromov?"

"It is the intent of the Military Collegium to act as the temporary government of the Russian Federation until the threat has been eradicated. However, I am prepared to exercise authority in the name of the collegium and the Defense Council, if that is their wish. I am prepared to shoulder the burden. I don't share your timidity, Mr. President."

"Be careful, Gromov, as you grab for the laurel crown. The goal may exceed your grasp, as it has other would-be caesars."

Gromov gave a small smile. "The goal is well within our grasp, President Milyutin. Now, I must ask you and the other members of the council to approve the martial law decree. And you, personally, will hand over your powers to the Supreme Committee for National Salvation."

"And that committee would be headed by you, of course?"

"I believe the other military members of the committee will agree to such an arrangement to ensure the restoration of order."

Milyutin looked across the table at the chief of the General Staff. "And is that your position as well, General Pankratov? Do your concur with General Gromov's becoming Russia's military dictator? That seems to be what the defense minister is suggesting, if I'm not mistaken. I find it hard to believe the members of the collegium would acquiesce to such a scheme."

Gromov gave Pankratov an alarmed look. "President Milyutin, there is no disagreement among us. Isn't that correct, Pankratov?"

Pankratov stood up slowly, a bit unsteadily. "Not quite correct, General Gromov. I was quite prepared to accept the collegium ruling jointly with the Russian president, but you have now changed the terms of our agreement in ways I find extremely disturbing. I must now question your motives and intentions. The Defense Council must review the whole situation."

Now it was the generals' turn to disrupt the proceedings as they began shouting at one another, but Pankratov quickly hammered on the table with his fist.

"Enough," he yelled, "let me finish what I have to say. We can argue about its merits in a moment. For now, I am inclined to concur with President Milyutin's judgment that the introduction of martial law would be premature. I do not approve of the manner in which you have addressed the issue in this body, General Gromov. Totally supplanting the civilian authority was never discussed. And your conduct toward the Russian president is intolerable. I cannot condone such behavior, such gross insubordination, on the part of a member of the high command."

"*You* cannot . . . Pankratov, what the hell is going on here!" Gromov shouted, his unblinking eyes filled with fury. "You sanctimonious son of a bitch! We agreed. You agreed! If there's any insubordination in this room, it's on your part, and you will be judged accordingly after this evening."

"General Gromov," Milyutin interjected, "if there are any judgments to be made, they will be made by the Russian president and the courts. They will certainly not be made by you, because as of this moment I have accepted your resignation as minister of defense. Should you decline to submit your resignation, I will have you placed under arrest for treason."

At Milyutin's signal, a dozen members of the security service entered the room, joining a half-dozen others who now rose from their seats along the walls, where they had been discreetly disguised as members of Milyutin's staff. Several other generals started to get up from their seats but thought better of it as the security service personnel closed in on the table.

Milyutin glared at the other members of the collegium who had conspired with Gromov. "I expect all of you to submit your resignations, or suffer the consequences. I would hope all of you realize the former is the proper course of action, for your sake and the sake of all your comrades in the military. You have dishonored yourselves; do not dishonor your fellow soldiers by embroiling Russia in a crisis that could well destroy her."

"This is absurd," Gromov shouted. "You have already destroyed Russia, you fool! I will not resign. I will walk out of this room and give the orders and you, Milyutin, will be gone."

Milyutin shook his head. "Gromov, there is no way for you to issue such orders. And even if you could, those unit commanders who would follow them have been detained for questioning. There will be no commands issued to those units, other than my order for them to stand down."

Gromov staggered toward the table, and as he did so, he pulled a revolver from under his coat, pointed it at Pankratov's head, and discharged several rounds before anyone could act.

Everyone stared, terrified, at Pankratov's body sprawled on the floor, the force of the point-blank shots having thrown him backward in his chair. Horrified that they could be the next target of the defense minister's rage, they slowly—almost imperceptibly—pushed themselves deeper in their chairs. Gromov, slowly raising his pistol at Milyutin, was only vaguely aware of the movement to his left as Dmitriy Pankratov walked swiftly toward his father's assassin, placed his own revolver firmly against Gromov's temple, and calmly pulled the trigger.

Pankratov dropped his weapon to his side with the same composure he had displayed in executing Gromov. He stared at Gromov's body, then spat upon it. Milyutin, steadying himself with the back of his chair, looked at the young officer and then down at Gromov.

"Thank you, Major," he finally said, barely able to mouth the words.

Pankratov continued looking at the floor. "I did not do it for you, Mr. President. I did it for my father and for Russia. My country would not have survived a man who could so easily murder another Russian officer."

"Yet you said or did nothing to prevent it until now," Milyutin said softly.

"Look at the rank on my shoulder, Mr. President. Look at the dead man on the floor. To whom did I owe my first loyalty? The one who did nothing stands before me. You and the Army continue to stare at one another incomprehensibly. You are afraid of what you don't understand; they don't understand your fears. They simply want leadership, but you have failed to provide it. That's how all of this started. Gromov was a product of your neglect. He deserved death for what he did to my father. What he desired for Russia and its armed forces was beyond reproach. I condemn his actions, but I honor his patriotism."

Ken Currie

Milyutin quickly regained his composure in the face of Pankratov's insubordinate scolding.

"Major, you must be forgiven those comments because of all that has happened, but I trust you will in the future remember your place. The Russian Army is not the only part of Russia I must worry about."

Pankratov looked around the table, snapped to attention, and saluted his president. "With all due respect, I don't give a damn if the president forgives my remarks or not. As far as I'm concerned, the president can go straight to hell. Now, if you will excuse me, I have to mourn a father, a member of the Army who died defending you."

Pankratov walked around the table, knelt down over his father's body, and made the sign of the cross. He bent forward and kissed his father's cheek. Then he whispered in the dead man's ear. "I have witnessed so much deceit in the past few days, Father. I have deceived you. And now you are its victim." Pankratov glanced back at Milyutin, who was excitedly conferring with the civilian members of the Defense Council. "It is all an illusion," he sighed, "and we are all its victims." The younger Pankratov, still tightly clutching the pistol that had been forgotten in the commotion, placed the barrel to his chin and followed his father into oblivion.

Chapter Forty

The agents boarded the ship at the Alexandria wharf without resistance. They found the missiles below deck. All except one were crated, still in their launch canisters. The exception lay on the cargo deck, removed from its container, surrounded by a few pieces of antiquated electronic equipment. There were no personnel on board the ship, save for the engineer's mate and a simple sailor. Neither spoke English. The agents deduced that the terrorists had been tipped off and had fled, forced to leave their valuable cargo behind. Congratulations were extended all around that another terrorist attack on Washington had been averted at the last moment.

The seizure of the missiles had been made possible by a tip from the Iranian ambassador to the United Nations, who had met privately with the U.S. secretary of state. Professing his country's desire to ease tensions with the United States, he had provided the information regarding the whereabouts of the weapons as proof of Teheran's sincerity. Iran had discovered that the missiles were bound for the United States aboard a Serbian registry freighter. The information was being provided to the Americans at considerable risk to Iranian agents, according to the ambassador. The secretary of state had pressed him for additional details, but he politely demurred, stating he had provided all that he safely could.

The secretary of state promptly called the White House. The White House promptly called the FBI, and agents were promptly dispatched. As the whole scene on the waterfront unfolded, it was witnessed by a small group of customers at a nearby sidewalk café. Among them was a tall young man with two canine companions. He slowly sipped his Irish whiskey and gently rubbed the surprisingly somnolent springer spaniel behind the ear. "Looks like a bit of excitement on the boat, eh, lads?" he cooed to his pets as he watched the agents scramble about on the *Nizhniy Novgorod*. "Too bad the Chechen bastard can't see this."

The young man jumped as a hand touched his shoulder. "And just how is the Chechen bastard these days, Kevin?"

Kevin relaxed and smiled as he turned in his chair. "Ah, Yakov!"

"Jacob. And not so loud, you dumb mick."

"It's good to see you, Jacob, it is. You're a tad early, aren't you, or couldn't you resist comin' back to the scene of the crime?"

Jacob sat down at the table, looking around as he pulled his chair closer to Kevin. The rottweiler raised its head warily as the newcomer slid closer, then loudly flopped back down when there was no reaction from his master.

"I repeat my earlier question. What's the news from Izrailov?"

Kevin grinned. "And why wouldn't the Foreign Intelligence Service be knowin' such a thing instead of me, a lonely Irishman? I thought the SVR knew everything?"

Jacob grabbed Kevin's arm. The rottweiler once again raised its head, this time with a growl.

"You know, Kevin, I really don't like you. The IRA didn't like you. You're too independent an operator. The only reason I can think Izrailov brought you into this is because vermin attracts vermin."

Kevin winced from the increasing pressure on his forearm, then forced a smile. "And would that be the attraction for you as well?"

Jacob released his grip and leaned back. "I've never shared your enthusiasm for mayhem."

Kevin nodded toward the *Nizhniy Novgorod*. "For certain the captain of that ship would not agree with you. You and I are brothers in arms, Jacob, whether it be to your liking or not. I've no more use for Izrailov than you."

Jacob wrinkled his nose. "The very last thing we are is brothers," he said as he stood up abruptly. "Enough of this. Just tell me what I need to know. Tell me how it turned out here. Did everything proceed as planned?"

"Like clockwork, it was," Kevin said with a laugh. "We were blessed with a most congenial band of marionettes."

"And Joshua?"

"Your brother's safe, beyond their reach. Izrailov has asked me to make sure the two of you are united soon. And knowin' what it's like to be worried about family, that's my desire as well."

3 September, 1435 hours EDT

At the crash site in Maryland, investigators had completed a preliminary survey of the scene. The discovery and tagging of bodies was proceeding very slowly, partly because of the nature of the explosions aboard the aircraft, but also because the team's attention, at least for the time being, was focused elsewhere.

"What do you mean there are no missiles?" Jeff Farley shouted over the phone. "There have to be missiles. Look harder, damn it!"

"Mr. Farley, what you fail to understand is we have a crash site roughly the size of Prince Georges County, with bodies strewn all over that area. Our priorities need to be centered on recovering those bodies."

"Your first priority, Agent Levine, is to locate the remains of the cruise missiles. The bodies aren't going anyplace, are they?"

There was a profound silence at the other end of the phone. "You're one sick son of a bitch, you know that, Farley? Look, there's absolutely nothing here that remotely resembles a cruise missile. What we do have is a bunch of computer parts lying all over the place. It looks like a Radio Shack exploded here. We'll keep looking, of course, but there's nothing here. The NTSB guys are really putting the heat on to let them get on with the recovery of the remains. We'd appreciate it if your office could back off the pressure a little bit. And I'll be sure to tell the family members who are starting to gather in the area with the press corps that the White House chief of staff says, 'Don't worry, the bodies aren't going anywhere.' "

"Press corps? Listen, Levine—"

"Goodbye, Mr. Farley, I have work to do. Take it up with the director."

3 September, 1500 hours EDT

The Iranian ambassador to the United Nations stepped to the microphone. Impeccably attired in an expensive double-breasted suit, he surveyed the crowd of reporters for a moment, then spoke in perfect English.

"Ladies and gentlemen. I have a very brief statement. I'm afraid I can't answer any questions afterward, so please bear with me for now. The Iranian government, in an effort to reduce tensions in the Persian Gulf and to join with the other members of the United Nations in the battle against senseless international terrorism, has just provided valuable information to the United States regarding the whereabouts of cruise missiles stolen from an American cargo ship several days ago in the Indian Ocean. The particulars regarding the name of the ship and the fate of its crew we trust will be provided to you by the American government. I have just been informed that agents of the American Federal Bureau of Investigation, acting on the basis of the information provided by my government, seized all twelve cruise missiles missing from the American arsenal. We are most pleased that our actions have prevented what would have been a devastating attack upon the American capital and its many treasures that the American people, our friends, hold sacred."

The ambassador walked quickly away, ignoring the questions shouted after him.

"Penelope, this was supposed to have been a secret meeting? What the hell happened, Penelope? Talk to me, Penelope."

"Mr. President, I am as upset as you." The secretary of state fidgeted in her chair. A quiet academic office was a tantalizing prospect at the moment. "The ambassador gave his word our discussions would be treated in the strictest confidence. I have asked for another meeting, to express our outrage, but I'm being put off."

"Well, the bastard's put us in a box. I can't very well tell the American people that we're mad as hell at the Iranians because they told the world they helped us recover the missiles. But I'll tell you one thing, it will be quite some time before I agree to any more private sessions with them."

"Mr. President, I don't have the impression they're looking for any more such meetings anytime soon."

"Damn, Penelope. What the hell is going on?"

"I'm not sure, Mr. President."

3 September, 1625 hours EDT

Majority Leader Harvey stepped to the microphone. He had the slightly emaciated look of a long-distance runner. His hair was unkempt, and he kept pushing his glasses up the bridge of his beaklike nose. The somewhat comical appearance concealed a formidable intellect and an uncanny political sense. He was Noonan's most unremitting Harvey's countenance was stern, but he was in rea' voring the moment.

"Ladies and gentlemen of the press," he beg you know why I've asked you to come here The shoot-down of the airliner by United craft is a tragic affair. My colleagues and I share the victims' family members' grief. I want to assure them that the Congress will do everything in its power to examine these events. We will determine culpability in this affair. If we determine that those responsible for this tragic event have violated the trust of the American people as well as the laws of this country, the Congress will act in accordance with its constitutional obligations. I'll take the first question."

"Senator Harvey, there are initial reports that the president himself ordered the shoot-down of the aircraft. There has been no confirmation from the White House, and we don't know when President Noonan will meet with the press. Would you care to comment on these reports?"

Harvey grabbed both sides of the lectern and leaned in the direction of the questioner. "We are certain that the aircraft commanders did not act on their own. Unlike some situations we've witnessed in the past, there were no military cowboys involved here. The orders very obviously came from a higher authority. We'll want to know, of course, if those orders came from the Pentagon or from the president. And we'll want to know the information on which those orders were issued." He paused thoughtfully. "We've heard nothing from the crash site that would indicate the aircraft was engaging in evasive maneuvers or threatening hostile action before or during its interception. We'll want to talk to the pilots, of course, to find out what they saw before we rush to any judgment, however. Next question."

"If the Congress determines the order was issued by the president, and that there was no threat posed by the aircraft or its holiday passengers," the questioner paused as his comment provoked a titter among the other reporters, "will the House and Senate look into the possibility of impeachment?"

"We're a long way from that. But I would rule nothing out at this point."

Williams found her puffing on a cigarette in the hospital parking lot.

"Those damned things'll kill you."

She turned toward him, smiled, then leaned her head

against his chest. Sensing her exhaustion, he did not pull away but wrapped an arm around her shoulders.

"It's amazing what bad habits you'll reacquire if the time's right." She pulled back and looked into his eyes.

"Who's going to keep you out of trouble when I leave?" he asked.

"Haven't you got that a little turned around?" She put her hands on her hips and smiled, thankful for the meaningless banter. "How many times did I have to bail your ass out of jams this week? These things are less of a threat to my safety and well-being than you've been, Boy Scout." She turned her head toward the hospital and grew serious. "I assume you've heard what happened?"

He nodded and then looked down at the pavement, seemingly lost in thought.

"What a mess," she said. "Oh, by the way, we found your missiles."

He jerked his head up. "At the crash site?"

"No, afraid not. They haven't found squat out there. No, your little toys showed up on a freighter tied up in Alexandria."

"How many?"

"All of them."

"Jesus."

"Yeah, no kidding. I think you can deduce what that means about what they'll turn up at the crash site. There is one slight problem, however. A couple of them were missing their guidance systems, or so I've been told by people who really understand these things. Maybe the Iranians kept a prize. Who knows? I do have one more bit of news. Jennifer Underwood is alive."

Williams could only stare.

"Evans lied. Or else the poor bastard was clueless as to what was really going down. I'd vote for the second. Ironic, isn't it? Underwood tries to play hero—"

"I have to leave, Carolyn. I've been ordered back to Scott. Actually, General Price ordered me out of town. He thinks it'll protect me from the wrath of the chairman."

"Smart move, if it works. Can I come with you? I'll sleep

in the kid's room. Maybe that son of yours can whip me up a disguise. I have a feeling there are a lot of people in this town right now who would like to disappear. I'm certain there are a few that would like *me* to disappear."

"You're welcome anytime. Erica would love you."

"Yeah, maybe, but I'd probably hate her." She savored his confusion for a moment before she added, "Because she got one of the good guys."

He gave her an embarrassed smile. "Why, Carolyn, you're shameless. I do believe you're flirting with me."

She blushed. "Don't flatter yourself, flyboy. You're forgetting I've had to be your mother this week, and only a mother could love that face."

He gave her a little smile as she tugged at his ears. "Cute. Look, I really do have to get going, but I couldn't leave without a proper farewell. You take care of yourself."

"You, too. Go back to those cozy cornfields and have nice, safe dreams about the heartland. Forget about this place."

He gave her a hug, turned, and started walking toward the waiting taxi. As he reached for the door handle, he called out to her, "Even though the last few days have overfulfilled my quota for Washington, I have a sneaking suspicion I'll be heading back this way."

Carolyn smiled, then whispered, "Count on it."

She watched as he drove away, then reached into her purse and fished out her cigarettes. She studied the almost full pack for a moment, then wrinkled up her face in disgust and tossed it over her shoulder. She hurried across the street toward the subway entrance. In a moment, she had disappeared down the escalator, lost again in Washington's noise and confusion.

JIM DeFELICE

COYOTE BIRD

The president is worried—with good cause. Two of America's spy planes have disappeared. Soon he—and the nation—will face a threat more dangerous than any since the height of the Cold War. A secretly remilitarized Japan is plotting to bring the most powerful country on Earth to its knees, aided by a computer-assisted aircraft with terrifying capabilities. But the U.S. has a weapon of its own in the air—the Coyote, a combat super-plane so advanced its creators believe it's invincible. Air Force top gun Lt. Colonel Tom Wright is prepared to fly the Coyote into battle for his country—and his life—against all that Japan can throw at him. And the result will prove to be the turning point in the war of the skies.

_4831-0 $5.99 US/$6.99 CAN

CHINA CARD

THOMAS BLOOD

With the Russian economy in a shambles, and the hard-line leaders in power, renegade KGB operatives an ultra-secret document detailing the exact location of over one hundred tactical nuclear weapons secretly placed in the U.S. during the height of the Cold War. Thousands of miles away, in Washington, D. C., a young prostitute is found brutally murdered in a luxury hotel. The only clue—a single cufflink bearing the seal of the President. These seemingly unrelated events will soon reveal a twisting trail of conspiracy and espionage, power-brokers and assassins. It's a trail that leads from mainland China to the seamy underbelly of the Washington power-structure . . . to the Oval Office itself.

__4782-9 $5.99 US/$6.99 CAN

R. KARL LARGENT

RED WIND

When a military jet goes down off the California coast, killing the Secretary of the Air Force, it is a tragedy. When another jet crashes with the Undersecretary of State on board, it becomes cause for investigation. When a member of the State Department is found shot in the back of the head, his top-secret files missing, it becomes a national crisis. The frantic President turns to Commander T. C. Bogner, the only man he can trust to uncover the mole and pull the country back from the brink before the delicate balance of power is blown away in a red wind.

___4361-0 $5.99 US/$6.99 CAN

Dorchester Publishing Co., Inc.
P.O. Box 6640
Wayne, PA 19087-8640

Please add $1.75 for shipping and handling for the first book and $.50 for each book thereafter. NY, NYC, and PA residents, please add appropriate sales tax. No cash, stamps, or C.O.D.s. All orders shipped within 6 weeks via postal service book rate. Canadian orders require $2.00 extra postage and must be paid in U.S. dollars through a U.S. banking facility.

Name_____
Address_____
City_____State_____Zip_____
I have enclosed $_____ in payment for the checked book(s).
Payment <u>must</u> accompany all orders. ☐ Please send a free catalog.

THE
JAKARTA
PLOT
R. KARL LARGENT

The heads of state of the world's most powerful nations—the United States, Russia, Japan, Great Britain, Germany, and France—are meeting in Jakarta, on the island of Java, to issue a joint declaration to the Chinese government. China must stop its nuclear testing or face the strictest sanctions of the World Economic Council. But a powerful group of Communist terrorists—with the backing of the Chinese government—attack the hotel in which the meeting is taking place and hold the world leaders—including the Vice President of the United States—hostage. The terrorists have an ultimatum: The WEC must abandon its policy of interference in the Third World . . . or one by one the hostages will die.

___4568-0 $5.99 US/$6.99 CAN

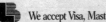